THE
BEGINNING
~ OF ~
CALAMITIES

To Arnold Weinstein —

THE
BEGINNING
~ OF ~
CALAMITIES

a novel

—

TOM HOUSE

*in appreciation of your many
Teaching Company lectures, which continue
to influence my writing & thoughts —*

Tom House

BRIDGE WORKS PUBLISHING COMPANY
Bridgehampton, New York

Copyright © 2003 by Tom House

All rights reserved under International and Pan-American Copyright Conventions. No part of this book may be reproduced in any form or by any electronic or mechanical means, including information storage and retrieval systems, without written permission from the publisher, except by a reviewer who may quote brief passages in a review.

Published by Bridge Works Publishing Company, Bridgehampton, New York, a member of the Rowman & Littlefield Publishing Group.

Distributed in the United States by National Book Network, Lanham, Maryland. For descriptions of this and other Bridge Works books, visit the National Book Network website at www.nbnbooks.com.

FIRST EDITION

The characters and events in this book are fictitious. Any similarity to actual persons, living or dead, is coincidental and not intended by the author.

Library of Congress Cataloging-in-Publication Data

House, Tom, 1962–
    The beginning of calamities : a novel / Tom House.—1st ed.
        p. cm.
    ISBN 1-882593-69-3 (cloth : alk. paper)
1. School children—Fiction. 2. Amateur theater—Fiction. 3. Boys—Fiction. I Title.

PS3608.O94 B44 2003
813'.6—dc21

2002152049

ISBN 1-882593-69-3

10 9 8 7 6 5 4 3 2 1

®™ The paper used in this publication meets the minimum requirements of American National Standard for Information Sciences—Permanence of Paper for Printed Library Materials, ANSI/NISO Z39.48–1992. Manufactured in the United States of America.

This first one is for my parents,
Maryanne and Jack,
my sister, Debora,
and my brothers, John and Don.

And in a small way, too,
for little English,
though he wasn't much of a reader.

Be constantly on your guard! For you will be delivered up even by your parents and brothers and relatives and friends. You will be manhandled and persecuted and tried by governors and kings on My account and have to testify your faith before them. This is the beginning of calamities.

—A COLLATION OF THE WORDS OF JESUS FROM THE GOSPELS,
THE NEW AMERICAN BIBLE

THE
BEGINNING
~ OF ~
CALAMITIES

Preface

No doubt there are still residents of East Islip, Long Island, who'll remember having heard of young Danny Burke and his infamous Easter play. Perhaps they'll recall a story told by the old Our Lady's nuns, justifying a controversial motion to expel the boy; or one told by Carol Burke herself, citing why she removed her son from the school before any consensus could be reached; or even one told by Elizabeth Kaigh, Danny's teacher, who, ever after apologetic and remorseful, also left the school that June—to study, it was said, the violin. But more likely they'll remember a clipped version from one of the many students at the performance, trying to make sense of a shocking and tumultuous moment in an otherwise predictable school career, or from any number of parishioners and neighbors who weren't involved at all, but, having gotten wind of a striking detail or two, wrote their own "Danny Burke's Play," and presented it as an amusing anecdote at a bar or party, whenever conversation turned to "strange things that have happened in this town." Therefore it seemed best to me, possessing the most complete knowledge of the whole sequence of events, to create a full account, so that whoever wishes to may read, from the vantage points of the principal players, all as it unfolded in early '73.

And so now, my friend, come back with me, down among the gray, leafless streets abutting a humbler Montauk Highway—streets with Indian names like Secatogue, Matinecock, Wyandanch, flanked by parcels of ragged-edged lawns and rows of converted ranch houses. At the center of this grid Our Lady of Perpetual Help looms all in white, with her boxy bell tower and four-faced clock and, high above, a verdigris cupola resembling nothing so much as a conquistador's helmet. On a Friday noon the parking lots behind the adjacent school are teeming, not with the Fords and Chevys of wor-

shipers, but with fifth-graders, their shrieks and their navy blue: navy-blue parkas and trousers and the navy-blue-and-white plaid jumpers and blazers and ties. And it's here, at the edge of this crowd, near an island of oaks and pines, that we find our boy, alone with his worries.

The Gospel According to Danny

All winter he's dreaded March—the longer, milder days, the vanishing of the last, cherished patches of ice and dirty snow on the walks, the announcement, so final today, that students would be allowed outside for recess. In the swirl of cheers, Danny smiled faintly, as if he hadn't prayed that morning that it wouldn't be so, hadn't knelt on the bench at seven o'clock Mass, the only child present, *One more day, God, please one more day.* But now it seems he may as well have been praying for straight brown hair because those petitions, too, had had little effect. Tight, brassy curls continue to crowd across his head. "Curly girly," the other boys continue to jeer, the same ones throwing Superballs now around the vast, empty parking lot: Brian Kessler, Joey Flynn, Kevin Lukas. What noise they make— calling out, choosing teams, racing all around! How defiant they are! Everyone knows Keep Away's not allowed, is the *most* not-allowed of games, but still the yard mothers look the other way. Danny doesn't know what to do and so continues to skirt the lot, trying to stay far enough away from the boys and the ball and yet seem part of it. Twice, when all the players have their backs to him, he raises his hand and murmurs, "Here," this mostly for the benefit of the girls, some of whom, glancing over occasionally from their chattering circles on the walks, are still nice to him and don't know yet how bad at sports he is, how spazzy. But in truth, he fears the ball will actually be thrown in his direction, that it will hit him—or worse, he'll put his hands up to catch it and miss. Yet even if he could catch it and throw it to someone else with any kind of skill, he wouldn't want to risk the anger of Sister Regina Mary Murphy, the principal. Sister

Regina often nods at him and calls him bright, devout, an example to other students. And though the boys will make fun of Danny even more afterward and say, "Who wants to be like Curly?" how terrible still if he were among those sent to the office, and she were to scowl at him and say, *You?*

Just ahead, Paolo Moreno, the dark-skinned boy, is skirting the lot as well, though he's much better, Danny fears, at pretending to be in the game: calling out loudly, sprinting all about, and sometimes, in the middle of a dash, he'll leap way up, eyes wide, showing their whites. Paolo's hair isn't straight, either, but bent and frizzy in places, the ends rolling under strangely at his ears and neck. And now here, by a far corner of the stockade fence, Danny tries to speak to him, boyishly. "W-Whatchadoin'?"

"Noth'n."

"K-Keep Away?"

"Mm."

"Me, too."

But Paolo looks at him warily, sidelong. Clearly, he doesn't want to talk to him and it's because, Danny realizes, he's just Curly, and not one of the boys across the way, in the thick of the rushing, whooping swarms. Yesterday, the boys called Paolo *spic*. "I'm not a spic, I'm Italian!" he yelled back. "*Siciliano!*" But they didn't believe him, and then he started to cry, which is the worst thing you can do.

"Are not," he accuses Danny now.

"Y-Y-Yes, I am."

"You don't want them to throw it."

"Y-Y-Yes, I do." He raises his hand again to demonstrate his willingness—briefly, so no one sees.

"How come you're all the way over here, then?"

"How come *you* are?"

"I had the ball before."

"No, you didn't."

"Yes, I did." His eyes stretch wider. "I *did.*"

"When?"

But the boy's turning and running off again, leaving Danny in the open by himself, and so he runs, too, but the other way, back to the island and the racks of bikes between the trees, and he squats down behind them, opening and closing the combination lock on his Stingray and looking through the bars and spokes to the game, the girls. At last he sits on the curb, dispatching Our Fathers and snippets of Psalms, all the while wincing beneath God's stern, tremendous face. *I know I have not been good, I know I should not ask.* And soon he turns to Jesus, softer-eyed: *Please make the bell ring, I beg you. I will do anything. I love you so much.* Next to the Blessed Mother, the "interceder": *Won't you please ask Them to make it ring?* And on to Saint John, Saint Peter, Saint Francis . . . but unfortunately, it's Stephen Hinch, the fattest boy, who lumbers by.

"Hi, Danny," he says, breathlessly and right out loud, and Danny blushes and squints up, marveling at the length and the strange, yellowy color of his face. Stephen's the least-liked boy of all, much less than himself or Paolo. The other children will say things if they're seen talking together; Stacy Ryan will say, *Ew, you were talking to Stephen Hinch at lunch!*

"Hi, Stephen," Danny says. He doesn't know what else to do, with him standing right there.

"Why aren't you playing Keep Away?" the fat boy asks.

"I was before."

"Oh." Stephen doesn't like Keep Away, he explains. He can't run for very long and gets awfully tired—he says *awfully.*

"Mm."

He says that when he runs the boys call him thunder thighs and pig-butt.

"Really?" Danny says, glancing nervously through the bars. "That's mean."

"What?"

"That's mean."

The boy looks down at his shoes—long, shiny black shoes with buckles that no one would ever wear. "How come you're nice to me?" he asks. Danny blushes again because he doesn't feel nice. And in a moment, when the bell finally does ring and he rushes ahead to the line, knowing the boy won't be able to keep up with him—that doesn't feel very nice, either. Yet once the boy's far enough behind, he forgets all about him and returns to his former worries. This kind of thing will happen every afternoon now: the ball playing, the looking for a place to hide. Eventually the boys will see him and know he's afraid. *Hey, Burke, what are you sitting over by the bikes for, huh? Fag!* Everyone will laugh, then, even Frances Fitzer, Ginger Holley, Patty Dupree, girls who are themselves fags, *Ah ha ha!*

How he hates to imagine that and yet he does, over and over throughout the afternoon. And he imagines it again later, walking the six blocks to his house, *Ah ha ha!* and all during dinner, and at various points throughout the evening and night, and in between his bedtime prayers. By the next day, Saturday, the chuckles have become cackles and hoots, the hoots growing in volume and duration, *AHH HAA HAA!* Steadily before him, an array of bared teeth and metal braces; glad, crinkling eyes behind big plastic glasses. *No!* he tells them, *Don't!* and, soon after, is struck with the idea for the play.

It comes to him in his small, slanted-ceilinged room upstairs, as if borne by a tardy angel. All at once, while reviewing his vocabulary unit and making practice tests, he looks up from his desk, remembering second grade: how, when they put on *It's the Great Pumpkin, Charlie Brown*, the players were allowed to stay in at recess to practice. And he wonders now if Miss Kaigh would allow their class to do the same thing, should he write a better and longer play and not just one about the Peanuts gang. *It's the Great Pumpkin, Charlie Brown* wasn't even a play, really, just a skit he wrote from his comic books. Peanuts are for little children, he knows that, and has long since stopped bringing those books to school. Still, he can clearly picture the afternoon Mrs. O'Brien took them up to the seventh and eighth grades to put the play on there at the front of the classrooms. How high the older children's desks were! They towered over him as he crouched at the foot of the aisle, awaiting his cue. He hears again the howls and cheers when he ambled to the front on all fours, his black earmuffs on, playing Snoopy. "I can't stand it!" one of the girls cried, "He's so cute!" And one of the boys, "Go, doggie, go!" swatting him on the felt tail Mrs. O'Brien had pinned to his trousers. Then Danny, emboldened, had said, "Woo-woof!" and the laughter had doubled. How good he felt! How he wishes that could happen again, boys and girls cheering and smiling, *So cute!*

But those seventh- and eighth-graders have graduated now, he realizes, and the children who were in the fourth and fifth grades are in the seventh and eighth, and there are different ones, younger than Danny, in the second, who weren't in school at all then. He's already *three* years older than they are! He wishes he could still be younger, in Mrs. O'Brien's class, ambling up the aisle. Would it be better to still be younger? Maybe. Though he remembers, too, that his sister, Sharon, was in the seventh grade when they put the play on, and she cursed at him and yanked him by the hair as they were walking home that afternoon. "You come into my class with earmuffs? You *woof* like a freakin' retard?" And so it might be better he's not, and that she's towns away at Holy Family, where his brothers had once gone. *High school*. He can't imagine what it's like, how enormous. Everyone so tall and learning *algebra!* He never wants to go there, yet it seems he'll have to, in just three and a half years . . .

Then possibly because his mind is on big things, he thinks of his field trip in the third grade, when they took the long bus ride to see the *Christmas Spectacular* at the place called Radio City Music Hall, the surprise when they emerged from the tunnel amid all the gray, gleaming towers, so many stories you couldn't see the roofs! He felt so tiny and shadowed-over beneath them, as if rolling past the toes of dinosaurs. And later, on the wide sidewalk, they were buffeted by taxi horns and the shouts of the mothers and the children, and the bray of a man on the corner, selling big, doughy pretzels. Danny tucked his nose beneath his jacket, so as not to breathe in the exhaust from the wall of idling buses. And he remembers the way Sister Theresa, when she saw the black groups arriving—whole classes of them, with black monitors—frowned and gathered them closer together. *Spectacular*, what a special word that is, how strong. And there was a kind of play called a *pageant* in it about the nativity, *a nativity pageant* with real animals and a great glow that arose from the manger; they all oohed and clapped. And now what if he, what if, with Easter a few weeks away, he were to write a play about Jesus' sufferings and the crucifixion? A *crucifixion* pageant! "Cool!" he bursts out and imagines Miss Kaigh, nodding and awestricken, *Oh Daniel, what a super idea!* "The Pageant of Christ," he'll call it, or, no, "The Passion of Christ." Yeah! Can he? Because that seems such an amazing title, and *Passion* itself an even more amazing word, with its serious, whispery sound. He's always admired it, the many times he's come across it, capitalized that way. It means *great suffering,* and he associates it with Jesus' taut, pain-ridden face lifted *beseechingly* toward heaven, with the drips of blood flowing from the tangled crown of thorns. But that would be hard, wouldn't it, to write such a play? He himself could never do it, a boy. Though the story's right in the Gospels, all the different parts of it, and what if he were just to read the passages and write down the quotes? Would that be cheating?

He doesn't know yet shoots up from his desk anyway and runs to the hall, over to the small case where the holy books are kept, just above the numbered spines of *The Book of Knowledge* encyclopedia. Oh, but the Bible's so big, he's forgotten just how. And heavy! So many chapters! How will he ever find just the one part about the crucifixion in it? But then just beside it are the smaller companion volumes—also beige, with the same gold marbling on the covers—books he's never thought to look at before, and, remarkably, one's called *The Life of Christ.* There are quotes inside: *fishers of men, hell of unquenchable fire;* Jesus' words all in red, and won't that make the play even easier to write, always knowing when He's speaking that way? Sure. And now he stops, magically it seems, at the part called "The Beginning of Holy Week." Before the chapter "Triumphal Entry into Jerusalem" is an illustration of Jesus in a white robe, riding a white donkey. Thick crowds are holding palm branches and laying down carpets, their mouths open with cheer, welcome. "Wow," he says, imagining himself in such a robe, seated on such an animal, emerging onto a huge stage like Radio City. And just then in the hall, he raises his arm in a slow, magisterial way, as if addressing multitudes: *Fear not, O daughter of Zion! Your king approaches you on a donkey's colt.*

Of course, in his own play, it wouldn't be possible to have a real donkey. For a second, he considers Duke, their springer spaniel, but he's much too small to sit on and never does anything you ask him to. Danny can't imagine bringing Duke to school—what a terror he'd be, tearing down the halls! He's not even allowed in their house because after they got him he wouldn't stop peeing on the carpets and chewing the furniture. "There's something wrong with that animal," his father explained. Poor boy, he's in the garage this minute, lying in his wooden box with his matty-eared head between his paws, the way Danny finds him whenever he goes down to the den and opens the heavy, scratch-marked door. He should go down there and play with him right now; he should play with him a lot more than he does. When was the last time he did? Days ago, probably.

There are more illustrations, one of Jesus at the Last Supper. He looks much cuter here, with the soft glow shining down on His golden-brown hair, glow on His neat, golden-brown beard. And oh—oh *right*, all *twelve* apostles are at the supper. That would be nearly half the class! He may have to begin the play after that, then, in the Garden. Isn't that where the suffering really starts anyway? He believes so and, paging ahead, finds proof of it—vivid pictures of Jesus' scourging, of Jesus falling on the Road to Calvary. And, "Oh no!" he says, coming upon the plate of Him hanging on the erected crucifix, not so much at the gory depiction of His torture, which is familiar enough, as at the fact that, in the three-quarter close-up of His face and upper torso, you can clearly see His left tittie, and it occurs to him that whoever plays Jesus will have to go bare at the end, down to the special, knotted cloth. His cheeks warm to imagine himself so exposed, his arms stretched wide, *Father, forgive them, for they know* not *what they do;* everyone staring at his chest, his *bellybutton*, his *feet*. He could never stand before them that way, ever; and, putting the book back in the case, he shakes the thought from his head—maybe there can be a way around the bare-titties part—then races down to the kitchen, where his mother's standing beside the stove, chopping onions for meatloaf. *Mom?* he's about to ask.

Surrounded in avocado—avocado linoleum, avocado wallpaper, placemats, toaster cover, appliances (even a dishwasher finally)—Carol Burke is on the verge of tears. Not real ones, of course, but still she combs her memory for the big boo-hoos, trying to match her mood to the welling in her eyes: her miscarriages, her hysterectomy, her boys moving out. Despite her best efforts, however, the welling remains just that, nothing falls, and so she sniffles and tries to straighten up a little, feeling like a phony. Were it not for this tendency to hunch, were she not this mother-of-four-pushing-forty, her big-boned Irish-Italian frame would look taller than average: five-ten. Or maybe just five-nine and change now, with the accumulating crush of gravity. Today her teased brown hair, which usually flips up at the ends like Dear Abby's, is gathered in the back with an extra-long barrette. So, too, the tail of her cream blouse hangs, in a casual, weekend way, down the ample seat of her knock-around blue polyesters. She'd say *ample seat*; her husband, Gerry, would not be so kind. Fat fanny, he's fond of blaring; and in the summer, when she wears her one-piece, unavoidably baring the cellulite ripples on the backs of her thighs, he calls her Michelin Man—right in front of the other husbands sometimes, he calls her that. But all the wives have those, Carol's quick to justify, which is why they're always running back and forth to Weight Watchers and drinking Tab; also like many of them, she works in the business office at the public school up the street (a convenient, walkable distance, as Gerry's always been against her learning to drive), and sometimes thinks of herself as psychic, particularly in regard to the kids. Now, for instance, she intuits by the speed of Danny's approach that he's about to make some impetuous demand, probably wants to use the kitchen table for another school project. Oh, that crazy planet thing last week, with the clay and the box and all that construction paper! She was picking up little black scraps for days.

"Mom?"

"No," she says.

"But I haven't asked you yet."

"We're going to be eating soon."

"Can I take one of the Bibles in my room?"

"The *Bibles*?" she says in an overly shocked tone, even to her own ears, as if he's just asked for a cigarette, maybe, or a condom. Still, her shock is understandable enough. When's the last time someone asked her about the Bibles? Has anyone *ever* asked about them, all the years they've had them? Which has to be eighteen, nineteen, by now; they bought them around one of the boys' christenings. She remembers the awkward moment when Father McGann asked if they had a good Catholic Bible at home, and she and Gerry exchanged glances. "I'm sorry, Father," Gerry said, "we haven't gotten one for the new house yet." "No Bible?" Father said, and right away arranged to have someone come to the door with the proper ones. Had to have a special seal on them, or signature, some archbishop's. Carol herself would never have chosen such a deluxe set, but Gerry's a sucker for that kind of prissy religious stuff. "It's a once-in-a-life-time thing you buy," he'd said, and the salesman was quick to pick up on that, "Treasure all your life." Even so, *a hundred and twenty-five dollars*; they had to buy it on time. It seems even more of an extravagance now: Gerry's forgotten they exist. Ha! Once in a lifetime he ever sat down with them, maybe. And the only thing *she's* ever done with them is dust the covers.

"The *family* Bibles?" she says again, her tone softening, for she doesn't see how she can forbid him to use the books. "What do you want them for?"

He glances away to the Formica counter. "I have an idea."

"You don't need the big one, I hope."

"No. Just *The Life of Christ*."

"Is that what those little jobs are?"

"One of them."

She pauses. "Is this for religion?"

"I want to write a play."

"A *play?*" She squints at him, vaguely recalling some Charlie Brown thing he put on in the basement a few years back with a couple of the old neighborhood kids. Cast himself as the dog! Didn't say a single word the entire time. Which was smart in a way, she remembers thinking, a relief to her. "About what?"

"The crucifixion."

"The crucifixion? Of Christ? Where'd you get an idea like that?"

"I don't know. I just thought of it."

She returns to her chopping. Well, his subject matter's certainly getting more serious. But she's not sure she likes this one; it seems gruesome to her, always has, the Good Friday stuff: all that whipping and those big nails. Every year they have to remind you of it, and right at the beginning of spring, just when things are getting nice. *Contemplation of the suffering.* What a concept! You'd think there'd be another way to get your blessings. Why do they always have to strangle the life from everything, cover it all in black? Oh now, what kind of thought is that? She glances quickly at Danny, as if he may have heard it, but he's just biting his lip, eyebrows high, waiting for an answer. She may as well say it now. Go ahead, be careful. However, just as she's about to, the uninvited image of her own sliced finger invades her mind: the disembodied tip of it, like the heel of a raw hotdog, rolling across the cutting board and settling, with a little bloody wobble, right next to the pile of diced onion. Oh! She winces and says distractedly, "Wouldn't you like to write about something more cheerful?"

"No, Mom, it's for Easter."

"Oh, I see. You want to write a play about the crucifixion for Easter. 'Contemplation of the suffering,' right? That's very nice, I guess. All right, go ahead. Just be careful with it and make sure you put it back when you're—"

But he's already fled the room, began to at *very nice*. She can hear the swift patters of his feet on the stairs, the swiping of the book from the bookcase, then a dull rumbling. Something falling? "Danny?"

A muffled response: "Getting something from my closet."

Dredging something up, from beneath one of the many piles: the old black Royal, which, last seen, was transferred to his room after his brothers moved out. What his mother hears are flying Lincoln Logs and Matchbox cars, old reports scuttling downslope, followed by parts of a never used microscope kit. Damn. Well, he'll fix all that later, and, slamming the closet door shut, he lugs the heavy machine over to his desk, wondering again what *dorm* means, which is where his oldest brother, Gerry, lives now. Robby's place he can picture better because it's supposed to be a kind of house, but in another town; he lives there with his friends and his girlfriend, Missy, a *good-for-nothing slut*, though Danny's not supposed to know that. He overheard his father using those words once; his mother, *floozy*. There was hollering just before Robby left, shoving, fists thrown in the playroom, because of something he'd done again, stolen—gas, maybe, or car parts from the junkyard. Danny didn't see the fighting, only heard it, his brother crying as he raced down the stairs, "I can't believe my own father punched me! I'm never coming back here again!"

He threads a sheet of looseleaf through the roller, and now his stomach flutters as he pushes down the caplock, hunts through the strangely jumbled keys, and picks out THE PASSION OF CHRIST. Then beneath it, SCENE ONE: THE AGONY IN THE GARDEN, followed by what he believes will be the first lines of the play, spoken by the NARRATOR: *Leaving Jerusalem, Jesus and the disciples soon reached the Garden of . . . G-E-T-H-S-E-M-A-N-E. Geth-so-many? This grove of olive trees had been a favorite retreat of Jesus in happier days, but tonight it had no charm for Him, for His soul was troubled with His coming Passion.*

See, there it is already! Capital P! Oh, but then—he was afraid of this—the very first character to speak is *JESUS*, to *PETER, JOHN* and *JAMES*: *My soul is sad, even unto death. Sit here and watch with Me. Pray that you may not enter into temptation.* In fact, it's *only* Jesus who speaks in the entire agony scene—the disciples keep falling asleep. Three times He gets up to yell at them, then goes back to pray. All that moving around, all by himself! A *solo*. Is that what it's called? What a relief when *JUDAS* finally enters (*followed by THE GUARDS*): *Hail Master!*

Judas, would you betray the Son of Man with a . . . ?

Oh yes, he forgot about this part and blushes now to think of it: a boy kissing a boy! But on the cheek, which is different. He used to kiss his father on the cheek; there was nothing wrong with that once. His mother would even tell him to, "Go kiss your father goodnight," and then he'd slowly shuffle into the den, approach the silent man stretched along the couch, one hand cradling the undershirt-hill of his belly. "Goodnight, Dad," peck, and the mumble behind him as he swept back out of the room—a grunty, throat-clearing sound that meant goodnight, also, and maybe his name. But of course, Danny doesn't do it *anymore*, hasn't for a long time. Imagine doing it now in front of everyone? They'd all laugh again; say, *So-and-so kissed you in the play!* Who? Who would kiss him? No one. Brian Kessler. He pictures the blond boy's lips brushing over his face, a soft, tender pressure, no hard look or funny smirk; betraying him but also not. And well, what if he just says, *Do you betray the Son of Man?* and leaves off a few words? That's an idea. But once he's backspaced to *with*, and his finger is hovering over the X key, he stops and spaces ahead again, arguing, with a wilder bout of flutters, that it's not right, especially with the red Jesus-words, to do any kind of changing, and so types *kiss* after all. Maybe there can be a way around that, too.

Sure, but in a moment he has a different kind of worry, mechanical: the print grows dim, then very dim, leaving just ghosty-gray impressions. When he takes off the typebar cover, he sees the ribbon isn't moving and remembers this was a problem before, and why the typewriter was put in the closet in the first place. He also discovers a trick—pressing the *release* button and now and again advancing the ribbon by hand, which means typing without replacing the cover and thinking the exposed typebars look like a kind of skeleton, a half-moon of thin, metal ribs. And this method works, though not perfectly—the print keeps going from darker to lighter, and when the ribbon is too loose the tops of the tall letters get chopped off—until, just between *PETER*'s second and third denials, he comes to the end of the spool and is forced to take it out and flip it over, and in the process drops it on the floor, the long ribbon uncoiling. He snatches it up and rewinds it by hand, bemoaning its sorry condition—see-through all down the middle, and dotted with little holes, like runs in his mother's stockings.

Then it's not until he looks down at the book again to type *I tell you I do not know the man!* that he notices the dark smudges he's left on the margins of *The Life of Christ*, a whole trail of them, like someone very tiny and dirty-shoed has just traipsed across the pages. He looks at his fingers, each one stained with an oval of ink. Of course they are, wasn't he just touching the ribbon? And he should wash his hands this minute, remove the smudges from the pages somehow with his pink wheel-eraser. Yet he goes on typing the line, and even pages over—lightly, he tries not to really touch the pages—and finds the high priest's line, *If you are the Messiah, tell us*, which he likes very much and sets to typing at once, along with the rest of the trial scene. But before he has it completed, the ribbon tightens up suddenly and stays that way no matter how many times he presses the release button or swipes at the *reverse* lever. "Oh, come on," he says to it. "Ooooh!" Then his whole fist comes down on the keys, sending a dozen ribs shooting up at the roller and catching in a hard, inky, frozen-up clump. Somewhat stunned, he raises his fist and examines the fleshy side of it. A couple of red impressions, a whitish scrape, but no cuts or blood, surprisingly little pain. "Ha!" He brings his fist down again, and so more of them now, stuck in the clump. The growing mass of blackened typebar heads infuriates him. "You!" he says, pecking at the remaining raised keys, "And you! Stupid! Stupid *thing!*"

And now his mother hears him again—not words exactly, but foot stomping, unintelligible grunting. "Hey, what's all that banging about?" she yells from the kitchen, then makes her heavy-footed way down the hall to the stairs. Still, Danny's unable to squelch another "ooooh!" or keep himself from giving the typewriter a little shove. "Hey, I said," at which point she starts ascending. At the sound of her rushing steps, he quickly pulls the keys off each other, freeing the last ones as she enters the room.

"I-I-I-I can't get the ribbon to go right," he explains immediately and, as she looms up behind him, moves the reverse lever back and forth, simultaneously typing fffffff to demonstrate its stuckness, the ghostiness of the print. "Look."

"All right," she says, not as angry. "Don't ruin your script. You'll have to white all that out now."

But his stomach's in knots; there's a little fury caught in his mouth. "I don't care," he snaps, and types more pale f's. "Look," he says again and brings his fists down on his desk, not as hard as he'd like to. "Ooooh."

"Stop that." She smacks his shoulder with the backs of her fingers. "Have more patience."

"Do you know what's wrong?"

"The ribbon's not moving."

He clicks his tongue. "Do you know how to make it move?"

"No, I don't know how that old thing works. Maybe your father can help you when he comes in."

"Dad?" he says, picturing the man's broad, hunched back in the plaid CPO coat, the way it would look if he were to glance out his window just now and see him squatting somewhere in the garden. He imagines his hands—big hands, rough, dirt in the knuckle grooves—fumbling with the ribbon. "He doesn't know, either."

"He might."

"I need it fixed now."

"Uh!" Oh sure, the whole world has to stop because he can't get his little ribbon moving. Kids kill her sometimes, their selfishness. The whole bunch of them, spoiled rotten. Maybe there's a few things she'd like right now. Of course, that would never occur to them. "What do you want from me, Danny, miracles? I'm not a typewriter technician. Can't you write the play longhand?"

"But I wanted to type it."

"Well, you can't if the typewriter's not working, can you? You'll just have to—Jesus *Christ*," she says, gaping down at the open book. "The fingerprints you're getting all over!" She smacks his shoulder again. "Will they come off? Let me see your hands."

"W-W-What?" he says, covering the smudges, his face flushing again.

"Is the rest of it like that?"

"No," he says quickly. "I'll use my eraser. Don't worry."

"But it's *the Bible*."

"It's not the Bible, it's *The Life of Christ*."

"It's holy. All these books were blessed by Father McGann."

"*Sorry*," he manages, and hopes now she won't demand to see other pages.

But in fact, Carol's mind is far from this, trying to recall her own schooling at Immaculate Conception in Queens, catechism lessons with dour Sister Clare Bailey and her rubber-tipped pointing stick. "Is it a sin to get fingerprints on a holy book?"

"I don't know. I'll get them off."

"You'd better." But as she retreats, she can't help thinking, Such a temper. Where does he get it from? Not her side of the family. Then in the doorway, she stops again. "Do you have a name for this play, Danny?"

And he tells her without turning around.

"'The *Passion* of Christ?'" She nods gravely. How does he know a word like that? Then suddenly its other meaning occurs to her, and she envisions couples embracing on the covers of paperback romances, chesty girls in little newspaper ads for the X-rated theater in Islip. But he wouldn't know about that side of it yet, would he? Little Danny? And the next second, as if to save herself from the answer, she comes up with a kind of joke, "Who gets to be the star?" But when he doesn't look up from his typing right away, her smile drops. "Danny?"

At last he glances over his shoulder, cringing slightly.

"I asked who you thought would be playing Christ."

Then opens and closes his mouth, not knowing quite how to tell her.

"Not you," she says, shaking her head. She can hardly believe he'd consider it—*him*, Jesus Christ! What happened to his sense? His humility? His days of playing the dog in the basement? Doesn't he know he'll stutter and blush and make a fool of himself? She can feel her own face grow warm just thinking about it. "Oh no, Danny, you'd be much better off behind the scenes, directing."

"What?"

"I mean—" And here her face grows warmer, to have said this aloud. "You're the writer, the director; you can't be the star, too."

"Why?"

"Why? Because—because you have to be the one organizing everything, telling everyone what to do. That's the most important job of all."

"No, it's not."

"Yes, it is. Without the director, everything falls apart. He's like the glue, he's like, I don't know, the quiet father."

"The quiet father?"

"Yeah. And who could do that as good as you, who'll know everything about everything, right?"

He shrugs, grudgingly.

"Right. And so," she adds, not as softly as she hopes, "so you get one of the bigger boys to play Christ, someone outgoing, with spunk." Then her heart sinks as she watches his gaze drop to the floor, but better to get the idea out of his head right away. "Maybe you can do one of the bit parts. What do they call those? Cameo. Like Alfred Hitchcock. You know what I'm saying?"

He does—"Pontius Pilate?"—and at once regrets his example. *He,* sentence the Son of God to death?

"Exactly," Carol says. But those names are all one and the same to her. "What does Pilate do again?"

"He gives Jesus over to be crucified."

"Oh, that's right. And he washes his hands. He doesn't want to give Him away."

"Yeah."

"But the Jews cry, 'Cuh-*roo*-cify Him! Cuh-*roo*-cify Him!'" she says in a nasal twang.

And when Danny looks up again, she's staring wide-eyed at a patch of paneled wall above his head and wagging her fist in the air, the flabby pocket of her triceps jiggling vigorously.

"'Cuh-*roo*-cify Him! Cuh-*roo*-cify Him!'" Carol cries louder. She likes the feel of acting out the line. What fun, to be in a play; she almost wishes she had her own to practice for. Almost, but now she thinks, for the first time in years, of the *Oklahoma!* fiasco at Astoria High. She auditioned and everything: O, *what a beautiful mornin'* . . . Never shook so much in her life, or sang so awfully! She had old Mrs. Beatty, the choir mistress at Immaculate Conception, to thank for that, that she even tried at all. Mrs. Beatty and her fuddy friends (of course, Carol didn't know they were fuddies at the time): "I just love when you sing at Mass! You have the sweetest voice I've ever heard on a girl!" Had her thinking she was the next Patti Page. Yeah, and then you get to high school and find out just what a little fish you are. She squints angrily and, seeing this now as a cautionary tale, drops her fist and looks back down at her son. She's right to discourage him. "So you can be that, then, Pilate."

"Okay," he says to quiet her, and she is quieted by it, thinks he sees her wisdom. Still, she watches a moment more from the landing as he hunches over the book again, feels the task absorb him in stages, draw his concentration to a point. A strict, almost fearful concentration, as if so much suddenly depends on the writing of this little play! *Relax, Danny,* she wants to tell him as she walks down the stairs, *don't take everything so seriously.* But she knows he will anyway.

And she's right, of course, he takes it all very seriously, devoting the rest of the weekend to poring over *The Life of Christ* or, when the book sometimes paraphrases important scenes, the actual Bible. He crouches before it in the hall, stealthily hunting down the passages listed at the tops of *The Life*'s chapters and in the process leaving—though he tries not to see them and clicks his tongue in passing—more dark smudges across the pages, *across the pages of the Bible itself!* And oh, it's true; it's so hard to find anything! All the chapter numbers! And the numbers inside the chapters! And the letters themselves so much smaller, in long columns, oceans and oceans of tiny gray words.

Then sometimes, in the death scenes for instance, Jesus says different things! In one Gospel, *My God! My God! Why have You forsaken Me?* In another, *Father, into Your hands I commend My spirit.* And in still another, *Now it is finished.* And how can that be? Because Sister Bernadette, in the fourth grade, said God was with the writers, filling them like water in a cup until all the holy words flowed out, and so they can't be wrong. Yet the lines aren't the same. And it's all so confusing that more than once he rushes to kneel before his model altar— the one he made of cardboard and tinfoil earlier in the year, with mini chalices and wine decanters and bread plates—and there prays like a giant priest for God to help him pick the "right" right lines, or even to fill him like those others long ago, so he can write in new words the way God would now like the story to be told: a *fifth* Gospel, *according to Danny.*

But then at his desk, the fantasy passes, and there's just plain, anxious choosing, this line and not that line; there's his concern about Jesus' back. He'd never really thought about His back before—His hands and feet and side, yeah, but His back, not much. However, as *The Life* points out, Jesus was whipped with leather thongs tipped with metal, maybe even *more* than forty times; His back was an ugly mass of blood and shredded flesh. And then to picture the heavy cross laid on top of that flesh, its hard, splintery edges rubbing into the raw gashes, the extra sears of pain every time the cross jumps on the rough, cobbled road! Danny imagines the pain like a hot iron pressed flat to his back, that all the while he hangs on the cross and people gaze up at his front, there's a great scorching behind that no one knows about. How unfair they don't know. He should add a line to the play, just so they will: *My back! My back!* he can say, just before *My God! My God!*

Oh, and then this, too, this especially—on one of his trips to the Bible, Danny stumbles on a picture of a naked boy! A whole full-page illustration of a scrawny, tan-colored, black-haired boy, naked, running toward a man on a camel. *Poor son,* the caption claims, *of Abraham and an Egyptian slave.* You can clearly see the poor son's heinie; his heinie, in the picture, is as clear as anything: long skinny cheeks. Not like Danny's or Danny's brothers', the rare glimpses he had of them once in the bathroom. Maybe like Drew Dwaney's, the skinniest boy in the class, but Danny's only ever seen his in underwear. No one ever strips down further than that the afternoons Miss Kaigh and the girls wait in the hall while the boys change into their gym clothes. And many, like Danny, take their trousers off first so their shirttails hang down over everything until they can slip their shorts on. Some even come to school wearing their shorts under their trousers—you can tell by the lumps the hems make across the thighs. And yet right in the Bible this naked boy, running along a dirt road toward the man on the camel, and the man looking back over his shoulder. And now suddenly Danny reddens, realizing just what it is the man's seeing, and wishing to cover the boy, but at the same time not wishing to, and imagining himself the man, and the boy getting closer and everything becoming clearer and more detailed . . . and so, would it be tanner, skinnier than his own? And would it be bouncing from the running, all out free like that? Yeah, he decides, bouncing like crazy: up, down, back and forth. He even predicts a slapping sound, and, giggling noiselessly, thinks he, too, might like to run naked one time, just so he could see how much it would in fact bounce, and if there would in fact be any sound. But then, how could he ever try such a thing? Where? And anyway, the boy would be upon him by now, huffing: *Give me a ride?* —*Okay*, Danny says, and the boy climbs onto the back of his banana seat, arms circling his stomach—they have to, so he won't fall off. And then his legs press up against Danny's hips and thighs and the sides of his shins; his bare feet curl over the tops of Danny's All-Star Pro-Keds, to help him pedal. *I'm sorry I don't have anything to give you to wear.*

That's all right. I can stay naked.

Okay. Danny peers over his shoulder as they talk and sees it again, nested on the sparkly plastic: the tan worminess, the rosy-brown sac.

The boy notices him looking: *That's all right, you can look down at it. There's nothing wrong with that.*

But Danny's pretty sure there is, and that a boy would never say there isn't. *Hold on,* he tells him, because he's about to pedal really fast. *Hold on tight!*

I am!

Tighter!

I am!

Then he feels the wind rush up against them and hears the boy's laughter and the wild snapping of the handlebar streamers. And while he wants to think more about that and to keep looking at the picture, he closes the book—though not without noting the page number first and repeating it to himself three, four times as he hurries back to his script.

~ 2 ~

Our Lady of the Curling Iron

Monday morning in 5B, Danny presents the finished draft to Miss Kaigh: a twelve-page, longhand work in Bic-blue and Bic-red, the latter reserved *Life*-like for words spoken by Jesus, and all in the slanted, meticulous cursive that, in the second and third grades, won him first-place penmanship awards. He barely managed to re-copy the last of the half-typed, half-printed, edited and annotated pages by secretly staying up until one in the morning. Now as he waits beside the big teacher's desk for her to finish shuffling through them, he's groggier than usual and fairly rigid with anxiety, which partly explains why he interprets her wrinkled forehead and darting eyes as signs of outrage, as if she's suddenly uncovered a kind of sin in the play he's written. *Oh, how shameful. I'm so surprised at you, Daniel.* It's a strange, confusing fear, one that falls away the instant she looks up, kind-faced, smiling.

Elizabeth Kaigh, known as Liz to her parents, a telephone repairman and a telephone repairman's wife, whom she lives above in her child-hood home in Patchogue. Just recently, her father took out a loan to convert her brother Dennis's old bedroom into a kitchen and to build a small deck outside and a separate upstairs entrance. Now every morning her beloved mother knocks at the new door and, together with Cleopatra, Liz's lethargic Siamese, they have their coffee and cigarettes and Nine Lives before she leaves for school. In her entire family's history, she's the first to have gotten a college degree (from Dowling, where she majored in English and had a largely companionable relationship with Artie McClaren, then a pre-law student, which formally ended over the holidays, to no great sadness on either part), and her hope, still, is to eventually complete the education courses required for certification, so she can apply for a position at the public school. In the meantime, she's gaining valuable experience at Our Lady's, fussing over lesson plans, adopting the practice of calling the children by their proper first names, and struggling—too much?—to forge a kind of "mod modesty" in her appearance.

This morning, for instance, her layered brown hair is rolling in just so beneath her jaw, while flipping up in orderly sweeps at her shoulders, a style she admired in *Cosmopolitan* and managed to re-create with a two-handed, magician-like wielding of curling iron, hair dryer, round brush and can of Adorn Super Hold. At least, she fantasized herself a kind of magician; more a wish, really. Wouldn't it be nice if she could just wave the iron at her limp tresses and *poof*, every strand perfectly arranged, without the whole long, tortured ordeal. But then, coming away from the mirror, she did finally decide she looked pretty. She can be, some people say so: her eyes, how large and doe-like, and these crowned lately with high, plucked brows that give her face an ever-alert expression. On the other hand, her nose is long, narrow between the eyes and knobby at the tip, and roosting above wide, thin lips that peel back slightly when she smiles, exposing a healthy set of Irish teeth. She's always been slim but on the shorter side of medium height and, above all, young-looking; she has a young spring to her step. A blessing, her mother says, but Liz feels also a curse. All that fall, teachers continually mistook her for an aide or a sub. Now, of course, they recognize her, and seem to smile the minute they see her coming, but not always in the kindest way, she fears, maybe even patronizingly, *Oh, here's the new girl.* Just a little while ago, in the lots, she thought she saw Sister Margaret, from 5C, smirk at her brightly patterned cowl neck sweater. She adjusts its bulky acrylic collar now as she speaks to Danny: "*You* wrote this?"

The boy produces a string of nearly intelligible sounds, roughly: "I was just thinking—because it's-it's just another month—and there's, well—so I wrote this play because—"

"For Easter," she finishes, nodding with interest. "You're asking if you can put this on here, at school." Her eye catches one of the red lines, Christ in the Garden: *Father, if it is possible, let this cup pass Me by*. She's always loved that, so human. And you know, it might really be something, a holiday show put on by her own fifth-graders. She can't remember ever having heard of a student play at Our Lady's. "Did your mother help you write this?"

"*No,*" he says worriedly.

She sees he's misinterpreted her and tries to assume a reassuring, teacher-like voice. "I don't mean to say there'd be anything wrong with that, Daniel, just I can't believe you wrote this by yourself."

"I did. I swear. Fr-Fr-From the Bible—and *The Life of Christ*."

"Oh yes." But quite honestly, she hasn't read it. Is it well-known? She hopes not. *Her* family certainly doesn't have a copy.

"It's just about Him. It starts when He was born."

"Right," she says, imagining the Burkes a professional, middle-aged couple with glasses and overcoats, serious demeanors. She feels barely educated in comparison, a glorified babysitter, and remembers her anxiety that fall on Parent-Teacher Night, how she toyed with privately mentioning to them, should they have shown up, that Danny might be better off in a different school. *I'm afraid we can't teach him enough.* Imagine if she had? They might've gotten angry, blamed *her*: she couldn't find challenging enough assignments for gifted students. Blamed Our Lady's: what are we paying tuition for? what's all the bull about superior education at Catholic schools? And if Sister Regina had gotten wind of it, boy, it wouldn't have gone well for her at all. "This was a book you had at home?"

He nods.

"Sounds like your family's very religious."

He nods more eagerly. He's sure this must be true. Is it? His mother? His father?

"That's very good. How many priests are there? I mean—parts."

"Seventeen. But you only need—they can be just—"

"Some of the players can do more than one part. I see. But when will you practice for a play like this? You'll need to practice a lot, won't you?" The boy looks down at his chukka boots, and Liz marvels at the color blooming over his face, how truly red it is; she can almost feel the heat, radiating. But why should he blush at such a question? "Daniel? Have you thought about that?"

And so he clears his throat and makes his timid suggestion.

"Recess?" she says, a bit surprised, though in an instant, sees she shouldn't be. He's always the last to finish his lunch, even behind the girls, little lingering lamb. Almost comical, the tiny bites he takes of his sandwiches, the endless chewing. Something in it, too, that reminds her of a rabbit: nibbly, nose-twitchy. Meanwhile the other boys, the Brian Kesslers, can't wolf theirs down fast enough before they're saying, "Miss Kaigh, can we go outside yet?"

"But the reason for recess is to get a *break* from work. Time to stretch your legs, socialize, be carefree." She smiles urgingly—and insincerely; she doesn't really buy all that garbage about exercise in the middle of the day. Seems a disruption more than anything, the coming in sweaty and all riled up.

"Th-This would be like a break."

"Mm." She tilts her head, biting her lip. "I don't know about that." And exercise is one thing, a hundred fifth-graders running wild in the parking lot for thirty-five minutes is another. Nothing but a couple of mothers out there with whistles. She can just imagine what goes on! Equivalents of "Frizzy Lizzy," lifted skirts; it's not so long ago that she's forgotten. Even in high school she'd ask for passes to the library rather than sit in the lawless cafeteria. And so she looks closer at Danny, examining the endless convolutions of reddish-brown curls across his bowed head, the whorled cowlick at the rear of his crown. A play might be just the thing for a boy like him—structured, group activity. Picturing him in a ring of classmates, talking, cooperating, she exclaims, "I think it's a super idea!" at which he looks up again, pale-blue eyes glinting hopefully. "Of course," she adds, teacher-like again, "first I'll have to read it through carefully and get permission from Sister Regina."

"P-Permission?" Danny says, biting his own lip now.

"But I can't see why she'd say no."

He nods eagerly again and, turning from her desk, starts, almost surprised to see them—the thirty-four other boys and girls in plaid ties and jumpers, looking up with mute, quizzical faces. *What is it?* they seem to be asking. *What is it?* And Danny, not a little proud and nervous, blushes deeper and hurries back to his seat.

"I think I remember saying that if you didn't keep the noise down, you weren't going to be able to talk at all during lunch," Liz says with a shrill, nun-like voice, then shuts the door loudly behind her—too loudly? did the classes down the hall hear it?—and bit by bit, though not as quickly as she'd wish, the shouts and laughter fade to a low buzzing of scattered whispers. "I should think I'd be able to trust you enough to leave the room for five minutes. Kevin Lukas, can I trust you enough to behave yourself when I'm not in the room?"

"Yes, Miss Kaigh."

"I can? Well, then, how is it that just a moment ago I could hear your voice from down the hall?"

The smirking, shaggy-haired boy doesn't answer, and Danny, across the aisle, looks from him to Miss Kaigh's right hand, casually clutching the script. "Would you like me to extend your punishment another week?"

"No, Miss Kaigh."

"At this rate you won't be going outside till May."

But now the sternness drops from his teacher's face and she turns up Danny's aisle. He straightens and waits, heart thumping, and then suddenly she's beside him, tapping two pearl-colored nails on his desktop: "Very impressed, said go right ahead."

He covers his mouth, stifling a yelp—of joy, sure, but not just of joy, because suddenly, as he watches his teacher return to her desk and position the script beside her own lunch, his ears are hot, his arms tingling with goose bumps.

Liz smiles at the red-faced boy and unwraps her sandwich. So excited, good for him. She feels a wave of satisfaction and notices her own excitement again, fanned higher by her talk with Sister Regina, the way the nun's pale, stoic face had animated, "A *Passion* play! How marvelous!" "Yes," Liz said, and went so far as to wave the script. "There's so little of this for them here—the arts." "Oh, I agree," Sister said, and mentioned again the speculation about a new science laboratory and a crafts studio, perhaps as early as next year, "depending, of course, on the success of the fund drive." Then as Liz was turning to go, Sister Regina stopped her and said, "You know, when *I* was a girl, I wanted to be Madame Curie." Liz laughed, as much from surprise as amusement. She'd never imagined a Sister having wanted to be anything else, and it was strange to picture her suddenly, in the white lab coat, handling test tubes and Bunsen burners.

She chuckles again now, raising her tuna fish on pumpernickel, and looks for her place in the script: back in the Garden, the *cup pass Me by*, Judas with the guards. *Do you betray the Son of Man with a—?* Hmm, that could be a problem. Next the cutting of the ear. She imagines *this* part going over with the boys. *Those who live by the sword, die by the sword.* Wonderful. She could pick up on that. Has anyone ever heard this line before? And did you know it was from the Gospels? When all the hands drop, she'd say, This is one of the joys of studying Scripture and literature, to find the sources of things, to see that others have had the same thoughts as you, even before you were born. She reads on. It's really a very gripping story—*greatest story ever told*, she muses. Well organized, too, the way he has it here, in four parts: the agony, the trial, The Way, the crucifixion . . . yes, but then, shouldn't there be a fifth?

While she searches for it, Danny nibbles anxiously at his baloney and mustard on white. Go *right ahead*, he hears Sister Regina say, his stomach fluttering again as all around him the conversations swirl. Here and there he catches a snippet—Joey Flynn doing a practiced imitation of Patty Dupree's orthodontic lisp; a group of girls singing, "Two all-beef patties, special sauce, lettuce, cheese"—though mostly the voices mute together, like a moving sea, and he a piece of something floating on it: small, pale, separate. And just now he remembers the naked boy from the Bible, and pictures riding off together over long, yellowy sand-stretches; and in the distance, palm trees, a sun-bleached village, men in robes and headdresses, like on so many Christmas cards.

"Daniel?"

Once again, as he hurries up the aisle to his teacher's desk, he worries that now she may say it, *I'm so surprised at you. How could you have written such a thing?* But instead she asks, "Is this finished? I can't find the last scene."

"The l-l-last scene?" he parrots, staring at the remains of her sandwich, splayed on a rumpled square of wax paper.

"The resurrection. It doesn't just end here, does it?" She runs her pen along the final line of the script: *My God! My God! Why have You forsaken Me? (Hang head.)*

"Oh."

"He has to come back at the end. Weren't you going to have Him come back afterward?" She raises her skinny-tailed eyebrows, and Danny, in lieu of explaining how the play is only about the Passion, nods earnestly.

"You couldn't have it any other way. Without the resurrection, the suffering has no purpose. It's like there's no reward, no heaven. What kind of Easter show would that be?" She flips to the first page and points to the title. "See," she says, crossing it out, "I didn't pay enough attention to this before. It should be called, 'The Passion *and the Resurrection* of Christ.'" She writes the new title in smaller teacher's-script above the old one. "Right?"

He keeps nodding.

"Because *The Passion* means just the suffering." She thinks a little more, then flips back to the end. "And the *Forsaken-Me* bit," she says, drawing a squiggly line beneath the words, "this isn't the last thing Christ says. He cries out here, He's in pain, and has a—" she doesn't want to say *momentary lapse of faith* "—but then He regains his composure. His dying words are 'Into Your hands I commend My spirit' or 'It is finished,' aren't they?"

"Um . . ." he says, trying to remember all the differences he found.

"And what about 'I thirst' and the sponge? And 'Mother, there is your son'? Are you going to include those?"

"Well . . ." he says, and, "Do you want me to?"

"I think it would be good to have a scene with the Blessed Mother and Mary Magdalene at the foot of the cross. There isn't much for the girls to do."

"B-But, Miss Kaigh," he says, and she looks up, raising her pen. "He says different things."

"Who does?"

"Jesus. In the books."

"You mean the quotes aren't the same in all the Gospels?" Again her forehead wrinkles. *Are* they different? She can't remember. Worse, she suspects she may never have known. When would this have occurred to her before, the question of which lines are in what books? And then just as she's making a mental note to check the Bible at home later, he asks,

"How come they're not the same?"

"How come?"

"Do you-you know which is the right one?"

"The right Gospel?" It seems an absurd question, almost unreligious. "Well, they're *all* right, Daniel. I mean, there's no right one per se." And now she's totally contradicted herself; he has every reason to gape at her like that. She looks back at the script. "What I'm saying is— what I—I think the question you're asking is very complicated, and I'm not sure I can explain it all right now. Let me think it over, and we'll discuss it again tomorrow, okay?"

"Okay."

"But these are very good questions. Very bright. I'm not surprised at all." Quickly, she plucks up her pen again and runs it down the last page. Something else she noticed, what was it, before he—Oh yes. Where did you get this My-*back*! thing?

"M-M-My back?" he says, flinching involuntarily, though Liz barely registers the movement, not too far afield from his repertoire of tics and stutters.

"Does Christ say that? I don't think so. I've never heard that before." She removes the added line. "So just work on the last page some more; otherwise it's excellent. You should be proud." Which is the boy's cue to return to his seat, yet he stalls another moment, script in hand, as if, it seems to Liz, he wants her to say more. And she should, really—widen her eyes, add, *very proud*—because she suspects it's not just excellent, it's extraordinary, a fifth-grader writing a play about the crucifixion from all the Gospels, and one so good! But something makes her not want to praise him too highly. She can't say what exactly, or stop herself that moment from glancing critically at his fastidiously tucked-in shirt. Why? What would she rather, his tail hanging out? His buttons undone? Another Kevin Lukas? She averts her head again, wincing.

But Danny, mind whirling off like a waterspout, perceives none of this; he's thinking solely about the script, recess. "You mean fix it t-t-tonight?"

"Sure, tonight if you like."

"Can I-I do it now?" he murmurs.

"Now?" She looks at the clock on the wall behind him. Only a minute or two before they go outside—*outside*, of course. She nods and says properly, "You may."

"Thank you, Miss Kaigh." He turns again, suppressing a smile. But as she says behind him, "Then tomorrow we'll tell the class and assign the parts," a new cloud passes over him, and he imagines asking, *Assign all the* other *parts, you mean?*

And those are more or less the significant events at school that day, except that Danny's first recess indoors is marred slightly by the presence of Kevin Lukas, who, even after Miss Kaigh positions him at a desk facing the corner and says, "Daniel, Kevin is not to speak while I'm gone," several times tries to engage Danny in conversation: "Pssst. Hey, Curly. Dude. Whatcha workin' on?" and, "How come you're stayin' inside if you're not punished?" Danny keeps shaking his head in reply, only once raising it enough to catch a glimpse of the boy, craning around, his small, rascally teeth clenched row on row. Then at one point in the afternoon, as Danny's thoughts drift back again to the naked boy, he begins to call him *Arram*—just suddenly it's come to him, this magical-sounding, secret-command-like name. It reminds him, too, of *harem*, the ladies in the sheik tent, *I Dream of Jeannie.*
     Later, once he lets himself into the house and runs to take Duke out—a prolonged affair, as the dog bolts out the garage door before Danny has secured the leash to the choke and eludes him all the way to Dixie Lane—he stops again at the bookcase at the top of the stairs and riffles through the Bible for the special page. And there, miraculously, the picture continues to be. He stares fixedly at it and, though he knows no one's home, looks over his shoulder before running his finger down the boy's tan back and heinie and down his long, skinny legs. *Arram*, he says, touching his finger to the boy's raised hand, *come on.* And the boy turns and emerges from the book, bigger, big as Danny; and when he's fully out and standing alongside, Danny leads him down the hall. *This is my room*, he explains, and shows Arram his schoolbooks and the trophy he won in the Town of Islip Halloween window-painting contest. And while the boy's deeply interested in these things, he knows Danny has to work on the play. *I don't mind*, he says.
     But what will you do?
     Sit here. He climbs onto the bed.

That's not enough, Danny says, thinking for him. *I know; you can read.* Fetching *Call It Courage*—about the island-boy, Mafatu, who was afraid of the sea—he lays it opened on the spread before him. Then, *Why were you running after the man on the camel?* he asks, sitting down at his desk.

Oh, the man? And though Arram doesn't say why exactly, he admits he doesn't like the man.

Me, either, Danny says, turning to his script, but then immediately looks back at the boy, pitying his skinniness. *Hey, aren't you hungry? I can get you food.*

Can you?

Danny imagines rushing down to the kitchen and piling a plate with cold cuts and hero-bread. Also deli pickles, cold slaw, potato chips, Oreos, maybe even some honey. Do they eat honey in the Bible? *Here*, he says, and looks on gleefully as the astonished Arram grabs at the food like a little monkey, like a wild jungle boy. Crumbs fall to the spread and floor, and Danny pretends to sweep them up. *Look at the mess you're making! What if my mother sees?* Then quite coincidentally, he hears the actual scraping of the key in the front door downstairs, her voice, "Danny? I'm home." "Hi, Mom." "Doing your schoolwork?" "Uh-huh." He stares past the doorway to the hall, imagining her walking to her room to change out of her office clothes, and for a moment, he's torn between running to tell her the news about the play and watching Arram. But the boy is so interesting! He eats and eats! Especially the cookies, his grinning teeth all speckled with brown. And when he's finally had enough, he gets sleepy and stretches his arms out like Danny's father: *I like a nice nap after a big meal.*

And so he clears the plate away and fluffs up his pillow. *You can nap right here.*

Okay, but you have to nap with me.

Oh no, Danny says. *My mother, the play.*

Just for a little while.

All right. And when he lies on the edge of the twin bed, Arram turns sideways and loops his arm around Danny's chest. Everyone agrees this is okay for him to do, even Brian and Joey. *Oh, those guys are such good friends*, they say, smiling and sad for themselves.

We're friends, right? Danny asks.

Friends, Arram says, and drifts off, snoring softly. Yet his arm remains, and Danny's unable to move or get up from the bed, and so he continues to lie there, studying the side of Arram's face: his closed, thickly lashed eye; his smooth, tan cheek. Sending the boys away, he kisses it softly. *Do you betray the Son of Man?* And later, opening his own eyes again, time has gone by. He checks his watch—forty minutes!—then bolts down to the kitchen. "Mom!"

Carol, at the table, looks up from her new Dell crossword book at her sleepy-eyed son. "Were you napping just now?"

"Miss Kaigh says we can do the play."

She cocks her head, shifting gears. She's been thinking of work, Mr. McVee's sarcastic remarks that morning about the budget report being late. "Play?"

"'The Passion *and the Resurrection* of Christ,'" he tells her.

"Oh." She looks at him skeptically. "You mean you finished it already? How long is it?"

"*Twelve* pages," he announces, clearly impressed with the number.

"*Twelve?*" she says, matching his emphasis, and at the same time wondering if that's very many. Maybe for a kids' play. "Get out of here."

"I swear."

She sucks in her breath and shakes her head, her usual expression of awe, then adds, "Jeez," and notes the smile it produces. Though in truth, she finds this more than a bit unnerving, the way his wild ideas become things so fast. She prefers when ideas stay ideas, though she wouldn't like to admit that, particularly since she's constantly yelling at his father and sister for never completing anything. *No stick-to-it-tivity,* she'll say, quoting her mother. Of course Gerry would use this as another excuse to call her fickle. *You know what you are, is fickle, is what you are, fickle.* Is she? "Well, good for you, Danny," she says, looking down at her puzzle. "Stick-to-it-tivity, I tell ya. That's just great."

Danny stares at her bowed head and at the dark flip of hair about her ear, his smile fading. It seems she hasn't noticed the change in the title.

But then, "Hey, wait a second," and she glances up again, eyes worry-widened. "You mean you're going to put it on now, too? In front of the whole school?"

"*No!*" he says, startled at the mere notion. "Not the wh-whole school."

"Who, then?"

But he hasn't really thought about whom it would be for yet, and pictures again the way they stood at the front of the classes for the Peanuts skit, boys having moved the teachers' desks so they had room; it seemed like there was a lot of room then. Only now when he imagines himself on a kind of cross before the blackboard, there isn't as much. "Just for the class, I guess. Maybe a couple of classes."

"Oh." She looks back down. "That's not so bad." Still, she remembers there was some problem with this play, some hesitation she had about it, and tries to think back to Saturday.

"Miss Kaigh put *the Resurrection* in the title. It used to be just 'The Passion of Christ.'"

"*Passion*, right. I remember that word."

"Miss Kaigh read the whole thing during lunch."

"Oh, did she? Huh," Carol grunts. Of course, she herself hasn't read the play.

"And then Miss Kaigh went down to ask—"

Oh, all right already, she thinks. Miss Kaigh this, Miss Kaigh that. What is she, some kind of saint?

"And she said she was very impressed, that we could go right ahead."

"Who did, your teacher?" This with more annoyance than intended.

"No, S-S-Sister Regina."

"She got the principal involved?"

"She-She had to ask for permission."

"Oh. Yeah, well, that makes sense. Boy, she's really getting her two cents in, this Miss Kaigh. Why doesn't she go write her own play?"

"What?"

Carol shakes her head and considers saying, *You didn't tell her I haven't read it yet, I hope*, but stops herself, then says it after all.

Danny squints at her, momentarily derailed. That she might read it has never occurred to him. "N-No," he says and, waving the question off like a passing mosquito, jumps back into his story—Miss Kaigh calling him up to her desk at lunch—and so Carol doesn't bother murmuring, *Because I will, you know . . . eventually*, and instead looks down at the book again and experiences a mosquito of her own. Something about the play still that's bothering her. She wonders if she could be having a premonition—is that what it's called? Prescience? Some kind of prescience or other, telling her this play may not go well for Danny? Huh. She'll ask Madame Sarah the next time she calls her. "You yourself have psychic powers," Sarah said once, "but you block them out. You're afraid to know things." And here Carol, who likes to think of herself that way—a girl with hidden, untapped powers—adjusts her reading glasses. But still he's going on, something about what Jesus says just before He dies, some controversy or confusion, she doesn't know. Well, how's this for a guess: *Somebody get Me down from here!* She chuckles devilishly to herself, then pats his arm mid-sentence. "All right now, Danny, why don't you finish your homework while I get dinner started?" Not that she plans to for another half hour yet, but this is the first moment she's had to herself all day, and she can feel a headache coming on. She should take a couple Tylenol, but doesn't feel like getting up. Probably just hungry; she threw most of her sandwich out at lunch. Can't really enjoy it when she eats at her desk. But at least she got everything in by four, and now she'll have Mr. McVee off her back again for a while. She looks at Danny. "What did you say, hon?"

"I said I did finish it, but I have to fix the end of the play some more."

Yet even after he rushes off and she turns her full attention to the last, unsolved corners of the puzzle, the subject continues to buzz about her thoughts: the potential trouble, Miss Kaigh. Above all, she doesn't want his teacher to think she's some lazy, uninvolved mother. She can't quite picture the girl, has she met her? Parent-Teacher Night maybe, the Christmas Fair? Then as she winces a little, realizing she hasn't been up to the school in a while—ages, really—she imagines a matronly, churchy type frowning at her.

"Ooooh," Danny mutters upstairs. He's having trouble with the order of the death-scene lines—*seven* now, instead of just two. He especially doesn't see where *Mother, there is your son* can go except for before or after the *Forsaken-Me* question, and that worries him, because the first seems like such a quiet thing to say, and the other like a great cry. He imagines looking down at Mary and John one second, up at God the next, his loving gaze changing to an anguished grimace. Or should he grimace first and then look down, lovingly gazing? He's not sure and glances helplessly at the bed, where Arram is again, sitting on the edge of the mattress. *I don't know the order*, he tells him, and the boy nods sympathetically, but he doesn't know, either. *Then I have to write the whole resurrection.*

Yeah, but that part's easy, Arram says. *All you have to do is walk back in and say, 'I am risen,' then show your hands. You can even keep a red magic marker with you and color in circles on your palms before you come out.*

Oh, that will look good, Danny agrees, *real. Thanks.* And at the same time, because the boy's legs are just dangling there, wide open, he takes affectionate notice. He's becoming used to it, the darker tan color, the long worminess, though here, in the midst of his appraisals, something else occurs to him, *Want to see mine?* and his mouth drops open, his cheeks grow instantly warm. *Only kidding*, he adds, but too late, for now Arram's saying he has to show him because he's seen his—all day he's seen it, whenever he wants. *That's true*, Danny says, eyeing the open door and realizing it can be closed, even though it never is. *All right.* He walks over, heart drumming, and slowly pushes the door into its frame, then slowly, too, presses the button-lock, twinging at the sly, metallic *click*. Yet he rushes to the bed, undoing his belt and zipper and pulling down the side of his underwear. First he shows Arram his right, snowy hip and the diagonal line where his leg meets his belly. *Hinge*, he calls it, not knowing if that's the right word, then peels the front of the band down a little, exposing the tubey, pink beginning. But Arram shakes his head, dissatisfied. *The whole thing?* Danny asks and, with one motion, pushes his pants to his knees.

Arram nods happily now, feasting his eyes while Danny sits beside him, holding it in his palm. "Head," he says, stroking a thumb over the tip like a lady smoothing her hair, puffy hair that flares out at the ends, and he looks for the lady's eyes in front, below the ridge of parted bangs. No, *this* is the eye: the hole at the top, sealed, sleeping. Then he pulls the lids apart, and it's an open, empty eye, a gaping fish mouth. He closes and opens it, *Hi, my name is Dickie*, then looks at Arram. *Make yours talk.* And just as the boy's about to, there's a loud banging at the bottom of the stairwell, his mother yelling up, *"Danny?"*

He jumps to his feet, hiking up his pants, tucking in his shirt. "Y-Y-Y—"

"I was just thinking—"

"—Y-Yeah?"

"Where are you? Do you have your door closed?"

"I'm right here." And, inching toward the landing, he finds her on the bottom step, hand on the bannister, peering up.

"If you bring the script to the office after school tomorrow, I could run off a few copies."

"Copies?" He blinks at her. "You mean, on the Xerox machine?"

"This way everyone has their own, and you won't have to keep passing the original around. Right? I mean, what would happen if you lost that thing? Did you ever think about that, Mr. Couldn't-Find-His-Head-If-It-Wasn't-Attached?"

"Oh," he says, blushing at such mention, then nods excitedly, his waning half-moon of fear behind him, in the bedroom. "Can you?"

~ 3 ~

Fishers of Kids

When Liz sees the revised script the next morning, she's struck by how exactly he's followed her advice—added all the lines she suggested to the crucifixion, brought Christ back on at the end. And it's much more interesting now, with the Mother and John and the earthquake (she pictures a boy drubbing a silver, gong-like instrument offstage), and then the resurrection scene itself she finds pleasingly dramatic, the women throwing their hands up and crying out. She loves the look of the cries on the paper, *He is risen! He is risen!* and, hearing them now in her mind, feels her spirits lift a little and imagines the spirits of the students in the audience lifting along with hers, *Let's join in, class: He is risen! He is risen!*

"Now *this* is how a play should end," she says to Danny, standing again beside her desk, and at once he sighs with relief.

"You mean it doesn't—I-I-I don't have to make any more—?"

"No, it's perfect now. Super," she says, flipping back to page one, rewritten to accommodate the added words of the title.

"Is it okay, then, if my mother—can I give it to her so that she—?"

"What would you like your mother to do?"

"She said when it's finished I can bring it up to her office—"

"You mean she's going to make copies of the script for us?" Liz bobs her head enthusiastically. "By all means. That's so kind of her." But oh, how idiotic she hasn't thought of it herself! Copies, of course. And what a blessing, because it'll save them the trouble of rewriting everything on mimeograph paper, and her the mess of running off the duplicates, one of the things she hates most about her job: the ink, the smell. She's sure wherever his mother works they have one of the beautiful new Xerox machines, so neat and quick and easy. And now come to think of it, "Office?" she asks gingerly. But the boy merely nods in reply, and she has to venture a second question: "Is it far away?"

"No. It's-It's right on M-M-Main Street, at the East Islip Junior High."

"Oh really? Is she a teacher, too?" she asks—excitedly, it seems to Danny, and he thinks about shaking his head because he knows his mother's an *office girl*, the type called *bookkeeper*. Once she even showed him how to spell it: the two O's, two K's, two E's. "Double your trouble," she joked. Still, when he looks up again at Miss Kaigh and her eager, raised eyebrows, he nods and says, "Uh-huh," so as not to disappoint her.

Yet she sends her son to Catholic school, Liz remarks with admiration and wonders how many children there are in his family. Have there been other Burkes at Our Lady's? She'd like to ask, too, what grade his mother teaches but stops herself, for fear she's pried too much already. Has she pried too much? "What grade does your mother teach?"

"Grade?" Danny asks, clearing his throat.

"At the junior high."

"Oh. Um—s-s-seventh."

"Seventh grade?" Liz says, but in a thoughtful, restrained voice Danny can't quite interpret. Could there be something wrong with teaching the seventh grade?

"And-And the eighth."

"The eighth, too?"

"All of them," he says.

"Oh. Does she teach one of the special subjects?"

He knows of only two, art and music. And maybe because he's often heard his mother humming over the stove or remembers her once alluding to a childhood hope of becoming a singer, he picks the second.

"*Music,*" Liz repeats dreamily. To her mind this makes perfect sense, that his mother should herself be creative, a woman of the arts—culture breeding culture, that sort of thing. How else to explain her interest in his projects? She may even play an instrument.

Liz pictures her, for some reason, with a violin, sitting before a small black stand, easily interpreting the hieroglyphic-like marks in the open book before her. And how troubling, in the face of such expertise, to think of their miserable little program at Our Lady's! A class every other week with Mr. Riley, the church organist, to practice hymns and folk songs sung at Mass. She wonders if Mrs. Burke is aware of this and assumes she must be, but now here the boy's pressing index cards on her, cheeks aflame with that singular Irish blush. "And what's this?"

"The list of c-c-characters."

He's even indicated which can be played by the same actor. "Wow," Liz says, pointing to the bracketed duo *SAINT PETER, SIMON C.* "I take it these two aren't in scenes together?"

He shakes his head. "And I-I-I made sure—they h-have to have time to change costumes."

"Oh yes." And as she tells him how smart it was to have taken that into consideration, in her mind she rolls her eyes and says, *Costumes;* she hasn't given much thought to them, either. How many parts did he say there are? She refers to the cards. Seventeen, not counting the narrator. They're going to need soldiers' armor, Roman tunics, all kinds of robes and veils. She can see it already, up to all hours the night before, cutting and sewing. And now she asks herself, Could they be biting off a bit more than they can chew? but quickly dismisses the thought. After all, it's only the first day. If the play's not until the Wednesday before Easter, they'll have three weeks to work everything out—that's plenty of time. Besides, she's already told so many people. Her mother thinks it's a lovely idea. Her brother, too: "It sounds like *Godspell* or something." "*Godspell?*" Liz echoed, not having seen the show; neither, she believed, had he. Still, she'd felt a surge of butterflies, imagining it to have been quite breathtaking. She wouldn't want to disappoint Sister Regina now, either—or, for that matter, Sister Margaret or Mrs. Sullivan in 5A. And then it's quite possible Mrs. Newman, the secretary, heard her talking about the play outside the office yesterday, as well as Mrs. DeLauriello, the nurse. And oh, the reverend himself! She spoke with him just this morning in the parking lot. "That reminds me," she says to Danny now, "I have a message from Father McGann."

"F-F-Father?" Danny says, immediately tensing as he pictures the tall, narrow priest, his oiled black-gray hair, gray teeth. And at the same time, he sees him at a distance, walking gracefully across the churchyard in his wind-rustled cassock, pensive head bowed. What message could Father have for him?

". . . about the Gospels," Liz explains, a bit tentatively. She hadn't really been prepared for the talk. It would've been better if she'd looked up the different crucifixion passages in the Bible first, as she intended, though somehow, once she cleaned up after dinner and graded all the spelling quizzes, she'd, well, forgotten. But then there he was, coming down the side steps of the church just as she was getting out of her car. "He says your question's very astute."

"Astute?" Danny says, smiling at this exotic *smart*.

"He was very surprised that it should come from one of my fifth-graders!" she says proudly. "They *do* vary, he told me, and Christ does say different things, and this is because—" she consults her notes, scrawled on memo paper, "—they're separate accounts of His life, written at different times and in different places, and for different groups of people, believe it or not. Some to Christians, some to Jews. And so each of the writers stressed the things that were important to his specific audience. Do you follow what I'm saying?" But upon perceiving his rumpled, red eyebrows, his mumbled *yes*, she adds her own clarifying analogy: "You know how when people see the same thing happen, their versions of it can be very different?" She waits for his nod. "Well, it's like that, different people giving their different versions of the same event. And while one is stressing this detail, another's stressing that. While Matthew's including this quote . . . uh . . . ." She snaps her fingers.

"Luke?" Danny suggests.

"Luke's including that one. And it's not like any of them are wrong, or more right than the others, but rather, Father says we need to read all four stories together, and that gives us the full picture of what really happened." Here she thumps her hand on the desk, so right does this explanation seem to her.

Danny nods because he sees she's very convinced of what she's said. Still, it perplexes him that the versions should differ if God sent the Holy Spirit to help the writers. Wouldn't the Spirit have told them the same thing? And on the heels of this thought, he has the strange vision of the four bearded Gospel writers standing at the foot of Calvary with parchment scrolls and quill pens, like ancient news reporters.

"All right, then," she says, breathing in excitedly again and placing the script and cards to the side of her desk. "I'll make the announcement before lunch."

For the rest of the morning, they go through the mechanics of history, spelling, math, Danny listening with one ear to Miss Kaigh's clearly enunciated lessons. One ear is enough, really, to follow the gist of what she's saying, and to snap through the long division exercises in the back of his textbook, all the while anticipating the moment she finally picks up the script again and looks at the class.

"People? I have something very special to tell you."

And now as she pauses, allowing a hush to settle over the room, he bows his head in all humility.

"Daniel has written an Easter play."

Then he raises it again, flashes a smile at the staring children, and waits.

However, there are none of the immediate *oohs* and *wows* he expected; no hands shooting up, *Can I be in it? Can I be in it?*; no eager, questioning looks. Instead they all just sit there, as quiet and dull-eyed as when Miss Kaigh recited the list of new vocabulary for the week.

It's almost a sound, the hearts of boy and teacher falling at once, falls of some distance as, until this moment, neither has considered the possibility that the others wouldn't be as excited about the play as they are. But while an embarrassed, panicky heat floods Danny's body, and he imagines the silence to mean the instant death of his idea, Liz is less daunted, and her heart buoys partway back up. The students simply haven't understood what she's said. Maybe the concept is so odd to them they can't comprehend it all at once; this, or they're just being shy. No one wants to be the first to raise his hand, afraid to look *uncool*, as it were. Volunteering for anything is uncool. And so, still cheerfully, "What I said was that Daniel here—" she smiles at him, "—has written a really super play about the crucifixion and resurrection of Jesus Christ, and Sister Regina's given our class permission to perform it. So we're looking for volunteers, anyone who'd like to be in it, or help out . . ."

Now at least there's some movement: little shifts and shuffles and crossings of ankles, some expression in the eyebrows, furrowed or raised, their owners for the most part looking down at their desktops, the floor. A few throw glances around the room or return them, smiling slyly or rolling their widened eyes, but nothing more.

"Okay," she says, a disgruntled edge in her tone, "I guess I'm not being clear. If anyone would like to be in the play, please raise your hand. There are quite a few parts and we need a minimum of . . . a minimum of . . ." She remembers the number but can't bring herself to state it in the face of the zero they're now confronted with. And so she looks over at Danny again and the boy, blushing anew, supplies the answer: "Ten, M-M-M-Miss . . ." Then as if a particularly bad catch on the M isn't enough, he squeals out the rest of her name—"*Kaigh*"—a sudden shrill warbling that unleashes a chain of giggles and titters.

"Well," she says, unruffled, as if the squeal and laughter haven't happened, "nine. You'll be one of the players, won't you?"

He nods stiffly.

"Yes," Liz says. "And so . . ."

Again there's no response.

"Wouldn't *anyone* like to be in the play?" She frowns and glares from row to row, and the shifting becomes more pronounced, the cheeks of the bowed heads more crimson, especially those of her better students: Patty Dupree, the Fitzer twins. And she's wondering which of them to call on, when it occurs to her that these are just the ones she shouldn't appeal to, the goody-two-shoes, teacher's pets. If they're the first to join, the others never will. No, the kinds of students they need are Joey Flynn, Brian Kessler—particularly Brian. She walks to his aisle, eyes lighting hopefully on his downcast, blond-and-brown mop, its bright, feathery tips awning out softly over his ear. Such lovely hair, she admits, for a boy. He reminds her of a little Jimmy Schaeffer, the conceited basketball star at St. Anne's whom the girls had terrible crushes on. Liz herself wasn't so impressed, yet it's clear to her that this one, too, is bound to have a bevy of his own at his beck and call one day. Though for now, before all the nonsense has begun, it's the boys who love him, in their emulating boy-way. Even this moment, she sees them looking from the corners of their eyes, measuring his reactions. *Come on, sweetheart, raise your hand; it wouldn't kill you.* And she imagines the succession of hands behind his, how they'd be fighting each other to be in the play, how there wouldn't be enough parts to go around . . .

But he doesn't raise it, and his face, though red like the others, isn't flustered or cowed by her nearness; rather, it seems it could continue to look down like that for some time. She wags her head, eyeing his smooth, pink cheeks, the almost-white down on his round jaw and the back of his slim neck. Such a little boy to decide so much for all of them. Does he know he decides so much? Not entirely, she imagines, not yet. Still it seems perverse to her, extremely unfair, and she turns away angrily, glancing at Joey, Robin to Brian's Batman. He has the short, parted brown hair of a Robin; duller, impish good looks. And from here to Stacy Ryan, an exceptionally pretty girl in row four: shimmering, cocoa-colored hair clipped back neatly with white enamel barrettes. But they, too, keep their heads decidedly bowed. Briefly, she considers offering them extra credit for religion or exemption from some very involved project she's going to assign the rest of the class. Ha! That would definitely raise some hands! Though of course it's not possible—to blackmail them like that.

And then just at this moment, as if to save her, as if to save it all, there's movement again at the back of the class, renewed giggling and tittering. Without turning, she sees the lone, brave, plump arm angling into the air, the arm, she realizes, of the least-liked boy in the entire grade, possibly the school, an arm of certain calamity.

"Ah, *Stephen*," Brian scoffs, followed by more suppressed laughter.

Now her heart falls the rest of the way, and she feels a warm prickling behind her ears. Pretending not to notice the hand, she walks back toward the front of the room, closing in on Patty Dupree, a girl who's several times given her flowers and once, at Christmas, Jean Naté cologne. She stares down at the ghostly part in the center of her long black hair. Morticia, the students call her—aptly, she thinks. At last the girl's diverted eyes begin to shift, the fingers in her folded hands to wiggle. In the back of the room, the arm is waving, the whole expanse of the boy rocking with the motion. Several students are clearing their throats and looking from Stephen to her. Any second, one of them will speak up, *Miss Kaigh, Stephen's raising his hand.* And so, despite herself, even apologetically, she clears her own throat, and it's as much to say, *Won't you please look up?* which the girl then does, slowly, a hand to her mouth.

"Yes, Patricia?" Liz says, though the girl's dark eyes and all of her long, pale, solemn face seem to be on the verge of saying absolutely nothing.

"Mmm-mmm," she mumbles, low and throaty.

"Patricia, take your hand away. I can't hear you."

"Nothing, Mith Kaigh," she says, her wayward teeth, in a prison of wires and metal brackets, clenched in a half-smiling, half-wincing expression.

"Weren't you going to say something?"

She shakes her head and shrugs, examining the snaky ends of her hair. "Juth wondering—"

"Yes?"

"Like what do you have to do?"

"To be in the play? Oh, is that the trouble?" Liz looks up at the others now, carefully avoiding Stephen's corner, though the boy's arm—tired, it would seem, from having been raised so long—has folded down behind his head, plump fingers tapping at the side of his neck, plump elbow pointing skyward. "Well, first of all," she embarks brightly, "we're going to practice and, uh, make costumes and . . . props. Right, Daniel, props?"

"*Yes,*" he murmurs.

"Like the cross, and swords for the soldiers . . ." She glances at the boys for signs of interest and, finding none, scrambles for some other exciting way to explain the project. When nothing comes quickly enough, she adds, "It's really going to be an awful lot of fun." And, reaching for a piece of chalk, "Should I write your name on the board, Patricia?" Not hearing her answer, she spells it out neatly, just below the heading *Players (Dramatis Personae)*. Then she's looking for a ruler to underline the heading, when the girl actually does respond: only if she can be the something or other.

"The what?" Liz asks, looking to Danny again and shaking her head at his stuttered attempts at translation. Did he just say she had the same part in *It's the Great Pumpkin, Charlie Brown* in the second grade? What could a Peanuts skit possibly have in common with a Passion play? "Oh," Liz says, *"narrator."* Played by the lisping Morticia! "That's a very big part," she says gravely to the girl, who, to her dismay, nods more eagerly now. "I mean," she attempts to qualify, just as a hand goes up in row one—jittery, half-raised. Turning, she's shocked to see it belongs to Ginger Holley, the nervous, cross-eyed girl with coke-bottle glasses, same fearful soul who wouldn't speak in class the entire month of September. *"Virginia?"* she says in too wary a tone, for immediately the girl slaps her hand to her chest and looks around her.

"Me? Oh, I was just, um—I was just, well—" She bites her lip, then throws her head down on her desk. Stacy Ryan, pushing back her cocoa hair, leans across the aisle to ask what she's doing. Ginger shakes her head in her folded arms and, on one of her frantic half-turns in the pretty girl's direction, mumbles something in that scrambled language, *". . . oing-gay oo-tay . . ."*

"She wants to know when you're going to practice," Stacy relays.

Patty looks up now, also. "Yeah."

"I see. Well, that's a good question," Liz says to the girls. "We've given this some thought. And we thought . . ." But here she begins to stammer, realizing suddenly that the other boys aren't going to want to give up their beloved time outdoors, of course they aren't. And instantly, her misgiving is confirmed by a lower-key chorus of gripes and boos.

"I'm not staying in at *recess*," Joey says. "What, like you were going to be in it, anyway?" Brian says, the others laughing and repeating, "What, like you were going to be in it, anyway? He wasn't going to be in it." "Oh yeah," Joey says, "that's true," followed by Kevin, late and even louder, "Yeah, I don't want to stay in at *recess*."

"Hey now, wait a minute," Liz says, about to object to such a free-for-all, when Brian cries, "You have to anyway, you're always punished!" and there's a bigger, more general burst of laughter.

It appears to Danny now—sinking in his seat, arms crossed tightly over his stomach—that the prospect of practicing after lunch has met with unanimous disapproval. Likewise to Liz, admonishing them again to quiet down, not very successfully, though she does, in a glowering sweep of the class, note a few who aren't complaining: Patty and Ginger, drawing back from their unruly neighbors with widened, fearful eyes. Frances, too—the girl-half of the platinum-blond Fitzer twins—is clearly weighing something, her nearly white eyebrows raised, lips pressed together. Then with a quick, checking look at her brother, Rory, in the second row, she shoots her hand up and says, "Miss Kaigh, I'd like to be in the play."

And these words, so articulated and forthright, take Liz by such surprise that, in the hush that follows, she blinks for an instant, as if she doesn't quite understand them. Then, "Oh," she says and, turning to her growing list of undesirables, realizes she might've predicted as much: the Fitzers are individuals, as a pair, anyway; they do unusual things together. She remembers those loose, fuzzy, almost identical landscapes they brought in last month; made them at home with their father, a weekend watercolorist. Lots of very bright green. Still she paraded them around, because, my God, someone had actually gone to the trouble to *create* something. But even the teachers didn't seem to care very much, gave them a wrinkled-brow one-two. And the boys had snickered; evidently painting was sissy stuff, a diversion for nerds. Turning from the board again, Liz glances worriedly at Rory, who's even less popular, a little tattletale. But to her relief, he continues to frantically ink in the white spaces on his composition book cover, "first boy" stigma as yet outweighing his panic at a potential separation from his sister. Neither has he overcome it by the time Juanita Gonzalez, the one Hispanic girl, raises her hand.

"Miss Kaigh?" she says, her round, caramel-colored face ensconced in a great black puff of hair.

"Ah, *Juanita*," Brian says, laughing again.

"Shut up, Brian," Juanita says. "I have a right to be in the play, too."

"*Juanita*," Liz says, "we don't tell people to shut up."

"He's laughing at me. You big galoon." She wags her fist at him and he laughs harder.

"I'm not laughing," he says.

"And we don't call people *galoons*. Where did you hear a word like that? It's not even English."

"I don't like him, he's very rude," she says, then turns, abruptly smiling and batting her eyelashes. "Miss Kaigh, can I be Mary?"

"*Mary?*" Liz squints at the girl, her long wiry hair standing straight up on end and believes she resembles, for all the world, a dark dandelion. At the same time Joey howls and, quite eerily, says her thought aloud: "She can't be Mary!"

Liz spins on him, face flushed with confusion. "Who asked you?"

"Yeah, Joey," Juanita says.

"Quiet, Juanita," Liz says.

And now Frances, "But *I* wanted to be Mary." Ginger, too, has an urgent look in her eyes.

"Nu-uh," Juanita says. "I called it."

"I volunteered before her," Frances says.

"Miss Kaigh," Ginger whines.

"I called it. I'm Mary," Juanita says, patting the airy, black halo, "the Mother of Jeeeesus."

"No," Ginger says.

"That's not fair," Frances says.

"All right, girls." Liz holds up her hand. "Let's not fight over parts. I know it may seem like Mary's the best role, but actually it's very small. In fact, I don't think she has *any* lines. Does she, Daniel?"

Danny starts and shakes his head, and now the girls sit back, grumbling, "No lines?"

Then Juanita raises her hand again. "I know what she can say. How about—" and looking heavenward, hands clasped high on her chest, "Oh, my Son! My Son!" And as the class shrieks in unison, turning to each other with shocked, delighted eyes—"She's crazy!" "Hail Juanita!"—she says it louder, "My Son! My *Son!*"

Liz smiles grudgingly at the glowing performer, her yellowy-brown cheeks darker now with the blush. "That's very good, Juanita, but I don't think the Blessed Mother is the type to wail." This is much appreciated by the others, who titter again and say *wail* as she leafs through the script. "I see Mary Magdalene has a line at the end. Also Pilate's wife, in the trial scene."

"Oh, I want to be Mary Magdaleeeeene," Juanita sings now, bouncing in her seat.

"But you just said you wanted to be Mary," Brian says.

"Make up your mind, Juanita," Joey says.

"No no, Mary Magdalene's much better," Liz says, at once jotting MM beside Juanita's name on the board. "She's the first to see the risen Christ."

"That's right." Juanita wrinkles her nose at the boys. "And what do I say, Miss Kaigh?"

"'Master!' And, 'He is risen! He is risen!'"

"Oh, He is risen! He is risen!" she cries out, in the same rapt, clasped-hands style, but to considerably less laughter and notice. "Give it up," Brian says. Others are looking at their watches and glancing at the closets, where their lunch bags wait.

"Okay," Liz says, "I think we've got enough girls at this point, but we're going to need more boys. We only have—" she glances at Danny, voice faltering, "—one so far. Is that right?" Then looking back at the board and seeing she's never written his name, she quickly aligns it to the right of the girls', a little way down from the top. "Yes, one. And the majority of the parts are for boys." Finally she clears her throat and turns with it, the one last thing that might spark their interest, that couldn't fail to: "Above all, we need someone to play *Christ.*"

She pauses again, to let it hover.

"Now I only want you to raise your hand if you're *very* serious. Christ has a lot of lines, and He's onstage the entire time. It's a difficult part to play, the most important of all. *Pivotal,*" she adds, "does everyone know that word?" and turns to write it, too, on the board. "How do I explain this? The pivot is like the part that everything depends on. I mean, if I make my left foot my pivot," she says, tapping it on the floor, "then I can swing my right foot around like this." With arms outstretched, she moves her body in a stiff arc from the center point, as if she were a human compass. Then, staring down at her beige, open-toe heels, she hears several surprised giggles and becomes aware of the warmth in her cheeks and on the back of her neck. *Elizabeth Kaigh,* she hears her mother chiding, *what on earth are you doing?* "But only if the pivot is grounded firmly in place," she finishes, smiling punchily as she looks back up—at a small sea of puzzled faces. She's surprised how short they are; just children, really. "No? Okay, well, it's what you'd call the lead role, the *starring* role. In the movies, say, or the theater. Everyone's heard of *that,* right?" Juanita nods enthusiastically. "Yes. And so . . ." she says, dropping the smile and crossing her arms. "Who would like to . . . ?" Then uncrossing them again, "Would anyone like to . . . ?"

And though her expectations are by now lower, it still astonishes her, and delivers her to a deeper circle of disappointment, to find that even here they continue to stare at their desktops, arms folded, hands folded, every last one of them—not just uncooperatively but obstinately, spitefully, still. Every last one, that is, but Danny, twisting in his seat like a little wound spring, eyes darting fearfully about the room, as if, it suddenly dawns on her, one of the others may raise his hand before he himself finds the courage to. He himself.

She lets go a startled, incredulous "uh!" She'd never dreamed he'd been harboring such pretensions, had pictured him happily playing a minor apostle. But Christ? Someone so quiet and bashful? Wrong for the part in every way, even physically? Who'd ever picture Christ with curly red hair? She looks at him squarely, meeting his eager expression with an alarmed frown, a quick shake of her head. Immediately, the life seems to drain from him, and he sinks back in his seat with a stunned, white-faced look. Normally, it would pain her to see him so dejected, but at the moment she feels numbed, even irritated.

"We need a real leader to play the role," she says, looking sharply away from him. "Someone brave and mature. Strong. Is there anyone here like that?" She glances from bowed crown to bowed crown of mostly straight brown hair, then despite herself turns quickly to the soft blond one, the words rushing out before she can check them, "Brian, what about you?" But as if to seal her humiliation, he still doesn't look up, just merely twitches his right shoulder— "Wouldn't you like to be Christ?"—before shrugging and shaking his head. "No?" She frowns helplessly and looks to Joey, whose diverted, pink face appears to be holding its breath. "You, Joseph?" And he, also, shakes his head, then collapses to his desktop, rocking with soundless laughter, the boys around him snorting. She ignores them and turns to Matt Poppolano, a nice, bright-faced boy at the back of the class, very endearing with his little sister in the first grade; even plays piano, she believes. At least he has the decency to respond, "No, thank you, Miss Kaigh," which sets the boys exploding afresh, *"No, thank you."* And lastly, the skinny Andrew Dwaney in row two: "No."

"No," she repeats, fending off the urge to stamp her foot. "Not one boy would like to play Christ. The Lord and Savior." And she's about to add something more caustic, maybe *And here I thought I was teaching at a Catholic school*, when, in the far left corner of the room, Stephen

Hinch raises his hand again, to a new burst of chuckles and murmured scoffing: "Stephen wants to be Jesus! He can't, he'll break the cross!"

Finally she addresses him and his plump waving palm. "Yes, Stephen, I see you. You can put it down now. Thank you for volunteering, but I don't think this is the right part for you." Here the laughter resumes, and it's really very heartless laughter; and then to make matters worse, the boy nods amiably—happy enough, it would seem, to have been spoken to. "Perhaps something else," she says to salve her conscience, the dying chuckles just now giving way to a commotion around Herman Edwards's seat, Brian and Joey at its fore: "Go ahead, Herm. Come on, Herm."

Liz narrows her eyes at the boys, and at Herman, by far the shortest student in the class; looks, really, like a third-grader, with his freckled pug nose and bowl of straw-colored hair that just accentuates his pixieness. He keeps saying "nah" to their coaxing, but all the while smiles and glances up. What's going on here? Is this some new way of mocking her? Herman's no friend of theirs; she's heard them call him halfpint, midget.

"Miss Kaigh, Herman wants to do it," Brian says.

"No, I don't."

"Yes, he does," Joey says. "He started to raise his hand before."

"No, I didn't."

"Boys, let him speak for himself," Liz says. "Herman, are you volunteering?"

And now he looks at the eagerly nodding boys, and grins widely. "Oh, all right."

"Yea!" Brian and Joey cheer, and so, too, the boys around them, and in turn, most of the class. A chant begins, "Her-man! Her-man!" and Liz, feeling overrun by it, and by the sudden needling urge for a cigarette, lays aside her hope of finding a suitable player.

"Well, Mr. Edwards," she says to the gloating, pug-nosed boy, her voice stripped of emotion, "it looks like you're chosen."

"Yea!" the class cheers louder, everyone joining in now—with the exception, of course, of Danny, who cannot muster a false face. All this glad sound is not for him. He feels it closing in ominously on all sides, like walls of a contracting room. "Her-man! Her-man!" Within it, he barely perceives what happens next: his teacher asking if there are any other boys who'd like to be in the play; Rory's hand shooting up finally, then Stephen's, yet one more time; his teacher listing their names on the board and sighing, "I guess that will have to do for the first day"; the students hopping up and dashing for the closets; the room filling with chatter.

~ 4 ~

Judas Kisses

Too soon, he looks up from his nibbled ham-and-Swiss and finds them lining up at the back of the classroom. Up front, Miss Kaigh is rummaging through her big beige pocketbook, locating something, closing it again, slinging it over her shoulder. At last she approaches his row, avoiding his eyes as she extends the script. "I'll just be a moment while I drop these devils off. Get everyone together and begin reading through the first page." Then she starts for the door—as if, it seems to Danny, that's all she's going to say.

"Miss Kaigh?" he manages, and she turns impatiently.

"Yes?"

"Am-Am-Am I still the director?" he whispers.

Liz sighs and, glancing now at his fretting blues eyes, feels a belated pang of sympathy. And though of course she thinks of herself as the real director, she sees this as a chance to make up for her, well, gruffness earlier. "Yes, sure, it's your play. Whenever I'm not around, you're in charge." But he hangs his head, only partially consoled, and so she addresses the students who've remained in their seats. "Listen, people. When I'm not around, Daniel's in charge. Pay attention to what he tells you. Okay?" And now when she glances back at him, he nods and looks down at his desk. "Okay. Kevin, get to work; not one word from you. Come on, everyone. Quick."

And right away the scuffling shoes and subdued, murmuring voices; a slow parade of sound fading from the room, the hall, and succeeded finally by a heavy, expectant silence in which Danny visualizes turning to the students behind him and relaying Miss Kaigh's request. But it doesn't seem possible to do that: endure the gazes of so many eyes, be the only one speaking while the others just sit there, quietly listening. It's difficult enough to know they're staring at the back of his head, *his* head, with all the kinky Brillo curls, and so he continues to stare down at the script and his half-eaten sandwich, and the silence deepens.

Finally, "Are we supposed to be doing something?" Juanita blares, and Danny, starting, sees Patty at his left, shrugging and looking askance at him.

"Did Mith Kaigh tell you what we're thuppothed to do?" she asks, a flutter of interest crossing her mirthless face.

Danny bites his lip and, bracing himself, looks over his shoulder, the rest of the room swinging blurrily into view. It's just as he feared: seven waiting faces, fourteen squinting eyes. Then, as he swings back around, Herman's grin fuses with Kevin's small, smirking teeth to produce a particularly sinister sneer. He shakes his head at Patty.

"Didn't thay," Patty reports.

"So what are we doing, then?" Juanita asks. "Waiting for Miss Kaigh to come back?"

Danny nods quickly.

"Yeah," Patty says.

"Well, I hope she's not long, this is boring," Juanita says.

"Yeah, I don't wanna just sit here," Herman says, his voice so munchkin-like that Kevin laughs and sings in the same pitch, "Ding-dong, the witch is dead . . ."

"You're not supposed to be talking," Rory says.

"Butt out, Gumby," Kevin says. "Is your hair always that green, or have you been using it as a snot rag again?"

"Groth," Patty says. "Leave him alone," Frances says.

"I'm telling Miss Kaigh," Rory says.

"You would, you little fag," Kevin scoffs.

"How's he gonna blow his nose in his hair?" Juanita asks.

"It's not even long enough," Ginger ventures.

"All the fags are staying in to practice for the play," Kevin says.

"Shut up, Kevin," Juanita says, "at least we're not staying in because we're punished."

"I'd rather be punished than be a fag in a play."

"That's because you're a retard."

"Who you calling a retard, you little nigger?"

"I'm not a nigger," Juanita says, unfazed, "I'm a Puerto Rican!" Then as she raises her fist, "Brown! Brown is beautiful!" there's a sudden balloon of laughter and comments, chiefly from Kevin, about how crazy Juanita is—"Crazy nigger," he says—but it settles down just as quickly, and the quiet and the waiting resume, even denser and more complete than before; and Danny, holding himself very still, reads and rereads lines from the script, *The hour is on us when the Son of Man is to be handed over to the power of evil men. The hour is on us . . .*

What a surprise, then, when Liz, furiously sucking on a peppermint Lifesaver, rushes back in to find them still in their assigned seats, quiet as church. She gapes at the bowed heads and tapping shoes, at Danny, hunched over his desktop, hand shielding his face, and wants to say, *Why are you just sitting there?* but instead finds herself on the brink of laughter—not a merry kind, more anxious, almost tearful. Because it strikes her now, as she glances from Patty to Ginger to Stephen to Frances to Rory to Herman to Juanita to Danny, that what they have here is an assembly of the shiest, most awkward students in the entire class, a veritable company of outcasts and misfits, in short, a little leper colony.

Her face floods with warmth that she should think such a phrase, but also, truth be told, that she'll be associated with such a group, perceived, even, as its leader. *Queen of the Lepers!* And for a moment, she feels small and girlish again, and pictures herself hidden away in the St. Anne's library. Then, "Well, come on! Come on!" she abruptly booms, a lively, ice-shattering voice—one she realizes she might not have achieved had her audience been that other group, just set loose upon the asphalt. It has the desired effect: they all start and chuckle uneasily; Kevin says, "Whoa! *Miss Kaigh.*"

"We're staying in to rehearse, right? Not stare into space!" She walks to the top of the last row. "Over here," she says. "Make a circle." At once they jump up and descend on the desks, pushing and pulling them across the floor, a sudden, noisy commotion that Liz finds momentarily heartening: the sound, anyway, of productivity. And indeed they accomplish a circle, or at least a rough ellipse. "Today we'll just read the script so everyone knows the story and who the different characters are. Since there's only one copy till tomorrow, we'll have to pass it around. Those with the most lines should sit next to each other. Herman?" She pats the nearest chair back. "And who did we say was going to be the narrator? Frances?" She doesn't really believe this trick will work, and it doesn't: "No, *Patty*," Frances says.

"All right, then," Liz sighs, "next to Herman. The rest of you fill in around."

And here with sudden boldness, Danny rushes to Patty's left, fairly nudging Juanita aside—"Hey, I was gonna sit there!"—and at the same time clutching the script, still in his possession, though he feels it, bitterly, about to be taken from him. And within seconds, it is. He watches helplessly as the first page is transferred to Patty's small, nail-bitten hands.

"Leaving Jeruthalem," the girl begins unceremoniously.

But right away Liz, hovering behind her, says, "No no no. The title first, Patricia. As the narrator, you'll have to walk to center stage and announce the title of the play." Again she looks at her gravely. "Are you sure you want to do this?" To which the girl responds with a blasé shrug/nod combination. "Is that a yes or a no?"

"Yeth," she says, and Liz flinches as the words *passion* and *resurrection* whistle through the girl's braces, eliciting several suppressed giggles—or not so suppressed, as in the fiendishly amused sound that goes up at the back of the room. "Okay, Patricia, let's just . . . take it slower and try to speak as clearly as possible. E-nun-ci-ate," she demonstrates hopefully, but the girl, in attempting to, only makes the whistling more pronounced: "'The Pathon and the Rethur-rethon of Chritht.'" And now the company laughs outright.

"Oh boy," Liz intervenes. "On second thought—here, let me just— *I'll* say the title for today. 'The Passion and the Resurrection of Christ,'" she states crisply. "Now you."

"Leaving Jeruthalem, Jethuth and Hith dithiples thoon reached the Garden of—the Garden of—"

"Gethsemane."

"Geth-themane?"

"No, Geth*semane. Semane.*"

"*Themane.*"

"Never mind. Just say 'Garden. Soon reached the Garden,' period."

"Thoon reached the Garden," the girl says, leaving Liz to wonder, as the lisp-scarred speech continues, if there might be a way of editing most or all words containing S out of the narrator's part. But here she catches herself and sees this as a desperate, ridiculous scheme. It just isn't possible to have a narrator of an Easter play who can't pronounce the name Jesus properly. *Patricia, I'm sorry, but you can't be the narrator.* Too blunt? *Listen, dear . . .* Oh, and not only does she mangle every fourth word, but she says them *all* so lifelessly, just one long, sad, hissing drone.

Finally the page is passed to Herman. *"To disciples,"* he says.

"*Herman,*" Liz rolls her eyes, "don't read the words in parentheses. Those are stage directions. This is your first line, here," flicking a nail at it, "in red." As the boy says "oh" and shifts a little, readying himself, she notices Danny isn't looking at him; rather, he's pouting at his desktop, head leaning on his hands, the middle fingers of which are plugging his ears. And she's waiting for him to glance up so she can shake her head or frown again, when Herman squeals, "My soul is sad, even unto death," with a voice like one of The Chipmunks. Just awful, profoundly un-Christlike. "Sit here and watch with Me. Pray that you may not—"

A slow, snorting guffaw erupts behind her, the type, she recognizes, that's been building for some time and finally escapes. Other eruptions follow, nearer and louder, until the room is besieged with riotous glee.

"What's so funny, Kevin?" she yells, glaring at the beet-faced instigator.

"His voice," the boy says frankly, and the laughter redoubles, not least of all hers, which wells up traitorously now, toppling her angry expression. And once it begins, it isn't easily squelched: she laughs long, from her belly, the students laughing with her, until even Herman joins in, leaving Danny the lone, unsmiling presence. How could they laugh to hear Jesus' words recited so? It seems sinful to him, and he wishes Miss Kaigh would tell them to stop. Yet there she is herself, red-faced, squinty-eyed, hoo-hoo-ing.

Indeed, *Christ with the voice of Alvin the Chipmunk!* she's thinking, imagining the furry mite in robe and sandals, minicrown of thorns, *'Please, Christmas, don't be late . . .'* At last she collects herself. "All right, people. Herman, try to deepen your voice if you can. Speak with more . . . resonance."

"More what?"

"Gusto."

"Father, if it is possible, let this cup pass Me by!" he bellows, managing to sound a bit less like a chipmunk and more like a furious, yipping Chihuahua. She closes her eyes, wishing it were as easy to close her ears, and thinks abstractly about sound, how incomprehensible it is that something invisible and seemingly substanceless can have such an assaulting effect. She pictures the different shapes of the waves: normal, lisp, chipmunk . . . until, travesties later, the second page is passed to Rory, whom she designates as Judas through a quick process of elimination. Stephen's the only other alternative besides Danny, and she can't very well assign the role to *him*—that would be much too bitter a fate for one who'd hoped to play Christ. *"To guards,"* she reads, peering over Rory's shoulder.

"The man I shall—shall—"

"—embrace."

"Embrace?"

"Well . . . hug, the way you would greet a family member or good friend." She sees the students eye one another. "Remember Judas is Christ's good friend, an apostle, which is why his betrayal is so especially terrible."

"—embrace is the one. Arrest Him. And lead Him away. Taking every . . ."

"Precaution. Care, safety. That's two more for the vocabulary list."

"Precaution."

"Approaches Jesus."

"Hail Master!"

Liz reads nonchalantly, *"Kisses him."*

"What?" Herman says.

"Huh?" Rory says. "I have to kiss *Herman?"*

The others laugh again, especially Kevin, who, if she's not mistaken, mutters, "Homos."

She glances at Danny, their cheeks simultaneously coloring. Then several within earshot click their tongues and look up at her, and she scrambles for a response. "What you have to remember is that this is a different culture and a different time, with different customs. Men kissed each other in greeting then, as this suggests—on the cheek, certainly. Do any of you have Italian relatives?" But her question is met with wide eyes, shaking heads. "Because Italian men . . ." she trails off, looking at Juanita, and almost asks, *What about your family?* thinking of the famous Latin passion, the rhumba.

"Do I have to kiss *Herman?*" Rory repeats. Herman grimaces and shakes his head. "I don't know about this play."

"All right, let's not worry about it right now," Liz says to Rory. "But you will have to embrace him in some way. You can't say, 'The man I embrace,' and then not do it."

"Can't someone else be Judas?"

"Rory," she says sternly, "pass the script to Herman."

"Judas," Herman yips, "do you betray the Son of Man with a kiss?"

Again the giggling. "I can see we still have a lot of growing up to do." This as she briefly imagines Rory's and Herman's pink boy lips touching, as if with more than friendliness. Her brow furrows slightly, and she suffers through the next exchange, and through Herman's long scolding of Peter, temporarily played by Frances, for cutting off Malchus's ear. By the time "the apothtleth flee and Jethuth ith bound and led away," she feels exhausted again and suddenly finds herself saying, "Listen, people, I have to leave for a few moments. Can you continue by yourselves?" her voice thick with doubt and guilt. "Just exactly what we've been doing. Very simple. Daniel, I'll be back before the bell and you can tell me what you've accomplished."

Then she's sailing through the door and feeling for her Virginia Slims in her pocketbook, just holding the pack loosely within the bag, as if for reassurance. "You've come a long way, baby," she hears the woman in the commercial sing, as if to mock the smallness and ineffectualness she feels. *Did I hear you say what I think you said? —What?* Of course he would deny it. *—I thought I heard you say a very offensive remark in regard to a boy kissing another boy.* Thank God he didn't say it louder; then she'd have *had* to say something. Little troublemaker. And now inevitably her thoughts turn to Marylou Spencer, an old college friend, wild Marylou and the enchanting bonfire and folk music festival at Ocean Beach several years back. A full-moon celebration, vaguely pagan, and all that lunar light reflecting startlingly across bil-

lowy, fast-moving clouds. They'd wandered afield of the group, were lying on their backs watching the sky, when Marylou pressed a joint on
her, half-jokingly, and Liz took it. "Really?" Marylou said. "Oh, what
the hell," Liz said, "I've always wondered what it's like." And on one
of the passes, her mind flooding with elusive, brilliant-seeming
thoughts—she remembers singing along to strains of "Lucy in the Sky
with Diamonds," visualizing the incredibly high flowers and describing
them in detail to Marylou—her friend's hand dropped down softly and
grazed her breast with the back of her finger. It took Liz a while to perceive the finger, that it was in fact grazing her, and then what a tumult
and confusion proceeded! Questions rushing at her, about lines: why
they were drawn here and not there. For a moment, there seemed a
possibility of expanded borders, of the elimination of borders—allowings in, allowings out, of untried, unthought-of things—but the next,
the possibilities terrified her, and, as she reached out and pushed the
finger away, she felt the chaotic chasm close again. They returned to
the group. She didn't pal around much with Marylou again after that
or smoke any more pot. *Who are you to judge other people? Who are you
to call them names?* Queen of the Lepers. Oh, what has she gotten herself into? Who wants to put on a play people will only laugh at and not
take seriously?

Not me, she thinks, not *I*, pushing open the door to the faculty lavatory; thankfully, it's empty. She sits in a stall, lighting one of the long,
narrow cigarettes, and imagines herself in high school again, sneaking
a smoke between classes, fearing that at any second a teacher might
burst through the door and discover her. A teacher, she chuckles now
to think, not so unlike herself. But very quickly, the chuckle becomes
a groan, and several of the tears that she suddenly, inexplicably feels
trickle down her checks.

Meanwhile in 5B, a naked, tan-colored boy is making pig faces and
devil horns behind Herman's back. Herman doesn't even realize; he
just keeps reading from the script, ruining every line. *Arram,* Danny
says, *make* me *Jesus,* and, as if his friend were a genie, he crosses his
arms, nods, and it's so: they're standing in the Garden, surrounded by
guards. *The man I shall embrace,* Arram tells them, then turns to kiss
Danny—on the cheek, certainly. It's like a little touch of feathers, a

light, warm pressing that continues for a longer and a longer time; they're all waiting for the kiss to be over. *Come on, already,* Malchus says, hand poised on his sword handle. *Knock it off,* the others say, pushing at Arram's shoulder, only it's like he's asleep, kissing. *We're not homos,* Danny assures them, with the lips still on his cheek, but they look at him skeptically. *It's for the play,* he explains, *a different culture.* And then suddenly, "How long is this thing anyway?" Herman squeaks. "Do we have to stay in the whole recess?" and Danny straightens right up. "Can't we just stay in for half?"

No, he wants to say before the others can rally behind him. But then, to his surprise, no one does; and Patty even shakes her head in a slow, emphatic manner, reminding them Miss Kaigh said they should read through the whole script. "Yeah," the twins agree. And only now, as a half-formed idea springs to mind, does Danny manage to make some sound—though not, it would seem, a particularly coherent one. "What?" they all say afterward, and so he swallows and says again, "She-She didn't say *everyone* had to."

"Had to what?" they ask.

"Ev-Everyone doesn't have to stay in. Not the first day," he says, the words like a stream now, sluggish and little but running. And it's astounding to him that when Patty asks, "Who'th going to read Chritht'th lineth, then?" it's he who answers, "I will."

"You?" she says, eyebrows knitting. "You?" the others say. "*You're* gonna?" "Don't make me laugh," Kevin snorts.

"*Yes,*" Danny says, looking stiff-faced at Patty.

"But how'th *Herman* going to learn them if he doethn't practith?" she asks, and Danny squirms beneath her gloomy stare.

"I'll—I'll write them down. He can practice at h-home."

"Oh," she says, eyebrows still knit. It doesn't make sense to him, either, though Herman himself doesn't seem concerned with sense: "Does that mean I can go outside?" is all he wants to know. Then Danny hasn't even said anything yet—just half-smiled, teeth clenched—when the boy jumps up and, quite swiftly, exits the room.

"Wow," Juanita says. "Balls," Kevin says.

And Danny, feeling his face burn hotly, is filled with as much wonder as fear. Because how really like magic, the boy there one moment, gone the next, as if the few lines he'd spoken were a spell that made him disappear, poof! And now Patty simply purses her lips and begins to sputter through her next speech, about the mockery of Christ: "They blind-folded Him and thmacked Hith fathe and thaid, 'Play the prophet for uth, Methiah. Who thtruck You?'" Then the others look at each other and at the unfazed girl, and one by one shrug and turn their attention back to the play. Already the action's moving to the courtyard for Peter's denials, and Danny stiffens, anticipating his first line in the trial scene. And while he sends up an Our Father and an urgent appeal to Jesus, it's Arram who advises him: *Just say it like you say it in your room, by yourself.*

Finally Rory, as Pilate, extends the page, "You go," and Danny takes it tentatively, his blue-and-red-ink script familiar yet menacing, like a thing turned against him.

"Here?" he asks, pointing to the next line.

"Uh-huh."

"Right here?" pointing to it again.

"Yeah."

Like in your room, Arram says, and Danny clears his throat, *Okay,* and parts his lips, *Okay,* but his heart's thumping furiously now, his en-tire body trembling, making little helpless things of hands, the page rattling within them.

Minutes after the last bell, Danny rushes, head-bowed, coat unzipped, through the loud, laughing clusters of students, past their brown- and tan- and rust-colored chukka boots and Hush Puppies, past the chug-ging wall of buses looming along the curbs, all the way to the front of the school. And not until he reaches Main Street and passes Dr. Whitehall's office and the paint and wallpaper store does he slow to a walk, the tension in his back easing somewhat. "I can't hear him," he mutters, remembering how they squinted and frowned. "Man," Kevin snickered, "you really suck, Curly." Oh, and then he stuttered so badly in defense of himself! Again while reading, "It is you wh-wh-who say I am a k-k-k-king." And now he mutters more, "Damn! Dammit!" look-ing before and behind him. "Damn!" he says louder, scowling at the passing cars, the speed limit sign. That wasn't him. He means, it was, but he can do much better. "I hope he's not going to speak that way in the real play," Rory said. "In the real play, Danny isn't Jesus, Herman is," Frances corrected him. "Oh right," Rory said. And then Miss

Kaigh! She got so upset with Herman; she was almost yelling: "How could you have gone outside? You're the lead role! You need to practice more than anyone!" "That'th what I thaid," Patty added. "But—" Herman began to say, and Danny quickly shook his head at him and at Patty and said, "Miss Kaigh . . ." But Miss Kaigh cut them all off. "I'd like to see a bit more *commitment,* a bit more *responsibility,*" stopping short of saying Herman couldn't be Jesus anymore, and so for now he still is—although Danny, who managed to avoid copying the lines down for the boy as promised, remains the only player with a script. He's got one more day to practice it before anyone else can.

And here he starts to run again, past his block and up to the junior high, where, swinging open the side door to the business office, he comes upon the headsetted switchboard operator in the glass-partitioned booth. She looks up from her conversation and smiles and waves him on. *Inside,* she mouths, and Danny, shuffling awkwardly into the large room, nods at the many high-haired, bow-bloused ladies who look up from their desks as he passes. "Oh, Danny's here. Does Carol know?" "Hi there, Danny."

His mother, in the far corner, vaguely registering her name, looks up from the rivers of figures in the payroll books. "Oh my goodness," she says, spotting her droopy-headed, open-coated son ambling toward her. Still in his uniform; must've walked straight from school. She glances at the clock: yup, two-forty-five. She had a feeling he'd stop in today; just moments ago, in fact, she said to herself, *Danny's coming.* And now here he is.

She stands up, and Danny notes her extra-broad smile and the way she looks around before announcing, "My baby's here!" in the singsongy voice she uses with him around the ladies.

"Mom," he says, cringing.

"Oh now," she says, "it's a mother's right to call her youngest her baby, no matter how old he is."

"That's right," the nearby secretaries cluck good-naturedly. "You'll always be the youngest, Danny. You'll always be the baby." And so he stops squinting and quickly circles behind her desk for the next part: the peck on her waxy, creamy-tan cheek.

"Oh, *isn't* he sweet," Mrs. Gallifano, the short lady who picks his mother up every morning, coos, peering at him over the top of her typing glasses.

"What a dear," Mrs. Mercer, the frosted-haired lady who comes to Mah Jongg on Wednesdays, says. "I wish my boys weren't ashamed to kiss their mother hello like that."

Danny smiles nervously at them and at his beaming mother who says, "You didn't walk all the way from Our Lady's with your coat open, I hope." He shakes his head. "I was gonna say. It's not that warm yet." Then she laughs as he squats on the floor, rummaging through his book bag. "What's this now? Another hundred on a test?" glancing at Mrs. Gallifano. At last he comes up with it. "Oh right," she says, taking the now-rumpled stack of looseleaf. "The play, the play! 'The play's the thing!'" She snaps her fingers. "*That's* from a play, isn't it, Danny?" And he nods assuredly, like a boy with knowledge of many. "Which one, do you know?" But he shrugs, and she can see he doesn't, either. "All right," she says, "let's see here. Twelve pages . . . Hey, girls," and now all the ladies in the room look up, "Danny's doing an Easter play for school. Wrote the whole thing himself." She looks down at it again. "Called 'The Passion and the Resurrection of Christ.' How do you like that?"

"About Christ?" "A play?" "Oh, how wonderful." "It's marvelous."

"My little Shakespeare," she adds, placing her hand lightly on his shoulder. Danny, staring at the tile floor, has the urge to step back so the odd pressure will fall away.

"Are you going to be in the play, *too*, Danny?" Mrs. Gallifano asks.

That's what it was—the thing that was bothering Carol the other day. "He's the director," she says quickly.

"The *director*," the ladies croon. "Wow. That's the most important part."

"See?" his mother says to Danny; and to the ladies, "And maybe he'll play . . . Whatshisface."

"Pilate," Danny says.

"Pilate, oh yes," Mrs. Mercer says, "the king."

"You're playing a *king*, Danny?" Mrs. Gallifano asks, and Danny smiles, though he knows Pilate isn't one. He's what's called a governor or a word beginning with p-r-o-, *procura*-something, which is different, he believes, less. Still, he doesn't think he should correct them.

His mother, however, finds the misnomer useful. To her mind, the more this role is talked up, the happier he'll be to play it. Like he doesn't get to be the big king, maybe, but he can be a little one, a king with a *real* crown. She'll say this to him later: Pilate's a king with a real crown, Danny. But is that blasphemy? Probably. Isn't everything? "Yes," she says, nodding pointedly at her son's yet-bowed head, "a king. He's the king of Rome."

The ladies wow and oh-wonderful again, an especially long chorus Danny shrinks from, not understanding enthusiasm for the man who ordered Jesus' whipping and death. For an instant, their voices fuse uncomfortably in his head with those of the multitude that spurred the governor on, *His blood be on us and on our children!*

Yet to Carol, this is the sound of admiration, and as she smiles at her crooning coworkers, her stomach flutters with a thrilling, kidlike excitement. But why should *she* feel excited? She didn't write the damn thing. Hasn't even read it, she reminds herself. Oh, but—it's because he's such a good boy, really, whom she can be proud of. This one, knock on wood, is turning out for some reason; must've done something right for a change. *She* must have. He is *her* boy. And so now, "Come on, Danny," she sings, leading him toward the Xerox room, "let's go copy our masterpiece."

Inside, she removes her hand from his shoulder and they wait quietly, reverently, while the monstrous new machine whirls, firing volleys of light at the first page, rolling out the magical facsimiles below. Carol hums and smiles, thumbing through the rest of the bicolored script, so neatly, almost prettily, written. She frowns at the word *prettily*, though not deeply enough to threaten the bloom of her pleasant mood, and, Oh, here it is, she thinks, smiling wider, her part. JEWS: *Crucify Him! Crucify Him!* Honestly, it all looks so professional—the characters' names capitalized like that, followed by colons. Even stage directions in parentheses! She steals another glance at her son's bowed head, the tight, wiry curls, pale-pink scalp, and wonders again if he may be a genius, if this is what one is, and if she, Carol Burke, is the mother of one. Strange, she hasn't thought of this in a while, not since the results of the IQ. He was just a few points under; she was certain there'd been some mistake and hoped the tests could be retaken. She told the girls he got the score anyway. What is it, 130? 150? In retrospect, she feels kind of bad about that. But then, isn't this proof she wasn't wrong to have done it? Look at him. What other eleven-year-old writes a play like this? And so neatly!

The machine stops, rousing her from her thoughts, and she retrieves the stack of warm, chemically fragrant pages. "Spread them out face-down on that table by the wall," she tells Danny, which he does, happily, and then, "Mom, there's *twenty* copies," he reports.

"I know, we're making a lot of them," she says. "There's a lot of parts, right? And you need a couple extra . . ."

"You won't get in trouble?"

"What are you talking about, trouble? Betty's always in here, copying stuff for her kids."

She means Mrs. Gallifano. But then, "Oh wait," he says, clearly distressed. "Jesus' words aren't in red anymore!"

"What do you mean, not in red?" She takes the sheet from him and confronts the uniform blackness of the script. "Well, of course not, Danny; machines don't copy in color. This isn't 1984, you know."

"But they have to be in red."

She flips her hand. "What difference does it make?"

"No," he says, stamping his little chukka boot. "The holy words of Jesus, they have to be red."

At last she understands. "Oh, you're just saying that because *our* Bible has them in red. They just do that sometimes for effect."

"Effect?"

"Yeah. But you don't have to have it. Joan?" she calls to a secretary outside the door, "it's not every Bible that has Christ's words in red, is it?"

"Red?" Danny hears her say. "Gee, I'm not sure." Then there's a general consultation, after which the Joan-lady concludes, "Betty says it's only the fancy ones have that."

"Hear that, Danny?" his mother says, looking back to him. "Just the fancy ones. Like the ones we have at home," she adds louder, then glances at the ceiling with feigned wariness. "I don't see the sky falling down, do you?"

Not answering, he turns back to the collating table, and Carol takes the opportunity to roll her eyes. *The color of the Jesus words.* Stamped his foot like a five-year-old. "What, so now you're not going to be happy because all the words are one color?"

"No, I'm happy."

"You're sure?"

"Yeah."

"You could put a red box around them, if you want. I can give you some magic markers."

He looks at her, eyebrows raised. "Or underline them."

"Exactly." And so she hums along until the last pages are copied, then shows him how to staple each script three times along the edge so they open like books.

"Wow, Mom, these are great."

"So you like them now?"

"They're perfect."

"See, you needed those. Good. Your old mother can be helpful sometimes, right?"

"You're not old," he tells her, his stomach tightening slightly, and adds, "You look young," the thing he knows she likes to hear.

She laughs and waves him off. "Go on. I'll see you at home. No wait, where's mine?" She plucks a script from the stack. "Almost forgot. How will I ever get to read it?" Then he's out the door, all skips and smiles, and she carries the copy to her desk, a little salvaged bubble of good-will in her throat. But then she can't help it—just before she sits down, she raises her fist and bellows, "Cuh-*roo*-cify Him! Cuh-*roo*-cify Him!" At once the other secretaries look up, breaking into shrieks of startled laughter, none louder than Sandy Bernstein, the one Jewish girl. And Carol, suddenly sober, drops her fist and puts the play in a drawer—the second drawer down, one she doesn't go into very often. I mean, she thinks, it was funny, but it wasn't that funny; they are, after all, talking about the Savior of the human race.

Arram, look! Danny says, throwing down his book bag and producing the stack of scripts.

And the boy, perched on the edge of his bed, takes one and lays it across his naked lap. *Whoa! Everyone's going to like these!*

I know. But I don't want Herman to have one.

Me either, Arram says, and the two squint with shared hatred.

You be Pilate, okay?

Okay. So then you are a king?

It is you who say I am a king, Danny says, unstutteringly now—in his mind, but then quite softly, aloud. *How's that? Better?*

Yeah, Arram says. *Try it again, louder.*

All right. However, now he hears Duke barking with special frenzy in the garage: *ruff! ruff! ruff! ruff! ruff!* Poor boy, Danny hasn't taken him out yet. *Be right back!* he tells Arram and, downstairs in the cold concrete room, has trouble clipping the leash to the choke, the spaniel a whining, wriggling, black-and-white blur. No sooner does Danny throw up the garage door than he lifts his leg on the near yew, something that makes his father furious. "Not there," Danny says, yanking Duke away; and the dog, spattering pee, charges to the closest oak, whimpering and puffing as he lets out a long ongoing stream. Then he charges to the weedy division between their yard and the Mahers' and immediately squats and grunts and looks away, as if embarrassed. "Okay, come on," Danny says, hopefully, as Duke scratches the ground with his hind paws, but midway back to the house the dog sits, unbudging. "Duke, no. Come. I have to practice before Mommy gets home." More bargaining, more refusal. Finally, "Want a frankfurter?" and the matty ears perk up. "I'll give you a frankfurter." A bark, slight movement. "Frankfurter!" Danny shouts, and the dog jumps up and runs with him back inside. Instantly, Danny yanks the big door down, then tries to keep him away from the den door. "Stay, Duke. No, over there." Still the dog barrels past, slip-dashing down the hall for the kitchen and ransacking the garbage. "No!" Danny yells, rushing to the refrigerator for the Oscar Mayers. "Duke, look!" waving a redolent link close to his snout. The dog lunges for it, and Danny pulls back just in time and runs to the garage, the dog chasing. "Go get it!" he cries, flinging the wiener onto the concrete, the dog sailing after it. Then Danny, slamming the door, "Sorry, Duke," races back up to his friend.

Try it again, louder.

"It is you who say I am a king," Danny says, now with remarkable feeling and confidence.

Wow! Arram says. *That was really good.*

It's like it's just coming out of me, and, "The reason I came into the world . . ." he continues; and, *Cool! Great!* Arram cries—here, and all through the rest of the scene, until Pilate says, *Take Him away*, and Danny looks quickly at the boy, *Want to do the Garden now?*

Yeah! Arram says, smilingly slyly; he knows what Danny means.

It's especially terrible because we're friends, Danny says.

Hail friend! Arram says, approaching gamely before the guards. But as Danny turns to offer his cheek, the boy catches his chin in his fingers. *No*, Arram says, *here*, and, quite shockingly, kisses him on the lips.

~ 5 ~

Happiness in Scourging

The popular boy sets the standard, Liz thinks at her desk the next morning, while the class, just retrieved from outside, settles in for the day. The line sounds familiar to her. Something one of her own teachers said, maybe? Her mother? It has the ring of wisdom to it now, a truth of the ages, and she considers conveying as much to Brian and Joey later, pulling them aside during lunch. Or better, she could approach them out in the yard at recess—on their own turf, so to speak. And why not? Why can't a play be cool? Why can it only be sports? They need to be exposed to other things—pushed, if necessary. She glances furtively at the pair, talking intently across the aisle as they stuff their books in the compartments beneath their seats. About what? Some famous athlete, she imagines, some important game she knows nothing of. Is it football now? No, that ended a while ago: Super Bowl, inescapable event. Dolphins, Dolphins, that's all she heard; her brother, Dennis, in the TV room with her father and the men all day, cheering and drinking even more beer than usual. She might ask them. Well, not her father, he doesn't know much about children, but Dennis might have some idea of how to approach them. Damn. She should've thought of that earlier; she wants to talk to them today. If she could just get them to try it, the experience itself would win them over, she's sure of it. What boy wouldn't like putting on a costume and disguising his voice, pretending to be someone else? Who could resist the magic of theater? Some of her brightest memories are of plays: the traveling company that visited St. Anne's when she was young. Just the sight of their yellow moving truck in the parking lot gave her butterflies, as if it were depositing, right on the school steps, the contents of a whole other world. What was it they did? Some Mark Twain thing? *Prince and the Pauper,* maybe? *Connecticut Yankee?* And oh, the comfortable darkness of the auditorium before the show began, the hushed anticipation, and finally the great splash of light and music, the actors' booming voices, nimble movements. She never wanted it to end! But of course it did, so fast, and then they were right back to everything—the old halls, the old classrooms. And now suddenly also, a familiar stammering to her left: "M-M-Miss Kaigh?"

"Huh?"

Danny, flourishing a stack of papers.

"Oh, you've got them! Great!" she purrs, flipping through the crisp, securely stapled manuscripts, seventeen tacit symbols of his musician-mother's competence and industry. "Thank you very much," she says, placing them on a far corner of her desktop and wishing to return to the warm memory of the traveling company. However, the boy lingers, lips forming words they don't quite articulate. He doesn't want her to hold on to them, is that it? "Don't worry, Daniel, they'll be fine up here." And so he returns to his seat, but too late, the memory's receded beyond her grasp. And the next minute, the bell rings, and the announcements and prayers begin: the dull engine of the day, chugging into gear.

Yet at points throughout the morning, she feels a tentative resurgence of her former excitement. Somehow the fact of the scripts themselves, their piled, waiting freshness, is heartening, and later, during lunch, she gives it another stab. "Remember if you want to be in the play to stay in your seat when the others line up. Some of you may have thought it over last night and changed your minds. Or perhaps you'd just like to try it out for one day, to see if you'll like it. That's okay, too." But glancing at the boys, she finds them sealed obliviously in a small, yapping circle. Neither do they wait behind when it's time to go outside; instead, from the door at the end of the hall, they run shrieking down the steps, like freed animals.

Discouraged again, she returns to the quiet classroom, where she does find one additional refugee: Paolo Moreno, the Sicilian boy. *Do the men in your family kiss each other?* she imagines asking, but says only, "Joining us, Paolo?" all the while eyeing his bowed, nodding head, his straightened swab of coarse brown hair. "How nice. Paolo will make a good soldier. Don't you think, people?" There are murmured assents from the charter players, and Paolo smiles faintly, cheeks a hot, oxblood red. He seems generally embarrassed and sad, as if just his presence here is a humiliating defeat, as if he's forever locked in now, while the others outside run wherever they please. Liz sighs for him and clicks her tongue, then distributes scripts around the reconfigured ellipse, relinquishing each one slowly, almost reluctantly, like wards to a hapless fate.

"Mrs. Burke was kind enough to run these off at the public school for us," she says. Danny, sneering at Herman as he paws his personal copy, looks up quickly. "Mrs. Burke is the music teacher at East Islip. Right, Daniel? At the junior high?" The boy smiles tightly at her. "Didn't you say she plays the violin?" she fishes, but now he squints and vaguely shakes his head. "I thought you said she played an instrument of some kind."

"N-N-No," Danny says. "I mean . . . y-yes."

"Play . . . ?" she continues.

". . . the violin," he finishes.

"She does! Really. How incredible. I mean, the violin is such a . . . romantic instrument." And what a coincidence, to have guessed which one, out of so many! Couldn't she as easily have thought piano, oboe, flute? It's almost as if she knows the woman somehow. "We'll have to think of a way to thank her," she says, looking at the others, and right away Juanita remarks, "I know, Miss Kaigh. We can make her a card."

"A card?" Liz looks at the girl keenly. "Sure, yes, a card. Good idea." But then, not the kind *she* has in mind: folded sheet of construction paper, crayon scrawl, *THANK YOU!* "I'll pick one up at the stationery," she tells them. A tasteful one; have them all sign it, put some thoughtful note of her own at the bottom. Maybe include a reference to classical music, the *Messiah*. She's heard that at Christmas, of course, parts of it—the "Hallelujah Chorus," "Unto Us." So beautiful! No, *exquisite*. Yes, that's the word. *I have always adored so-and-so's 'Messiah.'* Have to look up the name.

"Now that we all have copies we can practice the action of the play, too," she announces, overseeing Rory and Paolo in sliding her desk into the corner, before sending Patty out into the newly empty space at the front of the room. But before the girl can assault them with her phlegmatic hisses, she suggests as a kind of distraction that Christ and the apostles enter simultaneously from the side, on their way to the Garden, so that by the time she's finished the opening speech, they'll be standing right in it, ready to go, and this is received as a kind of genius. "Oh wow. Cool, Miss Kaigh." "All right? Herman, you station yourself over by the windows. And he's got Peter, John and James with him, right? So—" But now, as Stephen Hinch's hand shoots into the air, she looks down at the script, aware of a numbers problem. "We're also going to need Judas and the guards in a moment. They'll come in from the right, by the door." She points without looking up. "That's seven boys, two more than we have." Two, how ironic; imagining the blue-coated duo wandering aimlessly through the lots outside, she has a mind to grab her coat and go right after them. But before she can resolve to do this, a second hand goes up, Danny's: C-Could they pr-practice with w-one apostle and one guard? "Oh," she says, frowning, because it's true the others more or less do just stand around. "All right. So . . . there's Christ." She glances at Herman, grinning from his perch on the radiator. "Judas and Malchus . . ." Rory and Paolo by the door. "And now Peter," she says, turning back to Danny, who immediately looks away. "How about it, Daniel? There's a line here before you use the sword on Malchus, and in the next scene you've got three." The sword bit isn't right for him, but she can see him managing the denials and the weeping. In fact, his stuttering and mumbling might work quite well here.

But *Peter?* Danny's thinking, the disowner of Jesus? Who runs away in His hour of need?

"This might be just the role for you."

Not to mention that once he does run off, he doesn't come back for the rest of the play. It's just a quick, any-boy part, even smaller than Pilate.

"We need another boy."

Now the others join in: "Yeah, Danny." "Come on, Danny." "Don't you want to be in your own play?" Stephen Hinch waves his hand faster, "Oh-oh, Miss Kaigh. Miss Kaigh, I'm a boy."

"Daniel," she orders, "go over and stand behind Herman."

With a dizzy, panicky feeling, he hobbles to the radiator below the windows, Herman grinning down at him. "Gimme five, Pete," he squeaks, holding out his hand, which Danny leaves hanging, chiefly for fear of his bad aim. "Okay, don't." But now Stephen, a second, silent apostle, looms up behind him like a heavy-breathing wall. To step away from one is to move closer to the other, and so he stands tensely in place until the title's announced, and Miss Kaigh waves them on: "Slower. Walk like a group, not single-file. That's better, like friends walking down the street. Herman, pretend you're talking to them." The boy looks over his shoulder, half-stepping and moving his lips silently up and down, like fish-breathing. Then as Miss Kaigh prompts him for the first lines, Danny moves to the other side of Stephen—out of sight, he thinks.

Liz sees him shrinking away and would say something if she weren't so concerned with Herman, how much more miscast he looks standing up: a whole head shorter than Danny, dwarfed in every dimension by Stephen. It seems absurd they should be following him, this bratty infant-king, this Alvin the chipmunk of saviors. And then as the mite concludes his squeaky speech, the three proceed to gape at each other and at her. "Well," she says, "do what he tells you. Sit down and wait."

But instead they look to one another, murmuring, "Where?"

"What do you mean, where? On the ground. You're outside, in the Garden."

"But Miss Kaigh," Rory calls from the door, "we're not allowed to sit on the floor."

"I know that. This is different; it's a play. Don't you understand what I've been telling you? You're not in school now, you're in Jerusalem."

"Jerusalem!" they say.

"Yes, Jerusalem, in Israel. All the way across the Atlantic Ocean, and the Mediterranean Sea, near Egypt and Jordan."

"Egypt!"

"A whole other world," she says. "Deserts and palm trees and camels and a great temple!"

"Wow."

"Yes. And I want you to imagine, too, that it's not 1973, but 30-something A.D., nineteen hundred and forty years ago. Can you imagine that many years ago?" "No," someone says. Did someone actually say no? "And you two," looking at Danny and Stephen, "are Peter and John, disciples of this—this—" here stretching her own imagination toward Herman, "*man*. And you're all in the Garden of Gethsemane where there's no place to sit but on the ground, and so you sit on it. Go."

They obey at once and Liz nods, satisfied with her speech. She believes she's just taught them something important, imparted some sense of a larger world, of history. But immediately these pleasant thoughts are dashed by Herman who, going off his stone's throw, kneels, swings his clasped hands, and giggles his exhortations to the Father, actually giggles them. "Herman, is that your interpretation of agony? Daniel, Stephen, shouldn't you have pretended to fall asleep already?" Here Stephen thumps back onto the floor, leadenly supine, his massive arms and legs outstretched cartwheel fashion, and the group explodes anew, more so when he adds the effect of a snore. In protest, Danny leans back against the radiator and closes his eyes. But soon he has to open them again and sit back up when Herman walks over to scold them, then pretend to fall asleep again when he leaves. At last Rory, with Paolo in tow, begins his stiff traitor's canter across the room, all the while pleading with Miss Kaigh.

"Oh, all right, so don't embrace him. I don't know what we're going to do about this." She's disgusted for other reasons, every reason—the way they gesture, walk, speak. It's all so . . . unnatural and flat. Not one spark of vitality anywhere, not an iota of confidence or, what is it? Stage presence? If she can use such a term. And now what's Danny doing? Hiding again, fussing with his uniform. "Daniel, Peter's not going to be concerned with brushing off his trousers as the guards arrive. And the rest of you, how about trying to put some life in your voices? And picking your heads up once in a while and actually looking at each other when you speak? You can't be reading from the script all the time. Next week, I won't let you use the script at all," this just occurring to her.

"What?" they say.

"Well, what did you think? Did you ever see actors on TV reading their lines?"

"You mean we have to memorize this whole thing?" Herman squeaks, rustling his script.

"Hey, wait," Juanita says, waving hers. "You mean like is this what the Partridge Family does before a show?"

Liz seizes the homely analogy: "Exactly like what the Partridge Family does!" However, now Juanita and Frances erupt into a passionate contest of just who has more pinups of David Cassidy in her room. Ginger claims she's filled an entire wall. "Let's not get into a discussion of David Cassidy," Liz says, and the girls shriek—just, it seems, that she should say his name.

"We should do a Partridge Family play instead!" Frances suggests.

"Yeah!" Juanita cries. "Miss Kaigh, you can be Shirley Jones!"

"I have absolutely no desire to be Shirley Jones."

"And we can be Laurie and Tracy," Frances says to Juanita.

"Let's sing, 'I Think I Love You,'" Juanita says.

"Let's not," Liz says. "I think you girls need something to do." She sets them up in a small group in the back to discuss and compile a list of props. Meanwhile Paolo, with the help of Rory, doubling as second guard, "seizes" Christ—that is, slowly, almost politely, interlocks arms with him—at which Herman ad-libs, "No! No! Let Me go!"

"Hey," Liz cuts in, "Christ doesn't scream." After further explanations of His calm acceptance of His fate, His dignified, silent suffering, there's another pause, and she looks down at the script—Peter. "Daniel?" All red in the face, whispering to Stephen. "What's the problem now? It's your line."

"There's no sword," Stephen relays. And so Rory picks up the yard-stick from the chalk ledge. "Miss Kaigh, can he use this?"

She doesn't see why not. "Just be careful."

"Here," Rory says then, waving it, and Danny grasps an end reluctantly. He was hoping they'd just skip over this part, as they skipped over the embrace. And now, as he glances at the three sets of expectant eyes, he knows he's supposed to lift the sword and bring it down close to Paolo's head—close, without actually hitting him—but instead the ungainly ruler, like a thing possessed, swings around sideways and swats the boy on the hip.

"What are you doing? *Mio Dio*, you're supposed to cut off my *ear!*" he yells over the laughter, the whites of his eyes shining out starkly.

"Daniel, raise the sword a bit higher," his teacher encourages. But quite suddenly he shakes his head, a meek but clear refusal, which surprises him and much more so Liz, who can't remember a time he's contradicted her. "What?" she says.

"I-I don't w-w-want to do it," he says, scraping the tip of the ruler across the floor.

"I'll do it, Miss Kaigh," Stephen offers.

"This is your part, Daniel."

Again he shakes his head, and she flushes with frustration and embarrassment. Clearly, she shouldn't tolerate this. How will she stop the next one from defying her? And the one after that? Envisioning her tenuous control collapsing about her like dominoes—and all because of Danny, the very boy this whole thing is for—she manages to say, "You really don't want to?" her voice wavering between hurt and anger.

"N-No," he says in the same maddeningly meek tone.

Finally Liz throws up her hands and looks away from him. "Sit down, then. Someone else, come on."

Stephen takes it up. "Lord, shall we use the sword?" he booms and, with a look of fierce concentration on his chinned face, brings the ruler down to one side of Paolo's head, smacking him square on the shoulder.

"Ow! That hurt, jerk!" Paolo screams, and Liz jumps up, not knowing which boy to scold first.

"I didn't do it hard."

"Yes, you did."

"Stephen, put that ruler down!" Liz yells. "Paolo, are you all right?"

"No," he says, then "yeah," and leaves off rubbing the spot.

What a circus, she thinks and, with quick decision, grabs up her coat and bag. "Everyone continue what you're doing. Boys, keep practicing. Girls, . . ." Vaguely, she promises to return.

She's already seen the zipping, miniature football by the time the boys, catching sight of her on the landing, halt mid-sprint, automatically affecting casual, strolling gaits and ongoing conversations. A husky 5C student believes he's craftily concealed the ball in the hood of his parka, and now as she approaches, the others back away, leaving him to fend for himself.

"I'll take that," she says, holding out her hand.

"Take what?" the boy says, flicking his brown bangs.

"The little football you've got in your coat."

"Oh that." He produces it, the scaredy-cats laughing nervously behind them, then she gets his name, Arnold Graybosch. "And what would this be for, I wonder, Mr. Graybosch?" she asks, examining the nubby red plastic and stenciled letters along the seam: *Peewee*. "Not Keep Away, I hope."

"Uh-uh."

"Of course not." She slips it into her coat pocket. "You can explain to Sister Margaret what it was for when recess is over." Then she turns to the others, "Brian, Joseph, I'd like to speak to you a moment," and once again they laugh and ummm, and Joey says quickly, "We weren't playing, Miss Kaigh."

She doesn't believe him; just lucky enough not to be near the action when she got out here. "Did I say you were? I said I'd like to speak to you, is all." And to the gawking extras, "This doesn't concern anyone else," and so they slowly drift in different directions.

"It's about the play," she explains to the boys privately and, when they both say "oh" and look down at the asphalt, adds, "The popular boy sets the standard," but too soon, without any lead-up, and now they glance at her with puzzled, almost scornful expressions. "What I'm saying is—let's be clear, we all know the others look up to you. They follow you, copy what you do. Do you understand what I'm saying? I'm saying—*you* have little brothers at home, don't you, Brian?"

He grunts affirmatively.

"Well, it's like that. You're like the ones they watch to see how they should act. Isn't that the way they are?"

But his icy-green eyes shift enigmatically.

"And so if these other boys think you don't want to be in the play," she says, sweeping her arm about the parking lot, as if to indicate the reaches of his kingdom, "they're not going to want to be in it, either. But if they think you think the play is—is *cool*," she adds, not as hiply as she hoped, and worse, Joey snorts here in a quick, surprised way that makes her stammer and blush, "then they'll think it's . . . cool, too." And now as she searches for ways to modify what she's said, the boys exchange glances, frowns, squints, in what seems an involved, secret communication.

"But Miss Kaigh," Joey says finally, "recess is the only time we get to talk and goof off."

"But what if you only stay inside sometimes? If you play the guards and soldiers, for instance . . ."

However, Brian shakes his head in the middle of this, and now Joey reports, "We don't want to stay inside any day."

Liz clicks her tongue. "Why? I don't get this. There's some other reason you don't want to be in the play, what is it? It can't just be giving up one or two afternoons . . ."

Again they shrug and exchange glances. "Because none of our friends are in it. Right, Bri?" Joey says, and the blond boy nods.

"But you could have all been in it!" Liz says exasperatedly. "You didn't raise your hands!"

"It's not our play."

"What do you mean, it's not your play? It's everyone's play." But she knows very well what he means. "Daniel only wrote it," she says traitorously. "He has a very small part."

"Yeah, but—" Brian begins, and Joey finishes the line under his breath, "—all the fags are in it."

"Joseph!" Liz steps back slightly. "I heard that." Yet here again she has the disconcerting impression the boy's spoken her own dark thoughts aloud. She blushes again to remember them: *company of misfits, leper colony.* "That was not a very nice thing to say." And now she looks behind her to the classroom windows. "How would you feel if you were one of those children inside and your own classmates were calling you names like that?"

"I don't know," he mumbles, and she can see that he really doesn't. Because when it comes down to it, he's not one of those children inside.

"'Whatsoever you do to the least of My brothers, that you do unto Me.' Didn't we just practice that hymn last week?"

"Yes."

"And do you remember who the Me was?"

"Jesus."

"Well, would you call Him a name like that?"

"No," he says.

"No. Not if you're Christian." She shakes her head above them. "I expected more from you two. Well, go ahead. Back to your *goofing off.*" As they trot away, she notes with bitter envy their graceful, confident movements, and notes what fine actors they'd make, possessing, as they do, the world's good regard. That's the difference, she understands suddenly, the thing that makes them free and spontaneous and able to walk with their heads upright. And now, as her hand clenches around the Peewee in her pocket, she has the urge to fling it at them—right at their backs, at the backs of their heads. Imagine? *You hit one of the children with a football?* Sister Regina's round, pale face, full of reproach. How would she ever explain herself? *It was a small football. —It doesn't matter what size it was! —I don't know what came over me.*

She spins around and rushes for the building. In the vacant stairwell, she considers lighting up—two fast, delicious drags and then stamping it right out—but immediately recoils from this second insanity. If anyone were to see her, she'd get severely reprimanded, maybe even fired. Yet it seems impossible to go back without having a cigarette; she's too frazzled, too much like a tiny twig about to snap. And so on her way to the lounge again, she pauses unseen outside her classroom door and takes in a lifeless swath of trial: Rory at the fore of a slumpy-shouldered arc of players, haltingly interrogating the silent, smirking prisoner, "Surely You hear. How many charges they. Bring against You?" Then the girls in the back, doodling on looseleaf and discordantly crooning, "I think I love you."

All the fags, she thinks, her frustration mixing now with pity. She won't let them go it alone; she'll move those boys yet, turn this thing around. And, here sensing Juanita glancing toward the door, she drops her head again and continues down the hall.

"Hey, everyone," Juanita announces, "Miss Kaigh was just watching outside."

They all look at the empty doorway. "Where?" "No, she wasn't."

"Yes. She looked like she was crying."

But the boys shrug her off, Rory standing alone at the front now, Stephen and Paolo having just taken Herman off "to a room inside"— that is, to the end of the blackboard near the garbage can—and from here they look to Danny and Patty, seated beside one another in the ellipse. "Now what?"

"Thcourge Him," Patty says.

"Objection!" Herman says, like a lawyer on TV. He's been saying this all through the trial, and no one thinks it's funny anymore.

"But we don't have a whip," Stephen says.

"Can they use their belts?" Rory asks, and Danny and Patty grumble doubtfully. But already Stephen's removing his, thick and reddish-brown; Kevin's urging him on with a striptease song, "Da da da *da!*" and the prop-girls, laughing, jump up to get a closer look. It seems to go on and on, the length of two belts, three.

"Whoa now, big boy," Herman squeaks, cringing dramatically. "Easy does it! Easy does it!"

But once Paolo, too, removes his own, regular-sized belt, Herman leans eagerly against the garbage can, baring his small, pale-blue-shirted back. Then the boys, cheered on by the arc of spectators, proceed to move their arms in slow motion, the belts winding through the air and dropping lightly down on either side of him.

"Oh! Ooh! Ow!" Herman cries, forgetting Miss Kaigh's silent suffering point, one Danny particularly harkened to, having read nearly the same line in *The Life*, *Christ endures pain silently.*

No! he wants to say, and, looking to Patty, whispers, "He sh-sh-shouldn't cry."

"Tell him," the girl says. *"You're* the athithtant director."

But he winces and shakes his head.

"Then am I the athithtant?"

He shakes his head again.

"The athithtant athithtant?"

"Mm," he says, half-nodding.

"Okay," she says, and barks, "Herman, you're not thupposed to thay anything."

"And he sh-shouldn't smile."

"And thtop thmiling."

"Really," Frances says, "he's being whipped. What does he want to smile for?"

"B-B-But," Danny says louder, goose bumps rising on his neck and arms, "Jesus *n-n-never* smiles, even when He's *n-not* being whipped."

He feels this must be true, though he hasn't read every Gospel from be-ginning to end. Still he claims, "He doesn't think *anything's* funny."

"All right," Herman says, trying to drop his grin, but it keeps sneak-ing back up as the soldier-boys lightly rain their belts down just to his left or just to his right.

"No, hit him in the butt!" Kevin shouts. "Really hit 'im. Hard!"

And now Juanita, "I don't think you guys are doin' it right. You gotta say something when you're whipping Him, push Him around a little, spit at Him. Like this, *tooh!*" sending an invisible lob Herman's way.

"Hey!" Rory says, first in a chorus of indignation and nervous cack-ling. "Juanita just spit at Jesus!"

"But that's what they do! It says it in the Bible. Here, let me show you," she says, relieving Paolo of his belt and swinging it a little harder, "Take that, you jerk!" just misses Herman's elbow. "*Tooh!*"

And now the swelling laughter swamps all further protests: "It's not funny!" Danny stands up to say; "Juanita called Jesus a *jerk!*" Rory cries.

"I'm not calling Him that myself," she says, pressing an innocent hand to her heart, "the soldier is."

"Yeah, she's just acting," Ginger says.

"Miss Kaigh said we're in Jerusalem," Frances reminds them.

"Does that mean we can call Him anything we want?" Stephen asks.

"Yeah!" Juanita says.

"Anything?"

"Yeah!" Kevin says.

"Fatass," he offers. "Thunder thighs."

"Wait!" Danny says.

"Spic," Paolo says.

"Four-eyes," Ginger adds.

"Scumbag!" Kevin shouts.

Then it's a whirl of names: "Weakling! Nigger! Crybaby! Shrimp! Dickweed!"

"You're just calling Him what everyone calls you."

"So are you."

"Shut up, retard!"

"You shut up, asshole!"

Finally, as they exhaust their lists, Paolo looks down at his script and reads the one written line, "Hail! King of the Jews!"

Things are equally chaotic later when they try to stage The Way without a cross, or anything that might serve as a makeshift, and everyone hollers suggestions. "We can tie the ruler and the pointing stick together," Rory says, and this is considered but finally rejected as too small and funny-looking. "We'll juth have to pretend to have a croth for now," Patty says. Then the debate reswirls as to who should play Mary: Frances or Ginger.

"I'm tired of this," Herman cries, unheeded by the quarreling group. Danny, seeing an opportunity to approach him privately, is about to say it might be all right for him to go outside again, when Miss Kaigh returns and yells at them for being too noisy, then settles the score with the girls. "Frances will play the Mother," she says, for obvious, unstateable reasons: she's the less homely of the two and has the longer hair. "Virginia can be Pilate's wife." Then soon the bell rings, and in the commotion that follows—the students pushing the desks back into rows, Miss Kaigh running to pick up the others outside—Danny's at least able to request that Herman return his copy of the script. "I have to make some changes to the lines," he explains, and the dumbly trusting boy doesn't even ask which ones before handing it over.

This same copy Danny brings home with him and lays on his bed for Arram to read; and several moments into the whipping rehearsal, as he stares silently and nobly at the drawn window curtains while swinging his doubled-up belt over his shoulder and smacking his own back, he remembers an important detail. *Hey—* he begins to say, but then, more prudently, has the boy suggest it instead:

Don't they strip Him first?

Danny looks at Arram keenly.

Remember? 'Our Savior's back was bared,' Arram quotes.

That's right! Danny says and, at the risk of belying his coyness, quickly fetches *The Life* from the hall and flips to the "Jesus Is Scourged" chapter. *'The soldiers removed His robe and forced Him into a stooping position.'*

See! Arram says, *cool!* and, indicating Danny's corduroys and velour shirt, *So remove your robe.*

Not me, you. The soldiers *remove them.*

Oh yeah, Arram says, eagerly tugging off his shirt and undershirt. And now Danny, the bedroom air swarming coolly over his naked shoulders, hurries to his mirror to gaze at himself as Arram would: at the skinny white waist, small pink titties. *You've got an outy,* the boy notes with less derision than Danny's sister, and Danny rushes to cover it. But Arram pulls his hand away: *It's all right,* he says, and smiles at the tiny baby-nose of flesh. *Now the pants.*

At once he lifts his arms, imagining Arram's tan fingers undoing his button and zipper, then quickly dispatches the pants himself and stands in his Fruit of the Looms. *We have to pretend these are the cloth,* he says of his briefs.

Arram frowns. *Unless we make one.*

Make one? Danny says. *How?* Next he's running for the bathroom closet and rummaging through the towels for the thick white one from the Holiday Inn; and he finds, too, in a canister beneath the sink, a big safety pin with a white plastic tip. *I've got it!* he cries on returning, and in no time, the two have the towel tucked about his waist in the fashion of Danny's brothers, how they once looked emerging from the bathroom after a shower.

Wow! Danny says, admiring their work in the mirror and simultaneously brushing off the worry, which just now resurfaces, of having to stand in front of the class like this. Won't he? In the little cloth? And then right when he's about to have Arram change the subject, he twists his hips in such a way that the pin springs open and the towel drops to the floor, exposing his briefs again. "Oops," he says, quickly gathering it back around him and bending the tip of the pin out until it stays put when he fastens it.

But, *If this is your underwear now,* Arram says of the cloth, *why do you need the ones underneath? That's two underwears.*

Right, Danny says, loyally slipping the briefs off and toeing them across the room, *Jesus wouldn't wear those.* Then they look at each other and giggle for no apparent reason. *It's like I'm wearing a skirt,* Danny observes, *it's all loose inside;* and, a hand held protectively over the pin, he shakes his hips like a hula girl, and makes his dickie knock up against the towel. But enough of this horsing around. *Do you want to bind my wrists first?* he asks, referring to the book again. *It says they 'bound His wrists together and tied them to the low whipping post.'*

Let's just pretend they're tied, Arram says, because Danny has his work cut out for him as it is, baring his back, reading from the book, and swinging the belt, all at the same time. *What's a low whipping post?*

The bed? Danny says, looking down at it.

Yeah, get down on the bed. And when he does—leans over on his hands, the book opened manual-like between them—*I'll beat your bare ass silly.*

No, don't say that. And he doesn't, really; Danny's father says that—sometimes, when he's really mad at them, makes a fist and says it. Arram says . . . what? Names. *Fag! Retard!* Still now he thinks of it: lying on his parents' bed, in nearly the same position, once with Sharon, their pants pulled down as they were told. And it was funny, because when his father came into the room, and saw their two pink heinies side by side, the angry look in his eyes paused, and his whole red face grinned for an instant.

'*Then they began their task . . .*' But where's his belt now? He grabs it up from the floor, doubles it again, and swings it over his shoulders. It makes a loud thwack, louder than he expected, but the feeling isn't painful enough, and so he tries it harder: thwack! thwack! —*What are you? Stop screaming like a girl.* —*I didn't do anything, Daddy.* —*Shut up. Lay still.* And now he swings it at his right heinie cheek, his left, even harder, because of the muting effect of the towel. *Take that, you jerk, you dick!* '*The Jewish scourging was set at forty lashes, but the Roman punishment was unlimited in intensity and duration. The exhaustion of the floggers or the death of the victim alone ended the punishment.*' Thwack! *You homo, you little shit!* —*Keep going, Arram! Don't stop till you're tired!* And soon, to much giggling and crying out, the boy thinks to lift up the back of the towel and whip him underneath—*Jesus' heinie!* Arram cries; *Hoo-hoo!* Danny says—and then he can feel it more, his cheeks tingly, warmer. And finally, as he's puzzling over the commentary at the end of the chapter, about how Jesus, in suffering the scourging, was atoning especially for the sins of the flesh that men of all ages would commit, and how it can be helpful, therefore, to think of the sharp, stinging pain Jesus endured—'*the enormity of this torture can help us re-*

alize the enormity of these sins, which are often presented to us today as attractive experiences no one can be expected to forgo'—there's an exciting development: Danny's dickie, pressing up against the towel, making a little white hurray. With a wild impulse, he pulls up the front and spins around. *Arram, look!*

And his friend's face wells with approving glee. *A boner!*

Lessons in Humility

Once again during religion, as Liz lists the Beatitudes on the board for the students to copy, she catches herself humming that dreadful song, "Lep-ro-sy is crawling all o-ver me." Woke up with it in her head for some reason. Did she dream about lepers, maybe? At the same time she sees her childhood girlfriends, running about in their yards: Didi Lippy, the gap-toothed tomboy, shrieking at the top of her lungs, "Kiss me quick! There goes my upper lip!" Something about a highball, too—"There goes my eyeball, right in your highball!" Little by little everything *went* in the song: nose, fingers, toes . . . other things, too, she suspects. And now suddenly remembering herself—imagine a song like that about cancer today?—she tries to shoo it from her thoughts. She is, after all, relaying Christ's declarations of blessedness from the Mount, just now the sixth: ditto, ditto, *the pure of heart*, ditto, ditto, ditto, *see God*.

Behind her, Brian and Joey and several other boys are whispering and passing notes, have been for some moments. She should've spun around by now, said something spinsterish: *I suppose you must know these all by heart*, or, *I wonder if you people expect to make your confirmation next year*; instead she's let them continue. She's tired, she tells herself, of keeping after them like first-graders. If they choose to clown around, they'll just have to suffer the consequences. Still, her heart's beating fast as she writes the concluding *for theirs is the kingdom of heaven* and turns around, slowly. But now it seems she might've been less subtle, for not even a shuffle to the window disturbs them from their conversations, or a piqued gaze down at the lone, squat spruce at the center of the convent courtyard. She glances from it to Danny, whom she catches staring at her, and he immediately looks away, checking his notes against the board for accuracy—not entirely for her benefit. Earlier, when she told the class the Beatitudes began Christ's instructions on how to live an ideal Christian life, his eyes widened ingenuously and he grabbed his pen. She nods at him and at the other lowly, conscientious ones, waits for the tardiest to finish recording the last of the promises for their happiness, and smiles meanwhile at their alarmed, sideways glances at the boys, their feeble attempts to shush them. Then without once looking in the direction of the seceded clique, she asks, "And does everyone know the unofficial ninth Beatitude?"

"Ninth?"

As she appends it to the list, *Blessed are they who pay attention, for they shall do well on the test this Friday,* there's a slowly spreading bloom of laughter. "Don't say I never told you anything," she adds before erasing the line, and, in turn, the rest of the board.

And now finally the boys tune in: "What's so funny? What did she just say?"

She hopes no one tells them.

"Hey, I didn't finish copying those yet."

Halfway through recess, after she's had everyone sign Mrs. Burke's card and winced and worried through as much of the crossless Way as she can bear, she runs off for the lounge and some luckily unavoidable business in the office, which spares her the spectacle of Herman standing before the blackboard, one "nailed" arm outstretched, the other holding his script, from which he reads his dying lines. Not long after, Paolo and Rory drag him off to the hall by his wrists and ankles, only for him to reemerge, proudly grinning and holding up his hands. Here the girls leave off tracing olive branches on green oaktag and come rushing and cheering to the front, Juanita's voice trumpeting above the others, "Make way for the women of the Tomb! The great daughters of Jerusalem!" Then, "Hey look, girls, Jesus is back!" As they proceed to coo and salaam and prostrate themselves before Herman, the stunned boys look to each other and their scripts, "What are they saying? What's she doing?"

"Improvising," Juanita explains from under fanning arms. "You're supposed to just say whatever comes to your mind."

"No, you're not," they tell her; yet she continues: "Oh, he's alive! It's a miracle!" The other girls join forces: "The great Son! Back from the dead! We missed You, Jesus! It's so nice to see You again! Do Your hands hurt? May we wash Your feet? I want to dry them with my hair!" And through all this Danny's trying to say, "Stop! It's-It's not funny. You-You have to be s-serious," until finally Patty shouts, "THE END!" with unusual force and volume, effectively drowning them out.

An instant's silence follows, after which Juanita, still on her knees, asks, "Does that mean it's over?" and everyone looks at Danny. "Yeah, what do we do now?"

"St-start again," he says, and there's a general grumbling before the girls return to their nascent olive trees, and the boys, who found the deposition somewhat novel and fun, take turns dragging each other off into the hall. Danny glares at them and turns to Patty, seated cross-legged now in the ellipse and shaking her head at their antics, but with her same pale placidity, as if this is merely another stupid thing the boys are doing, not some terrible blasphemy. Then just as he's lobbing another faint hail of stammered, disregarded objections, Herman comes shuffling up beside him again, hands on his hips. "I don't want to do this whole thing again," he squeaks.

Immediately Danny's stomach leaps; forgetting the irreverent game for a moment, he leans in closer to Herman's small, downy ear. "That's okay; you can go outside again."

Herman looks dubious. "Miss Kaigh got really mad last time."

"She won't now," Danny assures him; however, the boy asks why not. "B-B-Because we've finished the play, and b-because we all have our own scripts now, and y-you—" He gives other reasons, not as coherent, then resorts to points made last time, expressed in different words, and finally Herman looks up from it all and says "yeah?" and glances at Patty. The girl squints, not having heard them, and, before Herman can explain anything, Danny nudges him, "Go ahead." And so the boy, hesitating just half an instant, rushes down the aisle for the closets and his coat.

Minutes later, when Liz returns to find Danny mumbling before the guards, her face colors with anger and disbelief. "That's it!" she cries and rushes out again, leaving them to oooh and rub their hands with anticipation or, in Danny's case, to fretfully clench his teeth, and none too long—for immediately after the bell rings, she storms back in, leading Herman by the collar, the rest of the class filing in behind her. "Daniel!" she booms before them all. "Did you tell him he could go outside?"

"Out-out-out-out—?" he says, a crazy zinging, like a thousand ant feet, scurrying down his arms and neck, and he doesn't see how he could possibly say yes. "I-I-I—He-He said he didn't want to practice."

"Is that true?" she asks Herman, who merely points at Danny and says, "He—" and Danny says, "No, I—" and Herman says, "He—" and here Liz jumps in, wagging her head angrily at the shorter boy, whom she suspects is lying. "Enough of this. I want to know right now, mister, do you or don't you want to be in our play?"

"But—"

"No explanations, a simple yes or no."

And so he grimaces and shrugs and looks entreatingly from one smirking, unsympathetic player to the next, last of all Danny, who, as their eyes meet, shakes his head ever so slightly. "Not really," Herman says then.

The very next instant, amid the startled murmurs of the players and the spiteful cheers of Brian and his minions—like a little circle of fiends, Liz thinks, winning back some sinner to hell—and just as Danny nearly jumps up from his desk with elation, the bold words *Miss Kaigh, can I have the part, then?* on the tip of his tongue, there's a kind of deus ex machina—at least it seems so to Liz; to Danny, diabolus— in the form of Matt Poppolano, the tall, piano-playing boy at the back of the third row. "Miss Kaigh, I'll be Jesus," he says quite unexpectedly.

"What?" Liz simply stares at him—"Matthew?"—and at his bright, self-assured smile, so astonishingly independent of the snorts of the boys and the low claps of the lepers.

"Matt will make a cute Jesus," she hears Juanita whisper, creating a ripple of girl-giggles and backward glances that the boy ignores.

"I like feel sorry for you guys," he says.

"Oh. Well—" Liz bites back an indignant retort. What does a little insolence matter when, with a couple of obvious exceptions, they could hardly do better than Matt: reasonably liked, responsible, strong-voiced, and, yes, maybe even cute, as Juanita claims. "What an excellent surprise!" she says, looking about the room, as if for more hands, a profusion of miracles, and this giddy search uncovers but a cold, righteous stare.

It's clear to Danny now that it's his teacher, not God, who doesn't want him to have the part. Wasn't it *him* the play came to with the aid of the Holy Spirit? *Him* God chose to be a kind of apostle and Gospel writer? It's wrong of Miss Kaigh to interfere with their plan, and, ever more fervently now, he prays for guidance and the triumph of heavenly will.

That afternoon, over a small cloud of steam rising from the kitchen faucet, he finds his mother's card resistant to the unsealing technique his brother, Robby, once used to intercept letters from school. Giving up, he wonders would anyone be the wiser if he didn't deliver it at all; wonders, but then quails at the thought of Miss Kaigh asking him about it the next day. He's made up so much already! Teacher, music, violin. That's why you're not supposed to lie in the first place, he remembers Sister Regina once explaining, because you have to make up so many others to cover up the original, and each one a venial sin, requiring prayers for forgiveness before Communion. But now he thinks, too, of his mother's tendency to just glance at things before setting them aside and, hoping she'll do the same with the card, rushes up to his room while there's still time.

To aid the rehearsal, he reads to Arram from "The Crucifixion" chapter of *The Life*, how finally the tragic procession reached Calvary, and Jesus was offered the wine mixed with myrrh but didn't drink it, so the world wouldn't be deprived of any of His suffering. But before he even finishes the next line, *'Then they stripped Him of His clothes and laid Him outstretched on the cross,'* Arram interrupts to ask if he thinks Jesus might've been crucified in the nude.

In the nude? Danny blinks at the startling idea; then, *No,* he tells the boy, he doesn't think He was, because in all the pictures and crosses, He has the cloth.

Maybe that's because they can't show it, like they can't show Adam and Eve's.

So he reconsiders, because Adam and Eve were definitely naked, yet you only ever see them with leaves or tree branches over their parts. It's very frustrating.

Jesus could've been naked, too, Arram says.

Danny raises an eyebrow. *That means when He was up on the cross, everyone saw His dickie.*

Arram nods. *And His hair.*

And His nuts.

Everyone saw everything.

All the soldiers and the women.

His mother.

No, not His mother.

Yes, Arram says, *she was there.*

All right, Danny concedes, wishing he'd been there, too, now. *So does this mean you're going to crucify me in the nude?*

Uh-huh.

Cool, he says, unpinning the towel and tossing it on the floor. Then he just stands there, naked to his toes, an excited shiver wriggling through him, because he believes he might like standing around naked very much. He wonders, even, if he might like doing other things naked and, just to see if he does, walks from one end of the room to the other, opens his closet door and looks in, sits down at his desk as if to write something or do his homework, all naked. Then he jumps up happily and rushes to the mirror. *Arram, now I'm like you!*

But once there he frowns: his dickie looks little and pink, and not very Jesus-like. Jesus', even if it wasn't the biggest in the world, would've been bigger than his, and had the black bush around it. *Right, Arram?*

The boy agrees and suggests magic marker.

You mean draw right on the skin? Danny says, now pretending his hand, uncapping the pen, is Arram's.

Yeah.

So he sits on the edge of his bed and, with cool, tickling flecks of the felt tip, makes wisps and curlicues and squiggles all around the base, and up from the base, and over toward each hinge, his dickie stiffening a little from so much attention and jostling. Lastly, he puts a few wisps, beard-like, on the bottom of his nuts, then jumps up again to look in the mirror and gapes—because it does, it looks older now, and more like a Jesus-wiener, with the biggerness and sudden blackness.

Are we ready? Arram asks.

I think so, Danny says, assuming the *laid-outstretched* position on his brown shag carpet. There, as his fingers and toes wriggle with their terrible anticipation, he imagines Arram mean-facedly raising the heavy hammer, glancing secretly at his half-mast, smeary-maned dickie. And Danny himself, with expert restraint, barely flinches as the spikes are driven through his wrists and foot-tops, and all the blood is loosed. *'When they completed the rudest part of their chore, they heaved the cross upright, dropped it into a hole which had been dug, and tamped the earth in solidly around the foot.'* Leaving the book on the floor, Danny leaps up on his desk chair, arms out straight like a scarecrow, and prays aloud for his executioners. Then, "Ha!" he answers himself, furiously improvising, "Listen to Him cry out to His Father! The Father He calls God of the Most High, the King of Heaven! Where is the Great King now? Where are His legions of angels to take Him down from the cross? Why won't He save His Son?" And here a second voice, as if of another soldier, joins in the mockery, "What the hell are you *doing* in there?" Danny freezes, recognizing it as his sister's, then in one motion, leaps down from the chair and scoops up his corduroys. "What's all this *angel* shit?"

"N-N-Nothing. How come you're h-home already?" he yells, frantically tugging on his pants legs, his magic-markered dickie bobbing and shriveling back up like a salted slug.

"Are you *praying out loud?*" she says, trying the door.

"No! D-D-Don't come in!" He eyes the button lock, doubtful of its strength.

"Why? Are you *naked?*"

"What?" he says, twisting away from the door, as if she may be spying through it somehow.

"Are you *playing with yourself?*"

"No!" he says, though he's not sure he wasn't. Could that be the name for what he was doing? "I'm-I'm-I'm practicing for the play at Our Lady's." Finally he zippers his pants.

"Oh no, is it religious? Is that why you sound like such an asshole?"

"I don't sound like that," he says, fumbling with his shirt buttons.

"Thank *God* we're not in the same school anymore. I would *die* if anyone knew my own brother was in some faggedy-ass religious play. I'd never be able to show my *face.*"

"I'll tell Mommy."

"Go ahead. Tell her I said *faggedy*, asshole. Tell her I said *asshole*, asshole. I can't believe I have such a faggedy-ass asshole for a brother!" Here she pauses, as if for breath, "Did you get that?" then retreats from the door, hard boot heels clopping on the stairs and down the hallway. He hears the swing and slam of her bedroom door, the near-automatic blaring of "Maggie May" on her stereo. She shouts along with the record, and Danny imagines her dancing and kissing the poster of Rod Stewart above her bed, and he wonders did her basketball coach suspend her for smoking again.

Witchmouth, Arram hisses, much like Robby once would. *Nasty Broomhilda.*

Danny smiles meekly at him, listening beyond the music and his sister's singing. At last he identifies the other noise, like a muffled, steady drumbeat beneath the others: *ruff! ruff! ruff! ruff! ruff!* "Oh no!" he cries, grabbing his parka and stuffing his bare feet into his chukka boots. Then he's sailing down the stairs and across the living room for the garage, "Sorry, Duke. Sorry, boy," clipping the leash to the choke, holding his breath as he steps between dried smears of shoveled-away shit.

Later, when the house is quiet—after Duke settles down, that is, and Sharon leaves again, and his mother comes home several minutes afterward, hollering up her hello before changing and retiring to the kitchen to read the circulars and advice columns in *Newsday*—Danny hunches over the Bible in the hall again, thumbing through the Gospels for some mention in the crucifixion passages of just what Jesus was or wasn't wearing. However, each of them skips right over these details, saying only that *when they got to Calvary, they crucified Him and divided up His garments*, but not saying which, and if these might have included underwear. And so consuming is this question that when he goes down to the kitchen, intending to give his mother the card from Miss Kaigh, he comes right out and asks her, "Mom, do you think Jesus was crucified in the nude?" and she looks up from the table with knitted, pencil-line eyebrows, semi-horrified eyes: *"Nude?"*

It's just the last thing she expected him to say, although—she relaxes her eyebrows now, and tries to cop a less anxious expression—

there's nothing wrong with the word per se, it's not a curse or anything. Just doesn't sound right somehow, coming from him. From his brothers, maybe—they were always springing all kinds of crap on her—but not from little Danny. She eyes his diverted face warily, the round, freckly tip of his nose. Just turned eleven in January; eleven's still young, got another couple of years yet, year and change. And so she sighs with relief, only now, dammit, she can't help thinking of how miserably they handled the birds-and-bees bit with the others. Didn't handle it at all, really; never said a word about it. But that was Gerry's department, with the boys. She at least told Sharon what to expect around her twelfth birthday; gave her a box of Modess—poor thing, turned beet red!—and when the time came around, she even talked her through it from the other side of the bathroom door. Could've been a lot worse. Carol herself was told by Mr. Silverman, the pharmacist up the corner from their apartment in Queens, and how humiliating that was! "I, uh—" she stammers finally to her son, himself nervously crossing and uncrossing his arms, his right hand clutching some kind of paper or other. "Well, what do you mean, Danny?"

"I mean—" he says, a warm, bright blush in his cheeks—the very color, Carol suspects, of her own.

"—that He was nailed to the cross that way? With no clothes on?"

"Yeah."

Despite herself, she pictures it, Christ without the cloth, sad little V of hair, whatsis out for all to see, whatsis very similar in character to her Gerry's: the long, sideways turning shaft (longer than average, she's always believed); flared, snapper-turtle head; jewels swagging low like a basset hound's. But she shouldn't be thinking this. It must be blasphemous to imagine Christ with your husband's whatsis. Though honestly, you had to wonder sometimes what it *did* look like, the Son of God's. Must've had one, of course, part man and all, not that He ever used it for anything. Oh Jeez, now she's really getting herself in trouble! "Are you crazy, Danny? Of course He wasn't . . . like that. What would make you ask such a question?"

And now he backs away regretfully. "I-I-I don't know. I j-just thought maybe He w-w-was."

"He had the whadayacallit on . . ." She moves her finger in circles, but can't think of the name. "Swaddling." That sounds right to her, biblical. "That was the old kind of underwear," she adds, with the authority, suddenly, of a fashion historian. "They didn't have elastic then, and they didn't exactly sew."

"They didn't?"

"No." She shivers slightly, knowing this must be true, though how she would is a mystery to her. "Basically they just folded things, and draped them, and fastened them together with little strips of material and leather. Kind of like construction boot laces." She glances down at the floor; however, he's barefoot. "But they all wore the swaddling underneath."

He nods—disappointedly, it seems to Carol, as if he were hoping maybe Christ wasn't wearing swaddling, and why the hell would he hope that? She shakes her head; she didn't like this play from the beginning, now she likes it even less. It just goes to prove that all this contemplation of the suffering does is make people a little looney.

"Okay Mom, thanks," Danny says. As he retreats awkwardly from the room, she glances at his feet again. What does he think it is, summer? He shouldn't be walking around like that without any socks. And she's about to say just this when he rushes back in from the hall, waving the paper.

An envelope, it turns out. "For me?" she asks, and indeed, across the front, *Mrs. Gerard Burke*. "What do they want, money again? Don't we pay enough in tuition?" But opening it, she finds a pastel-blue card, its cover declaring *In Appreciation* in florid, silver script.

"It's from the class," Danny explains, "for the copies."

"Aha," she says, pleased, then suddenly self-effacing, "Oh, they didn't have to do that." Inside are all the kids' signatures in similarly styled, unsteady hands, mostly girls: Patricia, Frances, Virginia. *Juanita?* What kind of name is that? "See now, Danny? That wasn't just nothing I did. Right?" He shakes his head quickly and holds out his hand, as if for her to give it back. "I guess your teacher bought the card," she says, looking at it with more interest now, and, yup, there's her name at the bottom, *Miss Elizabeth Kaigh*. But here Carol has to purse her lips; it sounds a little highfalutin, like she's a damn queen or something. Why doesn't she just call herself Beth or Liz? "'*Daniel*'—she calls you Daniel?" Carol looks at him, brow wrinkled. "Why?"

"I don't know. You don't have to read it," he says, beckoning with the hand again.

"—has told us so much about you. No wonder he is so creative! Oh," she says, the sarcasm dropping from her voice as the pieces fall together: he doesn't want her to know he talks about her at school. A wave of gratification passes over her, and she eyes his red cheeks furtively, imagining herself tenderly touching one with the tips of her fingers. Just like their father; always have to seem so hard and aloof, but on the inside, if you could ever get there, it's all putty and mush. "That's nice, Danny. I wouldn't worry about that."

"No?"

"It's nothing I didn't know already."

"It's not?" he asks, eyebrows knitting.

"No," she says meaningfully, then looks back at the card. But, "What's this now? 'I have always adored' . . . what? *Messiah?* 'Perhaps you've even performed it?' What's she talking about?"

Danny shrugs and rolls his eyes ceiling-ward.

"What do I care what she's always adored?" she snaps, then recoils at her sharp tone. She shouldn't talk about his teacher like that in front of him, even if she is highfalutin. "I mean, I don't know what she's saying here; it's like she thinks I'm an actress or something." She laughs and, partly to distract him, stands up and shimmies a little to the left, singing, "Boop boop bee doo." But so easily and pleasurably do her stockinged feet slip across the linoleum, that she does it once again to the right, then waits, with open, feisty mouth, for him to smile— which he does finally, but Jeez, so thinly, so late; she swears he has no sense of humor. She stands up straight again. "Bet you don't know who that was."

He shakes his head.

"Marilyn Monroe," her aging self informs him. *Girl who got her skirt blown up on the subway grate,* she doesn't add, here trying to think back to the last time she and Gerry went dancing. Must've been years ago, someone's wedding—their own, she muses bitterly. "Do you think she could have me confused with another mother?"

"Maybe," Danny says.

"That's what I bet. But you wouldn't think there'd be many mothers who are actresses around." She raises an indignant eyebrow and tosses the card in the drawer to the left of the sink, in with all the other stray papers and coupons. And the next moment, after Danny flees the room and she returns to her *Newsday*, softly singing, "I wanna be loved by you . . ." she pictures his bare toes again on the linoleum, and looks up. "And put some socks on when you're in the house!"

But Danny, already behind his closed door, hears only a muted bellow and doesn't investigate. Instead, between conversations with Arram and the formation of their plan—despite professed historical truths concerning the cloth—to continue practicing naked, he winces privately at his close call with the card. "Sorry," he whispers toward the stairs, imagining the word traveling down to the kitchen and floating about his mother's ear, a little kissing wind, "I'm only lying for Jesus." And thus assured, he shuffles off remorse: he must continue this difficult work, just now inventing his mother's gratitude for when he sees Miss Kaigh the next day.

～ 7 ～

Speaking in Tongues

E arly that morning, just seconds after Danny hears his father start
the car and leave for the station, he rushes downstairs, book bag in
hand, for the kitchen.

"Oh!" his mother, in curlers and robe yet, starts and turns from the
counter with her coffee mug. "What now? How come you're dressed already?"

"I'm going to Mass."

"Why? Is it a holy day?"

"No."

"First Friday?"

"It's Thursday."

Know-it-all, she thinks, though he happens to be right. "What, it's
not enough to go on Sundays anymore?"

"I have a big test today," he says, pouring out a bowl of Apple Jacks.

"But Danny, wouldn't you be better off studying for it, instead of
spending the morning in church?"

He shakes his head; it's not a book-type test. "I already studied."

"Then you could have slept some more. Won't you be tired now?"

"I have to ask God to help me."

Oh give me a break, she almost says aloud, and considers the term *Jesus freak*. Could this be what her son is becoming, a kind of freak with
shorter hair? But she rejects this notion, vaguely aware those people
are different somehow, not exactly Catholics. Yet it does seem freaky
to her—the altar, the play, this weekday Mass. What will it be next,
novenas? The seminary? She pictures him at twenty, cassocked, white-
collared, his skin pale and untouched. She feels so . . . *carnal* in com-

parison, a fat, horsey human, and gathers her robe at the neck, as if to prevent any unbathed smell from wafting free of her body, some seamy trace of her weekly whoopee with Gerry last night. Should have fought harder for public school for them, it's clear to her now: the trouble they had with the boys, and with Sharon, Danny's new freakiness, all because of the Catholic brainwashing, the Catholic straitjacketing. Either makes you a rebel or a saint, and who can stand either one?

Then as she turns to the window, frowning at the gray sky and listening to Danny's hurried slurping and crunching behind her, she finds herself picturing, of all things, her parents' bedroom—in the early years, before her father left them—the bitty twin beds separated by a night table. And so, what? Some kind of quick visit in the middle of the night? Her father crossing the room, claiming his lawful due. What would her mother say to him, anything? *Aw, come on, Ron, cut that out.* She can't imagine her clothes being fully removed, just raised somehow, parted; pictures her rigid, closed-eyed, counting the seconds till it's over. Then her father going wordlessly back to his bed, her mother straightening her nightgown, praying for pregnancy. Is that the way it was? Is that why he drank? And here Carol sighs with relief for herself, how much better her own life seems. Gerry might not be the most expressive man, but at least he'll keep an arm around her afterward; at least they're in the same bed. And he's stayed with her; she's made sure of that. It's just that it's so horrible they could've lived without some bit of tenderness between them. Her mother was never very tender with them, either, always so much to herself, and so careful about everything, and forbidding, and her brother, Ronny, such a cut-up while she was the Mass-going goody. History repeating itself. She feels goose bumps rising on her arms; she's never marked the similarity this clearly between Danny's piousness and her own of long ago. Age of sweet religious feeling. Of course, it's a young age, before you realize all the hair pulling and punching's going to go on whether you're on your knees or not. What a disappointment it all is then, what a disappointment God is.

Suddenly she finds her eyes welling with tears and quickly wipes at the corners. Good thing she hasn't done her mascara yet. What got her started on all this? "Danny?" she says, turning around.

"Huh?" Already he's grabbing for his bag.

"The nuns and priests don't know everything. That's just one kind of life they've chosen."

But he looks at her as if she's just spoken Greek. "Okay, Mom. Bye," he says, and flees the room. She hears the screen door swinging shut, the latch catching. Didn't even brush his teeth.

Please, God, Danny prays in a middle pew, squeezing his eyes against the solemn backs of the white-haired couples and the long black blots of the Sisters' veils, *help me to make it so Matt doesn't want to be in the play anymore.* And all the while his tongue is working at the Communion wafer stubbornly adhered to the roof of his mouth, *and so Miss Kaigh will give me the part,* trying to peel it in a slow, respectful way, and at the same time feeling a lingering gratification at the smile Father McGann gave him earlier, when he received, *and then help me to act well and not get nervous and stutter,* the surprised, pleased look he gives him whenever he comes to morning Mass, as if each were the first time he did. Doesn't he remember the others? *And let everyone say, 'Oh wow, he really sounds like Jesus!' That's all I want, God.* Yet he winces at the word *all,* realizing this isn't such a little thing, that this in itself would constitute a miracle of sorts. And now here, as the wafer peels free and slides in a clump to his throat, he imagines the special process of digestion that sends the little particles of Christ to the very tips of his fingers and toes, and waits upon the Holy Spirit.

"But it wasn't any trouble at all. It was the proper thing to do," Liz says, nodding at the authoritative sound of her phrasing, *"proper* thing," as if she's a person who knows what is or isn't. And it seems to her now— or at least, in the twenty hours since Matt volunteered for the play— that maybe she is. The event's brought about a general resurgence of hope and confidence for her, finding its highest expression last night when she drove to the Patchogue Public Library and found *Biblical Costumes for Churches and Schools,* written by a woman—a teacher, it seemed—and filled with all kinds of diagrams and advice. Right away in the preface: *Care must be taken to anticipate audience reaction, especially in regard to laughter that is out of place,* which seemed like a thought from her own mind. She checked the book out immediately, then dared to drift over to the music section and flip through albums marked "classical," but blindly, fruitlessly. Sonata, oratorio, concerto; names ending in -vich and -noff. It reminded her of a college tour of the United Nations, all the delegates chattering in unfamiliar languages, and she'd been too ashamed of her ignorance to ask a librarian for guidance. For a moment she'd held a Mozart—he was supposed to be such a genius—and it was then the idea came to her. She turns with it now to Danny, standing again by her desk:

"You know, I was thinking your mother might be able to recommend some music for the play."

"Music?"

"Background stuff. Instrumentals," she says, and studies his eyes. But nothing in them suggests she may have erred in her terminology. To the contrary, they look addled, oddly fearful. "Without words," she explains, "like in the movies. I could reserve one of the phonographs in the A/V room, and we could get one of the extras to operate it." Stephen, she sees right away, is perfect for the job; it'll keep him offstage completely. "Don't you think it's a good idea?"

Danny nods, teeth clenched.

"Would you mind asking her for me, then? Or . . . would you rather I asked her myself?"

But he quickly shakes his head. "Th-th-that's okay. I'll ask her."

She's pushed too far—too quickly, maybe. "All right," she says, then grimaces again, remembering all those strange names. "If you can, get her to write them down for me, the composers and works."

"Composers and works," he repeats.

"Won't it be wonderful?" she says, imagining a great splash of cymbals and soaring violins as Matt, in a white resurrection robe, raises his pierced palms heavenward.

At recess, she consults with the girls regarding the trees—bright, shoulder-high affairs with polka-dotted octopus-tentacles passing for olive branches. "They need some sort of feet, so they'll stand up," she tells them.

"Feet?" the girls say, "Tree feet?" laughing and tapping their Earth-shoes.

Then she shows them how to insert a crosspiece into the base of the trunks to give them some stability, emphasis on *some*, for even afterward they continue to wobble with the lightest touch or breeze. "Work on these more. Try to make them stronger and heavier at the bottom." And from here, she watches with mounting delight as Matt performs an assured and affecting rendition of the agony, his booming voice even quavering slightly as he entreats the ceiling. Again she feels the entire endeavor smiled upon by his tall, commanding presence and so bursts out, post-arrest, "Bravo! Bravo!" enticing the others to begrudged applause. She should mollify them somehow, say, *Oh, you're all good, too, but this is Matthew's first time, and he did a super job,* but doesn't, because clearly he's so much better than they are; they'd see the insincerity of it. Don't you have to draw the line between encouragement and delusion? Shouldn't the exceptional be recognized as such? Still, as rehearsal continues, she can't meet the eyes of her long-faced lepers, particularly Danny's, whom she's privately dubbed His Disgruntledness since his reassignment to Peter. By the time the first trial ends and she warns them all not to get too loud while she runs to speak with Sister Regina, she imagines him glaring at her back.

But it's hardly a glare—a squint, merely, from where he slouches at the front of the room, a scorned king. And he turns with this squint to Paolo and Stephen, who continue to soundlessly jeer at Matt as the scene changes to the courtyard, then to Juanita, gliding up the aisle from the back of the room.

"Oh hello, everyone. I am the very first girl to appear in the play. Do I look all right?" she asks, smoothing her puffy hair.

"You're not the first girl, Patty is," Paolo stops miming to say.

"Patty's not in the play, she's the narrator," Juanita tells him. "I'm the first actress, the high priest's serving girl." She resumes her glide. "Onto the stage I stroll, and I see this man. 'Ho-ho,' I say, suspicious, because I think I've seen him somewhere before." Now she smacks her cheek, "I know," and, pointing at Danny, bellows, "YOU WERE WITH JESUS OF NAZARETH!"

At which they all cover their ears. "Don't scream like that!" Matt says. "Yeah, Juanita," Paolo says, "you're just accusing him, you're not like screaming." And Danny, who's supposed to say, "I do not know the man," balks again, loath to utter the faithless words. *Please,* he prays, reminding God of his morning petitions. But now the laughter's died off, and the players, including Juanita—who seems, for the moment anyway, to have stopped improvising—are waiting, and so he turns to the window and scratches his head, as if oblivious. If only he could think of some distraction, some reason not to continue. Outside, girls are practicing cartwheels and handstands in the real courtyard, shrieking as their skirts fall up to their chins, exposing navy-blue gym shorts; and suddenly, a sharp rustling behind him, and he turns around. The favored boy has tossed his script to the floor.

"You guys are the worst actors in the world!"

"No, we're not," Rory says.

"Not in the whole *world*," Juanita qualifies.

"*You're* like saying things you're not supposed to, *he* doesn't know when he's supposed to speak . . ."

He meaning Danny, the writer of the play, stopping now several feet shy of Matt and bending for the rumpled copy. Just before he snatches it up, he imagines the boy's nappy Wallabee stepping on it, *Leave that right where it is.* "P-P-Peter is very s-slow to speak," he explains and, suddenly inspired—perhaps divinely, God now working in strange ways—adds, "And he-he has f-fainting spells."

"Fainting spells?" Matt says. "What?" Juanita says, intrigued. "What?" the girls in the back say, standing up amid the wobbly olives. Incredibly, even to himself, Danny cups his forehead and totters slightly, then makes his knees tremble and, groaning, folds to the floor in a breathless, closed-eyed heap. At once there are startled laughs and yelps, a rush of shoe-slapping about his ears: "What's he doing?"

"Is he dead?" Kevin asks excitedly.

"Danny?" Juanita toes his ribs. "You didn't really faint, did you?"

"Maybe he's flipping out," Frances suggests.

"I think you're right," Juanita says. "Danny, have you flipped?"

But now, unable to hold his breath any longer, he lets it go with an explosive, giggling, eyes-opened "No!"

"Ah!" they all shout above him, a rocking cloud of laughing mouths. Danny blinks, imagining the red-faced, down-staring children as members of an enemy tribe, Juanita their dark chief at his right elbow. He can see the underside of her jumper and the tops of her yellow-brown thighs, and, high above, the great pom-pom of hair.

"I must admit that looked very real," she says. "I never expected it from you, but you do a good faint. Kind of makes me want to try one myself." And so with a much more voluminous groan—"Oo-oo-ah!"—she topples to the floor to Danny's right. Then, "Try it," she says, lifting her head to advise Frances, who happily collapses to their left—followed by Rory, Paolo, Ginger, the floor thudding with each new fall, and much more so as Stephen falls, and then Kevin, skidding down the aisle and pouncing on the boys. "What a riot!" Juanita howls. "I feel like I'm at a slumber party."

"I feel like I'm at camp," Paolo says.

"No, it's a group brawl!" Kevin screams, rolling frenziedly over Ginger.

"Ew! Get away from me!" The girl punches his shoulder. "You're gonna break my glasses."

And now, "Hey, Matt," Juanita calls, winking and patting the floor beside her, "come on over and faint by Mary Mag."

But the boy only scowls in return, then looks to Patty, the only other unfainted player, who continues to sit cross-legged in the ellipse, equably regarding the mass of schoolmates squirming over the floor.

"And-and after they faint, they speak in tongues!" Danny cries, emboldened by the chaos.

"In what?"

"Tongues! All the languages of the world! The H-Holy Spirit speaks them for you!"

"Okay," Juanita says. *"Habla español?"*

"Agua," Kevin says. "Flied lice."

"Mi chiamo Paolo."

"I only know Pig Latin," Ginger says: *"Evinkay isyay ayay erkjay."*

"But he said it could be anything. Ooo-lee boo-lee boo-lee."

"Careeba careeba careebamay!"

"Woka woka wang wong. Ooh looka Godzilla!"

"You guys are crazy!" Matt yells.

"No," Danny says, "it's-it's the Holy Spirit. He's m-m-making us speak this way."

"I quit immediately."

"You what?" Danny says.

"You can't quit," Rory says.

"Yeah, Matt," Danny says, and, "Wait, yes he can." But now the others look at him—knowingly? "I-I-I mean, if he wants to. We can't m-make him."

"It's a free country," Matt says.

"Yeah," Danny says.

"I'm not going to embarrass myself with a bunch of fags fainting and speaking in tongues," Matt says. "This is the most ridiculous play I've ever seen."

"Hey, who you calling a fag?" Stephen says, lumbering toward the boy.

"All right, you guys," Juanita says, dusting herself off as she stands up between them. "I'll handle this. Matt, you've only been Christ for ten minutes—"

"Yeah," Rory says.

"—you haven't given it a chance."

"Yeah, give it a chance."

"That's all we're saying," Juanita says.

"Ha!" Rory exclaims. "All we are saying is give Christ a chance! Like the song!"

"What song?"

And so he sings, "Give peace a chance . . ."

"Oh, I get it," Juanita says, snapping her fingers and singing along, "Give Christ a chance." Then Frances and Ginger join in, a kind of backup, "All we are say-ing . . ." And in a moment, as the four form a hand-clapping chorus, Matt's eyes widen with accumulating disgust. "Stop it!" he yells. "Cut it out!" and, ultimately unheeded, runs for the door.

Just minutes after, Liz slows down in the corridor to douse her mouth with wintergreen Binaca, breathless with her rushing and her good news: not only was she able to get use of a phonograph, but Sister Regina said she'd look into the possibility of putting the play on in the Music Hall. *"The Music Hall!"* Liz cried, its name alone sending butterflies surging through her stomach—despite the fact, as she reminds herself now, that the hall doesn't seem to be used for musical performances or performances of any kind; she's known it only to house fairs and bake sales, bingo. Still, it's quite large, a freestanding building near the rectory with an honest-to-goodness raised stage at one end. In fact, it could be the stage would prove too big for them, just the opposite problem from the classroom. But a much better one; the whole grade could come to a performance in there! She returns the breath freshener to her pocketbook and lays a hand on her stomach to still the roiling inside. She'll tell them about the phonograph but nothing else, not yet. It would be cruel to raise their hopes if Sister isn't able to arrange it.

But now, through the little rectangular window of 5B, she glimpses Danny at the front of the class again, occupying a too central position among the players, and doesn't see Matt at all. For an instant, she feels strangely disconcerted, as if it were suddenly yesterday again or still, with all its bleakness; back to the ungraced leper colony, the original group of untouchables. "Oh no," she says, heart dropping fast—but not, it strikes her now, unexpectedly. How could they have hoped to keep him? She imagines the boy out in the parking lot, tossing a Peewee with Brian and Joey. *We like it here*, they say, *we don't need to pretend*. Finally she throws open the door.

"What happened to Matthew?" she blares, and at once the entire group scuffles away, averted eyes proving what she fears: he, too, has quit, run—maybe wisely—from their cursed production of the Passion.

When he gets home, Danny hurries up to the playroom, where his brothers' old Magnavox squats dustily below the dormer window, a joint Christmas present years ago, and the only working stereo in the house besides Sharon's, which he dares not touch. His brothers argued loudly over who'd get it when Robby came back for his things, then again out in the yard, the day Gerry was packing his car for college. "That stereo was bought to be used in this house," his father, who never listened to music of any kind, said on both occasions, "it's staying right here." And so it has, to no one's benefit. Danny doesn't often think of using it himself; it seems theirs still, just as the room itself does, full of their not being there, and of their cursing and wrestling when they were, the sounds of bodies or furniture banging up against the walls, and the shouts he'd heard in the last, terrible fight between Robby and his father. "Come on, you think you're tough? Let's see how tough you are." "I'm not gonna hit you." "What's the matter, afraid of your old man?" Full, too, of their old smoke clouds and beer spills, and of the way, the few times he found the door open and stopped to peek in, they and their friends—ponytailed, tattooed, wearing their boots in the house—would glare at him from the hand-me-down living room chairs.

And so it's with a feeling of trespassing that he flips through the left-behind LPs below the player. Why they left them, he can't imagine. He'd never forget any of his own records if he were to go somewhere—his Partridge Familys, or his old Disneys, or even those of Robby's he secretly rescued from the garbage: Cat Stevens, Bread, the Jackson 5. Danny'd seen him throwing them out and asked if he could have them, but his brother'd said no way, they were girl music, shit music, music that shouldn't exist and that he wouldn't live in the same abode with. That confused Danny; hadn't Robby bought them once and sung to them? "What?" Robby said. He never bought any of that shit, girls had given them to him, and if Danny ever told anyone he saw them here he'd break his head, did he understand? He did, and only played them when everyone was out, and then very low, listening for the motorcycles and sputtering cars.

On a black-jacketed Grand Funk, he finds the song "Mean Mistreater," which maybe they could use for the whipping scene. However, it has words, lots of them, likewise those on the white Beatles albums, including the "Why Don't We Do It in the Road?" that his mother used to yell up for his brothers to turn off. And now, *Hey, Arram!* Danny calls, and the boy squats naked beside him. *Help me find music for the play.*

Okay, Arram says, and selects *Abbey Road,* "Maxwell's Silver Hammer." *This could be the crucifixion song,* he says as it winds and crackles through the speakers.

The crucifixion song? Danny echoes warily. *But it has words again.*

They're perfect!

They're not perfect. It should be the soldier's hammer, not Maxwell's; and, anxious anyway to start practicing, he says, *Come on,* and turns for his room.

No, here, Arram says, *to the music.*

Here? Danny says, running to the window and looking down at the empty walkway and street, then at his watch: twenty minutes yet before his mother gets home. Quickly, he strips and stands on the cool wood floor, wiggling his toes and looking down at his dickie, plain as the pink morning. It's the only room besides his bedroom and the bathroom he's ever been naked in, he tells Arram. And now as they jump and skip and wag to the "Bang, bang" of the silver hammer, Danny reimagines his brothers' friends sitting in the chairs and circles around each one, sometimes stopping to perch on the tattered arms and cross his legs girlishly. *What do you say to a naked lady?* he asks, quoting the posters for the *Candid Camera* movie. And, *Look how long their hair is!* Arram says, and they pull on the different kinds: frizzy, straight; dark-brown, sandy-brown. They pull on their sideburns, too, bushy face-frames, and sometimes spin around and poke their heinies at the owners of all the hair, right under their noses. *Ha! They don't even know,* Danny says. But then Harold Aiken, the mustached boy who once set the lot on Matinecock Avenue on fire, slyly tugs on Arram's skinny nuts.

Hey, he just yanked my stuff! Arram says.

Fresh, Danny says to Harold, and, snapping his fingers, *Go back to not seeing.* The older boy obeys: automatically smoking and slurping his beer and talking obliviously to the others.

But now Danny has a better idea and, dropping the long-haired boys, rushes out, naked, to his room and rummages to the back of his closet, where he recovers *The Jungle Book* LP. Then he races back to the playroom. *Remember?* he says to Arram, *Baloo and Mowgli,* pointing to the illustrations of the friendly bear and orphan boy. *You and Mow are like brothers,* he says, because of their skinniness and tanness and straight black jungle hair, and because they're both always naked—except, of course, in Mow's case, for the bitty cloth, though there was the one time in the movie when Bagheera the panther pulled on the back of it while Mow was running away, and you saw his heinie. *That was the best part,* Danny says and, knowing just what track to play, fairly trembles as he cues it up.

Right away Arram leaps up and down, stressing his favorite word, *The BARE Necessities!*

The simple BARE necessities! Danny cries, leaping along, both their dickies swinging like crazy bells. *Are you watching?* he asks Arram, indicating his own as he darts from one end of the room to the other, but can't get up the speed enough to really make it go, the wall comes too fast. *Like you, running after the man on the camel.*

Oh, Arram says, his smile fading as he remembers his Bible life, and Danny sees at once he was wrong to bring it up.

No, look, Danny says, now swinging it side to side, and in circles, and it makes definite slapping sounds against his leg, belly, leg. *You, too. Make it slap!* And before long, Danny's gets bonery, a swaying pointing stick, then Arram's, too, dueling swords, touché!

This will be our song! Danny says.

Every day we'll dance naked in the playroom to The BARE Necessities! Arram says; and *Eeee-ya!* Danny cries, nearly overwhelmed by the thought of so much future joy.

That evening at the public library, after Danny conveys Mrs. Kaigh's *wordless* and *instrumental* to the librarian at the reference desk, she leads him over the uncharted orange carpeting of the adult section, past long tables of whispering teenagers. It's the first time he's ever had reason to approach the tall, scarf-wearing lady he's often seen walking officially about the rooms. To his relief, she didn't scoff at him but listened to his stammered explanations with all seriousness. "You must be an Our Lady's boy," she says rather loudly now, looking over her shoulder to speak to him.

"Uh-huh," he says.

She nods solemnly. "It's just a remarkable idea, a children's performance of the Passion. Your teacher sounds extraordinary."

"Mm," he says, as she stops before a rack of albums marked "Classical" and frowns.

"By any chance did she say whether she wanted an assortment of music, or something from a single composer?"

"A-A-Assortment," Danny says.

She nods again. "That might be the best way to go. Then if you like one of the excerpts, you can always come back and get the entire work."

"Right," Danny says, as if comprehending, and watches her slender, ringed fingers flip through records in a special "Collections" folder. At last they select one titled *Classical Masterpieces,* its cover graced with a pencil portrait of a wavy-haired, muscly shouldered man.

"Here's one with all the favorites," she says. "Beethoven's *Fifth, Swan Lake.* Oh, and Handel's 'Hallelujah Chorus.' That might be just the thing for the resurrection. Though of course, it does have words. Do you know them?" And surprisingly now, she sings, "And He shall reign for ever and ev-er," and Danny becomes conscious of snickers from a nearby table of boys, all with dark, feathered hair and public school letter jackets draped on the backs of their chairs. "Don't they sing that at Mass?" she asks. "King of kings! And Lord of lords!"

"I-I-I think so." He glances back at the boys, laughing outright now. "Th-This is good." Then attempts to take it from her, but too soon it seems, for her arms cross around the muscly man's head, pressing him to her chest. And now her mouth opens wide again—to sing more, he fears—and so he says quickly, "C-Could you write down the n-names of the composers and works?"

"Why?" she asks, unhugging the album, "They're right here," and points for example to SUMMER in bold capitals, "These are the names of the works," then to the italicized V-word beside it, "and this is the composer." She looks at him. "Composer just means the name of the man who wrote it, who composed it."

"I know."

"Is your mother with you?"

"Mother?"

"You'll need an adult to check this out for you."

"Oh," he says. "I-um . . . She-she-she's—well—in the ch-ch-ch—, with my-my-my—"

The boys snicker again and the librarian, first frowning at them, taps Danny's arm assuringly. "I understand," she says, surrendering the album, and making it unnecessary, then, to add "little sister."

"Thank you," he mumbles, and walks immediately to the children's room, past the smaller bookcases to the farthest window. He stares longingly into the garden and dimly lit parking lot and tells himself that if the window weren't the unopenable kind, he might attempt to raise it and deposit the album into the bushes. Yet it's not possible to leave now without *Classical Masterpieces*, as necessary as it is to the play, and as much as he realizes that by the time he convinces his mother to come and charge it out for him, it could be gone. That is, if he's even able to convince her, and if she, in turn, is able to convince his father to drive them back up. She might not want to bother. She might just say, "Wait till the weekend." She sometimes says that about things, and then once the weekend comes, "Oh, not on the weekend," and round and round, and never.

And so he continues to fret until, moments later in the locked men's room, he discovers that the album, concealed beneath his parka, makes an obvious, square bulge. But once he takes the white-sleeved records out, and puts these alone beneath his shirt, and puts his coat on again, it's less noticeable, provided he leaves the coat unzipped to his stomach, so it doesn't pull in tightly at the sides. Thus arranged, he steps out onto the bright carpeting again, heart beating furiously, and, after tossing the empty jacket into a record case marked "Languages," is intending to continue directly past the checkout desk to the doors, when he spots the old man seated before them. He forgot all about him! How? He's always there, with his white hair and gold glasses, and sometimes he looks up from his book when people leave, and sometimes he just keeps reading. Danny can't imagine passing him now, least of all empty-handed; he feels sure that if he does, the man will look right at his stomach and know. So he walks to a nearby bookcase and thumbs through *My Side of the Mountain*, praying for nerve, even as he realizes it's a commandment not to do what he's asking for help with.

The next moment, as if providentially arranged, a blond lady in a jogging suit carries a stack of oversized illustrated books to the counter. When they're nearly checked out, Danny walks up behind her, and a second librarian gestures at his one book. "I'll take that over here," she says, not even looking at his coat, and, after putting in the slip, "You're welcome, now," retreats in the usual way behind the desk. Slowly, Danny returns his card to his pants pocket, allowing the blond lady to adjust her shoulder bag before scooping up the books, then follows closely, trembling, sweat trickling from his underarms and down his ribs, the paper sleeves of the records beneath his shirt softly sliding against each other. And the white-haired man who sometimes doesn't look up from his book looks up and nods at the lady, and then at him, trustingly.

"Good night," he says.

"Good night," they say.

But just as Danny's almost cleared the first set of double doors, he hears, "Good luck with your play!" and so turns, and it's the reference librarian, smiling and waving from the front desk. Danny waves back, then runs through the doors—to catch up, as it were, to his mother— and, in less than a minute, he's unlocked his Stingray and is pedaling frantically down Main Street, the generator light casting a brighter- than-usual glow over the uneven sidewalk.

Safe in the playroom again, he jumps back from the stereo at the first, fast shout of "Hallelujah!" How loud and fierce the singers sound, like a whole host of screaming angels! They grow even louder and fiercer as the song continues, teaming up, with more and more voices, high and low, taking turns or overlapping. He makes out the part the li- brarian sang and understands the He to be Jesus: Jesus will reign for ever and ever, at the end of the world! Goose bumps rise on his arms as he imagines the angels, robed and white-winged, beating their breasts, crazed with love. *Careeba careeba careebamay! Ooo-lee boo-lee boo-lee!* they shout, *King of kings! Lord of lords!* Others, high on pedestals, blow trumpets or saw furiously on violins, and the little ones, the golden-haired cherubim, naked but for the streaming banners over their parts, loop and flit through the air, and down about all the san- daled feet, like beautiful human moths. And last of all Danny, pro- ceeding through this din down a cloud-carpeted aisle at the center of the dividing angel-sea, waving his pierced palms to the host at his left, the host at his right, his long brown hair bouncing regally down his back, his white and purple robes floating on heavenly breezes. "Hal- lelujah! Hallelujah! Hal-LEEE-lu-jah!"

Meanwhile Carol, quickly bobby-pinning her last pink roller behind her ear and spraying down her whole finished head, leaves the down- stairs bathroom on the trail of the strange noise she's been hearing. No, she tells herself at the foot of the stairs, she wasn't imagining things, he's playing some kind of Christmasy choir music up there. Disori- ented, she squints and blinks, and has to remind herself it's the end of March, the very beginning of spring. "Danny!" she calls, "Hey!" bang- ing on the stair wall—just, it strikes her now, as she once did with the boys when they were blasting their rock 'n' roll. Once again, too, it's merely the music that answers her, only this time, instead of a few frog- throated, disrespectful brats, it sounds like an army of holy rollers, fren- ziedly screaming, "Hallelujah!" "Oh Christ," she says, not sure which is worse. She rushes up herself now, as if to save him from them, imagining for no reason she can think of that when she gets to the doorway, she'll find him lying unconscious on the floor.

However, he's most definitely on his feet, striding across the bare wood, waving left and right like the president from a motorcade. "Danny!" she yells, a hot blush racing to her cheeks. "What are you doing now?"

He spins around and, seeing her standing in the doorway, assumes an expression of such wide-eyed terror that Carol has to struggle not to laugh.

"M-M-M-Mom!" he cries, squeezing his fly and running to turn down the stereo. "I didn't hear you!"

Why do they always squeeze themselves like that when they're scared? "Is that what you do in the play?"

"N-N-No," he says.

"I hope not, you'll make an ass of yourself."

"I'm sorry."

"You know, I have a mind to call up this teacher of yours and tell her the whole thing's off. I'm telling you if—" But she stops herself in time. Nonetheless she has every intention of calling Madame Sarah tomorrow, and if she says this play is going to be a bomb or some kind of humiliation to them . . . well, then, Carol will be sticking *her* two cents in. "Come on, Danny," she says now, bending to pick up an armchair arm cover from the floor and return it to its rightful owner, one more frayed than the other. *The frayed covering the frayed*, she thinks, how pathetic. The boys really demolished what was left of the furniture; she doesn't remember it being this bad. Though she can't remember, either, the last time she was even in here and winces to think of the fight Gerry had with Robby, maybe in this very spot, the banging she heard from downstairs. "God," she says, and snorts at how empty the room looks without the boys' things all over. It needs an area rug and some curtains to hang over those old grayed sheers; any of the girls ever came up here, she'd be mortified. But now an even more frightening thought assails her, and she glares at her youngest again. "Were you just pretending to be Christ?"

"No."

"How can I know if you're lying?"

"I w-wasn't."

"You promised me you were going to be Whatshisface. The king. Didn't you?"

"That's what I was doing, Mom. I was pretending to be the King," he says, earnestly this time because she can't see his capital K.

"Oh," she says. That makes sense to her: president, king. "Where'd you get this music, anyway? Is it one of our Christmas albums?"

"No."

"Where'd it come from, then?" She approaches the turntable suspiciously, squinting at the revolving record label. *Classical Masterpieces*. Well, pardon me. "I know your brothers never listened to this kind of . . . " here editing *crap*. "What library is that?"

"Huh?" He spins around again. How could she know? "Wait, Mom," he says, flushing and wishing she'd move away from the stereo.

"It's got the public library stamp on it."

"It does?" he says, looking now, also, and indeed, there it is, right beside the album title, *PROPERTY OF . . .* What did they put that on it for? "I didn't get it from there."

"Someone did."

"Miss Kaigh must have," he says automatically.

"Your *teacher*? Are you telling me she's checking records out of the public library for you now?" Of course Queen Elizabeth would listen to classical music. "I suppose she thinks you don't get enough exposure to the arts from your backward mother and father."

"She doesn't think that."

"Huh," Carol grunts, then purses her lips and attempts to read the rest of the label; but the lettering's so small she can't decipher it. "Who does this song, Beethoven?"

"Who?"

"Beethoven?"

"It's Handel's 'Hallelujah Chorus,'" he tells her.

"Oh," she says, feeling the awe again, that he should know such a thing already, that he should have such a glue strip for a brain. Then she shakes her head and turns for the doorway. "Don't stay up too late being sophisticated."

Danny watches her retreat, all rollers and powder-blue fat-fanny robe. And not until he's counted her thirteen steps and three hall-swishes to her bedroom does he cue up the record again, setting the player to a low volume. And now with one eye on the door, he resumes his procession down the cloud aisle, past the many love-crazed angels.

～ 8 ～

Danny Transfigured

Friday morning, Liz's mind swims with worries again, several concerning the Music Hall, which it now appears they'll be able to use, the Wednesday before vacation. Sister Regina had been so excited, like a girl, pulling her aside while she was mimeographing the religion test. Liz had smiled, of course, and said, "Oh, thank you, how marvelous," yet had felt none of it. That isn't much more than a week away, and they've yet to find a Christ! How much worse it'll be on a real stage, if they wind up with one of the boys they have now. She shakes her head, unwilling to picture it, and, at her desk now, worries instead about the test itself, the copies hidden in a drawer. On it are short-answer questions from the recall and review chapter of *We Break Bread in Loving Thanksgiving,* and a second part, much harder, in which she asks them to list each Beatitude separately and discuss how it (a) is violated, (b) can be practiced in the world today. She sees the boys' eyes widening as they encounter the menacing space below the words *list and discuss,* the clear white sea on which they're sure to drown, and asks herself if she dares to hand it out. *But didn't you go over everything with them just yesterday?* she imagines Sister Margaret, notorious for giving pop quizzes, asking. The nun is further alluding to the time and supplies it took to copy everything when Danny approaches with a brown grocery bag. Liz looks at it quizzically. "Now what's in there?"

"M-M-Music," he explains.

"Oh!" she says, immediately lifted. She hadn't expected actual records, and so soon! Mrs. Burke must've had them on hand, she thinks, and is about to remark how giving and generous his mother is—first the copies, now this—when he reaches into the bag and produces a familiar double-record set.

"But, Daniel, isn't that the Beatles' *White Album?*" She squints at the audaciously blank jacket, omnipresent in her college days. "How could that be appropriate for a religious play?"

He stammers, removing one of the records, and she squints at the label, its parade of unsayable names: Dvorak, Shostakovich, Tchaikovsky. "Yes, good," she says, intending to look up the pronunciations later. The titles, too, will require research. *Eine Kleine Nachtmusik* must be either Dutch or German; how unforgivable not to know whether Mozart was Dutch or German. "Radetzsky March"? Not a clue. Oh but, Beethoven's *Fifth*—isn't that the *Duh-duh-duh-DUH, duh-duh-duh-DUH?* That's wonderful, so ominous! Certainly they could use it somewhere—after Christ is sentenced, maybe? Imagine, Beethoven in the play. *We're using Beethoven's 'Fifth'! And Mozart!* Yes, here they all are, a bowl of riches! And now as she imagines Mrs. Burke extending the bowl and she graciously accepting—*I will listen attentively to every track of these records the minute I get home*—she feels a soft fluttering in her stomach and runs a fingertip over the ornate flourishes of the album title.

"But then why are they in *here?*" she asks, wrinkling her nose at the portraits of the surly, long-haired antitheses inside the jacket, their list of repellent song titles: "Piggies," "Everybody's Got Something to Hide Except for Me and My Monkey." "Your mother doesn't listen to this . . . stuff, does she?"

"No," Danny says. "I-I just put it there, so it w-won't scratch. It's my brothers'."

"Ah." An older brother, she gathers, squinting at the upper-right-hand portion of the label, a couple of words magic-markered out there: *East Islip* something or other. *Public Schools?* "How old *is* your brother?"

"Nineteen," he says, thinking of Robby.

"Is he in college?"

"Uh-huh," he says, though Gerry, his real college brother, is twenty.

Mrs. Burke must be in her early forties, Liz surmises, just a few years younger than her own mother. She thinks of striking redheads—Ann-Margret, Jill St. John. Curls, too, could be lovely on a woman, though not as tight as Danny's; wavy, rather, flowing, without all the frizz and fly-aways of her own. "Does your mother have red hair, too?" she asks, lowering her voice.

But he shakes his head. "Brown."

"Brown," she repeats. So much for Ann-Margret. The red must be on his father's side, then. And come to think of it, she's never asked about his father, not even what he does for a living, and is just about to venture there, when something Danny says diverts her attention. "What's that?"

"She-she said we could use the 'Hallelujah Chorus' for the resurrection."

Liz slaps her heart. "The 'Hallelujah Chorus'? Is that on here? Oh, it is! From the *Messiah!* By—"

"Handel," they say together.

"Super!" she cries, so relieved to actually know one of the selections. "But—" she sits back now, "isn't it usually associated with Christmas?" She thinks of the refrains, *He shall reign for ever and ever, King of kings.* Well, sure, that could be appropriate for Easter. Very much so. Because isn't the resurrection a kind of rebirth? Of Christ's? And the rebirth of all Christians into everlasting life with God? She shivers with the recognition of it all—life through death, the whole spiritual round. What a mind his mother has! What a woman she must be! If Liz had any confidence at all, she'd invite her to the performance; she might be able to get a sub for the afternoon. Liz would shake her hand of course, venture a few carefully chosen pleasantries. They might even strike it off somehow, in that brief exchange, take an intuitive, instant liking to each other. *Perhaps we might have coffee at the O-Co-Nee Diner sometime.* Could she find the nerve?

And in this way, the whole other matter of the father is forgotten. Soon the bell rings and Danny returns to his desk, Liz to her former worries. And one moment she decides she'll give the test, the next she won't again, will, won't, period to period, until finally, halfway into the one before lunch, while she's allowing the students time to begin their spelling assignment for the evening, and telling herself that she definitely won't now, and is in a way relieved, she overhears a conversation between Paolo and Brian. And though it's nothing new—the Sicilian boy asking for an extra piece of looseleaf and Brian disdainfully shaking his head—it occurs to her now that Paolo leaves his tablet book home purposely, just to have a reason to speak to the boy, only to get continually rebuffed. And it's this understanding, together with Brian's expression reminding her of the one he wore during their talk in the parking lot—*All the fags are in it*—that immediately precedes her standing up, exams in hand.

"Clear your desks," she says.

"Why? What for?" they demand, as she counts out stacks of papers and places them facedown on the first desk of each row. "Is this a quiz?" Brian asks. "Yeah, is this a quiz?" Joey echoes, and, after several beats, Liz looks up, as if having just regained her hearing. "No, it's not."

"Oh good."

"It's a test."

"A *test?*" the boys say, and the room grows loud with grumbles: "A test!" "You didn't tell us about this." "Does it count?"

"Of course it counts," she says, turning on the questioner, Kevin Lukas. "You think I'm doing this for my health? You think I'd just like a little more paperwork at home?" The boy quickly shakes his head. "And let me repeat myself, mister: whoever doesn't pass religion this year will not be confirmed in the sixth grade." She snaps down the last stack, and finds each student quiet now and looking up at her with wide, frightened eyes. "And some of you," she adds, glancing back at Brian and Joey, "are barely squeaking by as it is."

"But Miss Kaigh—" Brian pleads.

"No 'Miss Kaigh.' First person in each row pass back the exam. You have twenty minutes."

"—this isn't fair."

And now with her back to the class, she winces before sitting down again at her desk. Then to distract herself from the many sighs and tongue clicks, and from her own mind's rehearsal of the sudden, shrewish lines she's just spoken, she retrieves her pocket dictionary from her desk and busies herself with the pronunciation of composer names.

When lunch begins, the noise level more subdued than usual, it's all she can do to steady her hands as she reads through Brian's five mangled Beatitudes: peacemakers inheriting the earth, poor of heart seeing God—the *poor* of heart, like an anti-Beatitude, synonym for *Ye of little faith.* "Blessed are the hungry, for they shall eat." Below this he gives the thirsty to drink, as if it were a test on "The Song of St. Francis." And yet amid all this mumbo jumbo, "Blessed are those who mourn, for they shall be comfort," nearly letter-perfect. "This is violated in the world today when someone is sad and no one helps him. This can be practiced in the world today by helping someone sad." No question he deserves full credit there. Still, he'll be lucky to break a forty, and now her face flushes hotly at the effectiveness of her handiwork: the grade's sure to drag his average solidly into the F camp. Maybe the boys were right, it wasn't fair. *You all did so terribly I threw them out, and I'm giving you another chance next week.* They'll think she's flipped—hard-nose one day, softie the next. She pictures again the fearful respect in their eyes when she yelled and admits to herself it wasn't entirely unpleasant. And how fair would it be to the ones who do study every day and did well? Did any of them do well? She flips through the papers again, as if for someone who might have, but stops instead at Joey's and skims through his six answers. He, too, got the mourners right, why? The peacemakers inheriting the kingdom of heaven now. But what's this? The hungry and the thirsty again. At the second appearance of *the poor of heart,* her cheeks flush with new intensity. "Oh no," she says aloud, several students at front looking up sharply.

"What's the matter, Miss Kaigh?" Frances asks.

And as Liz glances at the two cheats, their yapping, happy-go-lucky heads oblivious as ever to her, and to anything besides themselves, she feels her eyes drawing ever narrower, and her own last vestiges of remorse dropping away.

Not until recess, while Danny's temporarily playing Christ again, does the small miracle happen, this just after Liz has made the Music Hall announcement and remarked how much brighter Danny's eyes lit up than the others'—"Like Radio City!" he blurted out breathlessly; "Well, not quite," Liz said, a little breathless herself at such a grand comparison—and moments, too, after having praised him for getting every Beatitude correct and sent Kevin Lukas, who'd grumbled at his desk and called Danny a little kiss-ass, into the hall. Though she subsequently noted how much more pleasant the room was without the foul-mouth and how proud Danny looked—he straightened right up and almost seemed to grow an inch or two—even that hadn't prepared her. It was the lines, "Enough! Put back your sword where it belongs. Shall I not drink the cup the Father has given Me?" that finally raised her head from the worrisome pile of exams. So convincingly were they delivered, with such sudden force, it was as if she were hearing them for the first time.

And indeed, it's Danny, but Danny as she's never seen him: remote and unself-conscious, attuned, it would seem, to something entirely outside the room. She shivers as she watches him circle the players as though they were the actual guards and apostles, something panther-like about him, fiery-eyed. "Do you not suppose I can call on My Father to provide at a moment's notice more than twelve legions of angels?" he cries, indicating the sky and frowning at Rory, temporary Peter, with palpable disdain.

"Is that Danny?" Juanita asks, looking up from a sword-making project in the back of the room.

"Yeah," Rory says, equally amazed.

They all watch as Danny pounds his chest and turns upon Paolo, "Am I a criminal that you come after Me armed with swords and clubs?"

"Ah!" the girls scream. "He's doing good! What happened?"

"Hey, Curly," Kevin yells from the hall, "did you hit your head or something?"

Liz, too, tries to cheer and smile along, though in truth, she doesn't quite believe what she sees. "Don't pressure him," she says, glancing from one amused face to another; and her voice, it seems, is the one that finally gets through to him, for his head snaps in her direction, bursting, she imagines, the strange bubble that had just surrounded it. "You'll jinx him," she says, staring at his blue, blinking eyes.

"Yeah," Kevin yells again from the hall, "he'll go back to being himself."

"No one asked you," Liz returns, without enough anger.

And now Danny, squinting at the waiting, mostly hopeful, faces, sees them in all their close and intimidating detail again, as if scales have just fallen from his eyes.

"Go on, Daniel," his teacher urges.

"Yeah, Danny." "Come on, Danny," the others say.

"All right," he answers, "one second," dizzy and bereft now of the lovely, comfortable hum, the high, full feeling in his chest when the words rushed from him in a clear stream. Somehow his mind had become trained on his own movements and voice, or, if not on his own voice, on the one he'd spoken with: transformed, resonant, as if— could it be?—he was actually speaking in the voice of Jesus Himself! But when he finally continues, pushed too soon by the goading and staring, "B-B-But th-th-this is your-your-your . . ." his voice is mousy and lifeless again, not even worthy of a Peter.

"Oh," they all say. Then one by one they turn from him, those who can, or, in the case of the onstage players, fall back into their postures of bored waiting. Finally Liz, too, sighs and takes up the exams again, relieved that at least this other potential trouble should have passed. Because though it occurs to her that they may just have witnessed the kind of acting Danny'd be capable of if he were a truly confident boy, she knows it was but a lucky moment. It can't be depended on to resurface under the pressure of a performance. For all their sakes, she must continue to look for another player, she tells herself, and, with some effort, and a last pitying glance at the boy, stumbling on through his lines, succeeds in driving the strange scene from her mind.

Not so Danny, who thinks repeatedly and longingly of his triumphant breakthrough, the hum and feeling in his chest graduating in memory to strains of Handelian chorus music and a Spirit-infused ecstasy. And if it was visited on him once, couldn't it be visited again? *Please?* he prays, all through the afternoon, and his brisk walk down Main Street, right up to the very threshold of the playroom door, where the praying and hoping give way to other pursuits.

Ugga wugga wugga! they chant, cavorting with jungle-like abandon around the arm chairs in the playroom, their new theme song blaring away on the Magnavox.

This is the most fun I've ever had! Danny says.

I know! Arram says, and then, just at the craziest apex of their joy, cries, *Let's dance naked through the whole upstairs!*

The whole upstairs? Danny says.

Yeah! We have to dance naked in all the rooms!

Naked in all the rooms! Danny repeats, as if swearing an oath, and immediately skips down the hall to Gerry's, or to what used to be Gerry's, but is still called that by his mother. "Anyone home?" he asks jokingly, because it's so still and empty inside: empty hutch and shelves, empty desktop, dresser top. *Come on, Arram!* and they flounce across the nappy maroon spread on the twin bed, ever made—*Wrinkle it! Mess it up!*—then strut across the wood floor and little maroon oval rug and take turns sitting at the desk. *"ARRAM WAS HERE,"* the boy writes across the dust, but Danny quickly erases it and, with a bold impulse, stands on the chair and wiggles all around like a belly dancer.

Ooh, yeah! Shake it, baby, shake it! Arram cries. Then they skip on to Robby's room to do a similar flounce and strut around the identical furnishings there, except that on one of Danny's turns across the floor—just, it happens, as he's passing the window that faces the backyard—he stops abruptly and, naked as he is, imagines himself his brother, the way he'd show himself when his sister and her friends were outside. He remembers several times being among them, and the girls pointing and screaming, "Look! Look, he's doing it again! You can see his thing!" He'd watched them all squint up, then away, then back again, warier; and once, when he dared to look himself, he saw his brother's bare chest turning from the window, and there, near the sill, a quickly retreating swath of blackness—just the swath, because he'd looked too late—and then Sharon, red-faced, snarling up at the place where he'd stood: "Pervert!"

That was really bad, Danny explains to Arram, even as he judges, by the way the sill cuts across his belly, just above his baby-nose outie, that he's much shorter than Robby was. Anyone standing outside right now, on the grass or patio, would see very little of him. He'd have to go to great effort, jumping as high as he could, just to let them know he wasn't wearing a shirt. And so quite logically, he casts around for something to stand on, in order to get his whole front, right on down to the good stuff, into the frame of the window.

At the same time Carol, climbing the front steps a few minutes earlier than usual, gets a drift of the music upstairs. Here we go, she thinks, must be hitting that age—one day they wake up, and all they want to do is blast the stereo. What's he got on now, some kind of musical? Oh wait, she knows this. An old Disney thing, isn't it? That's strange. Fumbling with her keys and the lock, she calls up to him over the singing bear, Whatshisface, Magoo? "Danny? Daaaan-ny!"

But just now he's standing on his brother's old desk chair, knees bent and hips thrust forward, in order to effectively moon his dickie over the backyard, a balancing act requiring such concentration that it's another instant before he becomes conscious of his mother's voice.

"W-W-What?" he yells, jumping to the floor. "Wait!" Making fig leaves with his hands, he rushes across the hall to the playroom, shuts off the stereo, pulls on his clothes, and finally, inching toward the stairs, pokes his head out just far enough to clear his chin. She's standing down on the welcome mat in her tan overcoat, penciled eyebrows raised.

"Was that *The Jungle Book?*"

"Huh?"

"Didn't I just hear 'The Bare Necessities'?"

"M-Mom," he says, shocked she would name the naked-dancing song.

And so she stops, seeing his embarrassment; it *is* a little young for him. If the boys at school knew he was still listening to this kind of thing, they'd laugh their heads off. But personally, she prefers it to that scary choir music he had on the night before. And she'd take it, too, over the stuff that's constantly wailing out of Sharon's room. What is it? Alice Cooper? Guy with a girl's name, no less. And what's the other one? Rod Stewart, going on about that poor Maggie girl? "Well," she says, voice softening, "it's okay to listen to those things once in a while." She winks at him. "When no one's around."

"It is?" he asks, squinting.

"Sure. Everyone likes to be a kid again."

That same afternoon, he paints Jesus' face onto an old undershirt he finds in a drawer of his father's workbench—"Did I say you could go into that bench?" he yelled the time Danny assembled the Sparrow Motel—the shirt still smelling faintly of sweat and Old Spice beneath the sharper basement must. He notices the smell more at his desk, while trimming a square from the shirt with the scissor of the Swiss army knife he found near it—"Did I say you could use my tools?"—and especially when he holds the square over his own face, marking out his hairline and the tip of his chin and the places for his eyes and nose and mouth. Then after he draws in the shape of the head and outlines it sketchily with black paint, the project itself absorbs him: adding strokes of brown and yellow to the mustache and beard and long-flowing hair; hints of blue to the eyes; and all around the forehead, black slashes to represent the thorns; and in and around the thorns, dashes of red; and several drips of red down from the corners of the eyes, blood tears. Then he's only just wished they could be real blood, when he finds the nerve to prick his finger with a pin from the bathroom. *The Blood of Christ,* he thinks, smearing a bead across the face's forehead, smearing another down the jaw. And finally, when he finishes the painting to his satisfaction, he runs with it to the kitchen, the avocado air thick with boiling ham. "Mom, look."

"Oh my God," she says, turning from the stove. "What the hell is that?"

"It's Veronica's veil."

"Veronica?" She shakes her head. "Danny, why would you want to have something like that around?"

"It's for the play."

"You mean you're going to have an actual veil with the face on it?"

"Yeah."

"Well, don't you think you're getting a little too realistic?"

"You have to have the veil."

"You don't *have* to have it," she says, though in truth, it's an awfully good painting, despite its subject. "It looks so real." She squints at the sad, bleeding face, and now suddenly it reminds her of her husband, the frowning set of the mouth. "The blood's so . . . bloody."

"I know," Danny says, just as the phone rings, and they both jump at the sudden peal. "I'll get it."

"No. I'm expecting someone."

The instant before she says hello, he imagines it to be the singing librarian at the public library, *We have reason to believe . . .* His mother pressing her hand to her heart, *My son?*

But she doesn't say, *My son?* she says, "*Sarah,*" with genuine enthusiasm, then waves him away before stepping into Sharon's room and closing the door.

He ducks beneath the green extension cord, stretched like a tightrope from wall to room, and walks to the garage, there holding the veil aloft and dodging grubby-pawed Duke on the stairs and at the basement door. And so the dog scratches and barks as Danny, nose twitching at the onset of the gray mustiness, walks past the many cartons and old bicycles and lamps and rug-rolls, and stops in an area just below Sharon's room, perching warily on the arm of a corduroy Lazy Boy, a worn, mildewed, busted-springs affair long ago destined for, but never delivered to, the dump. And here, gazing down at the bearded face on his lap, he makes out occasional words of his mother's conversation overhead: "Please. My God," said laughingly, and "What?" quite eagerly, this as the blue veil-eyes glint up with urgency, a message, the painted lips part ever so perceptibly, *Danny! —I am here, Lord.* But now: *"Please,"* an actual begging, and a flustered "By who?" and automatically his stomach tightens. He hopes his mother isn't arguing with the Sarah-lady. *Make ready, for you know not the hour I will speak through you again. —Yes, Lord,* he says, then hears his mother leaving Sharon's room and hanging up the receiver, the sound effectively ending both conversations—for when he looks down again, the eyes have gone dull, lips closed. He counts several empty seconds before getting up and dodging the dog again at the basement door, and when he comes on his mother in the kitchen, she's at the table, scribbling on a memo pad.

"Who-Who was that?" he asks, but she frowns at the veil and seems to be on the verge of saying something about it when she stops herself.

"No one."

"No one?" he repeats.

"Well, of course it wasn't no one." But she'll be damned if she tells him. "I've a mind to put an end to it," she says instead, with deliberate vagueness.

"To what?" Danny asks, stomach tightening again.

"Well, you can have a mind to, dear, but I also see it happening," Sarah had said. "And you can't change the future." And of course, she knows all about that. "He's a religious boy."

"Yes." Carol had frowned.

"Confused," Sarah said.

"Danny, would you stop breathing down my neck for a minute?" He's hovering at her right elbow, trying to read her notes. She covers the words *twin* and *friend*.

"I'm-I'm sorry," he says and plods off with the horrid face, and so she crosses her legs and lightly bites at her pinky nail. What could he be confused about?

"I see it as a form of worship for him." Then this zinger: "He's not a twin, is he?" Imagine?

"Twin! Please, my God." She'd gotten understandably dramatic.

"I see two boys, worshiping. Oh dear."

"What?"

"He has a friend."

"Yeah?"

"You might not like the friend."

But that couldn't be true, either. She's always encouraged him to go over to kids' houses; he's the one who prefers to stay home, drawing and what-not. Take that veil, for example. And so she cut to the chase: "Is it a bomb?" Oh, and it was excruciating, the silence that followed.

Finally Sarah said, "It's a children's play; these things never go right. But I'm having some trouble . . . I don't see them . . . finishing? Is that it? Could they get started, and not quite finish? I get a sense of—oops."

"Of what? What is it now?" Carol said, terrified. What could be more terrifying than a psychic *oops*?

"No no," Sarah said.

"Please," Carol said.

"I've been instructed to stop."

"Instructed? By who? Why?"

"He'll learn from this; you both will. It'll be something you never forget."

The conversation had ended rather soon thereafter.

"Instructed," Carol grumbles, "flake," and at the same time appreciates the difficulty of approaching a Catholic schoolteacher with such information. *Sin against your religion.* Betty had said that, nose in the air, when the girls in the office first talked about going to Sarah. Carol never understood why she put it that way, "*your* religion"—it's hers, too. But how could she justify her apprehension otherwise? Claim she had her own vision, maybe? Is it a sin if you see it yourself? If you don't seek it out or anything, how mad could God get? Still, Miss Whatsherface is liable to think she's a screwball, might hold it against Danny. She better not say anything about psychic flashes or fortunes, better not say anything at all. A burden to know so much and not be able to tell anyone—story of her life.

~ 9 ~

Lessons in Villainy

Monday before lunch, as Liz writes the words to the "Hallelujah Chorus" on the board for the children to copy—this as a prelude to the song itself, already cued up on a school phonograph on the floor beside her desk: an old, green, box-shaped contraption, the lid of which, containing the speaker, swings open on a hinge—she's thinking in part of Mrs. Burke's bowl of riches and her own discovery Friday evening, on sampling it, of how barren her life was before. By Saturday afternoon, she was convinced her whole Patchogue childhood had been one extended cultural desert and soon found herself impelled to the downstairs kitchen. "Mom, how come you and Dad never listened to music?" Her mother, drawing back a little, had to think about the question, as if she wasn't aware they hadn't. Finally she offered a list of excuses, including the claim that she and her father couldn't really afford a stereo when they got married. "But you never even listened to the radio." "That's not true. When I was young, I knew every word to the top forty songs." "But I'm talking about when we were growing up." "When you and Dennis were growing up, we were happy for any peace and quiet we could get." Liz hadn't laughed or said what was really on her mind—*I mean real music, Beethoven, Mozart*—but instead dropped the subject and retreated upstairs again, vowing to herself to steadily weave the classical masters into her days.

And Lord of lords, forever and forever, she finishes, then moves to the next board, beginning the week's new vocabulary list. "Say the word after I write it, everyone. Ready? *Hallelujah.*"

"Hallelujah."

"And now read the definition."

"Praise the Lord."

How grateful she is to the Ann-Margret-like woman (she'd further pictured Mrs. Burke, during the Handel, in a smart navy-blue skirt suit, hair pulled back in a simple twist, exuberantly maneuvering her bow in an orchestra pit below the choir) for this life-changing bestowal. Loveliness upon loveliness: no sooner had *Swan Lake* thunderously resolved than the swirls of a Strauss waltz began. When Mozart debuted with his serenade—*Austrian,* she repeats to herself, *Vienna*—she was so charmed by his jaunty, joyous violins that, despite her anxieties and normal reserve, she'd gotten up and executed several amateur turns through her den, to the surprise of Cleopatra, who deigned to raise her head from the otherwise serene beige curl of her body. At last reaching a summit of *Finlandia*—Sibelius, accent on the second syllable, long *ay* sound; a Finnish composer; she'd imagined, jokingly, her own *Long Island*—she felt she'd truly discovered the meaning of the word *sublime* and ran to verify it with the dictionary: "Impressing the mind with a sense of grandeur or power; inspiring awe, veneration." "Yes," she'd said, looking up at the ceiling, but more, thought it could quite possibly *expand* her mind, that, could she somehow be allowed into the music, into some understanding of these works, they might bring her a new intelligence, a composure, make her more . . . faceted, or something else, maybe, something necessary.

"Say it, class: *om-ni-po-tent.*"

"Om-ni-po-tent."

"Meaning?"

"Almighty or infinite in power, as God."

Oh, and she has so much to learn! To her shame, she found she couldn't even say what in the Beethoven was responsible for that famously ominous growl. Something stringed, obviously, but which? She could only think of a Bugs Bunny cartoon, the rabbit sawing on a giant, standing violin-like instrument, *Duh-duh-duh-DUH.* A viola? The bass? She hopes to locate some *Introduction to Classical Music* manual in the public library, preferably one with pictures of all the instruments. Or better, a book and record set, so that as she's looking at the pictures, a helpful voice might say, *And now hear the sound of the cello. Now the clarinet . . .* While she's at it, she'll find out more about the works they'll be using, which she conceives of now as a group of four.

Ironically enough, "Summer" from *The Four Seasons* seemed the most appropriate for the agony, its cycles of weeping and frenzy. The very first parts of *Finlandia,* that creeping, unbearably menacing—melody?—also seemed just right for the trials. And yes, the crash of the *Fifth!* as Pilate washes his hands, additional sinister bits of it along The Way and during the crucifixion. And at last her "Hallelujah Chorus." What a grand finale it'll be! How grand the entire score! She'd even gone so far, amid her planning, as to think that the music itself might save the play, that no matter how bad the show, there would still be this certain beauty. "Everyone?"

"*Reign.* To possess or exercise supreme power or authority."

"Good. Follow along as you listen." And now, bending too eagerly for the phonograph, she inadvertently lowers the needle into a somber cascade of piano notes: Chopin, Franco-Polish. Clunky metal arm's hard to maneuver, she notes, frowning at the prospect of Stephen manipulating it with his fat fingers, and, nudging it ahead, here now the violins, the rushing-in chorus. But flat, hollow, compared to her stereo at home, like it's being sung in the next room. Disappointing, too, the giggles behind her. And now from Kevin, a mock-soprano "HAL-lelujah!" followed by bursts of laughter.

"That will be enough of *that.*" She stands up, glancing from the grinning, ignorant boy to her two cheats, snickering along with the best of them. Brian, especially, seems greatly amused, sliding down in his seat and covering his face. *Sissy stuff,* she imagines him thinking, and, looking to Danny now, who stares stiffly at his desktop, blushes herself with embarrassment, all her discovered riches falling away as worthless beneath this new pronouncement. But how ridiculous. She has everyone behind her on this: Mrs. Burke, the East Islip Public Schools, RCA records, and the entire history of music and music appreciation—not to mention the chorus itself, just now proclaiming, "And He shall reign for ever and ever." "It's one of the great classical masterpieces," she says with mustered authority, "by German composer George Frideric Handel." Now at last the smiles fade, throats clear, bodies straighten in their seats.

"I like it, Miss Kaigh," Frances admits. "The choir sings this song at Christmas Mass."

"Yeah," Juanita says. "The Hallelujah's my favorite."

"It's my favorite except for 'I Think I Love You,'" Ginger says.

"Oh right," Juanita says. "It's my favorite *church* song."

"It's beautiful," Frances says.

"It's beautiful," Kevin mimics, and the boys snicker again.

Let them laugh now, Liz thinks, acknowledging only the girl. "You're right, Frances, it *is* beautiful." She does lay aside, however, hopes of getting them to sing along on a subsequent hearing and, in fact, decides against another hearing altogether, turning the player off when the song's few minutes are up, and immediately retrieving the graded exams, just the sight of which induces groans. Yet she swiftly delivers them and in turn collects tongue clicks, *oh*'s, an occasional *phew*. "Excellent, Daniel," she says, "Good, Frances," and, lastly, walking down the aisle between the two boys, lays their papers on the desktops. When their mouths drop open, as red and round a unison as their grades, she finds, with some shame, that she has to bite her lip to suppress a smile—not one, she insists to herself, of maliciousness, so much as recognition: just how closely she's visualized these exact expressions. "You look surprised," she says, glancing from either to either.

"Zero?" Joey says, and murmurs ripple over the neighboring seats.

"I wouldn't be so quick to announce it," she says, face warming. "Any idea why?" she asks Brian, and now he, too, reddens and looks down at his desk without answering. "Hmphf," she says and, unable to recall any of the lines she's prepared, finally remarks, "Well, why don't I give you a little time to think about it?" and raises her head. "We'll go over these this afternoon. First row, get your lunches." As the students file to the closets and the room fills with a welcome rustling, she returns to her desk, back stiffening against the whispers. "Second row."

To calm herself while she eats, she turns the player on again at a low volume, "Morning" from *Peer Gynt*, the friendly flute, if it's in fact a flute. And the moments this tactic somewhat succeeds, and she's not rehearsing the looming scene in the hall, she steals appraising glances at Timmy Miller in the back, is impelled to, as he now represents their last, vague hope for a Christ. She can see now why she hasn't thought of him before: his way of fading behind his long brown bangs and gray-tinted glasses, his touch of stockiness and rumpled shirt. Not quite Timid Timothy but not bold or outspoken, either. If he distinguishes himself in anything, it's intellect, negatively: straight C's, and not for lack of trying. Her chief hesitation, in fact, is in trusting him to memorize his lines. Even his expression at the moment, as he minds his own business, splitting open his Devil Dog and licking the cream from the middle, doesn't inspire confidence. Still, she resolves to speak to him—after the other matter. Now again her stomach leaps, and she gives up on her half-eaten salami sandwich, rewrapping it to the twinkly *doo-doo-doo, doo-doo-doo* of the Sugar Plum Fairy.

At last, when the students have finished eating, she breathes in and stands up—"Matthew, will you lead the class outside today?"—then instructs her lepers to begin their practicing and prop making, before turning to the desks of the formerly dynamic, now silently waiting, duo. "Follow me and bring your exams with you," she says, leaving another flurry of murmurs in her wake as she exits the classroom and walks stiffly to the window at the end of the hall.

When the blond and brunet pair shuffle up like hapless flies, she steels herself and asks them to put their tests beside each other on the windowsill. "I want you to compare your answers very carefully," she says without preface, pointing to the Beatitude question, "and tell me what you find." Then she waits and, as they're in no rush to respond, suggests, "Similarities, perhaps?"

"Similarities?" Joey furrows his brow. "You mean like which ones are the same?"

"That's what I mean."

At length he reveals, "Five."

"Five. And *you* only have five answers," she says to Brian, the boy's pale-green eyes immediately darting away. And so she looks back to her counter: "And now, Joseph, how many of them aren't just similar, but exactly alike, word for word."

Again he puzzles and stalls. Then, "Three."

"Three," she says. "All right. Enough of this. Let me ask you flatly: Did you copy your answers from each other?"

The boys' eyes meet, shifting and squinting in that indecipherable code. This time, however, it appears the message is improperly transmitted, for just as Joey's brow contracts and he says, "No," Brian's head drops and he says, "Yeah." Then, "Yeah," Joey says, and, "Well," Brian says, and finally, "Yeah," Brian says again.

"Yeah," Joey concedes now, also, looking down at his Wallabees.

Liz raises her hands to her hips, then lowers them again, not comfortable with the pose. What to say? She wasn't prepared for honesty. Then it hits her: "Cheating on a religion test? Do you have any idea how reprehensible that is?"

"How what?" Brian asks softly.

"Low, despicable."

"Oh."

She pictures the addition to the day's list: *hallelujah, omnipotent, reprehensible*. "How do you think your mother and father would feel if they found out about this?" Right away the boy winces and shakes his head. "If I report it to Sister Regina, don't you think she'll call them?"

But it's Joey who answers her, "Miss Kaigh, we won't do it again," an urgent pitch in his voice. His father, whose rough hand she recalls shaking at Parent-Teacher Night, is the owner of Flynn's Construction.

And now her tone wavers slightly. "But I'm impressed with your honesty and am considering not reporting you because of it."

"Thank you, Miss Kaigh." "Thank you, Miss Kaigh."

"I didn't say I wouldn't, that depends on your future behavior. You know that at the moment both of you have failing grades in religion. You'll have to take the test over and pass it. Afterward, you'll be given extra assignments during recess till Easter vacation."

And though this latter part clearly registers with them, they have the sense not to complain aloud—now, or as they make their way back to 5B, leaving Liz to savor the lighter, more exhilarated fluttering in her stomach. To her mind, it's gone quite well. Particularly at the end, she'd been decisive and strict and to the point, to which the boys had shown little defiance. However, now at the door, an entirely different matter presents itself: the girls, swarming at her, Juanita at the helm, "Miss Kaigh, can I be Veronica?"

"Veronica? You're Mary Magdalene."

"Can't I be both?"

"Of course not."

"Can I be her, then, Miss Kaigh?" Ginger, Pilate's wife, asks—even more of a stretch, it would seem. "No, Virginia. What's all this about?" Then she sees the article itself, displayed aloft by Frances, "Look what Danny made!" and also finds it arresting, even disconcerting, with its strange mixture of loveliness and awfulness: sharp black thorns and red smears marring a graceful, faint rendering of the face. It has a kind of ancient-artifact quality, with the faded-looking colors and the yellowing cotton, its edges fraying and curling, like something you'd find in a glass case at a museum, maybe in the medieval section. "Oh, glorious," she says, taking it from the girl, her stomach leaping again when she thinks of it in conjunction with the music, as the first of things that might save the play. Now she holds it up herself, in clear view of the two boys, "All these wonderful props," then clutches it to her heart, half playfully, half earnestly. "You know, girls, I think I'd like to be Veronica," she says, getting away from herself, all her lepers laughing after her. She clears her throat and, placing the gauzy portrait carefully on her desktop—a man's undershirt? she guesses, wincing at the intimate, possibly inappropriate, nature of the material—gets them settled again in their respective tasks: Beatitude copying, prop making, practicing.

As Danny shuffles toward the front with the others, his elation at his teacher's praise of the veil—not at all the *What the hell is that?* of his mother—is quashed by the prospect of Brian and Joey's continued presence in the room. But Miss Kaigh, he thinks as she bends again over the phonograph, can't they do their punishments at home or in the hall? Can't she send them to the principal's office? However, he isn't able to come up with any justifiable reason for making such a request, and, as a series of slow, hair-raising notes rumbles from the player, reminding him of the theme from *Alfred Hitchcock Presents*, he's pushed by Paolo and Stephen toward Rory, wrongly smiling in the role of high priest, and stiffens with dread of speaking before the boys. Already, as Patty lisps through the scene's opening speech, he catches them glancing at each other, then reddening and hunching over their desks to hide their laughter. They'll do the same with him, even more so if he stutters; and now suddenly, "Daniel, that was your cue," the surging music having just unluckily ebbed, and he begins a late Our Father for a second small miracle. "Daniel . . ."

"It-It-It-It—"

Right away Miss Kaigh's head drops, her polished nails touching her forehead, and he looks down at his chukka boots, warmth enveloping his face.

"It-It-It-It—"

"Take a deep breath."

And now Juanita, yelling from the back, "Danny, try to say it like you did last time."

"Yeah, last time you did it good," Frances says.

"*Well,*" Miss Kaigh corrects.

He glances up again and, finding both boys' eyes shielded, right hands deliberately scrawling, blunders on. "It-it is y-you who say it."

Liz, too, is glancing furtively at the boys, wondering what judgments they're making behind their hands. None of this is remotely like the magical experience of theater she'd once imagined luring them in. Actually, it's a worse travesty than usual: they're all mumbling and stiff, as if it were the first day all over again. They need to be shaken, woken up; she can't just sit here and let them ruin everything this way. And now, goaded by Rory's robotic muttering, "You heard the. Blasphemy. What is your. Verdict?" not to mention an upswell of violins, cymbals, and horn-like instruments—trumpets?—she finds herself standing up and crying, "He deserves death!" to the head-snapping amazement of all.

"Wha?" Juanita says.

"Act! Be mean! Let me hear you! 'He deserves death!'" she cries again, a trumpet herself. "Come on, people. Come on, Kevin; you've got a big mouth when you want to."

"Okay," he says.

"He deserves death!" they cry together, the boy baring his teeth and clawing the air.

"Come on, girls; you, too," she says to them, all three standing up in the back now, fists clenched. "He deserves death!" they shout as a group. Finally she looks to Brian and Joey, the two gaping at one another with disbelief. "Boys, don't just sit there. Help!" And to her joy, they join in, "He deserves death!" albeit weakly, halfheartedly. "Is that all you can do?" she says—just the right thing, it seems, because now Joey, with a sudden, impish squint, springs up from his desk, points at the scarlet-faced Danny, and howls, "HE DESERVES DEATH!" with such ferocious volume that the room is instantly racked with laughter, Brian's foremost, the boy clapping heartily for his friend. And though Liz hesitates to join him—certainly this is going too far, "out-Heroding Herod," as the famous warning goes—better this than out-mousing the mouse, and so, just as the "horns" of her newly beloved *Finlandia* sound their final flourishes, she cries, "That-a-way!" in an awkward, gym-teacher-like voice. "Good job!"

Later she has even more success at Pilate's trial with "His blood be on us and on our children!" here both boys standing up and howling in unison. What naturals, she thinks, such believable venom spewing from their fierce, pink faces. And just after this, instructs them to start again with the high priest's trial. "On your own," she adds, putting on her coat. Then, "Do you mind if I take this with me?" she asks Danny of the veil, "I'd like to show it to Sister Margaret," and the boy, still blushing, shakes his head. Maybe she shouldn't have let them point and carry on so much. Of course, none it was directed at *him*. "Help them out from the seats again," she says to her budding villains. And the next instant, sailing down the hall, she blushes herself to think what a mockery of a punishment it's been, allowing them, between Beatitude practice, to scream those kinds of super-blasphemies like animals. Thank God no adult can see what's happening, she thinks, the yellowing square of undershirt fluttering from her hand.

Meanwhile in 5B, the criticism grows franker. "Man, you really suck, Curly," Brian says, stumbling so exactly on the line Kevin once used that the rascally boy himself notices. "That's what I told him!" Still, it's a sorer misery to Danny, much sorer, that the blond boy should also say it, and his ears turn hot and prickle.

"He's like the worst one, and he's playing Jesus," Joey says.

"I thought Miss Kaigh said he wasn't going to," Brian says.

"No, she didn't," Danny tries to say, but Paolo's quicker: "He's not."

"But that's what she told us," Joey shoots back, "in the parking lot. 'Danny only wrote it. He has a very small part.'"

"He's just substituting till we can get someone else," Paolo says.

But the boys wave him off. "No one's gonna wanna do it."

Yet their fondness for screaming for Danny's death and blood doesn't diminish, and they continue to do so with growing animation, and at every opportunity, until, just when things seem loudest and most out of hand, the bell rings; and Miss Kaigh, the teacher who spoke meanly about him in the parking lot, returns among the streaming-in children, one hand patting Timmy Miller's shoulder—"Give it some thought," he hears her say to him—the other holding the veil. "Both Sister Margaret and Mrs. Sullivan are requesting permission for their classes to come to the performance," she announces, "all after seeing *this*." Then she flourishes the Man of Sorrows' portrait like a matador's cape before pinning it to the front bulletin board, directly over her "dramatically humbled" construction-paper cross, violet hub of the wheel-shaped aphorism, "Lent Is a Time of Preparation."

First they sit in the easy chairs in the den, reading *Newsday* and watching TV. But when Danny goes so far as to lie on the couch and pretend to snore, his father appears in the doorway: *What are you doing lying naked on the couch as if you were me?* And so he jumps up, heinie cheeks peeling off the Naugahyde like Silly Putty, and they continue the downstairs BARE Necessities tour in the dining room.

Gee, *Dan*, white-haired Nana Burke says, her teaspoon clinking noisily in her cup, *you'd think you and your friend would put some clothes on for Thanksgiving dinner.*

Sorry, Nan, they say, and mosey off to the living room, sitting on the nicer, crushed-velvet chairs and, *Brrrr!* the cold brick hearth. Then in the kitchen, as Arram perches on the counter, naked-eating honey, Danny naked-talks on the phone. *'Please. My God,'* he says, pacing the room and winding the long, loopy cord around his finger like his mother. Next they naked-iron in the laundry room; they dance over the dirty clothes on Sharon's floor, stirring the shut-up, *Charlie*-awfuled air. At last they come to the closed door at the end of the hall, and pause.

We have to, Arram says, *it's the only one left*, and so they pass inside.

No mess on the floor *here*, everything put away, and the smell mixed, him and her—Old Spice, Evening in Paris. And in the drawers, the bigger Fruit of the Looms and funny handkerchiefs, the lacy bras and panties. In the sliding-doors closet, suits and skirts, pajamas and robes; the hem of an unusual bright-red one pools about Danny's feet when he slips it on and ties the sash. *So silky*, he says, rubbing the material against his legs and chest. And now, *Goodnight, dear*, he says to Arram.

Goodnight, pet, the boy says, like Gomez on *The Addams Family*.

After Danny Morticia-shuffles over, extending his arm, which the boy douses madly with kisses, *Mm-mm-mm*, he trades the gown for one of the dark-blue suit jackets with wide lapels, the sleeves reaching even to his fingertips, and pretends to twist a mustache.

Pardon me, my sweet, but I am not wearing pants.

Oh Go! Arram says, proffering his arm now, as if within the gown, and Danny, stretching its empty sleeve out before him like a recently deflated balloon, smacks his lips up its satiny length.

Oh, what joy, what love! they cry, and so kiss on until ten of four.

But now as he catches his breath—what a frantic dash, lifting all the shades again, redressing in the den, and getting back up to his room before his mother walked in!—his shame and worries from the afternoon fly back at him and he kneels before his altar, reciting the cries for aid in the Psalms in his religion workbook: *Be not far from me, for I am in distress.* And then just in time with the strong bulls of Bashan opening their mouths against him *like ravening and roaring lions*, his mother calls from the foot of the stairs, "Who pulled the shades down in the kitchen, you?"

The kitchen, damn. "M-M-Me?"

"Who else?"

"Um. Y-Yeah. It was sunny."

"Sunny?"

"I mean, getting dark. I was just trying to help," he says—to which his mother grumbles something about a way he might really help, if he wanted to. "Huh?" he says, perhaps not audibly, and, when her footsteps trail back to the kitchen, resumes his petitions to speak like Jesus before the boys tomorrow.

— 10 —

The Third Coming

In the morning his hopes are dashed again as Miss Kaigh, coming from another low-voiced conference with Timmy in the back of the room, sails up the aisle with the same forgetful excitement she'd displayed with Brian and Joey the day before. Then almost as an afterthought, she backtracks to Danny's desk to tell him the super news: "I've got Timothy Miller to play Christ."

"Who?" Danny asks, cheeks flushing, and, in his ensuing panic, blurts out, "You-you don't w-want me to be in it."

And now the two stare and blink at one another, in horror of the naked utterance.

"What?" Liz finally mutters.

"You-you-you only w-want me to have a very small part," he presses on, heart racing lawlessly.

"A very small part?" Liz says, her own face flushing as she glances at the nearby students, discouraging their lifting ears. "Why would you think that?" But even before he indicates the boys, she's squinting at them in their now permanent seats on opposite sides of the room. "What? What?" they say, not having heard; yet they smile anyway, just to see they're being talked about. But what is this now, freshness on *Danny's* part? Will he have to be reprimanded as well? "Go out into the hall," she says and watches him rush down the aisle, ducking his head to avoid the students' gazes. Then as she passes Joey's desk, she frowns at the up-staring blabbermouth, his eyes nearly concealed beneath his droopy brown bangs.

"What did we do?" he asks, a grinning pride in his *we.*

"You know very well," she says, "get that hair out of your eyes," and steps into the hall, closing the door loudly behind her to silence the murmurs. "Daniel," she says, launching an immediate offensive on the waiting boy, who has no bangs at all, really, just a kind of standing red briar above his forehead, "the only concern I've had is that you don't take on more than you can handle."

But at the moment "more than you can handle" means very little to Danny, trembling in the aftermath of his unexpected boldness, and with the incident of being sent into the hall, before now the exclusive province of Kevin Lukas and other bad boys.

Liz, reading at least his misapprehension in his blank, blue stare, begins again. "You've been playing Christ temporarily when the others have dropped out, and I suspect you've been hoping the role would just eventually go to you. Am I right?"

He purses his lips and raises his eyebrows. Then, surprisingly, his teacher crouches down beside him, eyes level with his and noticeably traced with brown liner.

"I have to be honest with you, Daniel, you're very shy."

"I-I-I am?" he says.

She nods. "You're the shiest boy I have, by far."

"But I—"

"Listen to me. The entire fifth grade is coming to the performance. Do you really think you'd be able to speak in front of an audience that large?" For mercy's sake, she doesn't refer directly to his stuttering. Nevertheless, "That's over *one hundred children*," she stresses, batting her thickened lashes.

And while Danny in fact finds this number quite intimidating, he manages to shrug. Surely the crowds that hailed Jesus were even larger than that; they were a multitude, which must be a very large number indeed.

"Do you know what stage fright is?" his teacher asks.

"Um," he says, drawing back a little from the ominous phrase.

"It's when an actor becomes *totally frozen with fear* right before a performance. He looks out at the huge crowd and can't imagine walking onto the stage in front of all the staring eyes. He starts to shake and his teeth start to chatter and he can't remember any of his lines. It's as if his whole memory were *erasssed*."

Danny's eyes widen at the hissed word, and at the picture of the poor actor's brain, like a wiped-off blackboard.

"He's unable to play his role, and everything's ruined for everyone. I'm afraid this will happen to you."

"It won't," he says without confidence.

"Daniel, it's already happened during practice, never mind what could occur during the actual performance."

"But once I did it right."

"*Once?*" She winces—at first with incomprehension, then as she realizes he's still clinging to his brief bit of luck several afternoons ago, amazement. "I'm sorry, we can't take the chance."

"But," he says, "God wants me to play Jesus."

"God *what?*" she says and, when he repeats himself, "Now how would you know that?"

"He told me."

"Oh no," she says, shaking her head at this desperate ploy. "Daniel, God wants every boy to 'play' Jesus, but it's better if someone else 'portrays' Him onstage next Wednesday. Trust me, this is different. Think of how terrible it would be if you were to humiliate yourself and all those hundred students were to laugh at you. You'd wish you'd never been Christ, then. Here, this is what I'm going to do." In the privacy of the hall, she goes so far as to take his small-fingered, rather dainty hand. "At the end of the show, I'll bring you out and tell everyone you wrote the play and helped direct it. Would you like me to do that?"

And while of course he would, and doesn't see why she can't do that *and* let him play Jesus, he's squinting and struggling to resist the urge to pull back his hand so captured in hers, so unpleasantly engulfed by the actual, moist warmth of her palm. And so to appease her quickly: "Uh-huh."

"Good. That's settled. We're going to need you to help Timmy learn his lines; he doesn't have that long. Will you promise to help him?"

Danny squints and purses his lips more, hoping this will pass for a yes. And as his teacher finally releases his hand and stands up, it seems to him it has, and he secretly wipes his palm on his trouser leg.

After lunch, when she hands out the boys' retest after giving them ample time to review their notes, they begin filling in their answers with the kind of immediate eagerness that normally marks the brighter, more prepared students—a good, if disconcerting, omen. From here, she confers again with Timmy before leading him to the front and saying, of the conspicuously silent yesterday's Christ, "Daniel's the one who wrote the play and who's helping me direct it," as if also practicing for her show-closing speech.

As the bushy-haired boy awkwardly offers his hand, a slightly plump, olive-colored hand, Danny looks up questioningly at Miss Kaigh.

"He wants to shake on it," she interprets, tilting her head. "Isn't that right, Timothy?"

"Yeah," the boy says.

Danny winces and diverts his eyes as their fingers unboyishly tangle, then quickly restores his hand to his pocket.

"Daniel can be a big help to you learning your lines," she says; and to him, "You know them almost all by heart already, don't you?"

As Danny, with restrained pride, says he does, Timmy looks down at his script and nibbles at his bottom lip. "You mean like all the stuff after *Jesus?*"

"Mm-hmm," they say together, one with uncharitable eagerness, the other, concerned encouragement.

"You have a whole week," Miss Kaigh adds.

"Only a *week?*" Timmy says, eyes stretching wider below the fringe of thick hair.

Then as Miss Kaigh quickly turns from them, giving instructions and attending to the phonograph at front, Danny, re-Petered, whispers, "Just one week," into this new false prophet's ear.

A little later, after they've taken their places in the Garden, Liz finds Timmy's kneeling prayers to the Father at least audible and clear—anything an improvement to the I-I-I of yore—but she also finds them wooden, very much the product of a boy reading lines from a script he's not at all comprehending. And it continues in this stilted way until, quite by accident, Timmy's first foray back to the sleeping apostles coincides with a frenzied-violins interlude of "Summer," and he has to shout over it while rebuking Danny, the first real modulation of his voice, which Liz is quick to underscore: "*That's* how you should say it, music or no." With similar coaching, she manages to extract from him the faintest hint of expressiveness during the arrest skirmishes.

"Not too bad for the first time," she says generously. As he's taken away to the high priest and the interrogation begins, she walks over to collect the boys' tests, now promisingly crammed with their worried, narrow scripts. "You mean to say you may have actually learned something?" she says to Brian, the boy reluctantly shrugging. Deciding to look the exams over right away, she tells the two they may either help with rehearsal or finish the Now We Recall questions at the end of unit seventeen in their religion workbooks. "But you're not to talk to each other or do anything else, is that clear?" she says, making for the door.

"Yes," they reply and, not long after she's gone, Danny sees Brian look up from his book—bored, it appears, by the questions there and by what he perceives as the pathetic trial under way, for this is the word he grumbles, "Pathetic," before looking across the room to his friend and saying, "Timmy sucks, too."

Joey, not to be outdared, says, "He's a lot better than Curly."

"Yeah, but anyone's better than Curly," Brian says, looking right at Danny, who flushes and wants to point out, *Miss Kaigh said you're not to talk to each other.* Instead he looks to Patty; but his sometime-assistant, who seems already inured to the boys' taunting, stares steadily ahead at Rory. "It is Your own people. Who have handed You. Over to me," he's saying to Timmy, and, as the scene totters forward, the boys tirelessly mimic his mechanical delivery: "Scourge-the-pris-o-ner. Re-lease-Bar-ab-bas," they say, and, "It does not com-pute! It does not com-pute!" like the robot on *Lost in Space,* until finally their attention's diverted when Paolo and Stephen, taking Timmy to the end of the blackboard near the garbage can, more or less now the scourging place, unbuckle their belts.

"What are you queers doing," Brian howls, "taking off your clothes?" Then as Joey says, "Yeah, Bri, it's the love scene! Pigbutt and Paolo wanna make *love* to each other," Danny pictures himself in his parents' bedroom trading arm-kisses with Arram, and a hot blush spreads to his neck and arms and even to his hands.

"N-No, they don't," he says faintly, beneath all the loud tongue clicking and whistling; and, above all this, "No, it's not the love scene!" Kevin shouts, laughing and deepening his voice like a game show announcer, "It's the whipping scene!"

"Whipping?" Joey says.

"That's cool," Brian says.

"What am I supposed to do now?" Timmy asks, looking, to Danny's horror, directly at him. But thankfully now, Patty answers, "Nothing. You're juth thuppoth to lean over and thtay quiet."

"You're juth thupposed to take it like a puthy," Joey says.

"Ha! You should know how to do *that!*" Brian says. And no sooner do Paolo and Stephen raise their belts to the new victim, braced over the pail, than the boys begin to criticize their whipping techniques: "Swing it like you mean it," they advise. "Yeah, you have to wind up. Don't just move your arm in girly circles." "That doesn't look like whipping, that looks like my grandmother trying to swim." "Ha! Water ballet," Brian sneers, then suddenly leaps up from his desk and rushes toward the players, Joey right behind him, and Kevin right behind him. "Kill! Kill!" they hoot; and now the girls, rushing up the aisle, "What's going on?" followed at last by Danny, "You c-c-can't do this!" And all the while Paolo and Stephen at front, "Wait! Wait!" cringing from the onrushing stampede.

"Hand over your weapons, you water ballerinas!" Brian yells, and they quickly comply.

"Hey, what are you guys gonna do?" Timmy says, glancing back at the scowling boys with an expression, it seems to Danny, both fearful and flattered.

"Don't hurt him," Juanita says.

"Kill the mother!" Kevin cries.

"No!" Timmy says.

"Silence, prisoner," Brian orders, doubling up Stephen's extra-long belt. "Prepare to have your butt whipped." Then after he snaps the halves loudly together, and the onlooking players start and squeal, Joey snaps Paolo's belt, a resounding echo, and they all squeal again.

"Hey, wait!" Timmy says, hands cupping his heinie cheeks, then all at once spins around and rushes from the spot and on across the room, the boys whooping and fast on his heels, chasing him down into the opposite corner; and there Joey grabs his wrists and presses them to the window ledge, "Get 'im, Bri! Quick!" and Brian's arm pulls back, the long belt whistling through the air and landing, with a ringing crack, on the radiator grill beside Timmy's left hip. "Ho-ly!" the prisoner cries, "that was close!"

"Careful!" Juanita says, "if you really hit him like that, his bee-hind will bleed!"

"Don't!" Timmy pleads.

"It'll split wide open!" Kevin embellishes. "And his guts will pour out on the floor!"

"Let me go!" the boy says. "Let him go!" the players cry, and "ahh!" as the second lash rings even closer to his hip and wriggling, squeezed-in cheeks.

"Yeah! Cool!" Joey and Kevin shout. "Harder!"

And just now Liz, jubilantly approaching 5B, graded exams in her folder, fresh peppermint lifesaver popped in her mouth, hears a very real-sounding commotion within. What's this? she thinks and, glimpsing the chaotic scuffle through the small window, freezes with fear. Oh no, a fight! *Shit!* she almost adds aloud. What should she do? A real *fight!* She's been so lucky so far, had thought it maybe a benefit of teaching at a Catholic school. Oh but she should've known better, those bullies! Like leaving a pair of Doberman pinschers in a roomful of kittens! At last she brings herself to throw open the door. "What's going on in here? Is anyone hurt? Stop, everyone! Stop at once! Stop, I said!"—much of this repetition unnecessary, as, quite remarkably, they've all grown silent and still at "What's going on?" She glances about frenziedly for blood, brokenness—arms, noses, teeth. What she finds, however, is quite different, and just as startling: "Whose belts are those? Why are you boys even out of your seats?"

"You said we could help," Brian says.

"Help?" she repeats incredulously. "What could helping have to do with it?"

"No, Miss Kaigh, no!" her lepers yell, all at once clamoring about her, as if just brought back to life. "They were acting! It's the whipping scene!"

"Pardon me?" she says, emotionally stalemated as her prior terror and new joy collide. "You mean you two were up here taking part in the play?"

"Yeah," Joey says; and, "Well, we weren't exactly taking *part* in it," Brian qualifies.

"Stupendous!" she cries. "Totally convincing!"

"You mean—?"

"I thought that was a real fight!"

And so they all laugh and say, "You thought it was a real fight, Miss Kaigh?" with the standard exceptions of Patty, sitting cross-legged in the ellipse, and Danny beside her, teeth clenched and arms folded, but now also Timmy, who appears to be quite shaken by the scene and suspicious of the entire expanded company—for here he quietly steps away from the group and stops, as if for refuge, beside Danny. "Did they whip *you* like that?" he asks.

"Yeah," Danny says, though of course he hasn't yet had the pleasure. "But they did it a lot harder."

"Harder?" the boy says, his brown, believing eyes reliably widening behind the gray lenses. And he wears this same look when he asks if he said his lines right and Danny answers, "Not really."

"What did I do wrong?"

"A lot," Danny says, and comes up with, "You said them too loud." But here his attention is drawn back to his teacher again, just now returning the exams to the boys. It seems they've gotten B's, Brian a B-plus.

"*Plus?*" Brian repeats, his own expression as shocked as Miss Kaigh's.

"Your best mark all year!" she tells him. "See what you can do when you apply yourself?"

And now Liz, beside herself that so much good fortune should befall her in one afternoon, realizes she must've swallowed her mint in her race from the door, for no trace of it remains in her mouth. So she clears her throat and pats her chest, unpleasantly imagining the little white ring lodged somewhere in her esophagus—a gesture that, to Danny's eye, seems one more instance of doting on the boys, a hand pressed admiringly to her heart, and he's quick to conceive of the three in cahoots: like a team of kidnappers, making off with his play.

He wouldn't have expected this terrible day to turn on a gift from God. Yet as he's rushing down his block from Main Street, muttering to himself all the meanest lines from practice, there it is: a more than man-sized, sideways-reclining refrigerator carton at the edge of the Mahers' lawn, a refrigerator carton! Nearly trembling with the urge to whisk it away—but of course he can't, it's much too big and someone might see him—he peers inside its open top flaps and finds it indeed empty, save for a treasure of broken Styrofoam and plastic cording. Rashly, he runs up the forbidden territory of his next-door neighbor's lawn, rings the bell, and, seconds later, Mrs. Maher appears, beady eyes narrowing suspiciously beneath a dip of teased black hair. "One of the Burke boys?"

"Good af-af-af-af—"

"—ternoon," she says, and, suffering the remainder of his stammered request, seems to believe his mother's sent him to tell her she can't leave the carton on the street. "Do you mean to tell me that woman has the nerve—" she snarls, finger jabbing at the air. "Well, you can tell her that that carton is staying *right* where it is till the garbage man comes to collect it on *Thursday*."

"Oh n-n-no, Mrs. Maher," Danny tries to assure her. "I was just w-w-wondering if we could use it for the p-play."

"For the what?" she sputters, and he attempts to explain more—for instance, that his mother isn't even home from work yet. "You want to take the carton?"

"Uh-huh."

"Oh." She steps back a little, her look of anger ebbing. "Well, I don't know. My own kids may want it. To make a fort, play roly-poly. You know how kids love big cartons. And they're younger than you are, Robby. They may never forgive me if I give that carton away."

And so Danny, misidentified and crestfallen, retreats down the steps and starts back across the lawn, only to hear Mrs. Maher punch open the screen door behind him.

"No, you know what?" she calls now, stepping down onto the slate path. "Take it, go ahead. It was never you we had the problem with."

While not fully comprehending this new shift, Danny heartens again and glances eagerly toward the street, then back at his neighbor's terrycloth slippers. Above them, her arms cross and she adds, "I haven't seen your brothers around much. Or the motorcycles . . ."

"They-they-they don't live home anymore," he tells her because she's giving him the carton and, as her eyebrows raise, runs toward it, crying, "Thank you, Mrs. Maher!" In no time, he's dragging the thing like dead game across their own property line, leaving, in his wake, the lady's unanswered "Oh, how come?"

Getting it in the house, however, is no easy matter. First he has to tie Duke to one of the oak trees before he can empty it in the garage, collapse the entire corrugated enterprise, and, with a series of pushes, folds, and pulls, force it down the stairs and into the basement. There, beneath the insufficient glow of a sixty-watt bulb, he hastily tears the carton open and spreads it end to end, big as a rug, then lies back, arms spread, pencil marking the edges of his fingers, the top of his head, the tip of his toes; and, springing to his feet again, he hunts up a folding ruler, and begins to sketch in the vertical- and then the cross-beam, a much more difficult and time-consuming task than he imagined, spreading over his naked-dancing time with Arram, and any chance to play Morticia-and-Gomez. And later, when he dashes upstairs in need of the heavy-duty, black-handled scissors from the junk drawer in the kitchen, his mother, home already, asks, "Where you going with those?" "I'm-I'm making something for school." "Not more veils, I hope." "No." "Well, make sure you put them back when you're done. And why are you still in your uniform? Go upstairs and change." Which he does, with all speed, and now in corduroys and a sweatshirt, plies the scissors along his precise, worried lines and into the difficult center corners, several times stopping to rub the ball of his palm, before he finally frees the shape of the cross and lifts it up, disappointingly wobbly. So he jumps up for the workbench again, and, poking through the shelves and drawers, half-breathing their rusty, steely smells, he settles on long wooden dowels and masking tape to reinforce the cross, then cuts out another cross and reinforces that, and sandwiches the two layers together with glue and more tape. And after fishing through his closet upstairs for brushes and powder paints—"I hope you're not making a big mess down there"—he colors the front a dark brown with his father's big, clean wall brush, then goes back with a smaller one to make light and dark streaks, blending in yellow here, black there, and even some of the pure red, like long bloody stains, blood that rivered down the grooves of the wood and pooled at the foot of the cross. And once both sides are finished and dry, and he's attached the *INRI* sign at the top—a kind of abbreviation for *King of the*

Jews, somehow not *KOTJ*—he leans the whole thing up against the wall and steps back.

"Uh!" he cries. It looks so big, so real! Frightening with the red! *Arram!*

And his friend, perched on an arm of a decimated easy chair, crows, *Wait till everyone sees* that!

Mm, Danny says, already balking at the thought of Timmy dragging his new creation around the classroom. Maybe he won't bring it in just yet; this way only they can use it. *Friday I will.*

Next week, Arram says.

Hurray! they cry. *The cross!* And just as they begin to cavort around it, there's the sudden squeal of the front door opening overhead, followed by the *thump-thump* of his father's shoes on the mat, and Danny freezes mid-skip, then scrambles to return all the supplies to the bench. But the brushes are stiff with dried paint; he can't put them back like that! So he tugs open a nearby carton and buries them beneath mildewed books—*Becoming a Teenager, How to Win Friends and Influence People*—then slides the cross itself behind the warped, folded-up Ping-Pong table, grabs up the scissors, yanks the light cord, and runs up through the dark stairwell for the den door, where, fingers on the knob, he stops again, thinking something's wrong somehow, missing. Finally he hears it, the forgotten, plaintive cry from the yard: *ruff! ruff! ruff! ruff! ruff!* Poor boy! Outside still, tied to the tree.

~ 11 ~

Toiling and Spinning

The next day at recess, when Liz gives Brian and Joey the opportunity to *not exactly* play the soldiers again instead of doing their religion exercises, they trade a series of arched eyebrows and wavering
half smiles before leaping up. "All right. Cool. We'll show you guys
how to really act tough!" And her lepers, led by Danny and Timmy, shy
away, emitting a flurry of squeals and meek exceptions: "I thought I was
the soldier," Paolo says; and, "I thought I was," Stephen.

"Not anymore," the boys say.

"I told you we might have to switch some of these roles around," Liz
claims, not recalling whether she actually did per se, and quickly reas-
signs Paolo to John—"I don't want to be an apostle," the boy says—
and Stephen to technician—"Who?" Stephen says.

"You'll control the phonograph and be responsible for sound effects."

"Sound effects?"

"Yes. We need an earthquake, a cock crow." Here some snickering
from the boys. "What's funny?" she asks, glaring at them.

"Nothing," Joey says, red-faced; and Kevin, "*Cock*-a-doodle-doo!"

"That's enough from the peanut gallery," she says, her own face reddening as she thinks of the other doodle-doo. But they wouldn't dare
allude to such a thing in front of her, would they?

"You mean I'm not going to be onstage?" Stephen asks, as she feared
he might.

"We're really going to need you more *off*," she answers, avoiding the
fat boy's pout. "And you can call out, too, whenever the crowd speaks.
The crowd's got quite a few lines, you know."

And now Kevin again, "Hey, Miss Kaigh, how come you never said *I* could be in the play instead of doing assignments?"

"You?" While Liz finds this prospect mildly horrifying, she smiles anyway at how things are turning. "I didn't think you'd want to be in our silly play."

"Yeah, Kevin," Juanita seconds, "you said——" but is quickly drowned out by the boy: "I'd rather be in some dumb show than do homework."

"Oh, well, dumb show," Liz says and, as it strikes her there might after all be some villain cameo that would suit him, adds, "I'll think about it, provided I have no more trouble with you."

During rehearsal, the nimble pair swaggers in, expertly brandishing the cardboard and tinfoil swords, seizing Timmy and skirmishing with the faint-hearted apostles, binding Timmy's hands behind his back with Brian's tie, pushing him off to the high priest. "Now you're in for it, buddy! Let's go! We'll show You an 'hour of darkness'!" And the shockingly dramatic scourging, performed with just-completed lengths of rope, frayed at the edges and painted black, gives her an actual chill. They're stealing the show, she thinks, chuckling giddily to herself. In fact the play's so enlivened that, once Juanita and the girls skip across the front of the room proclaiming the resurrection, it's all she can do to tear herself away, exclaiming, as she goes, a director-like "Take it from the top!"

Immediately upon her exit, however, Brian suggests they practice the whipping scene again, and an argument ensues, Juanita insisting Miss Kaigh said *top* not *whipping*. And just as Danny's also trying to bring himself to object in some way and assert his assistant directorship, Patty shuffles up and asks, of all things, if they're going to need an angel in the play.

"An a-a-angel?" he says, glancing confusedly at her pale face and metal-bound teeth.

"Yeth," she explains, "becauth in my lath thpeech it thezth, 'An angel rolled back the thtone and revealed Hith Rethurrethon to the world.'"

"Oh," he says, blushing at the oversight. "No. W-We're not going to have a stone, either."

"But it thezth, 'An angel rolled back the——'"

"I know," he says, and vaguely, "we're not going to show that. Angels are invisible."

Patty nods. "Ith the rock invithible, too?"

And while of course the rock isn't, he pauses as if to consider this possibility and, before he's answered, is luckily diverted by Timmy, who yells from the front, "Danny, do I have to get whipped again?"

"What're you asking Curly for?" Joey says. "We're the soldiers; you have to do what *we* tell you."

"Yeah, get your ass over that pail," Brian says. Then for effect he snaps his drawn belt, apparently preferring it to the lighter whips made by the girls, before cracking it on the floor beside the boy's Hush Puppies.

"Watch out!" Timmy cries. "Can't you whip someone else?" an idea that immediately appeals to them. Now Brian turns to the onlooking players, right eyebrow dramatically raised. "Which one of you other pussies would like to get whipped?" And Joey says, "Step right up, get your pussy-butt whipped." And Paolo says, "Oh, all right," dark face blushing as he leans over the pail. The understudied savior, fleeing the whistling belts and loud, laughing cries, takes refuge again beside the mum first assistant, confiding in him his fear of the boys.

"I know," Danny says, and then, even while gazing with real sympathy into Timmy's eyes, suggests this fear may be nothing, compared to other kinds. Other kinds? Does he know what stage fright is? The bushy-haired boy shakes his head worriedly.

"It's when an actor *freezes with fear* right before the performance," Danny says, the words rushing from him like a little river of grace.

"Freezes?" Timmy says.

"He can't move."

"Not at all?"

"No. He looks out at the huge crowd and can't imagine walking onto the stage in front of so many people. He starts shaking all over and can't remember any of his lines. It's as if his whole memory were *erasssed*," he says with the added hissing effect, and the boy's eyes widen. "He ruins everything for everybody." And widen some more. "Oh man," Timmy says, "I don't want to do *that*."

Up front, Stephen's changed places with Paolo, insisting it's his turn, and right away one of Brian's fierce lashes, before this cracking only on the radiator or painted cinder-block wall, lands with a duller snap on the broad, navy-blue field of Stephen's left heinie cheek. At the very instant of impact—as the entire group sucks in its breath and holds it for the short, silent second before the fat boy's howl pierces the room—Danny's groin contracts and his skin bursts with vicarious heat: "Ah!" he cries, one in a chorus of exclamations and laughter. And Stephen, chinned face contorted with pain, clasps his pudgy hand to the spot, hobbling in fast, bent circles—"What's he doing?" "I don't know." "Is he having a heart attack?"—one of these taking him close to the door, which he disappears beyond, Rory following.

"Bring him to the nurse!" Frances calls.

"You bullies!" Juanita yells. "You could really hurt someone!"

"We didn't hurt him," Brian says.

"Yeah," Joey says. "He can't feel anything, he's too blubbery."

"It's not bleeding!" Rory rushes back in to announce, for which he's sneered at and called a homo. "You looked at pigbutt's butt!" Brian cries. "I didn't look at it," Rory claims, but only Danny and Timmy and Patty hear this. The boys are busy laughing and saying, "Gross!" and the girls, "Was it red? Was it lumpy?" "It must be like five beehinds." "It must be like a whole *world*." And when at last Stephen reenters, shirt untucked, they run, shrieking and covering their eyes, to the back of the room, "No, go away! Fix yourself!" And now Timmy, shaking his head and holding his own heinie, is even more fearful, "That looked like it really hurt!" And Danny, nodding, says, "I hope they won't hit *you* like that," after which the boy refuses to practice at all.

Already Liz is zipping back through the halls, propelled by the latest development: it seems Danny's veil, which she lent Mrs. Sullivan this morning, went on to make a tour of the entire sixth grade—for no sooner had she walked into the faculty room than Mrs. Higgins, Mr. Rice, and Sister Mary John Cleary asked if their classes, too, might attend the play. "You mean you want to bring *all* your students?" Liz asked. "Oh yes," Sister Cleary said, "we think it will be a remarkable way to illustrate the message of the Gospels." Yet even as Liz paled at the thought of actually doubling the size of the audience, not to mention with older children, she was so taken by the enthusiasm of the teachers who'd barely ever spoken to her before, let alone asked her for anything, that she reflexively said, "Well, I don't see why not—if Sister Regina agrees, of course." "I'll speak to her right away," Sister Cleary said.

And now, coming upon her classroom, she makes a mental note to speak with Mr. Loughlin, the custodian, about chairs; they'll need over two hundred, over two hundred chairs! And she's so engrossed in her calculations and planning that, once inside, she fails to notice the stymied rehearsal as she calls her company together and launches into a discussion of robes: they're each to go home and ask their mothers for any old ones they may have around. "Preferably not too long; we don't want them to swim on you. And nothing too loud or bright, the plainer the better. Earth tones."

"Earth tones?"

"Tan, brown, cream, rust, anything in the brown family—with hoods, if you have them. And a blue robe for Mary. And then we need scarves. Girls, ask your mothers for something to wear over your heads."

"Ooh, ooh, my grandma has a shawl!" Juanita exclaims, the other girls' eyes widening enviously: "A shawl? What color? My mother crochets. I have a veil from Holy Communion."

"A Communion veil is fine. We also need white sheets," Liz says, "and we still don't have a cross," at which mention another excited discussion begins. Danny's heart beats worriedly until Miss Kaigh nixes the popular suggestion that Joey's father make one from wood scraps. "It'll be too heavy, and if it ever were to fall . . ."

At last he brings himself to say, "I-I-I can make the cross, Miss Kaigh."

"You?" Joey scoffs. "How's he gonna make a big cross?"

"Don't say that, Joseph, you saw Veronica's veil."

"Yeah, but that was small."

So she asks Danny, "What *would* you make it from?" and he tells her at length. "A refrigerator carton! Perfect. Do you know where you can get one?" In fact he does. "But we need it right away. Can you make it soon?" He'll try, he tells her, and pointedly bites his lip, as if doubtful such a creation could be rushed.

"Oh come on, Danny," Carol says with some annoyance when he puts the question to her the second she gets in from work, but just in the spirit of objecting to anything connected with the play. Her closet's nothing if not crammed with old robes—a timeline of Christmas presents from Gerry: every year another one from Gimbel's, often purchased on the Eve—and she welcomes an excuse to chuck a few. What's the sense of holding on to them, anyway? "I'll let you know," she says, dismissing him. After some hunting and successful dueling with sentimentality, she comes up with two blue acrylics, a light and a navy, both faded and nubby from washing. A scarlet red from the '60s, loud thing; what was he thinking that year? Made her look like one of those birds, what are they called? Cardinals. Ha, and maybe like the other kind of cardinal, too. Then the one and only tan number she bought Gerry years ago, which he's never worn. Nose went right up when he took it out of the box: "A *robe?*" as if that was something only a fairy would wear. Looks like it just came off the rack, and it wasn't cheap, either. Lastly an old white terrycloth of Sharon's she outgrew long ago; been hanging around the laundry room forever. And now this assortment that she carries to the bottom of the stairs seems a generous enough offering, yet the second he comes to the landing, he bug-eyes the scarlet-topped heap and says, "You don't have any earth tones?"

"*Earth tones?*"

"Miss Kaigh says they have to be in the brown family."

"Uh! No, I'm sorry, these are the only tones I have at the moment. If she wants something else, you can tell her she can go to . . ." and here she tosses them onto the stairs for him to take or leave, "the mall."

As it turns out, there *is* an earth tone in the bunch, beneath the red Morticia-robe: a thick and brand-new-seeming camel-colored men's, made of a special suedey velour, with a lapel-like collar and wide sash, and this Danny immediately tries on before his mirror upstairs. But like the others, it's much too big, the shoulder seams hanging down on his arms, the hem collecting in folds about his feet. Yet it would make the perfect Jesus robe, with its belling sleeves and buttonless front, if only it could be made to fit. Tossing it onto his desk chair, he rushes downstairs for the scissors and needle and thread.

"What are you going to do?" Carol asks skeptically, relinquishing a brown spool.

"I just have to fix something quick."

"Fix something?" But here she lets the matter drop, afraid he'll ask her to take in that robe of Gerry's. Her mother's the sewer and knitter in the family, and Carol didn't inherit any of that talent, thank God. However, as he turns right around, back on his merry way, she says, "Wait," and, with a twinge of guilt, passes him an old silver thimble. "Put this over your thumb so you don't stick yourself. I don't want to hear any crying up there."

But as the minutes tick by, she doesn't hear anything at all. In fact, he's so quiet that it's over an hour later, while she's in the middle of roasting a chicken, that she thinks of the robe again and, wiping her hands on a kitchen towel, walks to the stairs and calls up curiously, "Danny?"

"Yeah?"

"Let me see what you've done."

When he appears on the landing dressed in it, she can't help but wince—because now the robe, sagging miserably on his shoulders, is choppily and unevenly hemmed about his ankles. Likewise the sleeves, shortened to his wrists, have a rumpled, scalloped quality. "Oh Danny," she says pityingly, and at the same time stifles a not-so-gracious smile: here at least is one art he has no talent for. "Maybe you should let Grandma fix that up for you this weekend."

"But I'm not done yet."

"All right," she says, still fighting the smile as she turns for the kitchen, "suit yourself." Then halfway down the hall, discovering her pun, adds a quick, "Ha ha."

After dinner, as Danny's finishing his American history extra credit, a mimeographed reading about Harriet Tubman and an amazing underground railroad for long-ago escaping slaves, Arram makes a special appearance beside his desk to suggest a before-bed practice in the basement.

While they're home? Danny says reproachfully, then grabs his Pro-Keds and folded-up Jesus robe and tiptoes downstairs, past the closed door of his parents' bedroom, where his mother's watching TV now, and past the closed door of Sharon's room, empty because she's supposedly at a basketball game, and right on through the den, where his father, in his V-neck undershirt and baggy tan canvas pants, is sprawled and snoring already on the couch, one pale arm thrown across his face, the other dangling to the red circular rug, its fist loosely curled around a black temple of his glasses. It seems only Duke, springing up from the floor when he flicks on the garage light, takes any notice of his movements: at once he's upon him, whining and blinking and shaking his matty ears.

"Shhh!" Danny says, slipping on the sneakers and allowing the scruffy spaniel to follow him down the stairs, for fear of his barking and door scratching. And no sooner does Danny turn the knob than the dog head-butts the door open and charges, stubby tail high, into the dingy expanse, zigzagging from carton to carton, corner to corner, sniffing and sneezing.

What a maniac! Arram says, and, "Oh wow," Danny really says as he slides the crucifix out from behind the folded-up Ping-Pong table—because the poster-paint colors look brighter now, the details in the wood even more lifelike than he remembered.

It's like from a museum, Arram says. Danny accepts this compliment gravely. *First we'll do The Way,* he explains, donning the robe and tying the sash. *After, you can strip me at Calvary.*

Cool, Arram says.

Only now Duke, lying on the floor across the room, is chewing on something unidentifiable, and Danny remembers how, two summers ago, the dog gobbled up Gerry's fish cleanings, along with a hook, and had to be rushed to the vet. He remembers looking up from the back of the car, blood on his cutoffs and T-shirt, "He's going to die, Daddy! He's going to die!" And his father, pink-throated, turning to look at the dog in his arms before yelling, "Shut your goddamn trap before I shut it permanently. What the hell is wrong with you?"

However, on closer inspection, the thing appears to be just an old, half-eaten rawhide covered with dust and grayish-green yuck.

"Ew, get that out of your mouth," he says, attempting to take it away from him, but the dog wrinkles his nose and growls and chews faster. So Danny can only pull his hand away and hope Duke won't swallow the yuck and be poisoned. Then in Jerusalem again, he stands with eyes lifted heavenward as the cross is lowered to his shredded shoulder and back. He staggers beneath it, as if adjusting to its wood-heavy weight and the intensified burning of his wounds, before trudging slowly ahead, the reinforced cardboard heart sandwiched between his right ear and hand, the tail dragging sibilantly across the concrete, and, just as he passes the cobwebbed and rust-colored column closest to the door, drops, chest heaving, to one knee, exhausted and overwhelmed with pain.

Arram kicks at him and prods his tender back with the butt of his spear. *Get up, scoundrel! Blasphemer! King of the Jews!*

Unsteadily, Danny stumbles ahead until, quite near the oil burner and Duke's frenzied chewing, he falls again and is prodded and heckled with added meanness, to the particular horror of the weeping women huddled on the edges of the road. But now Veronica bravely breaks from them and dabs at his blood- and sweat-streaked face with her veil. *Forever will this kindness be remembered,* Danny says to her, as she regards the impression on the material with wonder.

Get lost, woman! Get up, scoundrel! Ya, ya!

As Danny wobbles to his feet again, the dog, who's been watching him intently from the corners of his eyes, stands up suddenly with the rawhide—to join the procession, it would seem—but then, possibly thinking better of it, lies right down again and resumes his chewing. And so Danny, trudging on alone, once again comes around to the Ping-Pong table, where he falls the third, last time and leans the cross on a tall carton, Simon of Cyrene. *Your kindness, too,* he says to the helpful man, then fast-forwards to Calvary.

Now for the stripping! Arram says eagerly. *Naked in the basement!*

Come on, Danny says, dragging the cross to the far recess and laying it down between his father's workbench and sawhorses. *This way if we hear anything, I'll yank the light cord and put my clothes on.* Still, his heart's racing. *I'll have to be fast.* And, eyes rolling heavenward again, he gives himself up to the soldiers, their hands moving roughly over his body, tugging off his robe and sandals, and lastly his swaddling.

Ha, ha! Look at the naked King! Look at the King's wienie!

The daughters of Jerusalem scream and turn away, then rush to support the Mother, collapsing with shock and grief. And Danny, tossing his Fruit of the Looms atop his pile of clothes on the bench, listens past the thumping in his chest for noises above and on the stairs, before lying down on the cross, his shoulder blades and the edges of his heinie mashing onto the cold, gritty floor. *Hammer me,* he instructs Arram.

But now suddenly a real sound and a rushing up beside him: Duke's stinky ears and breath raking over his face, followed by a volley of mushy lashes on his nose, cheeks, lips.

"Ew. No, Duke, stop," he whispers, pushing him off, the dog's long nails scraping across the concrete, "I'm getting crucified." Yet the unruly spaniel lunges back at him for a lick of his left tittie, a curious sniff of his wiener; Danny can feel his cold, poking nose, then his gooey tongue, slushing right across it. "Hey," he says, shivering and jumping up, "get away from my stuff!" He tries to push the dog off with his leg, but he simply wraps himself around it, bumping his own furry dickie against Danny's knee. "Get off! Stop it!" he says, slapping Duke's spotted shoulder. "I'll take the bone." At this the gnarly black ears perk up, and Danny's able to free himself and rush to the abandoned rawhide beside the oil burner; and, just as Duke's about to bark for it, he throws the gooed-up knob over by the door, and the dog races for it, grabs it up, and lies down again, chewing and growling.

Quickly, Danny runs back to the recess for his undershirt and wipes his offended parts, then stands very still, listening for sounds, calls, *What's going on down there?* But after a moment, when all he's detected is Duke's incessant chewing and the muffled, overhead drones of the two TVs, he decides it's safe to resume.

Let's pretend the nailing's over, he suggests, thinking it wise not to lie on the floor again. Picking the cross up and leaning it against the far wall, he places a dusty stepladder before it, climbs up, and assumes the nailed posture again.

Oo-wee! the jungle-haired boy says, freely eyeing his dickie, on a level now with his nose, then makes a crazy Duke-face and pretends to sniff and lick at it, *Yum, yum, yum.*

No. Danny laughs and shivers again because of the cool basement air and the memory of the dog's tongue slushing right over it. *Jeer at me.*

Ha, ha! So You were going to destroy the temple and rebuild it in three days! Save Yourself now by coming down from that cross!

My God! My God! Danny says. *Why have You forsaken Me?* Then he says it again, *My God! My God!* and has the strange, frightening urge to say it out loud, scream it right up through the ceiling until the whole house shakes, the way Calvary did when Jesus died, the ground splitting open and the curtain in the temple tearing from top to bottom.

That would wake him up! he thinks, imagining his father sailing down on the couch through a hole in the floor and glimpsing, on his terrifying passage through the basement, himself, little Danny, naked and nailed to the cross. *Truly he was the son of God,* his father would say, dropping like a penny to the center of the earth.

At school the next morning, Liz feels like the manager of a St. Vincent de Paul, one that specializes in sleepwear, as the children drop bag after bag of old robes at the front of the room. Who'd have expected the mothers to have so many? Mrs. Burke alone sent Danny in with a trove, his shopping bag so brimming with promise that Liz takes the first opportunity, when the announcements begin, to rummage through it, reminding herself as she does that she still hasn't picked up an invitation. "Just look at all of these," she murmurs, her stomach fluttering again at the very real prospect of the woman in the audience next Wednesday, as she holds up one and then the other of the blues. A tall woman, shops at Gimbel's, which surprises her; she'd have thought her more Macy's. But these are nice enough, certainly, well made. As if echoing this thought, Juanita says, "Oh, those are *pretty,*" her judgment met with girlish agreement, boyish scoffs. "Aren't they?" Liz says, here deciding that, though it'll take quite a bit of shortening to get them to fit Frances, these are the ones for the Blessed Mother, the darker worn open over the lighter, as on so many statues. But now, what have we here? she thinks, fishing out a brilliant red. A contrast in her personality? A special holiday robe? Either way, it's far too bright, even for Mary Magdalene. Just the sight of it now sets the children giggling; "Your mother wears *that?*" Herman squeals. Then as Liz looks up and sees the degree to which Danny's blushed, she says sharply, "Let's all mind our own business," and promptly trades the controversial article for a snow-white unisex swim robe. Child's size, thank goodness, and perfectly suited for the resurrection. Finally, a new tan-colored men's, quite lovely but for what seems a fresh and especially inept hemming job.

"Oh Daniel," Liz says, "did your mother do all this work for us again?" Then as the boy squints and nods, she finds herself suppressing a not-so-gracious smile: the superwoman, it appears, can't sew to save her life. Which is perfectly understandable—she's busy with her music, and with managing a career and a family—and fine, really, because Liz herself isn't too bad with a needle and thread. She can easily patch this mess up. "How nice," she says, displaying it aloft. "Ooh, wow. That's a good one," the girls say, their tailoring standards obviously lower. "Is that for Jesus? Who gets to wear it?" *Well, Daniel, of course,* Liz is about to say, but stops herself and, avoiding the boy's sharp glance, merely smiles at the question and mumbles, "Some lucky devil."

Again at recess, she has to shoo the girls away from the bags and get them back to work on the soldiers' helmets and shields. Then for the first time she has the boys attempt practice without scripts, and the result is so appalling she sits them down immediately and distributes index cards. "I want everyone to copy each of his lines on a separate one," she explains, "and write his cue at the top"—something, it strikes her now, she should've had them do long ago. "Daniel, when everyone's done, start again. And only let them look at the cards when they absolutely have to." Finally, "Help him," she whispers, worriedly indicating Timmy, hunched over his script and extra supply of cards.

After she's left and Danny's made fast work of Peter's four lines, he joins the fretting boy and, in a fair imitation of his large, wiggly script, scrawls out two or three to his every one, here changing a cue, there jumbling a line or copying one that isn't Jesus' at all.

So when practice resumes, Timmy's even more disoriented than before, coming in too early or late, and once saying, "What is truth?" like a Jesus with little faith.

"Hey, that's my line," Rory says.

"No, it's not," Timmy says, holding up a card. "I've got it right here."

"Then you wrote the wrong one," Rory insists. "Pilate says that."

"Yeah, Timmy," Stephen says. "Jesus knows what truth is."

"Oh right," he says, slapping his forehead. And indeed, his performance is so thoroughly hobbled that Danny, in the commotion just before The Way, is able to whisper, "I hope that's not what you're going to do in the play," the river of grace resuming. "The whole fifth and sixth grades are coming now. That's over two hundred children."

"Two hundred?" Timmy says, eyes bulging pitifully.

"At least," Danny says. "Think of how embarrassing it'll be if all those hundreds of students laugh at you."

And just after this, Danny's recital of the denials, in full view of Brian and Joey, is relatively unstammered, almost smooth, though no one, to his frustration, seems to take note of it this time, or to care, and soon they're drowned out altogether by Stephen's crowing, voluminously assisted by Kevin, "Cock-a-doodle-doo! Cock-a-doodle-doo! Know what *that* means?"

"*Yes,*" Stephen says, huffing indignantly.

"That's so not funny," Frances adds.

"How's it going?" Miss Kaigh asks, just now barreling through the door in another flustered state.

"M-Much better," Danny reports.

"Good. I want you to carry those cards with you everywhere you go and practice whenever you can—on the bus, in the schoolyard, before dinner. They have to be absolutely second nature. Does everyone understand? I'm speaking especially to you," she says, turning to Timmy, and the pop-eyed boy starts and nods. "I wasn't going to tell any of you this, but I've just learned that the fourth grade may be coming to the performance."

"The fourth grade, too?" Juanita says.

"Cool!" Brian says, making a fist. "We're gonna have a big crowd."

"That's three grades now," Frances points out.

"Over three hundred students," Danny whispers to Timmy.

"Oh man," Timmy says.

"Daniel?" Miss Kaigh calls, waving him over and questioning him anxiously about the cross.

"I'm almost finished making it," he tells her.

"Oh good," she says, sighing.

"But then I have to paint it."

"Oh," she says, anxious again. "Do you think you can do that by tomorrow?"

"I don't know," he says, biting his lip as before.

"Try, please. He needs to practice carrying it."

But the next day, Friday, Danny doesn't bring it in again. "I haven't finished painting it," he claims.

"Oh no! Well, how much more do you have to do?"

"A little."

"Daniel, we absolutely have to have it by Monday," Miss Kaigh says, literally putting her foot down. "I'm counting on you." And the next instant, the firm set of her jaw softens, and she produces, from the pocket of her lime-green jacket, a second sealed card bearing the inscription Mrs. Gerard Burke. "Would you give this to your mother for me, please? It's an invitation to the play. We want her to come."

"We-we-we do?" he says, face suddenly blanching.

"Yes. She's helped us so much and has taken such an interest in the play from the beginning. I'm sure she's expecting this."

"B-B-But," he says, "she works on Wednesdays."

"I know that. Give it to her anyway; she'll figure something out." And, copping a wisdom-of-the-ages tone, "Trust me, she wouldn't miss this for the world, her son's play."

"Mm," he mumbles, tucking the card in the back of his religion notebook.

Liz, feeling the pressure on her instantly multiply, spends the better part of recess on her knees, mouth stuffed with pins, as student after student scarecrows before her, in some cases twice.

"I don't understand why we have to have two different costumes," Joey says, complaining his arms are growing tired.

"What do you mean you don't understand? You're playing two different roles."

"But aren't the guards and the soldiers the same thing?"

"No. The guards are the high priest's men, and the soldiers are Pilate's."

He squints at her.

"One's Jewish and the other's Roman. Each ruler has his own army."

"Oh," he says in an offhand, unconvinced way. But Liz, puzzling over the diagrams in Biblical Costumes and attempting to replicate the "Ionic-style drapery" of a tunic with a white flat sheet, hasn't the presence of mind to explain any further. Rather, she's tempted to eliminate the difference between Jew and Roman herself now, just to save her a little work. Then she calls back Rory, the reluctant Judas, to stand for the only striped model, navy-blue and gray—an ingenious match, it seems to her, though not so the next robe, which, for want of something better, she's settled on for Christ: a chestnut-brown really more suited to Peter. It has a hood that can be raised for the denials and just seems more fisherman-like in general. Ironically, Danny's tan robe has the most kingly air of any, maybe because it's in the newest condition or because she spent a good portion of the previous night redoing the hems and taking in the seams. "I just finished off a couple of things your mother started," she explained. "Of course, she did the really hard parts." Now as she fusses with her pins about Timmy's ankles, she wants to suggest to Danny that he let the boy wear it but holds off, thinking that after she alters this hooded one, she'll be in a better position to get him to trade. And in a moment, when she tosses the pinned robe atop the growing pile on her desk and quails at the endless sewing ahead of her, she moves on to the next and then the next, until finally she gets up stiffly from the floor—a hand on her back, the other brushing the knees of her lime-green slacks—and straightens into one of the strongest cravings for a cigarette she's ever known. "All right, let's go," she says, quickly rounding them together for the first scene, then slipping out the door. "Try not to use your cards. I'll be right back."

Yet even for his opening speech, Timmy continually refers to his, creating so many confused disruptions that Danny, in the shuffle between the arrest and high priest trial, has cause again to ask, "Can't you remember *any* lines?"

"I'm trying," the boy says. "I keep getting mixed up."

"You have to practice at home."

"I did," he says. "I can't fit them all in my brain."

"They won't fit?" Danny says, genuinely horrified at the idea of such a small-capacity mind.

"It's like I can remember some, but then the others push them out. You know what I mean?"

"No," Danny says. "Maybe you've taken on more than you can handle. There's only a few days left."

"Can't I bring my cards onstage?" Timmy asks desperately.

"You have to look at the audience when you talk. And your hands have to be empty. Jesus never carried anything."

"He didn't?"

With the obvious exception, Danny realizes now, of the cross. But here the boy, instead of challenging him, comes to the longed-for conclusion. Just says it flat out: "Why don't *you* just play Jesus, then. You know all the lines already. Then I can play Peter; that's easier, right?"

"A lot," Danny says. "But Miss Kaigh wants you to do it."

"But what if I can't?"

Danny forces a glance at Timmy's bugging brown eyes, for surely a true sympathizer would look into them. Then slowly, he leans in closer to the poor boy's ear, so fretting-red, and offers his solution.

~ 12 ~

The Way of the
Cross on Main Street

Struck by new genius on Saturday afternoon, Danny steals off on his
Stingray down circuitous back roads and the long-stretching
Bayview Avenue, the heavy-duty kitchen scissors in his jacket pocket.
As he approaches the marina, the trees giving way to tall rushes on either side of the cracked concrete road, he jumps off his bike. With no
one in sight, he snips an armful of the taller reeds, plying the scissors
around their flutey trunks, then begins a more precarious and frenzied
pedal back to his house, steering with one hand and trying not to bend
any of his precious specimens, their feather crowns flagging delicately
in the breeze. With each car that passes, he turns his head away, an obvious reed thief, until he reaches the safety of his backyard, none of the
drivers having called out to him, no marina patrol sped up from behind, lights whirling. Just before dropping his bike onto the grass, his
bundle onto the patio, he smiles meekly at his father, picking dead
leaves from the garden by the shed. But his father doesn't acknowledge
him, is lost in concentration perhaps, and so Danny turns to his project, lining up all the stalks and evaluating each in terms of length,
thickness, beauty, strength—above all strength, for it has to be able to
withstand repeated *smiting:* the soldiers *smote* and *smote* Jesus on the
head with the reed, even while He was wearing the terrible crown,
driving the thorns deeper into His scalp. And now his mother, stepping down from the stoop, pencil-line eyebrows knitted, asks, "What
are all the reeds for?"

"The mockery scene."

It's another moment before she understands and frowns.

"They give Jesus a reed instead of a scepter . . ."

"Yeah, yeah," she says, waving the rest away and turning to feel a blouse on the clothesline stretching from the door. Still damp, it seems, for she climbs the stoop again empty-handed, telling him to sweep up all those little feathers when he's through, and not to leave his bike in the middle of the yard like that. As she disappears inside, he continues the evaluation, choosing semifinalists and runners-up, and at last, the lucky—or, depending on how you look at it, unlucky—winner that gets to be Jesus' scepter and head-smiter. And with it he proceeds, solemnly, stately, up to his room—like the pope or Moses or even just Father McGann, when he walks up the aisle of the church on holidays—and leans it on the wall beside his desk, before turning to the "Preparation for the Public Ministry" chapter of *The Life*. Just prior to it is an account of the favorite "Finding in the Temple," about how the boy Jesus (unfortunately twelve, a whole year older than himself) somehow remained behind in Jerusalem after the feast of Passover had ended and Mary and Joseph were returning to Nazareth. When the holy parents realized Jesus was missing, they went back and found Him in the temple amid all the teachers, listening and asking questions, and *all who heard Him were amazed at His intelligence and His answers.* Then His mother, astonished, said, *Son, why have You done this to us? You see that Your father and I have been searching for You in sorrow.* And Jesus answered, *Why did you search for Me? Did you not know that I have to be about My Father's business?* Such beautiful words, all in the special red type. *'The very first words of Christ recorded in the Gospels,' The Life* points out, *'are these spoken to His parents.'* Danny imagines having some reason to say them to his own mother, *Did you not know that I have to be about My Father's business?* then is repeating them to himself a third time when, quite uncannily, she calls up:

"I thought I told you to clean up that mess on the patio."

"I was going to."

"Well, it looks like a beach out there."

Sucking in his breath, he barrels ahead, "Don't you know I have to be about My Father's business?"

"Have to what?" Carol says at the bottom of the stairs. "What business? What are you talking about?" And while the line strikes her as odd, it seems vaguely familiar. "I want it done before dinner," she says of the reed mess. Then in the laundry room, as she's setting the washing machine and shaking some extra Bold over the large load she's collected from Sharon's floor, it hits her, the temple: poor Mary looking all over for her Son, and when she finally finds Him, He's got that little smart-ass thing to say, right in front of everyone. Well, with all due respect to the Queen of Heaven, she wouldn't let *her* son speak to her that way, she doesn't care who He is. "We'll just see about this," she grumbles now and booms back up the hall to the stairs. "Pardon me, Mr. High and Mighty, but would you deign to appear on the landing?"

"Huh?" she hears him say in his room. "A-A-Are you calling me?"

"I'm speaking to the Son of God, Daniel Jesus Christ."

"M-Mom?" he says, poking his head out cautiously past the stair-wall. And it seems to him now, as he looks down at her crossed arms and pursed lips, that she's recognized the line.

"You meant big *F*, didn't you?"

"What?"

"My Father's business, big *F*."

"What's the matter?" he asks, flushing.

"Look at my arms," she says, "a thousand goose bumps." And looking herself now, she does find quite a few. "God is not your father," she says flatly, for she feels it must be said this way.

"But God's everyone's Father," Danny says.

"I thought you'd say that. You know what I mean." She narrows her eyes, and he smiles appeasingly, teeth clenched. "God is not your father-father. Your father-father is Gerard Robert Burke Jr., whether you like it or not. And I'm Caroline Theresa O'Doolin Burke, not the Virgin Mary. And I don't want to be. Is that settled?"

"Yeah."

"All right," she says, a bit surprised at such quick and seemingly genuine deference, though just exactly what they *have* settled now she can't be sure of. And after a moment more of their staring uncomfortably at each other, she realizes she doesn't have anything more to say and lets him run off to his room again, while she pads to the back door to check the work clothes on the line.

In the morning, it's all he can do to stay calm when, the instant he opens his eyes, he's assailed with knowledge of the date: Palm Sunday, the beginning of the real Holy Week, and the first day of the week of his play. To make things worse, it's unusually mild outside, full of blinding sun and warm, grassy smells, the old winter quiet, pierced through with bird chirping and all the extra spring rustlings and cars and bicycles; light, careless voices calling to one another, laughing; and daffodils, so many suddenly, in full, overnight bloom about the yews. In their silent station wagon, Danny squints at the onslaught of so much unruly life; again at Our Lady's, as swarms of parishioners pour down the steps wearing pastel-colored jackets and holding palm fronds. And in their pew, during the three-priest reading of the Passion, Danny's mother, who only goes to Mass on holidays, grows increasingly agitated, clicking her tongue and shifting in her seat. "Oh, come on, already," she mutters to his dozing father, "how long are they going to go on with this?" And, even to the unknown lady beside them, "What are they going to do, read the whole Bible?" Finally, when Mass is over, Danny summons the nerve to ask for extra palms from the usher, and when they pass a second, arms laden before the exit, he whispers to his mother, "Get more." "Why? How many do you need?" "Please?" She shakes her head but then asks for them anyway, and the usher gives her two, not enough. He wishes he could take the entire bundle from the man and rush with it to the car and up to his room. And when at last he does get there, he has eight in total, of varying thicknesses, and lays them out like ladder rungs across his carpet, then doffs his shoes and socks. Although it occurs to him, as he walks over the blessed palms, saying, *Your king approaches! Your king approaches!* that this may be a kind of sin, he continues to anyway, over and over, the cool, curling edges of the fronds crackling underfoot.

This boldness persists throughout the day, its full flowering in the basement, when Arram leaves off his rounds of soldier jeers to say, *Next we have to be naked outside!*

Naked outside? Danny says, climbing down the stepladder before the cross and slipping on his clothes and Pro-Keds. *We'll need our sneakers.*

Jacketless in the cool night air, they round the side of the den, Danny's father grumbling inside for the dog to be quiet, then move out into the dark of the backyard, toward the creaky, black-armed oaks skirting the woods at the end of the property and, huddled just before it, Danny's father's shed, in every way his father's. He built it himself before Danny was born; he tells everyone that, whenever the subject of the shed comes up, not often. In it, among all the old ice skates and sleds, he keeps his yard tools and one-speaker radio and old wooden chair where he sits sometimes in summer, listening to ball games.

This'll be home, Danny says, unlatching the door. *We'll leave our clothes by the lawn mower and rakes. Then we'll come out naked and run to the first oak tree.*

No, the second! Arram says.

By Mrs. Maher's yard?

We have to touch it and run back.

That's far to run naked, Danny warns.

The farther the better! Arram cries. *Naked race!*

But now before the black, yawning doorway, Danny's beset with worries as to what might be lurking within—shed monsters and so on—and freezes, squinting at the far shadows. *Let's run naked tomorrow.*

No! Now! Arram says.

Eyes and ears adjusting to the dark, he doesn't perceive any hunched, unexpected shapes, any creepy animal movements or low growls, and so steps in, leaving the door ajar, and all at once is assaulted by gasoline and oil fumes, and by a dusty spiderweb-and-dry-leaf smell. Holding his breath, he strips with remarkable speed, then stands up, naked to his sneakers before the corner-dwelling wolfman: *Mm, yummy boysteak.*

All right, he says, *let's go,* and, *Oh wait,* plucking an old snow hat from a nail by the door, the kind that covers your whole face.

Ew! You want to wear that?

Yeah, Danny says, turning it inside out and whipping it against the doorframe to shake out old centipede husks and bug turds; then he pulls it on and sneezes. *It smells like grease.* And back outside, the air raises goose bumps all over his body, his titties shrinking to tiny brown darts.

We have to run to keep warm, Arram says.

You first, Danny says, and right away the boy races ahead—nothing new for him!—tan cheeks Jello-jiggling above his skinny, whooshing legs.

But, *No!* Arram says now and runs backward to Danny like a movie in reverse. *We have to do it together.*

Okay, Danny says and, with a quick glance at the kitchen window—lit, empty—and the den window—his father's distant form partially visible on the couch—*Go!* They run as fast as they can, right through the whipping wind and the open yard, over all the spongy clumps of new grass.

Whoa, look at it! Danny says, staring down at his fast-jumping, flip-flapping dickie. *It's going like crazy! Ga-bing, ga-bing, ga-bing!*

That's a high flapper, Arram admits, his own *ga-binging* with less zest because of its worminess.

And now at the oak: *Touch it!* slap, slap, and the race back to the shed, and the cool wind again, licking every little naked part. And Danny, sneakers thumping, boner swiveling, reaches the door first and rushes right in, panting and giggling with exhilaration, his hands leaning on the lawn mower handle—Arram's shoulders—and suddenly the darker-colored boy moves closer and kisses him on his acrylic-covered mouth. *Wait*, Danny says and raises the bottom of the hat, to better flick his tongue between Arram's lips, as if he wanted to taste something there: the honey he eats.

I love you, Jesus, Arram whispers, and licks him back, a cuter Judas.

Then their two tongues, tip-touching and running over each other until, *Ew*, Danny says, breaking off and wiping his mouth. *It's cold out here! We have to run again!*

Ready?

Go!

Meanwhile Carol, looking up from the end of *All in the Family*, hears the call of the strawberry swirl ice cream she bought at the A&P the day before and sidles off the bed for the kitchen. Sunday sundae, she coos excitedly to herself, thinking that had she given up desserts for Lent, as she briefly entertained doing last month, she'd still be entitled to this one now, on the weekly day of respite. And so it's just as her scoop is spoiling the smooth pink block, like a first step on a snowy field, that some unusual movements out the window catch her eye. In fact, if she's not mistaken, she could swear she just saw someone streak across the backyard.

"Oh, not this again," she says aloud, mind plunging back a few years in confusion—the boys and their gang of cutups, running through the trees; had the neighbors at the door and everything. That bitch Maher, threatening to call the police again, "I have young children in my house!" But they wouldn't still be doing that kind of thing, would they? And why here? They've got their own neighborhoods to terrorize now, she thinks, half-regretfully. But wait . . . yup! There he goes again! Definitely some kid out there, looks like he's wearing a ski mask. "So we're getting more discreet," she says, rushing to the door and banging on the storm before punching it open. "Hey, out there! What's the big idea? Get lost or I'll call your mother!"

And here the whisking form lets out a high-pitched yelp, then makes a mad dash to the shed at the back of the yard and disappears behind it. Pretty young-sounding yelp, if you ask her; probably just a boy, not much older than . . . She frowns and glances at the ceiling, but she knows he's up there doing his homework, heard him rummaging through his desk just a . . . while ago. No, that's crazy, she decides, closing the door and returning to her sundae making, imagining, as she does, Gerry grumbling in the den about the size of her derriere. Of course he's probably still sound asleep, even through all her racket. She steps back and glances in at the den couch, and, yup again, there he is, mouth hanging open, hands folded over his belly, blissfully unconscious. So nice to have a man around the house. And now with a spiteful flair anyway—because he *would've* grumbled it if he were awake—she drips a generous amount of U-Bet chocolate syrup over the lovely, striped scoops, and tops it all off with a shot of Reddi-Wip and a maraschino cherry. Casting another quick look out the window and finding all beyond obediently quiet and still, she retires comfortably to the bedroom and changes the channel. *Police Woman,* she likes that Angie Dickinson; and right away sliding into bed again and sinking her spoon into the ice cream, she ignores the idea, while the opening credits are rolling, of calling up to her son, just to see for sure.

At the same time Danny, in the dark garage, feverishly pets Duke to keep him from barking. He remains there several moments more, squatting beside the slobbering, wriggling spaniel, before finding the nerve to venture toward the den door. Miraculously, he squeezes inside, past his sleeping father, without Duke breaking into a new fit, then removes his sneakers again and tiptoes across the living room to the stairs. *I was in the basement,* he's prepared to say, should his mother appear behind him, *painting the cross*. No one knows about it yet; he could pretend he just made it. Still, it would seem suspicious, and not until he clears the landing and reaches his room does he relax, a little. How much did she see, he wonders, in the dark, from far away? He feels he must find out.

As Carol loads the empty bowl in the dishwasher during a commercial break, she spies his bare feet on the linoleum behind her.

"Who were you yelling at before?" he asks.

And is she imagining things, or does he sound a little out of breath to her, nervous? "Some kid," she says, pouring Cascade into the door compartment, "outside in the yard."

"Really?" Danny says, with all appropriate alarm, then dares to add, "What was he doing?"

"What do you mean?" she asks, "Why?" and, looking up finally, sees his hair is flattened and messy.

"I-I-I don't know. I was just w-wondering."

"Well," she says, locking the door handle, "if you have to know, he was streaking." This as she presses the on-button and water surges through the machine.

With his mother's unblinking, unmascaraed eyes hard upon him, Danny sucks in his breath, not altogether unnaturally. His heart, it would seem, is beating with the same excitement and frustrated wonder he'd feel if it had been the report of some other boy running naked outside, his body fighting the same urge to rush to the windows, as if he might still be able to make out, between the silhouettes of the trees, the fleeing, far-off shape.

Carol examines her son, brow furrowed. She doesn't want to consider that he may be lying to her or pretending in such an elaborate way—wouldn't that be nutty, for him to wave the subject right under her nose? Yet his expression's awfully like the guilty-fibbing look she's seen a hundred times on Sharon and the boys: the eyebrows a little too high, lips jutting out strangely, like a grinning fish. And despite herself now, she glances at her pious son's toes for bits of grass, dirt. Nothing obvious there. *Let me see the bottoms of your feet*, she imagines asking but shrinks from such a request; it seems so . . . personal.

"I don't like the look on your face," she says instead. "I hope you're not up to anything you shouldn't be." But then, "W-What?" he says with such genuine innocence and fear that she drops the matter altogether. "Nothing," she says, shaking her head and making for the bedroom again. "I don't know what I was thinking."

"Oh," Danny says, watching her retreat. "I wasn't up to anything."

"I know. I didn't mean you," and, as he hears her door swing shut, "Forget it."

And so he stands in the empty kitchen, toes wiggling on the cool linoleum, with a shivery, sweaty feeling on the back of his neck and arms. Did she see him? he wonders again, the warmth deepening and spreading to his face to think of his dickie, flapping up and down. Oh God! And does she truly believe it was some other boy, or does she know it was him? And if she does, why didn't she say so? He hopes— oh, he hopes something! And now his thoughts and worries race along so furiously that it's several moments before he can peel his feet from their spot in the middle of the floor and return to his room.

When he does, he's calmer, relatively so, and only for those moments until he remembers he's promised to bring his basement creation to school the next day, after which he's once again awash with dread and his reluctance to part with it. At last, just before going to bed, he finds himself hunting through his desk for his thickest black magic marker and sailing down to the basement, there briefly erecting the cross and, in lovingly meticulous script, signing the bottom, *Daniel Burke, artist.* Only then does he feel reassured enough to fall asleep.

But the night passes with terrible swiftness, the light of the new school week easily defeating the last dark of Sunday, and at once he springs from bed and rushes frantically about, not always with direction, tripping over himself, dropping his cereal bowl and spoon en route from cabinet to table. And immediately after breakfast he runs to pack his lunch and copy of *The Life* in his book bag, before interrupting his mother's extended grooming ritual in the bathroom and kissing her freshly made-up cheek.

"Isn't it still early?" she asks, eyeing him suspiciously in the mirror, blue teasing comb poised hatchet-like above her sleep-tousled tresses.

"I don't know, a little."

"You're not going to Mass, I hope."

"No, Mom. Bye."

"Bye," she says, attacking her hair with the comb again.

And in a moment, Danny, reaching the end of the walk outside, zips back up the driveway to the garage, dropping his bag on the asphalt. Then quietly, he hoists the big door up just enough for Duke to poke his freckled snout and paws through, and gropes for the cross he's leaned up against the wall inside. But the spaniel tries to nudge the door higher with his nose and, not succeeding, nudges and slobbers at Danny's hand and blazer sleeve instead, never once getting out of the way enough for him to maneuver it flat onto the floor and drag it through. "Move, Duke; watch out," he whispers to no avail and so has to raise the door much further and grab the dog by the choke. Then it's all he can do to keep the spotted huffer inside while he pushes and slides the cross out onto the driveway with his free hand and feet; finally, with a forceful shoo and a "sorry, boy," he yanks the door closed and turns the lock, all much too loudly.

And indeed Carol, her entire mane now standing on end in what she thinks of as the bride-of-Frankenstein phase of her styling, hears the rumbling from the bathroom and, alarmed, does what she'd never do: appear at the front door before her hair's finished. There, she's confronted with a truly shocking sight: her son shouldering an enormous, perhaps life-sized, crucifix, the likes of which she's never seen. It's so elaborately, grotesquely painted, so full of dark knots and grains and long swashes of bright red, it's as if the blood's running right off it, as if the wood itself is bleeding.

"Oh my God!" she says, fumbling to open the door and the screen, and in the process almost urges him to run, quick, as if the thing were one of those horrible, talking trees from *The Wizard of Oz* that might grab him or throw apples at him—all her life those trees have given her nightmares—but instead she cries, "Danny, no!" just, "No!" She can't think of anything else to say now in the face of this religious insanity.

Danny, halfway down the driveway, starts at the sight of her, for fear she might try to take his masterpiece away somehow. But also, because her hair's all standing straight up, like the bride of Frankenstein. "It's the cross," he explains.

"Well, I can see that. Where did you get such a horror? Don't tell me you made that, too."

He bites his lip and shrugs, but as far as Carol's concerned, he's answered by not answering. Oh, how she longs for the days when he used to copy the *Peanuts* strips and do his little linoleum prints of birds and sailboats and animal faces. "Danny, I've never heard of anyone making these kinds of veils and crosses."

"It's for the play."

"The play, the play," she says sarcastically; he can't imagine how happy she'll be when it's all over. But now, remembering her state, she holds a hand up in front of her hair and takes a half step back from the door. "Where are you going with it?" she asks, bracing for the obvious.

"I'm bringing it to school."

"Oh no. You mean you're *walking* all the way there with that big thing?" the full brunt of it hitting her.

He shrugs again.

Sure, no skin off his teeth; he's just a crazy kid. Don't worry about anyone at your mother's office driving to work. "Can't you wait till your father comes home? I'll have him bring it up to the rectory."

"No, Mom, we need it for practice."

She frowns at him. Anyway, she's not even sure it would fit in their old Ford.

"Take the back roads," she says, hating to concede on this; it's her last concession. She's also on the verge of suggesting a hat, or at least telling him to keep his head down, but he's too quick for her—already cleared the driveway and heading south—and that's not the kind of thing she wants to yell. Oh but—oh Lord, what a spectacle! In his plaid blazer and navy-blue trousers, book bag in one hand, huge cross over the other shoulder. He looks pathetic, like a real case. "I can't stand it," she says, quickly locking the doors again, and retreating inside to finish her hair.

But Danny, after making the first right on Dixie, doesn't continue down the long, quiet road toward Timberpoint and the rear of the school, but rather turns north again at the very next block and, some distance still from Main Street, lays the cross on the pebbly road and removes *The Life* from his bag. Then it's another moment before he can find a way to shoulder the cross, hold the bag and read, all at the same time, this finally accomplished by first slipping the hand that will hold the book through the handles of the bag and letting the bag dangle, albeit a little uncomfortably, from his wrist. And so he proceeds, nervously and jerkily, up the road, just then imagining himself pushing aside a curtain and walking onto a particularly long stage, the intermittent rush of tires on the asphalt ahead a kind of welcoming applause.

At first he doesn't read at all but just holds the book open to the proper, ribboned-off page, repeating to himself, *Via Dolorosa, road of sorrows,* the lovely-sounding words like a prayer to calm him and help him concentrate, *Via Dolorosa, road of sorrows.* But unfortunately, this attempt at conjuring a rapt and blessed state is almost immediately ruffled when, just as he's cutting across the small corner parking lot of Stanley's Bakery, Mrs. Maher emerges from the store.

"My word! Robby Burke!" the beady-eyed lady says, stopping with a large and fragrant white bag of rolls—an earlier riser, it seems to Danny, for her own hair is already whipped up and shellacked in place, its distinguishing dip cascading toward her right eye from its puffy heights. "Robby Burke!" she says louder, two other similarly high-haired women stopping beside her now. "Is that my old refrigerator carton?"

Danny nods, fearing any attempt at speech will further interfere with his imminent blessing.

"Well, you've certainly done things with that!" she exclaims, and, "He made this from the carton my new Kenmore came in," she tells the others, whom she may or may not know, six now including three of the white-smocked counter ladies, who have just crowded at the door.

"Will you look at that!" "Look at the red!"

"Can you eat a cookie?" the shortest one asks, proffering a colorfully iced bunny on a square of waxed paper.

"How's he going to carry it, Sue? Get him a little bag."

"Oh, I'm sorry," Sue says, rushing off.

"I said to him, 'Well, I don't want this carton. Sure, you can have it.' And look what he does!"

"Incredible." "Marvelous."

Danny, thrilled and petrified by so many eager adult eyes on him, smiles and nods, then quickly proceeds away.

"Don't you want to wait for your cookie?"

"Good-bye! Happy Easter!" another calls.

"Something for the Catholic school, I guess," he hears Mrs. Maher whisper. "That's where she's sent them all. Though you'd never know it, with some of the older ones. This one's like a mouse."

"Didn't say a word."

"Is he reading the Bible?"

Via Dolorosa, road of sorrows, he thinks, and, as he passes Friendly's, a gingham-aproned waitress stares and waves from behind the large front window. He mouths hello, then looks down at his book, swallowing and breathing deeply to still the butterflies in his stomach. *The place of execution was Calvary, a forbidding, ill-omened hillock about a thousand paces from the praetorium, where Jesus had been condemned to death.* A thousand paces, Danny remarks, seizing on the number; would it be longer than his walk to Our Lady's? He hopes not; he hopes it's exactly the same distance and begins to count from a hundred, allowing for those he's already completed: a hundred and one, a hundred and two. *According to the law, He was required to carry the instrument of His execution, and the weight of the cross made the journey an agonizing ordeal.* So Danny stoops a bit and imagines his strides more labored, the strength draining from him with each next step, and each next step. *The tragic procession moved slowly through the streets of Jerusalem*—a hundred forty-six, a hundred forty-seven—*At its head was a mounted centurion leading a platoon of soldiers*, then a burnt-orange Mustang, honking, *With them was a throng of people and many joined in the jibes and taunts,* a boy sticking his head out the window, *All His enemies seemed to have come to witness His final humiliation*, "Go, Jesus!"

Danny blushes, dropping his head further, and labors on. *He was fatigued to the point of death; He had not slept since Wednesday night,* and his arm, with the bag dangling from the wrist, is growing heavy now, *He was hungry and thirsty,* and he wonders how much longer he'll be able to hold the book up—two hundred sixty-five—*and His body, aching from sheer weariness as well as from the wounds of the scourging* (he mustn't forget the wounds: My back! My back!) *was caked with blood and dirt,* caked. "Uh!" he says, perhaps aloud, though he hopes not to have broken his word-fast. And now, to his left, outside the firehouse—three hundred twelve—two men in windbreakers, smirking and rubbing their chins: *Blasphemer! Dog!* they snarl, and Danny proceeds faster, as fast as possible; however, *Under the heavy cross*, at the Carleton Avenue intersection, *He faltered and fell to His knees. The soldiers kicked Him repeatedly and prodded Him with their pikes, until at last,* the light turning red again, *He stood up*—four hundred thirty-one. "Are you okay?" a stopped driver calls. He nods without looking. "Is that for Good Friday?" *and with the strength of His great will and obedience,* continues on, his arm somewhat rested.

Yet *He quickly tired again along the pocked and stone-filled road, and,* after several blocks, *after repeated falls,* a short, kindly-faced old lady, emerging from the delicatessen, *the soldiers were unable to get Him to His feet,* starts and drops her cigarette. *The centurion had his men seize a passerby,* he eyes it smoldering on the sidewalk, *Simon of Cyrene,* and thinks about stopping to pick it up for her, *Simon was on his way into the city, and as the great cross was laid on his shoulders,* but he promised his mother he'd be her one child who'd never touch a cigarette, *he undoubtedly wished he had taken a different road,* and so lets her struggle to retrieve it. *The priests and elders who walked behind Jesus,* "Hey, George, did you see that?" *resented His temporary escape from the cross and* before long a second car *redoubled the insults and indignities,* a sky-blue Volkswagen bug, *But there were friends of Jesus present, too,* swerves over to the curb, *the apostles had recovered their courage and were now following their Master,* a man with thick sideburns at the wheel. *With them were the other disciples and many of those whom Jesus had healed and comforted,* "Look at this nut," he says, *as well as a large group of the women of Jerusalem, including Jesus' mother and that holy woman, "Veronica."* "Freak!" the long-haired girl beside him yells, *Though a decree forbade manifestations of grief for one who was being led to execution, they could not restrain their tears at the sight of His suffering,* then they screech away, *and followed wailing and lamenting.* Danny turns his head, blushing deeper—six fifty-two, six fifty-three . . .

. . . and finally, in the disappointing eight hundreds, *As they started to ascend the slope of Calvary,* the north parking lot before the church is glutted with chugging buses and screeching first-graders, *a dark cloud gathered over the ugly little hill and* the children, seeing him crossing to the sidewalk, *began to spread rapidly across the sky,* fly up against the fence like birds, small fingers lacing through the chain-link. "Look at the big cross! Look at the big cross!" they shout, dashing his semi-blessed state and setting the butterflies surging wildly through his stomach, for it seems every child in the area is headed his way, all the bus drivers and yard mothers staring at him. "Off the fence, boys and girls! Hands off the fence!" one calls.

Quickly, before the entrance, he lays the cross down again on the sidewalk to return the book to his bag, the near children squealing and firing questions at him: "Is that real? Where'd you get it? How come it's so skinny?" He smiles nervously without answering—because, he tells himself, he's continuing his word-fast, not because he's unable to. It seems his claim is proved when, after steeling himself, picking his cross up again, and proceeding into the lot, the children swarm at him from every side, asking if they can carry it. "No," he says readily enough, first meekly, but then louder and possibly for the better. It may not have been right to ignore them. Hadn't Jesus said, *Suffer the little children to come to Me?* So he also tries to suffer them, their Oh pleases and Why nots. "No," he says several times more, "watch your hands. Don't scratch the paint," all as his heart pounds and he casts timid, eager glances about, amazed he should be at the center of a real crowd now, moving through the parking lot.

"Jesus! Jesus!" a girl with blond, barretted hair cries at his left, skipping and grinning and touching the hand that's holding his book bag. Danny, looking down at her, imagines she isn't joking or playing to call him this, but rather that a glint of secret recognition is passing from her eyes to his. *I promise you, today you will be with Me in paradise.*

"Jesus!" others are saying now also, "Jesus!" Then, "Sister Ernestine! Sister Ernestine!" to a squat nun emerging from the doors of the east wing, one Danny's seen several times in the yard, ever-smiling, crooked-toothed, with the same kind of black-framed glasses his father wears. "Sister Ernestine, look at the big cross!"

"Oh yes, oh *my,*" she says, signing herself as she waddles down the steps and through the crowd, stopped now before her. "Children, bless yourselves. Everyone, bless yourself when you're reminded of the suffering of Our Lord."

They all pause to reverently comply, then jump and clap and shout, "Sister! Sister Ernestine!" again.

"Careful now, James. Mark, step away; it looks delicate. And what's your name?" she asks, squinting at Danny, her pale forehead crinkling beneath a small show of dark, parted hair.

"D-D-Daniel Burke, 5B, S-Sister."

"Aha," she says jovially. "And where did you get such an impressive cross, Mr. Burke, 5B?"

Danny, carefully returning her smile, looks away from her terrible teeth. "I-I made it, Sister."

"Really! What for?"

"A play," he tells her. "'The P-P-P-Passion of Christ.'"

"Lovely! The cross is for a play, boys and girls," she announces, and at once they jump and clap again and ask if they can see it. Then she calls to a tall, sandy-haired teacher on the fringes of the group, "Mrs. Sales, did you hear that? 5B is putting on a Passion play."

"A play? How fantastic."

And now, "Mother in Heaven!" a different voice, familiar, and before Danny's located the speaker, an abrupt hush settles over the children, and they begin a slow, overlapping chorus of "Gooood Morning, Sis-ter Sis-ter Re-gin-a Re-giiin-a." Then directly to his left, the crowd parts, clearing a lane before him, and he finds the principal, official and tall in her black veil and overcoat, descending the east wing stairs.

"Good morning, boys and girls," she says, her round, inexpressive face tilted slightly as she approaches the extraordinary scene. "Good morning, Sister Ernestine, Mrs. Sales," but her slate-blue eyes are moving up and down the cross, seemingly taking in every grain mark and stroke of paint. And at the same time Danny, his throat closing with fear, imagines her face contracting indignantly. *How dare you mimic the holy road of sorrows!* she sputters, droplets of spit flying from her mouth. *How dare you walk through town as if you were the Son of God!* And though he's never seen her do so before, her rage is so great, his offense so terrible, that the back of her hand swings out at his face. *Oh!* everyone says, backing away.

But now, quite to the contrary, the nun's eyes enlarge and water; a hint of pink softens her pasty, rigid face. "Well, isn't that fine, Daniel," she says, and at once he sighs, all his dread falling away. "I imagine this is for the play Wednesday in the Music Hall?"

"Y-Y-Yes, Sister," he says, glancing up with respectful brevity at her teeth, which, in contrast, are white and straight, though small.

"This fourth-grader wrote an entire script about the suffering and resurrection of Christ from the Gospels," she informs the teachers.

"Fourth?" Sister Ernestine asks politely.

"F-Fifth," Danny says, wincing.

"That's right, fifth. Yes, of course, *fifth,*" Sister Regina says.

"How fantastic," Mrs. Sales says quickly, "a young writer."

And now the three exchange a series of earnest, approving nods.

"A fine artist, too," Sister Regina adds.

"Clearly," they say.

"Miss Kaigh showed me the beautiful veil you painted last week, also," she tells him. "A beautiful veil," she explains to Sister Ernestine, moving her hands apart like Father McGann blessing the bread at Mass, "with the face of Christ."

"Ah, for Veronica," Sister Ernestine realizes.

"Sister, will the younger grades be allowed to see this play?" Mrs. Sales asks gingerly. Here several of the bolder children break their silences. "Oh please, Sister Regina, can *we* see it?" And this, surprisingly, is tolerated by the nun, who merely shushes them and says, "We'll have to see. No promises. There's only so much room." And Danny, horrified by the prospect of even more students attending the performance, is scrambling for some way to remind her it's only for the fourth through sixth grades, when the bell rings and the children are directed to their lines more instantly than usual: "This way, everyone. Come right along."

"Oh," they complain and, shuffling off, call, "Good morning, Sister Regina! Bye, Daniel! Bye, cross!"

"Bye, Jesus!" the blond girl whispers, tugging his hand a final time.

Danny, too, is about to make for his own line on the other side of the building, when Sister Regina stops him, her face rigid and unreadable again. "Walk with me to the office," she says, turning toward the road. "I'd like Mrs. Mauriello and Sister Francis to see what you've made."

"Yes, Sister," he says, keeping the cross to the far side of the nun as they proceed. Once they come upon the sidewalk and round the corner of the wing, away from the stares of the children and teachers, she asks him where he lives and how he came to school this morning. When it becomes apparent to her that he's shouldered the cross all the way from his house, the hint of color surfaces on her cheeks again. "Through the entire town of East Islip, right down the main road! And people saw you, I imagine? They stopped on the sidewalks, stopped in their cars?"

"Oh no, Sister. I wasn't trying to—"

"How wonderful, Daniel! That's a proud Christian, a true witness! All those people now know of your love of Christ. You should feel blessed."

"Thank you, Sister."

After a moment's pause, she says excitedly, "Do you know what you were today?" as if it's just struck her. "A *pilgrim*. Are you familiar with this word?"

"Yes, Sister," he says, thinking of the black-hatted men and bonneted ladies of the *Mayflower*.

"A religious pilgrim," she repeats, "someone who makes a special journey for God. That's what you've done." She nods and then looks ahead, walking briskly, her flash of inspiration past now, it seems, and the color draining from her face again.

Danny doubles his speed to keep up with her and wonders if during this silence he might now mention his objection to the younger grades attending the play. But the instant he thinks of this, he hesitates, wondering if it wouldn't be better that more children attended, should Jesus choose to speak through him during the performance. '*Make ready, for you know not the hour.*' *Jesus! Jesus!* he imagines them chanting, a huge chant, filling the room. Brian and Joey, baffled in their soldier suits, looking from the crowd to Danny to each other. *Danny's cool now,* they say, outnumbered, *everyone likes him.* Oh, but it's all so unsure! Stuttering or blessedness, laughed at or cheered, and he wishes the play could be like the cross, beautiful and approved of and finished already. And now, hurrying up the steps to the office, Sister Regina tugs open the doors for him to maneuver the cross into the building.

Instantly, they're intercepted by the old secretary-Sisters and the school nurse, who offer similar words of surprise and appreciation, as do the teachers and aides stopping at the office or passing through the small lobby. "When is this play? Wednesday?" And so the announcements and morning prayers are already over by the time he arrives at the closed door of 5B, a late pass written by the principal herself in his blazer pocket, which, perhaps wrongly, he's read and memorized: *Please excuse us, Elizabeth, for detaining Daniel. We all could not help admiring his unique and passionately painted crucifix.* Knocking, he braces himself like a trick-or-treater, and, when Miss Kaigh appears—hair unusually disordered, eyebrows high with worry—her expression passes from disconcertment to delight, then to a kind of urgent elation: "Oh Daniel, oh super! Oh . . . *sublime!* You've outdone yourself!" Then as she pulls him into the room, "Class, will you get a look at this?" they burst into spontaneous applause, even Brian, even Joey and Kevin, all clapping in just the way he imagined earlier. At once his cheeks burn and his stomach leaps—an exalted, revelrous joy that lasts but an instant before it dissipates, and he finds himself brought low again. *Because,* he wants to tell them, *the cross is not the play: the play is much harder and yet to come,* and the anticipation of it presses on him like a great, unmovable stone.

— 13 —

Lunatic and Sore Vexed

It had surprised even herself, the urgency with which Liz had glanced at his ominously empty desk and asked, "Has anyone seen Danny? Did anyone see him walking to school?" the worst of her fears—irrational, in the light of lunch—that he'd not only elude them today, but every other day this week, that having gotten cold feet, he'd somehow removed himself, vanished with that essential prop, as completely as Christ into the desert. But when she saw him in the hall, eyes batting at the heart of that gnarled, bloody wood, she'd felt a rush of relief—that all would still proceed, and that her one fear, anyway, of having no cross for the performance, had been eliminated with such beauty and saving art. It lasted two minutes; then she was back to her harried state, fretting over the swelling audience—nine classes, nine teachers—not to mention the continued mystery of Mrs. Burke's reaction to the card. Danny didn't say a thing about it, hasn't all morning, almost as if it's a subject to be avoided. And here she suddenly lifts her head, "I hope you all practiced your lines," then bows it again and nibbles queasily at a corner of her roast beef and mayonnaise on rye.

She blames this added skittishness on not sleeping enough, and on the sheer drudgery of a weekend-long sewing session, her fingers even now stiff and tender-tipped. Yet to her frustration, she'd gotten just over half the costumes done, and these only with the help of her mother, who did a reasonable job with Mary and John. Liz herself had worked on the guards' and soldiers' costumes, and on the hooded Jesus/Peter robe, then devoted Sunday to the Pilates and the high priest before quitting in the wee hours. She'd no idea what she was in for, particularly with the Romans, all those pleats and royal borders! Were it not for the calming influences of Mrs. Burke's *Masterpieces* and the full-length *Finlandia* she found at the public library, or for the sense of sophistication and composure the red robe lent her those hours she worked in it—after tacking up the sleeves, that is, and the hem a good five inches—she fears she may have lost her mind. Then it was during one of her twirls through the den to Strauss and Dvorak, the open robe billowing about her and startling poor Cleopatra into hiding beneath the sofa, that Liz recalled how the soldiers draped a magnificent scarlet cloak over Christ during the mockery, a cloak that couldn't have been any redder than this robe. At once she knew she'd have to bring it back to school for the performance—though not a day before, so it would suffer the least amount of wear and tear.

Finally, after lunch is over and she's deposited the nonplay children outside, she finds the nerve to stride up Danny's aisle. "Did your mother say anything when you gave her the invitation?" But the boy, not having thought of the card since putting it in the back of his notebook on Friday, starts and stammers so incoherently that she says, "You did give it to her, didn't you?"

"Uh . . . um . . ."

"Um? What does *um* mean? You either did or you didn't."

And doubtful now he can convincingly claim the former, he divulges, "I-I-I forgot."

"Oh *no.*"

"I-I-I was d-d-doing everything," he says. "M-Making the cross. I'm sorry, Miss Kaigh."

"Sorry?" She clicks her tongue. "Well, you absolutely have to give it to her today. Can I trust you to do that? Or should I just call her myself? Perhaps I should have just called in the first place."

"No. No, I'll give it to her. You don't have to call," he says so earnestly that, for the time being, she's able to look up from him and attend to other matters, just now instructing the players to slip their finished costumes on over their uniforms or, in the case of the soldiers, send them out to the boys' room. When they strut back in with their sleeveless, knee-length tunics, crying, "Seize that man!" and

"Blasphemers!" the room breaks with howls and whistles and shy, girlish giggles. That is, until Liz, horrified at the spectacle of the boys' Wallabees and fuzzy navy-blue socks, discovers an anachronistic parade of chukka boots and Earthshoes beneath all the hemmed robes. "Wait!" she cries. "What about sandals?"

"Sandals?"

"You all need a pair."

"I have a pair at home," Frances and Juanita say. But, "We don't have any *sandals*," Brian says. "Sandals are very uncool for boys, Miss Kaigh," Joey explains. "Can't we wear sneakers?"

"No."

"Are flip-flops good?" Ginger asks.

Liz frowns. "Ideally they should be brown or black and lace up the ankles." "Lace?" someone says, and, "Ankles?" someone else. Oh boy, she thinks, flushing with frustration and heading for *Biblical Costumes* on her desk, a section she remembers on footwear. "It says if you don't have real sandals to look for old felt slippers; we can use the soles. Otherwise . . ." *corrugated cardboard cut to shape of foot . . . add a quarter-inch to length . . . larger will catch on edges of steps and long garments . . .* Wonderful . . . *lace strips of dark cloth through slits in cardboard . . .* "We'll have to make them tomorrow." And now with this "settled," she looks next to Timmy in the chestnut hooded and Danny in the tan regal, then sidles up to her assistant and hazards her suggestion.

"M-M-M-My robe?" Danny says.

"Well, yes, I know it's your robe, and—let's just see how it looks for a minute, can we? I spent a lot of time on this darker one. Timmy, come here, will you? Take that robe off. Here, put this one on," she says, facilitating the begrudged exchange, and "See?" to Danny, lifting the hood. "Hold this closed at the neck." As his face reddens within it, she tells him to squint and say *I do not know the man*, then waits. "Go ahead."

"I do not know the man," he mumbles.

"Fan-tastic!" she says, "Did everyone see how good that was?" glancing from Danny's bitterly shaking head to the other players' silent, tilted ones. Finally she looks to Timmy, and to the tidily cuffed sleeves of the tan robe—a last-minute, inspired detail she'd managed on Saturday. "Oh, that's so much better; you really can't have Christ in a dark color like that." And, "I'm sure Mrs. Burke will be honored that we chose one of hers for Him, don't you think, Daniel?" not looking behind her or expecting an answer. And he doesn't give one, just continues to squint beneath the dark hood— for in truth, this robe doesn't fit him at all; it's baggy and falling almost to the floor. And his own robe looks tight on Timmy, especially around the middle, the sleeves and the bottom riding higher than intended. Yet his teacher seems quite satisfied with the switch, pointing them now to their opening positions for a "semi-dressed rehearsal."

And in fact, Liz does feel a small, illogical surge of expectation, if for the one or two moments before it becomes plain to her that the better robe is doing nothing to improve Timmy's performance. To the contrary, he's moving more awkwardly than before, even stuttering Danny-like at times, and, worst of all, resorting again to the cards. "Oh please," she says, "don't tell me you still haven't memorized them."

"I just need a quick reminder."

"But you had all weekend! Did you practice every day as I asked you to?"

"Yeah, but—"

"But what, Timmy? You don't seem to know them any better than you did on Friday. Tomorrow's our *last* day to practice. Do you understand how little time is left?" But now as the boy's eyes bug, she instantly regrets her words; she's scaring him, scaring herself. Look, she thinks, glancing down at her hands, visibly trembling, and just then catches Juanita and Frances, noticing her noticing them, oh great! "All right," she says, with only marginal success at copping a calmer, less needling tone, "all right," but then hasn't quite brought herself to say *It's okay* or *Everything will be fine*, when there's a knock at the open door. Turning, she finds two second-grade teachers huddled in the doorway. "Oh my. Everyone say good afternoon to Sister Bernadette and Mrs. Sales."

"Good afternoon, Sister Bernadette. Good afternoon, Mrs. Sales."

"We hope we're not disturbing you," the petite, smiling nun says, the hem of her collared black dress touching the tops of her girlish knees, "We just wanted to . . ."

"There it is!" the sandy-haired Mrs. Sales exclaims, pointing to the cross leaning yet against the windows, where it appears even more striking now, semi-silhouetted and glowing about the edges with noon sun.

"Oh yes, it *is* quite remarkable," Sister Bernadette says.

"And such wonderful costumes," Mrs. Sales adds, indicating Brian and Joey.

Liz, blushing, gestures quickly to Danny. "This boy made the cross himself."

"Yes, that's the one," Mrs. Sales says.

"Remarkable," Sister Bernadette repeats, nodding briefly at him. And now to Liz, "Could we speak to you outside a moment?"

"Of course," she says, scurrying out, and the door's barely closed behind her when Danny steps closer to Timmy to underscore some important points. "There's only *one* more day to practice."

"One more day after today, right?"

"Yeah, but today's almost over," Danny says, looking at his watch. "How are you going to learn your lines in one day if you haven't been able to learn them in a whole week?"

"You don't think I'll be able to now?" the boy asks, nervously shuffling his cards.

Danny raises his eyebrows doubtfully, then indicates an overstuffed sleeve of his tan robe. "You know you have to take that off when you're crucified."

"I do?" Timmy says, wincing.

"You have to stand in front of everyone in just the towel," Danny says, touching his own hips, "like you're getting out of the shower."

"No undershirt?"

He shakes his head firmly. "Bare."

And now, suddenly, the ever-bugging eyes narrow. "Nu-uh," he says, "I'm only gonna do it if I can wear a T-shirt."

"But you can't. Look at Him." Danny points for evidence to the naked-titties figure on the crucifix above the door.

Timmy frowns at it. "I'm not skinny like that. Everyone will laugh at my belly." He clasps it protectively. "Maybe I'll ask Miss Kaigh if I can do it with my undershirt anyway."

"No," Danny says, "Matt already asked her that."

"He did?"

"And she said, 'Whoever plays Jesus has to wear just the towel at the end and I don't want to hear any complaining.'"

"She did?"

"She got really mad. You better not bring it up again."

And quite to the point, Miss Kaigh reenters the classroom nearly screaming, "Daniel, you didn't tell me about the parking lot!"

"The parking lot?" several ask.

"They're all talking about it downstairs," she says to him, ignoring their question.

"Who is?" Frances asks. "About the play?" Rory asks.

"The second grade, the third grade." And now she paces before the board. "I don't know what we're going to do."

"Do about what, Miss Kaigh?" "Are you all right?"

"Nothing. Yes. Back to Pilate, let's go." Oh, but shouldn't she have a cigarette first? Won't she have a nervous breakdown if she doesn't? "What time is it? Oh my gosh." Just minutes left, no chance at all. "Everyone in your places. Hurry!"

Rushing home awkwardly with his book bag and two shopping bags full of props—"These are terrible, Daniel," Miss Kaigh said, snatching up laurel wreaths, swords, helmets, "Can you do something with them? Tonight?"—Danny bitterly reviews the image of Timmy shouldering the cross to the front of the classroom, the undeserving lead flanked by the tunicked soldiers, and loyal John, and the weeping women-girls, all without costumes yet save Frances, and still it had looked *spectacular*, even Miss Kaigh said so. "That cross is really something. It makes the whole scene!" And Danny, from his seat in the ellipse outside of it all, could only console himself by imagining Timmy a kind of Simon of Cyrene, temporarily relieving him of his load until he could somehow, with God's grace, carry it himself on Wednesday. And now, just inside his front door, he drops his bags on the floor and rummages through his books, at last producing the sealed invitation and tearing it open.

Be Our Guest! the cover exclaims. And inside, over ruled lines, *Dear Mrs. Burke— I and the students of 5B would like to request the honor of your attendance at the performance of "The Passion and the Resurrection of*

Christ" this Wednesday, 11 o'clock, in the Music Hall at Our Lady of Perpetual Help. It's just as he feared, all the information so clear and correct! It would not be the same without you, who has given us so much professional assistance and guidance. I look forward to meeting you. Gratefully, Miss Elizabeth Kaigh.

As Danny reddens and touches his fingers to his lips, he happens on the idea of removing the first 1 in 11. That would be terrible, of course, his mother going to all the trouble to make it up to the school, only to arrive long after the play's over. Still, if she wasn't carrying the card with her, it could be blamed on her own memory: You must have thought it said 1 and not 11, he'd say, and, It's a mistake anyone might make, his teacher could add. And so he hunts for Wite-Out, the little crusted-capped bottles his mother brings home from work, ultimately locating one in the junk drawer not far from Miss Kaigh's first card. Then at the kitchen table, after practicing on a piece of scrap paper, he lightly brushes the liquid camouflage over the numeral and, patting it down with his pinky and filing the edges with his nail, proceeds to his mother's closet and takes a similarly sized envelope from a box of leftover Christmas cards and rewrites the inscription in his teacher's hand. At last he rushes upstairs with the resealed invitation, changes into his corduroys and sweatshirt, and steals out to the shed.

But a while later, he's still sitting on the wooden chair in his ski mask and Pro-Keds, the hard edges of the seat making grooves in his naked hams, not having found the nerve to streak across the backyard in the daylight. Time and again, he's approached the door, stuck his head out, peered all around the yards and over at the Maher house, seen no one, and yet retreated anyway. He can't shake the fear that there's someone somewhere, behind a window or door, who'll see, and so, for boredom's sake now, he fiddles with his father's transistor radio, then leans forward, elbows on his knees, folding and unfolding his hands, Watch the Yankee game yesterday, Dad?

Oh yeah, Arram says, leaning back and looking away, lips pulled in like a toothless Mowgli.

See Whatshisname get a homer at the bottom of the ninth?

Oh yeah.

Sheez, he's got some swing, that guy.

Oh yeah.

And just in the middle of this tortured exchange, the call comes: "Daaaan-ny Daaaan-ny!"

He jumps to the little window and spies her on the stoop in her beige overcoat and good shoes. Then she scans the yard and calls again, and he continues to watch, heart thumping, fending off the urge to get dressed, and even going so far as to imagine bursting out the door that second and racing across the yard in front of her. However, as she retreats and swings the door shut, he quickly dresses and dashes around to the front stoop, there fishing out his keys and unlocking the door. And not until he's wiping his feet on the mat and he hears her sharper voice, "Is that you, smarty pants?" does any dread awaken in him—that, for instance, Miss Kaigh may just have phoned.

"I was calling for you. Where were you?" she says, scowling as she emerges from the bedroom in her after-work slacks and blouse.

"Out-out-out-side."

"I thought I told you to take the back roads with that cross this morning," she says.

"Oh," he says. He'd forgotten all about the morning. "I-I-I—"

"Not one, but two of the girls at work said they saw you walking down Main Street with it. A *teacher* came in and said he saw you outside Stanley's Bakery."

"The b-b-b—?"

"Don't play dumb with me, mister. You went down to Dixie and then right back up to Main Street when I couldn't see, isn't that right?"

He raises his eyebrows and juts his lips out, making the lying fish face.

"You wanted to carry that cross where everyone would see, that's what I can't understand. I can't think of any reason why—"

"I was a pilgrim," he explains.

"A *what?*"

"It was a special journey for God."

"Special journey for God? Uh! Uh! Oh, this is too much now; I've had enough of *this*. Danny, you don't actually believe you're Christ, do you?"

He draws his head back, blinking.

"Do you? Because that's a—that's a—" She tries to recall the list from the *Psychology Today* article she once read: the alphabetized phobias, delusions . . . "*Messiah complex.* Don't tell me you have one of those."

"No," he says, repelled by the new phrase, its harsh *-ex* word beside the lovely Jesus name. "I don't have *that.*"

"I hope not. I don't want a lunatic for a son!" But regardless, he deliberately disobeyed her; she can't just let that go. *If this nonsense doesn't stop, I'll have to speak to your father,* she's about to say but holds back, because that was always the first sign of things spoiling before, pulling out the I'll-tell-your-father. And now quite unexpectedly again, she feels her eyes tearing. What is it with her? She shakes her head, steels herself. "I won't tell your father you deliberately disobeyed me if you promise there won't be any more of this pilgrim-and-special-journey stuff."

Right away his eyes widen. "T-T-Tell *Dad?*"

"I said I wouldn't."

"All right."

"But I don't want this to happen again. If I tell you something, you listen."

"All right."

"I explained to everyone that the cross was for the Easter play, that they asked you to make the props because you're the best artist in the school, that's all. And that's what I want you to say if anyone asks you about it, agreed? And if it's one of the teachers or administrators—" though how would he ever run into a teacher or administrator? "—don't tell them you wrote it and are playing the king, none of that."

"Okay."

However, now she remembers the streaking boy the night before and Danny's messy hair when he came down from his room. In fact, it looks messy again now—where was he just before? He never said, and she wonders if she shouldn't talk to Dr. Shapiro after all, just to make sure he doesn't have a complex, or even the beginnings of one. But just as easily, she rejects the idea—that kind of thing's bound to get around, her kid visiting the psychologist; it would label him. And her. And oh brother, if Gerry ever found out, he'd have a shit-fit. *You're sending him to a shrink? What the hell is wrong with you?*

"I thought you were the one kid I wasn't going to have any problems with."

"Huh?" Danny says, his mouth dropping open, and he wants to add, *I'm not a problem*. Is he? Like his brothers were, and Sharon? Is he *now*? "I'm sorry," he says. Still she frowns and walks for the kitchen, not saying *all right* or *okay*, and he lingers for a moment, wondering if he should follow her and apologize again. But before he can decide to, the thought *Tomorrow is the dress rehearsal* sails at him, and, with so many props to make and fix, he rushes to his room, leaving all else at bay.

There he works with special concentration and productivity, fashioning a cardboard ear to fall to the ground during the arrest skirmish and painting it in flesh tones and touches of red. Then he refurbishes the laurel wreaths and helmets and swords, accenting them with glitter and thumbtacks and painted macaroni shells. And finally, just as the phone rings downstairs and he starts and listens for the timbre of his mother's voice to betray whether it's someone she knows or doesn't know—knows, it seems—he turns to the crown of thorns, also made of cardboard, jaggedly cut, but to his mind not real or sharp-looking enough. And now as he hears his mother say "okay, see you then" and hang up the phone, he leaps up and grabs the invitation from his desk.

"Who was that?" he asks in the kitchen, and she looks up from the opened paper on the table, squinting annoyedly.

"Betty. Why, nosy?"

"Nothing," he says, handing her the card.

"*Oh*," Carol says, her stomach dropping intuitively as she recognizes the fastidious script. Then again it might just be another thank-you for the robes, she thinks, but this flicker of hope is immediately doused when she tears it open. Dammit, she was hoping to get away with not going. *Professional assistance*. "Boy, she's really got some fancy phrases. Well, you know, Danny, one o'clock is kind of late; it's not so easy for me to leave work for an hour in the middle of the afternoon." Which is absolutely untrue, many times she's taken lunch at one. "And why's she inviting *me*? I thought this was just for the kids."

"It is," he says.

That just figures to Carol: do them a little favor, try not to be an un-involved mother, and they lasso you into going to the whole perfor-mance. She sighs and gets up to toss the card into the junk drawer. "Guess I'm just one of the lucky ones, made the A-list." But as she sits down again, the snotty tone of her remark repeats in her mind and she glances guiltily at him. "I'll see what I can do," she says, already plan-ning to show up late. *The business manager insisted we finish the budget reports before lunch. I told him I had my son's play but he just wouldn't hear of it.* Or she could run up there a little early, make a quick appearance, and then duck out after it begins. *I may have to leave before the end,* she'll warn them, *the business manager's insisting we finish the budget re-ports this afternoon.* She'd like to duck out right before the king comes on. And now it hits her, "The Music Hall? Isn't that where they have bingo?"

"Uh-huh."

"That's pretty big in there." She frowns at the runaway highfalutin-ness of it all: invitations, *Classical Masterpieces*, music hall. Next they'll be selling signed catalogues. "Doesn't your teacher think she's going a little overboard? It's just your class play."

"I don't know," he says.

On the other hand, it might be easier to duck out of a bigger room, Carol thinks, looking back to her double acrostic. And Danny, for his part—as he slips out the backdoor now and walks toward the woods at the end of the yard—is relieved she didn't seem to notice the Wite-Out. In fact, he believes there's a chance she'll forget about the invi-tation altogether, if he doesn't remind her, which he has no intention of doing. And now, stopping in the shed for a pair of clippers, he con-siders some mismatched gardening gloves but decides against them, so his task will be more dangerous and lifelike, and, some yards into the undergrowth he finds, among the many budding oak branches, the faint olive-green vinings. He clips the thickest vines with the largest thorns, extracting them with difficulty from their winding, toothy neighbors, and lays them at his feet. After clipping half a dozen or more, he gathers them one by one, curling his scratched and stinging fingers between the prickers—a luxury, he realizes, Jesus Himself wouldn't have had—and makes his careful way back, the unwieldy sprigs bouncing menacingly before him.

When Carol looks up again from the paper, her mouth drops open, for now her son is holding what appears to be a sticker bush bouquet, like one of those sinister arrangements the long-haired girl on *The Addams Family* makes, snipping all the rose blossoms from their stems. He's actually bringing this thing into the house.

"Oh, you shouldn't have," she jokes desperately, but neither of them laughs, and he looks at her earnestly, as if to explain. "I do *not* want to know," she says, only hoping he doesn't intend to hit himself with them. What's that called, self-whipping? self- . . . something: monks. At this point, she wouldn't think it entirely out of the question. He may have read about the monks somewhere, seen them on TV, whipping themselves silly because they weren't holy enough or because they'd eaten a tiny bit of something delicious. cheese. *Danny, you're not going to hit yourself with them, are you?* But she can't say this; she's leery, on the one hand, of seeming as crazy as he does, and on the other, of putting such an idea into his head if it isn't there already, and so she merely grunts and frowns. Danny, too, remains silent, then proceeds to his room and drops the stickers on his carpet and sits down among them, braiding a custom-fitting, unholy halo, the layers bound together with string for extra security, some stained with a bead of blood from his fingers when the thorns pierce deeper than expected. Then at the end of his trouble, when he rushes to the mirror, carefully lowering the crown until the innermost thorns touch his scalp, his own mouth drops open, for never before has he seen one so terrifyingly, so beautifully real!

To complete the picture, he imagines his hair longer and brown and parted in the middle, imagines blood and soldier spit dripping down his face. But not content with the thought alone, he spits in his hand and smears the saliva onto his forehead and cheeks. Then he kneads out additional bits of blood from his pricked fingertips and mixes these among the spit; and while the resultant pink glaze is pleasing enough in its own right, it's not the running red he's after, and, quickly removing the crown and wiping his face, he rushes down to the kitchen, where, his mother luckily occupied in the bathroom, he grabs a handful of McDonald's ketchup packets from the refrigerator, then races back upstairs and redons the crown. With great fervency, he applies heavier doses of spit to his cheeks and squirts the sweet, pulpy contents of a packet across his forehead. And it runs, yes, in startlingly red rivulets into his eyebrows and over his cheekbones, making his stomach dry heave, his eyes sting with tears. Through them, he stares with awed horror at his besmirched image in the mirror, imagining the rough soldiers all around, jostling him and smiting him with the reed: *All hail the King of the Jews! Ah ha ha!*

∼ 14 ∼

Curly's Calling

In the mercilessly punctual school morning, Liz, bleary-eyed and on edge from having sewed into the wee hours again and *still* not finished all the costumes, runs headlong into a nightmarish and entirely unexpected snag: going out to retrieve her students from the lot, Christ isn't among them. At first she doesn't believe it can be possible, but when she checks the line of boys again, his tinted glasses and bushy hair are nowhere to be found.

"What's happened to Timothy? Why isn't he here?"

"I don't know," the students say.

"What's going on?" she asks Danny.

But the boy quickly shakes his head. "I-I-I don't know."

"Wasn't he on the bus?" she asks Ginger and Stacy, who ride with him.

"No," they say, "he wasn't."

"He is coming to school today, isn't he?" she says, trying to contain her panic, but when the girls say they don't know again, she clenches her fists and cries, "This is terrible! I hope nothing's happened," looking left and right to the entrances, bereft of rushing boys, in-turning cars. "What are we going to do if he doesn't show?"

But no one knows. And so she leads them upstairs and, as they're putting their book bags in the closets—or, in the case of several girls, stopping to hold up summer sandals, "Look, Miss Kaigh!" "Not now," she says—paces across the front of the classroom, paces for the second time in as many days, when she's never known herself to pace before; it feels so old-fashioned, so idiotic, yet she's not inclined to stop. Maybe she should check the office, she thinks, staring at this new empty desk with disbelief. It just seems cruel to her, a kind of plot: six grades coming and their lead not showing up for the dress rehearsal, their lead who hasn't completely memorized his lines yet. "Six grades coming," she says aloud, "and no Christ."

"*Six?*" several say.

"First through sixth," she says.

And even Danny, head bowed to hide his breathless hope, thinks that's extremely vast now, a multitude or more.

"That's almost the whole school," Frances notes.

"You guys better be good," another says—Herman.

Liz spins at the pug-nosed boy, ready to lash out, *Keep it to yourself, you deserter, you imp!* But before coming up with an utterable equivalent, she spies a woman in the hall in a windbreaker and plain slacks and flats. A yard mother?

Now the woman knocks on the open door, "Miss Kaigh?"

"Yes?" Liz says, rushing over, and just beyond the doorway, cowering out of sight, there he is—hair, glasses, and all. "Timothy!" she says, and then to the woman, whose own hair is of a familial bushy-brown, "Mrs. Miller! Of course. You don't know how happy I am to see you."

"Well, maybe not," the woman says.

"Maybe not?" Liz says, quickly stepping into the hall and pulling the door closed behind her. "Is something wrong?"

"Timmy wanted me to—"

"We were all so worried when he didn't show up. You know he's playing Christ in our Easter play, the lead role!"

"Well, you see, that's just it. He's so upset about that darn play. Last night I caught him crying in his room."

"Crying?"

"Mommy, don't tell her."

"Yes, Timmy. Then this morning when he got up, he begged me to come here and speak to you. He's terrified." And now as she puts her arm around him, he actually does begin to cry, covering his face with both his hands. "He thinks he's going to forget his lines, and everyone will make fun of him. It's all right, Timmy," she says, patting his back, her own eyes gone glassy.

Liz steps back from the sobbing embrace, casting a blushing look around the hall—empty, thank goodness, otherwise he'd be a laughingstock. "I don't know what to say," she manages. "I don't understand why he's so worried. We've been practicing every day, he's been doing so well. Have you considered that it may just be a case of stage fright? That's so natural. Everyone gets nervous the day before, the best actors in the world. I'm sure he'll be fine; everyone will love him, and clap. You'll be fine, Timothy, really," she says to the boy's moist, shielding fingers, and even smiles and claps herself, this more for his mother's benefit. Yet despite this ardent performance, Mrs. Miller shakes her head decidedly.

"I'm sorry, but I'd rather you had one of the other boys play Christ."

"Pardon me?" Liz says. But indeed, the woman repeats the request: another boy play Christ. "Oh my."

"I know it's very soon."

"Oh no, not just soon, *tomorrow.*"

But now Mrs. Miller looks at her squarely and frowns, on the verge of saying something unpleasant, it seems, something quite firm, when Liz rushes in with, "Well, of course, of course. If he's so upset, he doesn't have to. It's all volunteer, it's—I thought he would've wanted to play Christ. It's such an honor." And here she adds, "Everyone wanted to, but we chose him," assuming the boy won't contradict her mid-fit. "He can play one of the smaller parts if he wants. Timothy, would you like to be one of the apostles, instead?" Finally the boy drops his hands, nodding and sniffling. *How about Judas?* she thinks, bitterly picturing him in the striped robe.

"That would be fine," Mrs. Miller says. Then after her son's collected himself and she's made her triumphant, flat-footed exit, Liz leads the boy back into the classroom.

"Oh!" the students murmur, and "He's here, Miss Kaigh!" Juanita observes.

"I'm aware of that," Liz snaps.

"Aren't you glad?"

No, she nearly says, sending Timmy to his seat and glancing at Danny. But the scarlet-cheeked redhead immediately looks down at his desk, unable to meet her eyes, and now her glance becomes a glare. He's caused this to happen, she intuits suddenly, caused it in some direct, malevolent way. Maybe terrorized the boy when she wasn't around, whispered all kinds of poison in his ear. She can just see it, wolf in sheep's clothes, angel-faced Iago; had her fooled all along. But no, what's wrong with her? *Is* she losing her mind now? He's just a boy; she can't blame him for Timmy's fearfulness, for his babying, meddling mother. And yet, if he didn't cause it directly, then indirectly, by the sheer force of his will, his enormous little will that's hung over this project from the very beginning—and this will combined with the force of a thousand prayers, for no doubt he's been praying every day of the past week for Timmy to quit like the others. Well, they say God hears the prayers of children, and maybe it's true, for He certainly doesn't seem to hear any of the adults'. Then all at once she spins to the board, alarmed to discover her own eyes are welling. Oh please, not here, in front of them, she thinks, snatching up a nub of chalk, as if to write something.

And now behind her, all heads crane toward the back of the room. But the boy, under a barrage of whispered questions from his neighbors, keeps his bushy head bowed, refusing to acknowledge anyone. Danny faces front again, his thoughts a whirl of worries as to what Mrs. Miller said in the hall. Did Timmy tell on him? Is that why Miss Kaigh looked at him so meanly? And will he be punished now? Banished from his own play?

Finally, "What's the matter, Miss Kaigh?" Frances asks. And Matt, "Do we have an assignment to do?"

But Liz, staring at the blurry board, shakes her head and manages, "I'm trying to . . . um . . ." all the while tapping the chalk until the tears have safely receded. Then she places the nub back on the ledge, turns around, and begins the day's lessons as if the mother hadn't come, the play not been ruined. And she proceeds this way throughout the morning and on through lunch, shaking her head whenever thoughts of their new fate press at her, and avoiding the eyes of Timmy and Danny. Later, as the students file outside for recess and her players, still seated in their desks, look up at her, she parts her lips, as if now to face it and tell them, but instead says, "I've arranged for us to have our dress rehearsal in the Music Hall. Everyone grab something and follow me." Then she leads her excitedly murmuring company, with their big cross and Garden trees and brimming bags of props and costumes, down the hall and north stairwell, and on across the parking lot.

Here Danny, at the rear of the procession, finds nerve to ask the silent, straggling Timmy what happened—to no avail, for the boy only stares at his plodding feet and shakes his bowed head. "Why won't you look at me? Why won't you tell me? Please, Timmy?" Still he hasn't answered by the time they reach the gray building near the rectory and climb its creaky side ramp to a door beneath a worn placard proclaiming, O   ady's   sic Ha ; and there Mr. Loughlin, the ever-stooping, pink-faced custodian, meets them with his ring of keys.

"So these are the little stars and starlets," he says with a lingering brogue.

"Oh yes, ha ha," Liz says, the children giggling behind her with more ease and sincerity.

"Did you ever see such a cross?" he says, kicking the bottom of the door as he turns the lock. "And what have you there? Ferns?"

"Olive trees."

"Oh sure. It's quite a production." And now the door swings free, and he reaches inside to turn on the overhead lights. "'Fraid I haven't finished the sweepin' yet. Have it all done by tomorrow. Got to lug over a bunch more chairs!" He whistles and rolls his eyes, then rushes off to his countless other duties, telling them to break a leg, to break all their legs, every last one of 'em.

"Thank you," Liz says. "Everybody say thank you to Mr. Loughlin."

"Thank you, Mr. Loughlin."

Then as they enter the hall, Liz, tilting her head back to take in the whole high ceiling, replete with pockmarks and tea-colored water stains, has the immediate impression of them as so many Jacks pattering across the floor of the giant's castle, their little murmurs and squeaks pinging off the tan-paneled walls, stirring the dust-moted air. "I didn't remember it being *this* big," she says. Danny, terrified too by its size, is even more unnerved by the light streaming down from the unshaded windows. It's not at all cavelike and comfortable, as he remembers Radio City, the audience nestled in row after row of blankety shadows. Here they'll be able to see everyone, even way in the back; it'll be like putting a play on outside in the bright daylight. "Look!" Kevin and Paolo say, dropping their bags and bending for translucent red and blue disks between the legs of scattered folding chairs. "Bingo chips!"

"Oh wow!" Juanita says. "I want some."

"No, leave them," Liz says, grimacing at the dust and crushed cigarette butts, as welcome as one of the latter would be in its former, ignited state. "This floor is filthy."

"You mean, we're going to put the play on up *there?*" Joey says, pointing at the ridiculously high stage to their left, as if it were a distant shore.

"Cool!" Brian says, running for the steps on its left side, his loud foot slaps reverberating violently against the walls and ceiling.

"Hey, where are you going?" Liz yells. "Get back here!" And the hall yells back, *Get back here!* To her relief, the boy turns around. "Is everything going to echo like that?" she asks.

"I don't know!" Kevin shouts. *I don't know!* the walls say.

"Oh boy. Well, I hope it won't be so bad when—" she's about to say *all the children get here*, but stops herself and instead brushes off the seat of the nearest chair and sits down, a handful of the students following suit.

"Miss Kaigh, aren't you excited?" Juanita asks. "It's so great! A real stage!" And the others, "When can we go up there? Are we starting yet? Should we put our costumes on?"

"No," she says. "Quiet, everyone." And as all of them now—with the exception of Timmy, sitting on a chair at some remove—gather about her, she's intending to use the straightforward word *quit* in her explanation of what the boy's done, but it comes out as, "Timothy has resigned from the role of Christ," and the rest of the players grouse in unison, none louder than Danny himself, their heads snapping back at the boy, who immediately looks at his feet. "Resigned?" "Resigned?" they say, as appalled by the word, it seems, as what it represents.

"The way it stands now," Liz continues, "we have no lead. And without a lead, there's no play."

"No play?" they say.

"N-N-No play?" Danny repeats, struggling to stay in his chair.

"Do any of you other boys feel you know Christ's lines?" Liz asks, looking doubtfully from Rory to Paolo to Joey to Brian, each of their heads bowing in succession. And it's clear to Danny, then, that she's deliberately not looking at him, as she isn't at Timmy, as if he were as out of the question. "Well, you have to know some of them, you've been hearing them every day."

"Yeah, you guys," Juanita says, "'It is you who say I am king.' 'What do you, betray the Son of Man with a kiss?' Want me to try, Miss Kaigh?"

"No, Juanita. The boys are going to. Let's have the robe," she says, pointing to the bags. And after Frances and Ginger pick out the article and carry it over by the shoulders, she has Rory put it on first and kneel before the group: "My soul. Is sad. Even unto. Death," he says, launching his short-lived audition, followed by Paolo's, Paolo's by Joey's: "My soul is sad," "My soul is sad," one more horrendous than the next; and the tan robe, passing hand to hand. At last it's given to Brian, who offers the most impressive rendition of the line by far, so impressive Liz gets up from her chair. "Oh, why couldn't you have volunteered on the first day? Look how good you would've been!" Despite the hour, she has the players in the first scene climb onstage and set up the Garden—Danny among them, placing the wobbly olive trees, then feigning sleep on the dusty floor as yet another boy, the best boy of all, asks to have his cup taken away. And the opening goes well enough to worry him, and for Liz's heart to uncrumple ever so slightly—but briefly. Even by the end of the first speech, Brian begins to trip over the lines, then to read them word for word from a tattered script.

"*Yesss,*" Danny hisses into the crook of his arm; and, "Oh no, oh no, it's terrible," Liz says, shaking her head. "You'll never learn them all."

"But what else are we going to do?" Rory says.

"Yeah, what are we going to do?" Joey says. "No one knows them. No one but . . ."

Then one by one their eyes turn to him, sitting up at Brian's right, arms crossed over his racing heart.

". . . Curly."

And the girls begin to argue his case: "Miss Kaigh, he's done it before." "He's done it when no one else would." "He did it after Herman and Matt quit."

"I know all that," Liz says, "but—" *he'll stutter, he'll freeze with fear. It'll be ruined either way, with or without him.*

"But, Mith Kaigh, he'th the only one left." "It's tomorrow." "It's better than not having the play at all." "We've got all our costumes." "And the cross." "And six grades are coming." "Please, Miss Kaigh?" the girls say, and then the entire troupe, "Please?" "Please?" *Please?* an insistent, echoing chorus; and finally, grudgingly, and for the first time since the morning, she looks at the bracing, open-mouthed boy, particularly at his hair. Then against all markers of good judgment she knows, and with the dim hope of picking up some kind of costume wig at the five-and-ten on her way home, she says, "All right, Daniel, it looks like you've gotten your wish."

And now as he wobbles to his feet, real cheers on every side, "Yea!" *Yea!* "We'll have the play!" *We'll have the play!* he stares at the opened robe the blond boy proffers, dazed as if struck by hammers. "Go ahead, put it on," the players say. "Come on, Danny," Brian says, roughly working one, and then the other, of his arms into the sleeves—familiar and fitting, his father's scorned Christmas present, returned to him. "Yea! Danny's Jesus! We'll have the play!" *We'll have the play!*

"I'm Jesus," he murmurs, and all at once a delayed, electric jolt zings through his body, and he stiffens with terror.

~ 15 ~

The Power of United Prayer

And the terror lingers about him, a constant, bedeviling companion, as his former rival is quickly Petered—"Basically all you have to say is 'I do not know the man.' Can you manage *that?*" "I think so"—and all the while Miss Kaigh directs them to the storage areas to the left of the stage, two of which, cluttered with old podiums and music stands and a disassembled altar, she designates as dressing rooms, the third, empty but for collections of lumber scraps and a small wooden ramp, the offstage tomb. Then the terror's fast on his heels as he emerges with the others, and they race and collide and stagger across the stage in a chaotic, abbreviated rehearsal. "That wasn't enough; we'll have to run through it again tomorrow morning." And it dogs him on their way across the parking lot, and all through the worried debate of how the cross will be kept upright now that there's no chalk ledge to lean it against, and the equally worried decision that Joey's father will make a slotted stand that the base can be slipped into, and drive it over in his truck. And then it sits beside him in the classroom during the sandal-making project that spreads out over what would've been science and math, Miss Kaigh repeatedly warning them not to make the soles too big. "Is everyone checking to make sure they're not too big?" "Yes." Just after this, as it becomes clear to Danny that she wants the players to run through the entire script from their desks, the terror bristles and growls.

"B-B-But M-M-Miss K-K-Kaigh," he says, raising his hand and boldly approaching her desk without permission, "you mean n-n-now?" Because, he wants to point out, there are other children present, nearly twenty of them.

"Well, yes, of course," she whispers back, brow furrowing with strain.

"In fr-front of everyone?"

"What do you mean everyone, Daniel? This is just a small group of students, your own class. If you can't do it in front of them, how will you do it tomorrow in front of all the others?"

And so he sits down again, flushed and sweating, and the reading begins, "My-My-My-My s-s-s-soul is s-s-s-sad," and right away the giggling and snorting, first restrained, then unleashed. "Cut that out," Miss Kaigh says, herself blushing. "Louder, Daniel!" she tells him when his voice drops, and "Louder!" she tells the others when theirs do, and "Listen for your cue!" when they come in late.

"You guys don't seem ready at all," Matt observes between scenes.

"How is that constructive criticism?" Miss Kaigh barks.

"I'm just saying."

"Well, don't."

Only later, when Brian and Joey bellow their jeers during the scourging, does her expression lighten and do all the students cheer and clap. Then as the Roman trial resumes, and the offstage characters, led by Stephen and Kevin, speak in the voice of the crowd, she looks to the others and says, "Come on, everyone, let's help them out: 'Crucify Him! Crucify Him!'"

"Crucify Him! Crucify Him!" they say, at first meekly and dissonantly. "Louder! Shout! Like an angry mob!" Miss Kaigh goads, and their voices lift and join together, "Crucify Him! Crucify Him!"—a vociferous, terrifying chant. And Danny, looking from one to another of their shaking fists, their pink, snarling faces, feels his breath catch, as if he were indeed about to die.

Go! Arram says, and they bolt out the shed door, racing for the second tree.

Oh my God, Danny cries, looking left and right at the whizzing blur of woods, lawn, neighbors' windows, *we're running in the light!*

Naked in the light! Arram yells.

Cool! Danny says, heart drumming wildly as the sun and wind swaddle his stiffening, ga-binging dickie. And now, *Slap! Slap!* and they race back, bursting in through the shed door with laughter so breathless and violent that, if not for the figure in the powder-blue pantsuit Danny spies stepping down from the Mahers' back stoop, he fears it might have gone on to choke him or literally split his side. But at once the laughter stops mid-spasm, replaced by an all-pervading dread, for now the figure, its teased dark hair sporting its distinguishing dip, ventures closer to their yard.

"Who was that? Is someone in that shed?" she yells, stopping at the property line and planting her fists on her hips. "Is someone there? I said. Answer me."

He ducks down from the window, frantically dressing and hiding the ski mask, then tosses a crumpled and web-sticky tarp over the mower and seeder handles and crouches warily beneath it. But quite soon, when the legions of imaginary spiders creeping over his neck and scalp get the better of him, he springs up and sits in the chair and dials the radio to the Carpenters' "Sing, sing a song" which, under different circumstances, he might've danced happily to with Arram. Now, however, he imagines his neighbor peering in through the window and pulling the door open, *There is someone in here!*

Oh hello, Mrs. Maher.

Don't play dumb with me, mister. I saw you running naked across the lawn!

Oh no, Mrs. Maher. I've just been sitting here with all my clothes on, listening to the radio. I've just been singing. 'La la la la la . . .'

All this time you've been singing?

Yes. It must've been some other boy you saw.

Hmm, she'd say, then somehow leave. And only after imagining several of these scenarios and half hearing "You're So Vain" and "Ain't No Woman (Like the One I've Got)" does Danny find the nerve to inch up to the window again and peer out. His neighbor's yard empty, he dashes to the house and up to his room, where he paces from window to door, door to window, blushing and muttering, "Is someone there? Is someone in that shed?" until all at once he hears them: the muted, angry voices on the street.

He leaps up and runs to the playroom and its window that faces the street; there, beside the telephone pole and small, isolated birch tree at the far corner of their lawn, his mother and neighbor are scowling and waving their hands at one another. "Oh no!" he says, fumbling to lift the sash.

"*Robby?*" his mother's saying. "Robby doesn't even live at home anymore."

"I just saw him," Mrs. Maher counters shrilly.

"Then maybe you're seeing things."

"I most certainly am not seeing things. I saw a naked boy in a ski mask run right into that shed of yours in the back—"

"Well, maybe so," his mother says, "but how am I to be responsible for every naked kid that decides to run into my shed while I'm not home?"

"—and it's not like they haven't done it before."

"That was years ago."

"At least that was at night! Now they're doing it in the broad daylight!"

"Lower your voice!" his mother yells.

"I will not lower my voice!" Mrs. Maher yells back. "You lower your voice!"

"I will not lower my voice!"

"Fine!" Mrs. Maher says, crossing her arms.

And "Fine!" Danny's mother says, winning with the louder *fine*. "I'm not going to stand here and listen to this," then she turns sharply for the house.

"Oh yeah? Well, let me tell you something, lady," the neighbor says, dogging her to the very limit of their driveway and shaking her fist at his mother's rapidly receding back. "If I see another naked boy in that yard, I'm calling the police. And I'll press charges!"

"Press them up your ass," his mother grumbles, rooting through her pocketbook now for her keys, and Danny can see, from his breathless perch above, that her hands are shaking.

"What did you say?"

"I said, Have a nice day!" his mother shouts over her shoulder.

"I will when you move out of here!" Mrs. Maher shouts back.

At last his mother steps into the house, slamming the door behind her, and Danny runs to the landing. "Mom, what's the matter?" But she glares up at him, eyes wild and unfocused.

"Did you hear how that . . . that . . . ? I've never heard such . . . such . . ." she sputters, nose and lips twitching with stifled, savage curses, and finally, "Little smart-ass son of a bitch. I've a mind to—oooooh!"

Then she storms down the hall for the kitchen, only to storm back again to the stairs. "Danny," she demands of her son, who freezes mid-descent, "was Robby here?" Because on second thought, it doesn't seem entirely implausible that he might return to wreak some old-time vengeance.

"R-R-Robby? H-He doesn't come into the house."

"I know that. Was he out in the yard? Did you hear his motorcycle?"

"I-I didn't hear anything."

But just then Carol, after peering out the window to make sure her neighbor's gone, notices her son's hair is once again messy and flat, and groans. "All right, what's going on?" And at the same time madly considers they may be in cahoots: his older brother haunting the house when she's not around, spoiling her last white sheep. "Who is this boy? Do you know something about him?"

"B-B-Boy?" Danny says, backing up a step.

"The streaker from Sunday night. He was out there again today in the broad daylight."

"H-How do you know?"

"Mrs. *Maher*," she cries, lips curling around the hated name, "said she just saw him. Oh God, and now she's probably on the phone already with Mrs. Vesely. She'll have this story up and down the street in five minutes." But here, Carol suddenly recalls Madame Sarah's warning about a friend and grasps at it, her tone momentarily lightening. "Danny, is it some boy in the neighborhood or at school? Some troublemaker you're hanging out with you don't want me to know about?"

Danny squints fearfully, as if she's peered into his thoughts, but then, assuring himself that she must be referring to some actual boy, says, "I-I-I didn't see anyone."

"You didn't?"

"No," he says honestly.

"Is it you?" she blurts out.

"Huh?" he says, stomach leaping fiercely.

"I know that boys do this sometimes, for God knows what reason. I didn't think you were the type to, but now I'm not sure. Why's your hair so messy?"

"My hair?" he says, quickly fluffing it.

"It looked that way Sunday, after I saw the boy. And yesterday, too, when I came home from work. Where were you when I called you? Out in the shed, by any chance?"

"The sh-sh-sh—?"

"I want to hear you tell me you're not this boy."

"I'm-I'm-I'm not, Mom."

"Would you swear on the Bible?"

"Yes," he says, believing it a hypothetical question, but then she tells him to get it, and he stutters with special intensity, "G-G-G-G—?"

"Did you hear me?"

Dashing to the bookcase, he hoists up the volume, then walks down again, slower, stopping on the third step just beyond her reach—for fear, also, that she'll take it from him and inspect the pages.

But in fact, she doesn't reach for the book at all, or even regard it much, as she tells him to lay his right hand on the cover. And so he cradles the tome lengthwise in his left arm like a heavy, squarish baby and places his trembling hand directly over the ornately bordered picture of the Holy Family, blinding them to the proceedings.

"You're a Catholic schoolboy and you're swearing on a blessed Bible," she informs him. "If you lie now, you're lying to God, and terrible things will happen to you, far worse than any punishment your own father could give you. Do you understand?"

He looks away, barely nodding.

"Now repeat after me: 'I, Daniel Burke—'"

"I-I-I, D-D-Daniel B-B-Burke—"

"'—am not the streaker boy.'"

In an attempt to save himself from mortal sin, he looks straight into his mother's eyes, so as to hold them while he crosses the fingers in his left hand, partially concealed beneath the book. And indeed, it's this earnest expression which, together with Carol's conviction that her son's fanatical piousness wouldn't allow him to swear falsely to God, persuades her to take his declaration to heart: "—am-am-am not the st-streaker boy." Then, "I don't know what sh-sh-sh-she's talking about," he adds, extra venom in his *she*; and, just as he hoped, his mother's lip curls up reflexively.

"Oooooh!" she says, leaving him holding the book as she retraces her storm path to the kitchen. "Never in my life have I heard such . . .

such . . ." As she picks up the phone and quickly dials—"Betty? Oh good, I caught you"–he tiptoes to the bottom step and thrusts an ear into the hall. "Yes, I am. Unbelievable. That witch next door again . . . Well, I'm walking home from the office, and who comes running out of her house all in a huff, 'Excuse me, Mrs. Burke! Can I have a word with you?' . . . Just wait. 'A word?' I said. 'Do you have any idea of the kinds of things that go on at your house while you're at work?' . . . I kid you not. 'What do you mean,' I said. 'Just a little while ago I saw a young boy in a ski mask running around naked in your backyard.' . . . That's what *I* said," his mother says, emitting a sharp, joyless laugh. "'A ski mask? In the spring?' . . . No. I'm not even sure there was a boy. Danny was home the entire time and said he didn't see anyone . . . I know he wouldn't . . . I know . . . I think she's flipped her lid . . ." And suddenly, "Danny, are you still down here?" and he starts and loses his balance, foot thumping heavily on the landing. "Go upstairs."

"Okay."

After making several loud thumps on the bottom step, he pauses to overhear her murmured, "'Press them up your ass, you son of a bitch!' . . . Oh, yes I did. I didn't care, I was furious . . ." then climbs the rest of the way and puts the Bible back on the bookcase, wondering if she believed him, and if his crossed fingers had been enough to invalidate the oath, or would something terrible really happen now. *I didn't mean to swear against You, God, please don't be angry*, he prays and turns to strengthening his cardboard sandals, and to whispering a rehearsal of the Roman trial. Then he whispers the entire play from beginning to end, moving with great drama and sweeping arm movements across the small run of carpet between his bed and dresser.

And after dinner, he practices and prays some more, all the while picturing how his mother enacted the scene with Mrs. Maher at the table:

"What do you mean, some kid in the backyard?" his father said, never once looking at him.

"She said there was some kid," his mother said, likewise not looking.

"I find some kid in the backyard, I'll smack his bare ass silly."

"Not a neighbor's kid," his mother warned.

"I don't care who he is," his father said, "little wise guy."

And still Danny practices, still he prays, way past bedtime, until well after midnight, and then until after two. He can't seem to breathe calmly and quietly or even to completely stop sweating, a perpetual bead forming above his lip. At two-thirty, saying he cannot practice anymore, he gathers the last, important items to be brought to school—his sandals and crown and Holiday Inn towel, his fragile reed scepter and army knife and ketchup packets—and arranges them carefully in a shopping bag. Then he strips and turns off the light and lies down naked, pulling his sheets up over him like a shroud and staring into what's left of the quiet darkness. Occasionally, as the stone-like heaviness bears down on his chest and legs, he dips into an anxious sleep, only to start breathlessly awake shortly after, thinking, *It's today*, or, *It's in seven hours, in six hours.* And at five-forty, when there are just five hours and twenty minutes until the play, he awakes again and gets up and kneels before his altar. *Make me Jesus, God, I must be Jesus.* Then he showers and parts his hair in the middle and combs it down as straight as possible, and, careful not to be seen by his father moving about below, smuggles Sharon's brush and blow-dryer from the bathroom, locks his door, and turns to his final preparations.

Seconds after his father leaves for work, he races down to the kitchen in his uniform, superstitiously swallowing spoonfuls of Lucky Charms—exactly seven—before grabbing his bags and walking for the front door. But there, when he opens his mouth, no sound comes out, and it's only after summoning all his determination and force that he successfully emits, "Bye, Mother." And that instant, on hearing the rustling of her sheets, her dreamy, disoriented grunt, he's beset with a rush of reluctance and fear. He should stay home, beg her to call the office—even now he feels genuinely light-headed and queasy. "Bye, Mother," he says louder.

"Huh? Danny? Is that you?" she says, getting up. "What time is it? It's not even light yet." Then as she opens the door, she squints first at the reed sticking out of his bag, "Oh, is it today? Today's Wednesday?" before looking up at him, her eyes fully opening. "What did you do to your hair? It looks like you blow-dried it straight."

"N-N-No," he says, blushing.

"Honestly, Danny, it makes you look very . . ." *girlish*, she doesn't say, and a bit like Alfalfa from *The Little Rascals*, ". . . strange. If I were you, I'd go stick my head under the faucet and let it dry again naturally."

"I don't w-w-want to."

She shakes her head. "I'm telling you, that's not making you look any more like a king." And now, as he clicks his tongue offendedly, she notices his unfocused, zombie-like stare, probably up half the night fretting.

"And what are you going to do now, go to Mass and pray again?" But he doesn't answer, just stares at his shoes. "All right," she sighs, "but there'll be no more of this leaving at the crack of dawn after today, is that clear?"

He nods and turns slowly for the door. Then as she watches him shuffle, head bowed, down the walk, and imagines him emerging in the same lackluster way onto the Music Hall stage—O, *what a beautiful mornin'* . . .—her stomach leaps with surprising force, and she has the urge to call him back. *Danny, wait! Don't go. I'll tell them you're sick. I have nothing but terrible, terrible feelings about this play.* But she knows it's useless; there's as much chance of keeping him home today as there is of the Second Coming. So instead she says, "I'm going to try to make it, but I may have to leave a little early," and he murmurs a "that's okay" or an "I don't care" from the road. And finally, "Good luck! Try to be confident!" she yells, for what it's worth—very little, she's afraid, at this late hour.

Outside, the weather itself—mild and breezy and brightening, the sky a stubborn, unbroken blue—seems but another cross to bear as Danny turns the corner to Main Street and shuffles up the sidewalk past the bakery and Friendly's. He'd hoped for grayness and rain, a chill wind, distant rolls of thunder. But now, when the children file into the warm, sun-filled hall, they'll be smiling and restless with spring cheer. How could he ever face such smiling children? How could he face any children at all? He can't, he tells himself, and considers turning down Bayview Avenue and walking its entire miles' length to the marina and spending the day hidden in the reeds, for it seems it would be enough just to sit and look up at the sky for hours on end, so long as it kept him from the hundreds of eyes that would soon be trained on him.

Oh, but then poor Miss Kaigh, when the first bells rang and he still hadn't shown up, would pace and pace across the front of the classroom, *Six grades coming and no Christ!* Sister Regina, too, would become frantic and call his mother at work. How worried his mother would be! And how angry when she found out the truth. *That's it; now your father's going to hear about this.* Perhaps he'd get suspended from Our Lady's, or kicked out altogether and sent to the public school. What then? And what if the police were called, and he was stopped by a patrol car on his long walk back to his house. *Are you Daniel Burke? —Yes.—Get in; we're bringing you to the station.*

Clearly he could never let such things happen and so trudges on, step by step, block by block, to the squat, still-slumbering school; crosses its gray mote of still-carless lots. As he enters the church, he finds it not only empty of people but, to his greater dismay, of its usual peace and comfort, as if the protected flame in the red glass holder had just sputtered out, the Spirit of God flown away.

Nevertheless, he kneels in his middle pew, offering eleventh-hour petitions until, at several minutes of seven, the white-haired ladies plod in on canes or with their arms linked to white-haired men. Then the Sisters come, genuflecting and scattering silently across the first rows, some of them teachers who'll attend the play, and who won't be sitting with their backs to Danny, but staring right at him, witnessing his every stutter and blush. Then Father McGann himself enters and Mass begins. Danny stands and sits and says the responses aloud; in no time, Communion's given, and back in his pew Danny resists the urge to swallow, so the host's powers will remain in contact with his mouth for as long as possible, envelop and transform his tongue. *Please, God, the hour is drawing near. I need You inside me, I need You to say the words.* But soon he's forced to down the liquefying pulp, and he watches Father return the ciborium to the tabernacle, and bless and dismiss the small group. Then the Sisters step briskly out, followed by the hobbling ladies and men; and Danny's alone again, petitioning God even more fervently, when Miss Kaigh appears—hesitantly, through a side door— in a startling red-and-white outfit, her hair a new, complicated arrangement of light-brown flips and waves. Neither has he seen this particular diamond-checked blouse before, or the red shoes and matching belt pinching the waist of her pressed, white slacks. Such unexpected stylishness further intimidates him, and he slides down in his pew, dreading the moment she turns around.

But just now Liz, bowing stiffly before the statue of Mary behind the baptismal vat, is overcome with embarrassment to be wearing so much scarlet in the face of the Virgin's humble blue. So, too, her hair— which she had done at the beauty parlor yesterday, and whose set she's been at pains to preserve—strikes her as showy and vain. Not a wisp of Mary's strays beyond the scalloped edges of her veil, motherhood having come, it seems, and tucked her tresses permanently away. Yet despite her awkwardness, Liz presses on, *Hail Mary, full of grace . . .* until, thinking it best to sit down if she's going to pray, turns, and, oh my, there he is, slouching and biting his lip. Is that him? Yes, certainly. It's just that his hair, for some reason, is straighter than usual, and curling under at the ends like a pageboy. What on earth did he do to it? "Daniel?"

"G-G-G-Good m-m-morning, M-M-Miss K-K-Kaigh," he whispers reluctantly; he was hoping not to speak at all until the play began, so as not to fritter away the blessing on his tongue.

Liz blushes and waves her fingers nervously. *Well, we need all the help we can get,* she considers saying, but stops herself. Imagine? Joking in church? And with a student, no less. Instead she nods, as if in tacit approval of their similar intentions and, installing herself in the second pew, inwardly cringes at how otherwise pale and exhausted Danny looks, beneath the dreadful hairstyle. *You're a wreck. Didn't you sleep?* she imagines asking, quite like her own mother, who came up to wish her luck before she left the house. "Some," Liz answered, though in truth she'd only closed her eyes a moment. Late last night, just when she was lying down and thinking the costumes were finally finished, she remembered Barabbas and sprang right up again, descending on one of the leftover robes and slashing it with a scissor to give it a been-in-prison look; then the next thing she knew, it was nearly six o'clock, and she had to race around to get ready. Now she sighs, eyes fluttering beneath the heavy, incensed hush of the building. How lovely it would be to just sink into bed and forget about her fragile hairstyle, forget about the whole damned performance . . . But of course, that's not possible, and so she opens them again: *The Lord is with thee . . .*

Danny, staring up the pews into the swirling layers of her hair, is halfway heartened that they should both be praying at once. *'Wherever two or more gather in My name,'* Jesus said, *'I am there.'* And so he stares at the flickering candleholder with new intensity. *Please bring Your blessing now. Please bring Your peace.*

Liz, too, leaves off reciting prayers and begins to speak plainly with God or Mary, or some kind of amalgam or joint panel of the two, at first modestly requesting that they keep the play from being a disaster: *Even if it's just nothing to be terribly ashamed of at this point, that would be enough . . . And please don't let all those students laugh and make fun of me,* Danny adds . . . *I'm so afraid of being humiliated in front of so many people,* Liz admits . . . *Especially Brian . . . Especially Mrs. Burke. She'll think what a terrible teacher I am, and won't even want to speak to me . . . 'See, Curly can't play Jesus' . . . And dear God, strengthen Danny. He's white as a ghost . . . Make him be amazed and start to like me now . . . Help him to be confident and keep from stuttering . . . 'Danny, you were the coolest Jesus!' . . . I just can't imagine it, I just can't imagine that happening . . . If You will just send the Holy Spirit back, that will happen . . . But I'm losing faith. I'm sorry, God. There was that one time during rehearsals when his lines came out so powerfully . . . and my voice will be just like Jesus' . . . Perhaps it could be arranged for the fluke to happen again?*

And what if it does? Liz wonders. What if, despite every indication to the contrary, the play comes off like a charm, and Mrs. Burke and Sister Regina rush up to her afterward, *I had to keep reminding myself they were children! Have you directed before?*

But just as quickly, her smile drops again and, conscious of the boy behind her watching her every move, she stands up. She shouldn't have come; she feels like a hypocrite. When was the last time she stopped in church before school? She can't remember and is sure that if she ever did, she must've wanted something then, too. Maybe if she were just to light a candle instead. She glances hopefully at the racks of cobalt holders before the Virgin, half already glowing with the earnest petitions of other parishioners. She's seen it done, coins dropped into the money box, people wielding the long, wooden matchsticks, lighting new candles from old—sometimes two or more, which struck her as possibly improper. It's not a raffle, for Pete's sake. She herself would light only one. And who knows? It might help.

Danny, surveying her walk to the aisle, feels his heart misgive him: they haven't prayed long enough. However, it seems she may not be leaving but approaching the votive rack before the statue of Mary. Oh good, oh great, a candle! Burning in church while they're in the Music Hall! And after she dips the long, flaming matchstick into a new holder and crosses herself, she quickly drops more coins into the donation box and lights a second, and a third. *Three* candles! Only once she replaces the stick in the sand tray, she doesn't kneel before them but turns and waves awkwardly to Danny again. *Not yet,* he wants to say, waving back, and then thinks of asking—as she exits the building, and he listens to the fast-retreating clacks of her new shoes—if he can stay here, praying. He'd like to pray in the dim, empty nave of the church all morning, even until eleven o'clock. Imagine the blessing he'd have by then, how thick! And he could walk, in the holy trance, directly to the hall and onto the stage, the words streaming from him boldly and fluently, like beautiful, sad music. And there would be startled cries, tears; Sister Regina, *Never have I been so moved as when this boy . . .*

But already he hears the buses rumbling outside, the children descending to the lots, squealing and shouting. And if he doesn't have time for many more rosaries, perhaps he has time for one more. So he hurries through the first decade, races through the second, prayer after prayer—for peace, for the hush, for the gentle ignition of his blessing—and oh, exactly midway into the fourth, it comes: the clear, terrible peal, shattering all hope.

The Trials of Liz Kaigh

No sooner does Liz push through the doors at the back of the school than she hears the murmurs of the students on the curb below: "Is that Miss Kaigh?" "Look at Miss Kaigh!" Oh boy, she thinks, stiffening before the many keen eyes trained on her, then descends the stairs as quickly as safety and composure will allow.

"G-G-Good morning, Sister Margaret," she says with sudden difficulty to the black-frocked 5C teacher.

"Good morning, Miss Kaigh," the nun answers, squinting at the open throat of her blouse. "Ready for your performance?" she asks—sarcastically? Liz wonders, then swallows, meaning to say something pleasant and positive, but finds she can merely wring a quivering smile from dry lips.

"Miss Kaigh, I like your hair. Mith Kaigh, Danny'th not here," Frances and Patty say as she reaches her class's double line, followed by a half dozen others: "I like your hair." "Danny's not here." "It's so pretty. Did you get that done for the play?" "I like your outfit, too, Miss Kaigh." "I like your diamond blouse."

"Thank you, girls."

"And look at her shoes!"

"Red," Kevin slurs.

"Pardon me?" she says to the boy.

"Nothing," he says.

And, "Daniel's here. I just saw him," she announces.

"Where?"

She imagines him still in his pew, by now a frozen knot of prayer. "He'll be joining us shortly. Follow me," she tells them, jumping ahead of the other classes waiting to enter the building. Just moments later, amid the cacophony in 5B—"Players, don't put your jackets away"—a sharp rap comes at the front door, and she turns to a hunched, pale-jowled nun in a nappy black cardigan.

"Sister Ruth," she says, straightening before the retired teacher, on a rare excursion from the convent. "Thank you so much for coming," she adds, unnerved by the nun's promptness and by the fact that, as Sister Regina just informed her, this particular excursion is to last until after the play, which she and the other rarely seens have arranged to attend. "Class, everyone say good morning to Sister Ruth."

"Good morning, Sister Ruth," they say from the closets and aisles.

But the nun merely frowns and pads breathlessly to the front desk.

"Oh here," Liz says, hastily clearing the top. So dramatic is her fuss that it's several instants before anyone notices the ghost-faced Jesus stepping sheepishly through the rear door.

"Hey, he's here!" Herman squeals.

As the others twist one by one in their seats, Danny, even now continuing his rosaries, has to concentrate more than ever not to lose his place: *And blessed is the womb—is the fruit of thy womb—*

"Look at his hair!" "Hey, Curly, what happened to your curls?" "It looks like he ironed it." "*Ironed* it?"

"No, he blow-dried it. Right, Danny?" Juanita says.

"Danny, did you *blow-dry* your hair?" Brian asks.

"You gotta watch it doesn't frizz now," Juanita cautions. "Did you spray it good?"

"*Spray* it!" Kevin shrieks.

And Liz, who feels entirely justified now to have picked up the costume wig at Janel's, scolds the chorus and says to the pale, silent boy, "Stay where you are; we're going right over. Brian, Joey, Juanita, Frances, let's go, line up behind him. Everyone else is to stay here with—" She gestures deferentially to the aged nun, precariously lowering herself into her desk, "—Sister." And now as Liz hovers closer to be of some assistance, the nun, risking her balance, flicks a gnarled hand at her.

"Oh, I'm sorry," Liz says, backing off into a swell of grumbles and tongue clicks from the seated students: "Can't we go, too?" "How come we have to do all this work, and they don't?" "Are they going to have to do this for homework?" And, glaring at them for taking her to task in front of another teacher—albeit a semi-senile, hard-of-hearing substitute—she yells louder than she might have, "Excuse me! You all had a chance to be in the play weeks ago. Now your assignment is on the board, and I don't want to hear any more noise." And then, "No more noise!" the until-now-silent Sister Ruth barks suddenly behind her, one bony hand landing on the desktop with such a shot that, despite herself, Liz jumps; and the children, bully hearts fainting, straighten in their seats and open their books with remarkable speed, so remarkable that Liz's eyes narrow and she has to bite back the word *hypocrites* prickling on the tip of her tongue. Then she lowers her head, refusing to meet the eyes of Sister or students as she leads her troupe from the room.

When they reach the hall, it's still locked and dark, and she has to send Brian and Joey to find Mr. Loughlin. Eternities later, as the stooped man appears with his ring of keys, he's full of apologies and explanations: from what she can gather, an overflowing toilet in the second-floor boys' room. "Gonna need a snake," he says, kicking open the door, but she doesn't inquire further. "Soon as I'm through, I'll get started on the sweepin' and chairs."

"Started?" Liz asks.

"Should be back in about an hour," he says, illuminating the still litter-strewn expanse.

Stepping in behind him, "An hour?" she repeats too loudly, for now the walls deliver the shrill, panicked question back to them. *An hour?*

"Water all over." He waves his hand before his nose. "Bit of an emergency. We'll have you ready in time, don't you worry."

"Eleven o'clock!" she reminds him—*o'clock!*—as he rushes down the ramp again.

"Don't I know it! Need a few of your whippersnappers to help cart those chairs over."

"Of course!" she calls after him, and, *Of course!* the walls reiterate. And soon, after warning everyone to keep his voice down—"I find this echo very hard to tolerate. Doesn't everyone find the echo hard to tolerate?"—and after eliciting from Joey just when his father said he'd drop off the stand—"In the morning." "He didn't say what time?"

"Not exactly"—and after brushing off player after player, half of whom seem to be vying for her attention or pulling at her sleeves like little children, particularly Juanita, "Miss Kaigh, I have to talk to you." "Talk to me later"—she tells them to collect their costumes, all save Danny, whom she asks to sit on a nearby folding chair. But the boy, coming to at her left as if from a trance, looks up now with a mute, questioning face. "Sit. Sit," she repeats, as if to a poorly trained dog. Then not until she's groping through her bag of supplies does she think to ask, "Why are you so quiet?" But again he merely shakes his head. "Is something wrong with your voice?"

"No," he mumbles finally, defusing her alarm. Then quickly, "I'm saving it."

"*Saving* it?" She squints at what seems, even to her, an unnecessary precaution, and, at last extracting the long shimmering wig from its package, watches him clap his hand to his chest. "We'll have to trim it," she allows, next producing scissors and placing them on the floor. Then before he's able to squander another syllable, she brushes aside his feebly protesting hands and snaps the netting over his brilliant copper fleece.

As the synthetic hair falls about Danny's face and shoulders, blacking out the hall and stage beyond, and as the students' cries and cackles echo off the walls—"Look, Miss Kaigh's putting a wig on Danny!" "He looks like an Indian!" "He looks like Cousin It!" "No, Morticia!" Kevin shouts, closing in for a better look. "Now *he's* Morticia!" "That'th not funny," Patty says—he's overtaken with concern for the fate of his own carefully styled hair, jammed up beneath the netting and breaks into full-fledged speech, "M-M-Miss Kaigh, do I n-n-need a wig?"

"Daniel, Christ had shoulder-length hair; yours barely touches your ears, and it's . . . not dark enough, for one thing. No one will know who you're supposed to be."

"But this one is-is-is black."

"Yeah, Miss Kaigh, it's a witch wig!" Kevin laughs, indicating the packaging, replete with photo of a fanged, black-fingernailed girl below the gothic scrawl VAMPIRESS.

Liz scowls at the boy and quickly slips the package back into her bag before Danny can see it. Clearly, it isn't an ideal match; she would've preferred a brown wig, had the cashier been able to find one among the store of last year's unsold Halloween supplies. "I'll take it if it's all you have," she'd said, laying out her own money, "at least it's long and straight."

"It isn't a *witch* wig," Liz says, "its—"

"—for the bride of Dracula," Frances finishes. "Look, it has the white streak."

"Well, the streak is coming right off," Liz says, snipping it with the scissors and letting the hoary lock fall to the floor before them all. "Now get dressed." But as she sets to removing some of the wig's general length, her hands prove so unsteady that several times she has to pause and exhale so as not to nick an ear, the same as she chops the ends unevenly and teases bits here and there, in hopes of achieving the wavy, layered look of that *King of Kings* actor with the intense blue eyes. Yet by the end of her trembling efforts, the boy, she finds, still looks very much like a vampiress, especially with his face so bloodlessly white. Finally, throwing up her sweating hands—"That's the best I can do"—she holds a black pirate's beard up to his face. "Yes, that will help. We won't glue this yet, but I want you to practice with the hair." And so the boy, stammering unintelligibly—in fact he's trying to tell her just how hot and itchy the wig's become—stands up. "No, wait." And she reaches into her pocketbook for bobby pins and fastens the wig to his own hair, the boy all the while squirming beneath her fingers. "I'm sorry," she says, "otherwise it'll fall off," and, placing the last pin, hesitates before awkwardly brushing the cut hair from his shoulders and back. "All right, get into the robe. The good tan robe," she adds for consolation. And now here once again, "Miss Kaigh, I have to tell you—" "Not now, Juanita. We have to rehearse," upon which she reaches for *Classical Masterpieces* and groans.

"What's the matter, Miss Kaigh?"

"We can't start yet; the music isn't ready!" she says, automatically fishing for her keys. "Who can I trust to carry the stereo in from my car?" Of the eager hands, she chooses the strongest: Brian and Joey and even Kevin. But first they have to get back into their uniforms and, running for the dressing room, stumble in their sandals. "What's the matter? Are the soles too big?" she calls after them. "You'll have to fix them before the play!"

As the boys invade the cluttered space, Danny, barefoot and in his underwear, jumps for his robe. "Ah, look at his skinny legs!" they say, "Bock-bock! bock-bock!" and he stumbles away, gathering the robe tightly about him and brushing the wig hair from his face. Then as they laugh and toss their tunics and robes to the floor, Kevin sneers, "Don't be looking at my body, fairy"—not without cause, for Danny, leaning now against the wall in the far corner, has been trying to stare without seeming to at the thicker pinknesses of their waists and thighs, the shrinking points of their goose-skinned titties, the actual, jiggling evidence of their dickies below the double layers of cotton. But too soon the trousers are fastened, shirts buttoned, replaced by lifeless blue. And from outside, "Boys?"

"Coming!"

"Daniel?" Miss Kaigh says as the three rush out, something about sandals while she's gone. Gone where? "Okay," he murmurs, wide-eyed and startled as he kneels on the hard wood floor in hopes of rekindling his grace. *Hail Jesus . . . Blessed heaven . . .*

Out in the lot, Liz has to struggle to keep from running and manages to only for fear of the alarming figure she'll cut—a teacher dashing across the asphalt with students. Yet a normal pace isn't possible, and so she leads them along at a brisk clip.

"You're walking really fast, Miss Kaigh," Brian observes.

"We don't have much time," she says. "Careful." In a moment, from the backseat of her father's old Nova, they unload the cumbersome speaker cabinets and the receiver/turntable module, which she trusts to Brian. However, once she's locked the car again and they're about to head back, she finds herself asking if they can make it by themselves; she'll catch up with them in a second. And, quite soon, shed of the fear of tripping children, she breaks into a trot in the opposite direction and rounds a corner of the school, calculating the time it will take to run to the lounge and back: too long. And, just now spying an outdoor stairwell leading down to the auditorium—the very stairwell where two eighth-grade boys, subsequently suspended, had been caught smoking several weeks ago—she casts a quick look around the yard before rushing down it. And there, at its concrete heart, unable to see anything above but bright sky, she lights up and draws heavily on a Virginia Slims, all the while imagining Father McGann or Sister

Regina darkening the top step, *Miss Kaigh, could that be you? Smoking in the stairwell?* "Oh God," she murmurs, the delicious, outlawed smoke floating freely up, like signals. Then she lights another and smokes it down even faster, before rushing up from the well again into the still-empty lot. Got away with it, thank God, she thinks, heart pounding savagely as she opens her bag and gropes for Lifesavers, although now, suddenly dizzy, she has to stop and catch her balance. When the whirling slows, she finds the contents of her bag on the asphalt. "Dammit," she says, picking up lipsticks, lighter, tissues, makeup cases. Mirrors broken? she worries but doesn't look, for fear of the bad luck it will bring and, at last locating the mints, pops two in her mouth and starts running again, despite the many windows above.

Back in the hall, Danny, still praying in the far corner of the dressing room, jumps up and unclasps his hands as the boys rush back in. "If he tells, I'll kill that little shit," Kevin's saying.

"He won't say anything, he's too scared," Brian says.

"What do you have to be such a spaz for anyway, Lukas?" Joey asks.

"I'm not the spaz, you are."

"You're the one who dropped it."

"But you were making me laugh."

Any speculation Danny may have as to what they're referring to is instantly squelched as they doff their shirts and trousers again.

"Hey Un-Curly," Brian calls, "what are you doing over there, practicing your agony?"

"He looks like he's in agony," Joey says.

"Too bad he can't look that way when he's supposed to," Kevin says.

Then they laugh and, fastening their tunics and robes, rush from the room.

This just as Liz, out on the ramp, pauses breathlessly before the entrance to the hall, startled by the spectacle of her students within, decked out in colorful robes and headwear—as if they're having some sort of play, she thinks. But then this odd, almost pleasing impression is overwhelmed by the realization that there's still been no sign of Joey's father or Mr. Loughlin. "Hasn't it been an hour yet? What time is it? No, don't tell me. Let's just get this—" And as she rushes to attach the speaker wires to her stereo on the floor, she notices Kevin's widened, diverted eyes. "Is something wrong?" she asks. Yet by the time she searches out an outlet, he still hasn't answered. "Something's the matter. What happened?"

"Nothing," he says, glancing at Brian and Joey. "Nothing, nothing," the boys repeat, looking down at the floor. Liz, stomach coiling tighter, turns to the stereo again, hoping that whatever they aren't telling her will go away. Then with the help of Timmy and Paolo, she spreads the speakers as far apart as possible at the foot of the stage and turns the system on—just as Juanita approaches her yet a third time: "I have to tell you . . . ."

"Oh, all right, all right. What is it?"

"I'm not allowed to play Mary Magdalene."

"You're what?"

"She can't play Mary Magdalene," Frances interprets.

"Yes, she can. What are you talking about?"

But now Juanita hands her a note, and Liz glances at the salutation, *Dear Mrs. Kay,* written in an unpracticed adult script. "My mother won't let me."

"*Your* mother now?" Liz nearly yells.

"She says Mary Magdalene was a prostitute."

"A who?" Liz blushes and glances at the other students.

"A prostitute."

"Well, I heard you the first time. That's not a nice word to repeat, Juanita."

"But wasn't she?"

"Well, I—I'm not sure exactly," Liz says, here recalling some debate in regard to the nature of Mary's *seven demons.* "I know some people say she was, but—Daniel?" She looks about her, as if to consult with the boy on this point, but doesn't find him near. "Is he still getting dressed? Daniel!" she calls—*Daniel!*—and the next instant assures Juanita that if Mary Magdalene ever was this . . . kind of woman, she repented and became clean again; Jesus cast the demons out of her. And the girl nods, understandingly it seems, yet "My mother says I have to play someone else," she states flatly. Liz, looking down at the note again, is alarmed to discover it's strongly worded: *I hope it is not because she is a Puerto Rican that you ask her to play this role. I hope that such attitudes would not prevail in a Catholic school.* "Oh but, Juanita, didn't you tell her you volunteered for the role yourself?"

"But that's because you wouldn't let me play Mary."

"I never said you couldn't play Mary! It was your preference, it was—" Over the girl's insistence that she wanted to play Mary first, Liz says, "Why is she only writing this note now, the day of the play? If there was a problem, you should've told me long ago." But it seems her mother only asked her last night what part she was playing and threatened to call Sister Regina Mary Murphy if no changes were made.

"Sister Regina! Why?"

"Because it's prejudice."

"What?"

"That's what she said."

With the boys muttering disdainfully behind her, Liz says it was nothing of the kind, and how ridiculous, and—because what choice does she have?—"Fine. We'll have to get someone else, then. We'll just have to change everything at the last minute. This is really going to mess us up now, this is really . . ." Here the murmurs become louder and the girl's eyes well with tears. "Quiet, boys," Liz says, and, looking now to the tunicked, spunkless, colorless Ginger, "Will you be the—Mary Magdalene?"

"Okay."

"But will your mother mind?"

"No."

"Mary has the last lines of the play. Do you know them?"

"Master," she recites, and, "He is risen. He is risen."

"Right, but you have to really say them; you're witnessing a miracle. The greatest miracle of all time."

"Okay."

"Okay," Liz repeats warily, "then Juanita will be Mary."

But now Frances begins to cry. "Miss Kaigh, I'm Mary."

"I have a better role for you. A *speaking* part," Liz stresses, realizing that with a bit of coaching, she might also be able to solve a long-standing casting dilemma. "Paolo, go get Daniel and tell him to come out here at once."

As she proceeds with the role swaps and costume trades, Danny, on his knees in the dressing room, pretends to be adjusting a sandal when the boy rushes in.

"Miss Kaigh says to come right away."

"Mm-hmm," he mumbles and waits for Paolo to leave again before slowly hoisting himself to his feet; then, blinking as if emerging from a cave, he shuffles onto the sun-drenched stage, *Holy Mary, Father of God.*

Liz, just now instructing the huffing, sausage-fingered Stephen on the delicate workings of the turntable, looks up and winces at the sight of the wig again, so startlingly black. "We're just about ready," she tells him and, the next instant, as Stephen again bounces the needle across the "Summer" track, shoos the helpless klutz aside. "Never mind, I'll do it myself," here hazarding her own shaking hand to lower the needle, and it wobbles only slightly before catching—but suddenly the left speaker is making a hollow, hissing sound, like a transistor radio. She adjusts the equalizer levers, to no result, then slides the balance lever all the way to the left, and the music drops out altogether, save for some faraway, tambourine-like sounds. Imagine: "Summer," with tambourines. "What's wrong with my stereo?"

Once more the boys slink away. "I don't know," Kevin says, tripping on a sandal.

But now Rory points at the boy. "He dropped the speaker on the ramp."

"Shut up, Fitzer. You tattletale."

"Did he, Brian?" And when the boy looks down again, Liz feels another surge of panic.

"Miss Kaigh, I'm sorry," Kevin says. "The wire got caught in my legs."

"He stepped on the wire," Rory reports. "It—"

"Are you saying it's not going to work now? My good speaker?" She looks at Brian urgently.

"The other one's okay."

"The other one? Brian, look at the size of this room! Two isn't even enough!" And, "Oh great! Oh, this is just—! This is just—!" she says, pacing before the now mono and mousy strains of Vivaldi emanating from the system. And even the speakers themselves, at the foot of the gigantic stage, seem pathetic and toylike to her, little baby's blocks; and suddenly she stops and clenches her fists, and has to bite her tongue to keep from screaming something venomous. Then just when it seems the venomous thing might leap from her mouth anyway, the hall door flies open and knocks against the wall with a reverberating bang.

"Delivery for ya, Miss," Mr. Loughlin says, red-faced and panting. With the aid of two upper-class boys, he drags the large wooden stand into the hall. "Boy's father dropped this off at the rectory."

"My father," Joey says. "Look, Miss Kaigh."

"I see," Liz says, already squinting at the unsightliness of the cube, made of scraps of raw plywood and beige paneling.

"Where would you like such a contraption?" Mr. Loughlin asks.

"On the stage, please," she says, directing them to the center of it, and a little to the back. Then the three drop it to the floor, dust blowing onto all their shoes.

Mr. Loughlin looks on as Liz bends to brush hers clean. "Be goin' to get the brooms," he says, eyes lingering over the bright toes. "After ten already."

"Ten?" Liz says, looking incredulously at her watch. "It can't be!" But here she stops herself and thanks the custodian and the two boys and, when they're gone, quickly examines the top of the stand, where she finds a thin gap between two strips of paneling, but nothing per se to slide the cross into. "Where's the slot? How are we going to stand the cross up?" She glares at the open-mouthed carpenter's son, then looks back at the ugly box and sends for the cross, Rory and Paolo rushing it over. But clearly, the double-layered base can't be slid through the small separation. "All right, well, maybe Mr. Loughlin will be able to do something with it when he comes back," she says, breathing loudly. "Stand the cross behind the box for now, boys, and hold it up while I look." She steps down from the stage and walks to what would be the first or second row, should the chairs ever be set up, and at least the thing appears to be of an adequate height. "Daniel, climb on there and hold your arms out. Let me see if—" But as the boy, slow to move, clambers ungracefully up, she hears a shifting and creaking sound she doesn't like at all. Then as he turns to face her, arms lining up with the gnarled crossbeams, and she's wondering if the stand is strong enough to support him, she hears a loud, definite crack—the very announcement of impending calamity. "Get off, quick!" she yells. *Off, quick!* the hall warns.

"Jump!" the students cry. *Jump!*

Rigid with self-consciousness, Danny hesitates and, the next instant, to the great resound of the top panels giving way, falls—ragged, splintery edges raking up his bare ankles—clean through to the floor.

In the brief, stunned silence that follows, Liz's heart flies to her mouth and her eyes squeeze shut; then amid the late, echoing chorus of squeals and startled laughter, she blindly asks, "Is he all right? Did he break anything? Is he bleeding?" *Bleeding?* And only when a distinct "No!" and "Not bleeding!" rise from the tumult does she dare to open her eyes again and rush up to the boy, sitting now on the floor beside the stand, robe hiked to his knees. "Everyone get back!" she says and squats down, examining the ankles without touching them. There don't appear to be any needles of wood lodged within the whitish scores. "Do they hurt, Daniel?"

In fact he can feel the burning where the jagged wood raked him, and the throbbing of the hidden splinters in his calves. Yet he resists the urge to complain or to rub himself, and instead shakes his head.

"Are you sure?"

He nods.

"Thank goodness," she sighs, not with any real relief—for then, looking back to the stand, the entire top of which is broken beyond repair, the sense of futility and doom she's struggled to stave off overwhelms her. It's not just the stand, but the entire enterprise, along with whatever heart she had left for it, that's broken, caved in on itself. She should call it off at once, before something even worse happens; that would be the sensible, the Christian, thing to do. Then she lifts her head and whispers her thought to Danny, "It's time to give up."

And now at last the boy speaks out with urgent, surprising clarity: "No, Miss Kaigh, please. We have to have it."

But she shakes her head. "It's going to be such a disaster; it'll be better for everyone if it doesn't take place."

"No, it won't. Please. We have to."

She'll send Frances to the office: *Miss Kaigh says she's extremely sorry, but we're not going to have the play.* Or she'll go herself; yes, she'll have to go herself. *Sister, I'm so sorry. I'm afraid we—* But now he's saying something else, about sewing? Is she hearing him right? Indeed, "You've done all this sewing," he repeats, and she pauses, because it seems such an odd thing for a boy to say—and yet, at the same time, terribly true. She's sewed more in the past several days than she has in her entire life, pricked her fingers repeatedly, even drawn blood. And all this just a fraction of the time and effort that's gone into the play. What a waste it would be to call it off now. And how humiliating, the talk that would go around: *Practiced for weeks for a play they didn't even put on; canceled it at the last minute; all the classes ready to go and she got cold feet.* Oh no, she could never let them say that. And now as Danny leaps up and looks eagerly down at her, vampiress hair clinging to his sweat-dampened face, "Come on, Miss Kaigh"; and as the others one by one chime in, "Miss Kaigh, are you all right?" "Miss Kaigh, is something wrong?" she grits her teeth and tries to gather up a last thread of determination. But it's not their pleas so much as the sound of the door banging open again below, the sight of the stooped custodian pushing a wheeled trash bucket into the hall, three push-broom handles sprouting from it, that gets her to her feet:

"Mr. Loughlin, we've had some difficulties with the stand."

— 17 —

Body Snatcher

In a moment, after the man winces at their collapsed cube and offers the wisdom, "Never meant to be stood on, that"; and after he drags it off to the tomb and distributes brooms and sweeping instructions to the whippersnapperiest volunteers—"Yeah, you're a live one. Yeah, you, too"—arming, it turns out, the same inept threesome who carried Liz's stereo from the car; and just after he trots bleakly off to see what kind of Calvary he can fashion from materials in his workshop, Liz looks again at her watch and confronts the inevitable: "Frances and Virginia, I want you to change back into your uniforms and go ask Sister Regina if we might postpone the play."

"Postpone the play?" the girls ask. "P-P-Postpone?" Danny's alarmed reiteration rises above the others.

"I'm sorry, but we can't possibly be ready in half an hour. We'll have to wait until after recess. Hurry, girls," she says, "but don't run." In the meantime, she sets the boys to sweeping and, with the help of the new Mary, whom she wishes to occupy with as menial a task as possible, tossing dustpans of litter into the bucket. "Fast, now. We have to have the whole hall done before Mr. Loughlin gets back. Brian, bring one of those brooms on the stage." All the while Danny's at her heels, stammering his irrational case for starting earlier, the one even more petrified than she, suddenly raring to go. "Daniel, quiet," she says, "you're distracting me," and there's an end to his noise, if not his pleading glances. Then many dustpans later, when the girls finally rush back in with a folded note—"She gave us more time!" Frances announces—his face seems to drain of its last trace of pink.

"Here," Liz says, grabbing the paper and reading its scripted message: *Dear Miss Kaigh— While I gather that there is much for you still to organize, I cannot allow the play to be postponed any later than seventh period. If you are not able to start by 1:00—*"One!" she says; "One?" Danny says—*I am afraid we will have to cancel the performance. And I believe I speak for all when I say I hope this will not be the case. I entreat you to consider that on this occasion it may be your own faith that is being put to the test. You must not succumb to the sins of self-doubt and despair, but rather trust that God will look down on your Passion play and all will be blessed.*

"Trust He'll look down," she mutters, resisting the urge to crumple the note in front of them all. Well, if He *is*, He's got a strange way of showing it. The rate things are going, she'd just as soon put her trust in Shakespeare or even Hamlet: his pep talk to the players she nearly memorized last night at her sewing table—"Speak the speech, I pray you, trippingly on the tongue"—at least that was solid advice! But now Danny again, asking isn't one o'clock too late. "Daniel, if we started tomorrow it would be . . ." Then all at once the reason for his distress dawns on her. "Oh no!" she cries, rushing over and plucking bobby pins from his hair. "Why didn't you say something? Go to the office at once and ask Mrs. Newman to call your mother at the school."

So he dashes to the dressing room, where he dons his uniform and jacket, and pockets his comb and, for diversionary purposes, his father's army knife, then hurries to the side door, smoothing his freed, frizzing hair.

"And Daniel, don't have her paged, just ask someone to deliver a message. It's disruptive enough."

"Okay," he says, scooting down the ramp and almost colliding with Mr. Loughlin.

"Watch yourself now," the custodian says, stepping aside to let him pass, then lumbers into the hall with a homely device made of milk crates and one-by-fours thatched together with duct tape.

What on earth? Liz thinks. Yet once he plops it onto the stage and slides the cross into a slot between the two crates, it indeed stands of its own, wobbly accord. "Yea!" the students cheer, and Liz—quickly instructing Paolo to cover the crate with a spare sheet, the result resembling a snow skirt of a Christmas tree—is about to join the clapping herself when the custodian turns and trots down the steps, presumably to fetch the chairs. "Oh, Mr. Loughlin?" she calls. "The play's been moved to one o'clock."

"One, now?" he says, slowing to a walk. "Give a chance for my blood pressure to drop. All right, fellas," he tells his threesome, rebanding about him, "we'll get the first load at our leisure."

In the stairwell on the side of the school, Danny, wavier hair recombed to the best of his blind ability, sits on a bottom step extracting tool after tool of the army knife, his heart racing with dread of being rushed upon by a Sister or teacher or, for that matter, any of the seventh- and eighth-grade students who sometimes come down here to smoke—for it seems to him, as he spies the two crushed filters on the concrete not a yard from his chukka boots, that they may have come quite recently. *Did you smoke those?* He imagines the witchy-faced Sister Margaret glaring down at him from the landing, then kicks the filters farther away before attempting to resume his prayers, prayers especially for his mother's forgetfulness or, should she remember to come after all, for the play to start much later than one, so she'll be forced to leave before it begins.

Finally, at twelve of eleven, having allowed ten minutes for his rush to the office, he pockets the knife and makes his stealthy way up the stairs and back around the side of the school, then runs out into the front lots, where, to his dismay, he finds Mr. Loughlin off to his right, steering a long, unwieldy cart loaded with folding chairs, Brian and Joey and Kevin jumping up and riding the sides, arms saluting the air. "Full steam ahead!" they shout and, catching sight of him, "Hey, Jesus! Hey, Blow-dry!" followed by the custodian's amused rebuke, "No teasin', fellas." Despite the throbbing in his calves, Danny races ahead, the laughter of the boys and man a chasing wave of scorn.

No sooner does he cross the threshold of the hall than Miss Kaigh is upon him. "What happened?" she demands.

"I-I-I—they-they sent a message," he tells her.

"Well, did they send it immediately? Are you sure she got it?"

"I th-think so."

"I hope you stressed the urgency of the situation. Did you stress the urgency?" she asks, just as Kevin rushes up the ramp: "Get out of the way, everybody! Make room for the train!"

"'Get out of the way,' Kevin? Is that how we speak now?" Liz says, her words lost beneath the rumble of the cart and Mr. Loughlin's shouted orders. Then the students mill and knock about like a pile of ants, unfolding the chairs and placing them in rough formations, the custodian straightening them all, until, moments later, there are three rows, divided by a middle aisle, stretching from wall to wall—only three, when they'll need dozens. She turns her worried glance to Mr. Loughlin.

"We'll go fetch us more," he says, and it's all she can do to keep from yelling, *Hurry! Move it!* But then it's nearly *twenty-five minutes later*— the time it takes Liz to review the role and line swaps again, and run the shuffled girls through their positions during The Way and the crucifixion and the scene at the tomb—before he and the boys return with the second load. Once again the entire company mills and knocks about endlessly, installing the three additional rows—enough chairs, Liz estimates, for a grade and a half. Yet when the last of the load's been straightened, Mr. Loughlin, clapping his hands and going for his empty cart, says he'll break for lunch.

"*Lunch?*" Liz says, touching her knotted stomach. How could anyone think of food now? "Now?" she asks.

"Sure." He glances at his watch. "Be near a quarter of noon by the time I get back there."

"But," Liz says, "will you—be long?"

"Nah. Ten minutes." Then in a gently rebuking tone, "I imagine your whippersnappers will want to eat, too," he says, as if she's so neglectful that she has to be reminded of such a thing. And while in fact she hadn't yet thought about their lunch, and had imagined spending the next hour practicing, most likely it would've occurred to her eventually.

But now the better part of the company, led by the inept threesome, bursts into a whiney chorus of "Yeah, I'm hungry, Miss Kaigh. Can we get our lunch? Can we get our milk?" and she clenches her teeth, breathing loudly again. They eat all the time, every day; couldn't they miss one meal? Or have it quickly afterward, before the buses come? If they leave now, they'll have to change back into their uniforms again; it's all such a waste of precious time. *Oh, come on,* she wants to say, *Christ fasted for forty days in the desert, and you can't wait another hour or two for lunch?* but doesn't dare to beneath the gloating eyes of Mr. Loughlin. "Okay, okay," she says, "we'll leave now, but you have to go right to your desks and eat, no dilly-dallying." Then as they placate her with nods and *mm-hmm*'s and she sends the still-costumed back to the dressing rooms, Danny's once again at her side, asking, of all things, if he can wait in the church until they come back. "In the church? Of course you can't."

"I-I-I'm not hungry," he says, and she glances down at him, so pale and squinting with dread, and manages a sympathetic frown.

"I know. Neither am I. But we still have to go."

After the excruciating changing delay, she conducts their hastily formed double line back to the classroom at a near trot, only to have their speedy progress arrested by Sister Ruth, who, once the players retrieve their lunches, spearheads an elaborate grace and midday prayer ritual before proceeding to distract Liz with stories of the class's conduct throughout the morning. Unsatisfactory, it seems, particularly Herman's: the boy not only answered his questions poorly but was twice caught whispering to his neighbor. Then after Liz stops to scold them all and, on Sister Ruth's advice, requires them to compose written apologies for their behavior before going outside for recess, the nun lowers her shrill, exasperated voice and tells Liz she'll take advantage of her return to have a "moment of privacy."

"Privacy?" Liz says, her own voice leaping as the nun rises unsteadily from the desk. Then, checking the impulse to assist her, she finds herself bathed in an ordained glare.

"If you please," Sister says.

"Oh, of course," Liz says, realizing now what she means. But then, glancing up at the clock—already several minutes after twelve!—she asks, "Will you—be long?" a question the nun doesn't even deign to acknowledge. She merely pads, in her proud decrepitude, out the door and down the hall—for which lavatory, Liz can't imagine; she only hopes it isn't for one in the convent, another building altogether.

Pacing across the room again, she passes Danny's desk and grows suddenly alarmed: the boy's eyelids are shut and trembling, likewise his pinched, blood-drained lips. She wonders, even, if he's unconscious or having some kind of seizure.

"Daniel," she whispers down at him, rapping on his desktop, and at last the lids spring open, revealing the pale-blue irises in their customary places. "Are you sleeping in your seat?"

He shakes his head, staring at her without seeming to see her at all.

"What's the matter?"

"N-N-Nothing," he murmurs.

"Eat," she says, pointing to his sandwich, still in its baggy, "you'll need the energy."

"I-I-I-I-I—" he says, then gives up. *Have enough*, he would've said.

"You don't want to be dizzy or faint onstage."

"F-F-Faint?" he says, one of the few disasters he hasn't imagined.

"Try to eat some of it, a few bites."

But now his stomach lurches and his cheeks puff out, even at the suggestion.

"Oh no," she says, "well, don't force yourself," and continues her pacing. Seven after! Should she ask Mrs. Sullivan across the hall to watch the class? But she'll be on her way to the lounge and then what would Sister think, coming back and not finding her here? No, she'll have to wait. And so she paces faster, *Hurry up and pee, goddammit!* then reddens to hear her foul-mouthed self again. Because isn't she, finally, under all her new-girl goodness gracious? Her true colors flying out with the least bit of pressure? How could she even hope to associate with the likes of Mrs. Burke, with classical violinists? And just at this moment, Herman and several of the apology-writing others have the nerve and bad timing to ask how the play's going. "How's it going?" she says, eyes widening madly, and she glances at Danny, as if for backup or an answer, but once again finds his eyes closed.

"Are you guys ready?" Matt asks.

Which seems an infinitely more cruel question. And now, "I suppose you boys think you're smart," she says, unable to stop the charge of words. "I suppose you think it's a real scream to ask us how it's going, and if we're ready, when you know we're not and that it couldn't be going more terribly, and no thanks to any of you, you boys with your nasty, bully attitudes. God forbid you'd tried to help us or had one nice thing to say to anyone about anything; all you care about is your sports and who's the most popular and can kick whom in the parking lot. You're *animals*." But now certainly she's gone too far and yet continues: "You've tried to sabotage this play from the very beginning, sabotaged us at every turn. And now there's nothing you'd like more than to see us humiliated in front of all these people today—" At last she pauses and looks at them, all startled and gaping at their desktops or each other, several of the girls close to tears. Even Danny blinks up at her with a confused, wounded look on his face. *I didn't mean you,* she should say, *the boys I was talking to know who they are,* but can't bring herself to, even to him, and simply proceeds to glower and pace, her heels clacking in the heavy silence. The ticking of the clock above her head seems to gain in volume and spur her on like whip lashes to a faster gait, a greater panic. And finally, when Mr. Loughlin's boys, the quickest eaters, loudly crumple their paper bags, she impulsively orders them back to the hall to help with the chairs. "Daniel, go with them."

"We don't need him," Brian says. "We can watch ourselves."

"Go directly to the hall," she says to Danny, ignoring the ridiculous suggestion. "Here, bring this with you," stuffing his untouched sandwich back into his bag. "Maybe your appetite will come back."

In the corridor, Danny walks several paces behind the boys, keeping his eyes to the floor and beginning a fresh rosary, perhaps his fourth. Yet there have only been instants of what seemed to him actual grace—or, if not grace itself, the shadow of its approach, as if all the various noises about him were braiding together and about to fuse into a single, bearable note, and the note become something lovely: a clear, lovely horn. He pictured himself, then, freed from his terrors and the knotting in his stomach and the cold tingling in his hands; he would step away from it all, like a serene ghost from its racked body. But always the shadow retreated, as it had when Miss Kaigh yelled *sabotage* and *humiliate,* quite far this time, and further frustrated now by wolfish whispers about how much he's going to suck in the play. "You're really gonna sc-sc-screw it up," Brian says. Then Kevin swipes the lunch bag from Danny's hand—easily, for he offers no resistance—and they toss it one to another until Joey opens it and describes its contents, a chicken-roll sandwich.

"I like chicken roll," Kevin says.

"You do? Mind if Lukas eats this?" Joey asks, tossing it to the boy even before Danny shakes his head. Then "Ring Dings!" he says and "Cool!" Brian says; and they scarf them down and toss the empty bag onto the floor. "Tell your mom we said thanks," Brian says, their laughter ringing in the stairwell as they push open the doors. All at once, piercing sunlight and shouts, the west-wing lots are filled with open-coated recessers: clustered girls, running boys, a Peewee cutting a red arc across the seamless blue. And now Arnold Graybosch, the 5C boy, easily catching it beside the island of pines, cries, "Hey, Kessler!"

Danny, shocked from prayer as the ball missiles toward them, turns quickly south for the hall—just the wrong direction, for quite unexpectedly the ball ricochets off Brian's fingers and, with a series of wobbly bounces, comes to lie on the asphalt not a yard from Danny's feet. "Pick it up! Hurry!" Brian yells, the ground vibrating with the hoof beats of onrushing boys. As Danny's hand closes over the strange, pimpled rubber, an unfamiliar dark-haired boy reaches him. "Here! Here!" he says; and Brian, farther off, "Here! Here!" He lobs it to the closer one, but widely, and the boy has to chase it and scoop it up, then he rushes off, laughing.

"You asshole!" Brian yells. "You gave it to the other team!"

"Team?" Danny says, blushing deeply and looking after him as the entire trio now races after the careening pack. "Miss Kaigh said we have to go straight to the hall," he calls feebly and, disregarded, rushes ahead alone, avoiding the stares of the girls on the sidewalks.

When he reaches the building, again he finds it deserted and locked. Fearing the imminent return of the boys, he runs to the side door of the church, entering as Miss Kaigh did this morning and immediately checking for the candles—all three flickering still, to questionable effect, beneath the Virgin's statue. He kneels in a front pew, glancing desperately from icon to icon; and then, halfway through his second Hail Mary—just as he's staring at the tabernacle in the northern alcove and regretting how much time has passed since he received, and how spoiled his mouth has become with all the unavoidable talking—his breath catches, the sudden sound resonating in the high ceiling. And just as suddenly he's mounting the aisle and kneeling on the step before the alcove, examining the double doors of the golden temple-shaped device; and, within seconds of ever imagining them touched by fingers not a priest's, the small knobs are beneath his own, resisting his tugs—a keyhole beside the right knob. He fishes in his trouser pocket for his house and bicycle keys, all much too large, then resorts to the army knife, jimmying and jiggling blade after blade into the slot, all in vain, until finally he extracts the long slim file, and, running it up the crack between the doors, a pressure gives way, and, astonishingly, the device clicks loudly open.

Again his gasp echoes in the ceiling and he looks over both shoulders, then all in a whirl strikes his hands into the gold-walled sanctum, removing the nested ciborium and plucking its cross-crowned lid, and oh, inside, a treasure of immaculate, consecrated wafers! The blessings of a hundred or more! He cannot, must not, touch them, yet with his own hand scoops up several at once—*Body of Christ, Amen; Body of Christ, Amen*—shoving them into his mouth and taking another larger handful and filling his pocket. Then he replaces the ciborium and pushes the doors closed, and pushes them closed again. Still they remain stubbornly sprung, loudly clicking open when he removes his hands; and here now another noise, from outside—someone running, several people. And, quickly swallowing the unchewed wafers, he dashes to the side door, about to push through it when he spies the boys, just this second bounding up the Music Hall ramp, and so stops short and ducks below the window.

"It's locked," he hears Joey say; and Kevin, "Where'd Curly go?"; and Brian, "Probably to tell on us." "I'll kick his ass if he does," Kevin says. "We'll beat the shit out of him," Joey says. "I'll do it," Kevin says; and now abruptly, "Look, it's Mr. Loughlin," Brian says, "he's waving, come on." Again the thumps of their shoes down the ramp and across the asphalt; and, after a moment's silence, Danny, touching the place on his throat where the hosts were roughly swallowed, peers out at the deserted hall, then up to the west wing, where he spies Miss Kaigh, a splash of red and white at the fore of the jogging company. Urgently, he scurries back to the tabernacle and examines the insides of the doors, then closes them in tandem and runs the file down the crack between. And at last, as they tentatively catch, he pulls his fingers back, wincing at the many prints on the golden doors, and races away without looking back—did he hear them click open again?—out the side door and down the steps and across to the hall ramp, where, just seconds later, Miss Kaigh reaches him, palms patting her jostled hairstyle.

"Why are you standing outside? Where are the boys?" she says and, bolting past him to the door, tries the knob and screams. "Locked! Do you mean to say . . . ?" And peering inside, "They haven't done any-thing? They haven't—?"

"There they are!" Rory calls; and Danny, hand arranged before his bulging pocket, turns now with the others toward the school and the loaded, approaching cart, the three boys who'd kick his ass riding the sides and saluting again.

"But it's twenty after! Mr. Loughlin," his teacher yells ahead, "it's twenty after! I thought you'd have most of it done by now!"

"Only so many hands," he says, muttering under his panting breath as he lumbers up the ramp with the keys.

In the echoing, unready hall, Liz turns from the colliding ants, their cacophonous unfolding and positioning, and asks Danny, "Were you able to eat anything?" But as he tenses and drops his hand casually from his pocket, his stomach, as if to betray him, churns loudly, and he clears his throat. "Apparently not enough," she says. "Try again in a lit-tle while." And here she orders him onstage before the new milk-crate stand. "Now climb up carefully. Will it hold you?" "Mm-hmm," he an-swers, lips sealed. "Okay, now step down. Okay, now step up again. Still okay?" "Mm-hmm." Then she collects several others and hurries with them to the boys' dressing room, where they sift through the props, separating them by scene and set. As she impresses on Rory and Paolo, the chief prop changers, which trees and chairs have to serve double or even triple duty—"Are you listening carefully?"—it strikes her that the most intricate array is for the scourging, for in addition to the wooden "throne" and Cleopatra's scratching pole cum whipping post, there's Mrs. Burke's scarlet robe, and the whips themselves, and the reed, and the wonderful, terrible crown. But now, where's the stretcher to carry Christ to the tomb? "Paolo, you said you were bringing your father's hammock!"

"I did," he says, pointing to a heap of tasseled blue-and-yellow fabric.

"*That* thing?"

"It's too bright. Right, Miss Kaigh? It's too happy-looking," Stephen says.

"Can we put one of the white sheets over it?" Rory asks.

"Yes, all right, cover it," Liz says; everything covered with a sheet. "But whatever you do, don't forget. You can't be carrying the martyred Savior on this kind of gaudy floral print." Then as Mr. Loughlin, having completed the next set of rows, leaves with the three boys again, she calls out to the remaining players, "Places, everybody. Scene one," in the clipped, director-like style she wishes she'd used all along. Well, too late.

And soon Danny, in Gethsemane, is forced to open his mouth and allow the mortal air to taint the holy residue on his tongue. Now he's sorry he ate the first three hosts so soon, for what good are they, wasted on rehearsal? "Daniel, why are you mumbling?" his teacher keeps asking, then makes him start over and interrupts with such frequent corrections that they haven't even finished the agony when the fourth load of chairs rumbles up the ramp.

"Oh, not now!" Liz cries over the commotion and watches vainly again as the players run to help and the rehearsal breaks apart. By the time the additional rows are installed—still not half what they'll need—they're down to twenty minutes; then after she's wrangled Mr. Loughlin's whippersnappers away and gotten everyone back in place, eighteen. And so they're forced to skip certain speeches and hurry through others, concentrating on scene transitions and on the troublesome raising of the cross at the crucifixion. With makeshift desperation, Liz has Timmy and Paolo hold up another sheet when the nailing's completed, to screen Danny while he climbs onto the stand. "As soon as he's in position and Patricia finishes the 'rude chore' speech, drop it. Okay? Now!" But the boys continue to hold up the sheet, looking behind them. "Well?"

"He's not on it yet."

"Daniel, what's taking so long? Let's go." And again, "Drop it!" she shouts. *Drop it,* the hall orders.

So they do, and now there he is, with his ghostly face and his arms stretched out before the beautiful cross; and the sudden sight is so striking and strange—all the more so because he's still in uniform—that she cries out, "Wonderful! Yes! Will you be able to do it like this in the play?" "Yeah," they say. And here she looks again at her watch—a mistake, for it's not just ten, but nine, almost eight, minutes of. "Right to the death, Daniel," she says, her voice more strained and high-pitched than she expected.

Danny, looking worriedly at the door, says, "F-F-Father, i-i-into Your hands I commend M-M-My spirit," then drops his head and sees, through slitted eyes, Brian raising the oval kitchen sponge impaled on a broomstick.

"Not *now*," Liz says. "He's dead already! You raise it when he says, 'I thirst.'"

"You mean we passed that?"

"Yes," she says disgustedly.

And here Danny, lips just feet from the boy's blond crown, whispers, "He-He-He is dead"; "He is dead!" the boy says, upon which Stephen shakes the cookie sheet below and Kevin pokes his head out of the dressing room, making quaking sounds from his own natural throat. "We don't need to *see* you!" Liz calls, in competition with the girls, squealing with stage horror, and just now Patty, shuffling up: "In the inthtant of Hith death all nature wath con— con—"

"Vulsed," Danny whispers, eyes still closed.

"Vulthed," Patty says. "The tholdierth fell to their kneeth and thaid, 'Truly He wath the Thon of God.'"

"Truly He was the Son of God," Brian and Joey say, falling, after which a too-lengthy silence ensues. Danny, knowing it a gross breach of his deadness, looks to Miss Kaigh—collapsed now on a folding chair, arms crossed, "Don't look at me; I'm not going to be able to help you"—then to Paolo: "L-L-Let us take Him down and bury Him."

"Let us take Him down and bury Him." Now Paolo reaches for the hammock—"Cover it first!" Liz says—and, when Danny collapses over it, the boys, attempting to lift him by the corners, say, "Whoa! Heavy!" and jostle him to and fro.

"You can't grunt like that! Watch what you're doing; you're dragging him!"

Danny feels himself tugged up more forcefully, his heinie raised from the floor.

"Daniel, drape your arm over the side," Liz suggests, vaguely recalling Christ's posture from a famous Italian painting. "Let it fall right to the ground."

And so, fingertips brushing the boards—"They took the body of Jethuth and carried it to the tomb"—he's lugged into the third room and dropped on the floor.

"Boys, be ready with the flashlights. Daniel, you'll be changing into the white robe."

"Okay," Danny says faintly. And then just as Patty says, "Early in the morning of the third day," and he's about to make his glowing reappearance, it happens: the ramp outside begins to rumble, not with the thunderous roll of the cart but with the unmistakable sound of feet, tramping feet.

Liz is the first to perceive them. "Oh my God," she mutters, glancing back at Sister Margaret and the first 5C students gawking at her from the doorway; and worse, behind them, on the dreadful horizon above their heads, she makes out other sections of the fifth and sixth grades, approaching like plaid warships on an asphalt sea.

— 18 —

Go Make You Ready!

In the business office, Carol rubs her eyes and looks up from her books, astonished to find it's already five of one; and she realizes, too, that her stomach's growling and that she hasn't taken her lunch yet. Not like her to let a meal slip by, she jokes at her own expense, but then quite soon this lightness gives way to a foreboding: is she supposed to be doing something right now, be somewhere? A meeting in Mr. McVee's office, maybe? No, not today. But here she wonders if the foreboding may be an intuition, something going on with her kids, one of them in trouble, needing her, and she looks around, vaguely, psychically worried, until all at once it hits her: the play. Oh no. How could she? When does it start? One? Yes, one. Oh no, because at this point, by the time she walks up there, she'll be fifteen, twenty minutes late. And now, even as she struggles not to smile—for twenty minutes seems perfect to her; she couldn't have arranged it better consciously— her heart hammers with dread to think of him standing offstage this very instant, watching all the kids streaming into the hall. He must be petrified, a beside-himself, stuttering mess.

Maybe she should be there; no matter what, by his side. What kind of mother is she? Late for her own son's play. And she hasn't even read the damn thing. Well, part of it: *Crucify Him! Crucify Him!* Maybe she could read the rest while she's walking up there? Where did she put her copy? No, forget it; she can't look now. And here she suddenly leaps up, so if anyone Danny's teacher knows were to see her, they'd say, *She leapt right up and rushed out to see her son's play.* Unfortunately, it's just Betty, at the desk opposite hers, who looks over curiously from her own accounting books.

"Lunchtime," Carol explains.

"Is it? Oh. Well, I haven't taken mine, either," Betty says. "If you wait a minute, I'll go with you for Chinese."

"Oh thanks, but I've got to . . ." But what Carol has to do she doesn't explain. The last thing she wants is one of the girls coming with her: *Oh, I'd love to see the play! I'll drive us up!* Of course, then she might get there on time, or at least, closer to on time . . . but no, it's out of the question. Betty'd tell the whole office when they got back, and then say what it was really like when she wasn't around. But neither can Carol think of what else she might have to do alone at the moment, and so just quickly walks off before her coworker can press.

"Is something wrong?"

"No no," she says, hoping Betty won't think she's some kind of snob or having an affair with an administrator. Well, she can't worry about everything. Punching out, she stops in the ladies' room to tease up the front of her hair and give it a good spray, then applies a fresh coat of lipstick and fastens the second button of her blouse—she is, after all, going to a crucifixion play. But as she's closing her pocketbook, she remembers, for the first time in months, her emergency Valium in her little plastic case, the several leftover yellow pills from the last time she renewed Dr. Whitehall's prescription; must've been just before the boys moved out. What's the shelf life of Valium? she wonders. Rooting down to the corners of the bag, she finds the case, and inside—yup, three. Does she dare to down one? A little late at this point, maybe, but by the end of the thing, just when she'll be feeling the most terrible, it'll start to kick in. And so, yes, she decides, furtively sliding one onto her tongue and swallowing it in the hall with a sip of water from the fountain. Supposedly the yellows are so mild anyway.

"Going to lunch alone today, hon?" Linda, the switchboard operator, asks as Carol makes for the doors.

"Uh, well, I'm—" she says. Outside, the grounds are flooded with sunlight and breezy warmth. Even the tulips in the beds are opening up now, cheerful dots of red and yellow and purple. Enough to make you forget your worries, she thinks, heading with no great speed up Main Street—at least for a block or two, for by the time she passes Janel's, those worries seem to be making a full-scale reinvasion, and she finds herself stopping in for a 100,000 Dollar Bar and a Tab. She *is* starved, stomach churning away, and there's no time for food-food. Come to think of it, she'd better pick something up for the way back, too, and so snatches up a Charleston Chew and a Nestle's Crunch.

"Oh, my favorites," the blue-smocked register girl says conspiringly.

Carol gives her one of her least-friendly smiles. *How could you eat such crap?* she imagines saying. *Well, you're eating them,* the girl might say. *They're not for me,* Carol could say. And the next moment, she's headed up Main Street again, slurping from the soda in one hand, shamelessly tearing at the oozing 100,000 in the other. Delicious, she thinks, oh absolutely.

Back in the Music Hall, a continuous double line of students and ever multiplying noise streams in through the side door: after 5A and 5C, the belabored entrance of Sister Ruth and the rest of 5B, then all three sections of the sixth grade, and those of the fourth interspersed with the third, the second, the first—the youngest filling in the front rows, and so on to the back, so that the heads of the sitting students are increasingly taller and mature, as if posed for "Stages in the Growth of a Child." All the while Mr. Loughlin, at the head of a new band of whippersnappers, lumbers up the ramp with armloads of chairs, trying to keep up with demand. "I'm afraid we still don't have enough!" Liz calls to him from just inside the door, where she directs the streams and greets the teachers and Sisters.

"I know it, I know it!" the huffing custodian says. "Got another cart comin'!"

Another coming? How? she wonders, and at the same time checks her watch again and scans the milling crowd for a lone, unfamiliar teacher. Could she have missed her? Shouldn't she be here already? "Pardon me," she says now, squeezing past Sister Theresa and the 3C and sailing up the side aisle toward the stage, where she finds two of her costumed players preening before the first grade: "No, *I'm* the Mother," Juanita's saying to Sister Ernestine, "she's Mary Magdalene," pointing to Ginger.

"But first I'm Pilate's wife," Ginger says, explaining her tunic.

"Girls," Liz says, hurrying them over to the stairs. "Tell everyone to wait for me by the dressing rooms. Where's Daniel? Is he still in the tomb?"

"I don't know," they say.

"Is he dressed?"

"I don't know."

And just as she's about to see for herself, the door at the rear of the hall swings open and a contingent of tall boys, each carrying folding chairs above his head, parades in, followed by the slender, mustached Mr. Walsh. *"Mr. Walsh?"*

"You mean the seventh grade's coming, too, Miss Kaigh?" Juanita asks.

"I don't know; no one told—" But now she straightens as, behind the man, an imposing, overcoated figure appears in the doorway. "Go!" she tells the girls, then sails back down the aisle as all rise and say, with deafening disunion, "GOOD AF-TER-NOON, AF-TER-NOON, SISTER REGINA MARY GINA MARY MUR-PHYYY."

"Good afternoon, boys and girls," *boys and girls,* the nun says, her steely voice reverberating to the far corners of the hall. "Please be seated now," *seated now.* "The remaining classes are on their way, and we'll be starting shortly. You will all have time to get back to your rooms before the buses arrive." Then as she turns to the chair-laden seventh-graders, and the hall begins to echo again with the murmurs and rustles of the audience, Liz rushes up to the nun, stammering apologies for the delayed performance and begging her pardon, but did she say remaining classes?

"Just the eighth grade," Sister's moon-face matter-of-factly relates.

"The eighth grade?" Liz says with disbelief, because that would mean—

"We didn't think it was fair to leave them out of it, and Mrs. Dillon was very keen on coming."

—the entire school. "Mrs. Dillon?"

"You know she studied drama in college."

"Oh yes." As Liz fixes her widened eyes on the last rows being formed and wonders where an additional hundred students—a hundred large students—will fit, Sister Regina, reading her mind, says, "If we run out of chairs, the rest will stand; there's no time to get any more." Then she adds, "I'm afraid the only one who won't be here is Father McGann."

"Father McGann?" Liz had forgotten all about him!

"He has a burial service this afternoon in Calverton."

Oh, thank goodness, she doesn't say. "I'm so sorry to hear that."

The nun nods gravely. "I'm sure he'd much prefer to be at the play." Now she steps closer. "How long did you say it was?"

"Long? Oh—uh . . . th-th-thirty minutes?"

"Thirty?" She glances at her watch.

"Not a *full* thirty minutes," Liz qualifies, and maybe it isn't; they've never gone from beginning to end without some disruption.

"I hope not," Sister says. "If it gets near ten of, we'll have to speed things along."

"Speed things along?"

"We'll use a system of signs."

"Signs?"

Then just as Liz is fretting over the details of Sister Regina's plan, and struggling not to betray her indignation—just trim off ten minutes, uh!—Carol, pausing before the side entrance of the hall, pales before the vast gathering within. This can't all be for the play, she thinks. It must be over already, and now the rest of the school is coming in for some type of assembly or Mass—that's what all the confusion reminds her of, Mass on Easter Sunday. Oh good, she thinks and, outwardly frowning as she steps into the hall, cries, "Oh no! Is the play over?" But right away two young girls in a nearby row inform her it hasn't started yet, and her frown becomes real. "Hasn't started?" She glances around with bewilderment. "But isn't this the Music Hall, where they have bingo?"

"Yes," they say, and Carol, searching vainly for Danny at front, feels her apprehension deepen as she regards the tremendous stage, empty but for a cluster of brightly colored tree cutouts occupying a tiny section at left, like a park for dwarfs.

"They're late," the first girl says. "Yeah, they're really late," the other says.

"And you're all here just for the play?" Carol presses. "Yes, yes," the whole row says.

"But I thought it was just for the fifth grade!" she says, almost a cry.

"We're the fourth," the first girl says, "and that's the third," pointing before her. "The fifth is back there . . ."

Carol doesn't listen to the rest but instead clicks her tongue and says, "Oh . . . boy," the only G-rated exclamation handy. As she searches for her son again and imagines dragging him out the door the second she sets eyes on him—*You can't.* —*I have to.* —*You're not.*—she discovers she's sweating and starts to fan herself and worry about her makeup and hair.

Liz, breaking from her conversation with Sister Regina, turns for the side aisle and immediately spots the tall brunet with the scowling, lost look on her face. On first glance, she appears to have the teased hair and penciled eyebrows of an office worker—an assistant to Mrs. Newman, maybe, or one of the mother-volunteers who come in to help with the filing. But on second, she believes she may recognize the woman's slightly crouched, apprehensive stance, her way of squinting about the room as if half-expecting something calamitous to happen. Could it be! "M-M-Mrs. Burke?" she calls, elbowing her way along the side aisle.

Carol, startled to hear her name, turns to the bounding girl with the flippy hair—a stranger to her, yet her big brown eyes stare up with such seeming recognition that she asks herself if they could've met before. A onetime aide at East Islip, maybe? Some kind of office temp or student teacher? "Yes," Carol says, temporarily lightening her scowl, "and you're Miss . . ."

"Kaigh. Elizabeth," Liz says, half-raising her right, twittering hand.

"Who?" the woman asks, not looking at it.

"Elizabeth Kaigh, Daniel's teacher."

"Danny's teacher?" Carol says, frowning at the loud harlequin pattern on the front of the girl's blouse, just the kind of thing she'd pass in the Young Miss department and snort, *Who the hell would ever wear that?* "*You're* his teacher?" she repeats with too surprised a tone, for then the girl shrinks back, unclasped hand dropping to her side.

"Well, yes."

Yet Carol presses, "Are you sure?" It doesn't seem possible—she's just a young little thing, looks barely out of school herself.

"Oh, I'm positive. Since September," she says.

In the confused instant that Carol adjusts her conceptions of Queen Elizabeth, her relief that she shouldn't be a finger-wagging old maid mixes with a general skepticism toward the school's personnel department. Obviously they're desperate for applicants, taking them right out of college; she wonders if this one's even certified. "Oh, I'm sorry. Of

course you're Miss Kaigh. Sure, Danny talks about you all the time."
This last line stripped of sarcasm. "That's some outfit," she adds, also
ambiguously, looking up from the shoes.

"Oh," the teen queen intones—recovering, it seems, for now she
steps closer, all smiling teeth. "It's just something I picked up at Gimbel's."

Gimbel's, no wonder, Carol thinks. Got the same taste as her husband.

Meanwhile Liz, her gaze dropping from the woman's lovely, deep-
blue eyes to her surprisingly conservative pantsuit and blouse—
evidently she's much more daring in her choice of sleepwear—wonders
if it wasn't a mistake not to have bought the skirt and jacket she'd had
in her other hand, instead of settling on this more bohemian ensem-
ble. Then again she did admire it, and aren't people drawn to just those
qualities in others that lie hidden in themselves? She hopes so and,
imagining herself now a kind of blazon of the woman's secret nature,
motions to a lapel of her jacket. "And your, uh . . . this color is so rich."

Carol nods. "It's royal blue."

And now the girl bursts out, apropos of nothing, "Oh, and—and you
as well."

"Me as well?"

"Daniel. He-He talks about you all the time; he simply adores you!"
Both hands now, beating the air like little wings.

"*Adores* me?" Carol says, skeptical but flattered.

"There's no question." And here a wing flutters up and beckons to
a forming group of scared-looking kids in bathrobes and sheets beside
the dwarf park. "Rory, where's Daniel?" she asks, and a towheaded boy
points to a room offstage. "Tell him his mother's here!" Even from this
distance Carol can make out the murmurs, "His mother's here, his
mother's here," and the other kids, too, in the nearby rows, all staring
up at her. Jesus Christ, did she have to scream it across the entire hall?
Then as if once weren't enough, she calls again, "His mother's here!
Tell him to come over!"

"Oh please," Carol says, "it's all right, he's busy." But now, as Danny
emerges from the room, both women blush and suck in their breath,
Liz because he's still in uniform and seems so wildly distraught to her:
big, bugging eyes darting over the hall; Carol because of how slight and

cowering he appears among the others. *Danny, stand up straight!* And oh, that namby-pamby hair—she told him to fix that.

"It's really warm in here," Carol says, fanning the deepening red of her cheeks.

"Is it?" Liz says, her own hands aflutter as the boy is pushed in their direction. "I'm so sorry. I really didn't expect so . . . many," here indicating the sea behind her without turning to look at it, lest Sister Regina hail her before she mentions the records, or Sibelius. *Yes, why so many?* Carol's about to ask but is prevented by Danny, who, head bowed, barely manages to stammer hello, his lips tangling hopelessly over the m's in *Mom*.

"I was just telling your mother what a pleasure you are to have in class," Liz says, at once upbraiding herself because she's not sure she'd gotten around to that yet.

That's not what she was saying, Carol thinks, narrowing her eyes at her son's blow-dried crown. She was saying another bit of bull: that he adored his mother, that he talked about her all the time. And now between her teeth, "Some class play," but he doesn't move or seem to hear her, just continues to stare at the floor as if he were a deaf-mute, a boy in a bubble. Liz, puzzling over the odd exchange—why won't he look at her? was that something unpleasant Mrs. Burke just whispered?—tells the woman how glad she is they were able to reach her.

"Reach me?" Carol asks, aiming her squint at the girl.

"We were having such terrible problems with-with—everything, but luckily we were able to get Mr.—and now we're running so—"

"Well," Carol says, brow wrinkled, "it's not that—"

"I hope we haven't interfered with your schedule."

"No, I just took lunch a little—"

"Later? Can you do that?"

"Sure."

"I see; this must be a free period for you."

"Period?" Carol says, scowling again. What does she think, the whole world's a little classroom?

"Or did you get a sub?"

"Sub?" And now as her son grunts and stutters louder, it occurs to her she actually does think she's some kind of teacher. What a riot!

Carol, who had to sweat out a general equivalency to land a book-keeping job at the public school business office, a *teacher*. Boy, she really can't keep any of the kids' parents straight, can she? Carol's got a mind to let her know right there she's really thinking of Mrs. Whoever but stops herself, for fear of pushing the girl off the edge she's so clearly teetering on. She half-considers slipping her one of her emergencies—though of course she doesn't and instead at last acknowledges her squirming son, "Yeah . . ." but then can't bring herself to say the rest of it and scoot him off to his dreadful fate. Didn't she say she was going to drag him out the door? Wasn't she going to object to the size of the crowd? However, now the girl's thanking her for something—records?—and, amid what seems an urgent plea from Danny, claims, "I've become such an admirer of Sibelius."

"Of who?" Carol asks, glancing from son to teacher.

And Liz, confidence shaken, carefully pronounces the name again: "Si-*bay*-lee-us."

"Mm. Well, sure you have, hon," Carol says.

Even as Liz's stomach flutters at the unexpected endearment, she worries about the woman's irritated expression. Maybe she herself doesn't care for the composer, however masterly his compositions? We all have our preferences, even among the great. "No, really," she says, going so far as to extend her hand to the woman's shoulder.

Carol sees the twittering thing coming and has to struggle not to shy away. But to her relief, it's just one little passing wingbeat before the dingbat adds, "It's made such an impact on my life." Then in the awkward silence that intervenes, she literally steps back from what strikes her as a force of nature: this large, already rolling thing, rolling on in spite of her. She feels as overwhelmed in its face as that little king who set his chair on the seashore and raised his hand to the waves. *Stop.* "I'm sorry," she says, glancing again at her son, who, maybe smartly, continues to avert his eyes. "You have to get started."

"Oh," Liz says, "but I'd love to—"

"No, I'll just—"

"You're more than welcome to—"

"—sit in the back."

"—up here." She points to the chair beside her own at the end of the first row, on which she's laid *Classical Masterpieces*.

But Carol shakes her head. "I'll be much more comfortable back there. I might have to leave a little early."

"Of course," Liz says, crestfallen she may miss the resurrection and "Hallelujah Chorus." "You-You have to get back to your classes."

"Right," Carol says, then repeats her morning "good luck" to her son and turns away.

It's all Liz can do not to follow or call her back—she hasn't asked about her music yet, the most important thing! And when will she suggest they meet for coffee? If Mrs. Burke leaves early, her chance is lost, completely lost. She must have made a terrible impression! That's why Mrs. Burke doesn't want to sit near her. Who would, when she's so nervous, and stuttering like a fool, like . . . ? And at last turning to Danny, himself stuttering and tapping relentlessly at her arm, she all but sneers—for in truth, she blames him for this attack of nerves, this-this *sickness* he's spread to her, to everyone. But now she sees he's pointing to Sister Regina at the center of the swelling commotion in the back, that the nun is frowning and indicating her watch: it seems Mrs. Dillon and the eighth grade have just arrived, the overflow filing up the side aisles and standing along the walls.

"Yes, Sister! Almost ready!" she cries, possibly unheard, and, brusquely turning the boy toward the stage, "The beard. Hurry!" She races up behind him and on through a clutch of lip-biting players— "Are we starting yet? Are we starting yet?" "Any minute."—to the boys' room, where she stops at the doorway, "Is everyone dressed?" before continuing in, lip-biters in tow. In no time, she punctures the tip of the spirit glue dispenser and dabs the thick, pungent adhesive along Danny's jaw and chin and above his lip and onto the coarse mesh of the beard, before pressing it in place. "Keep holding this down," she tells him, taking bits of black fuzz away on her sticky fingers, and then, "Oh, for Pete's sake," holding her hands away from her white pants, "Someone get me a towel!" Quickly Rory offers her Pilate's, and she tries to rub them clean. "Where's the wig?" she cries next, but here, too, hair collects on her fingertips as she pins it back in place. Doesn't that just top it all? After all her fuss, she ends up looking like a Neanderthal. She shakes her head, fighting back tears. "One more minute," she says to Danny, his hands pressed to his half-hidden face in a prolonged gesture of distress, "then get in costume, quickly."

However, here the boy murmurs something and she has to bend closer to hear: alone, he wants to get dressed alone. "Why?" she snaps, but then immediately surmises he needs a moment to collect himself. Don't even the very best actors require so much? "All right, yes, let's leave him alone now. Boys, follow me. Daniel, you have three minutes. As soon as Patricia says the title, start walking toward Gethsemane. Timothy, Rory, right behind him. Okay, Daniel?"

The boy looks up and mouths a response, unable, it seems, to utter a sound.

"Okay?" she asks, stomach free-falling.

But again he merely manages a nod.

"No. Let me hear you say it, the word. Speak!"

And now, "Y-Y-Y-Y—"

"Come on!"

"—esss," he whispers.

"What's your first line?"

He looks at her blankly, silently.

"What's the matter? What's the line?" she demands, glancing frantically at the other boys, for she discovers now that she herself can't call it to mind.

"My soul is sad, even unto death," Rory prompts.

"'My soul is sad.' Of course. 'My soul is sad,' Daniel. Don't you remember?" She struggles to contain her panic as the boy retreats to the corner, holding his face. "Keep saying it to yourself!" she calls after him. "Three minutes!" Wiping her fingers on the towel again, she pulls herself away and herds the others to the next room—"Girls, we're coming in"—then arranges them in a rough, shoulder-to-shoulder arc for a last-second inspection. "Okay, glasses. Hand them over." Here collecting Ginger's plastic coke bottles, Timmy's wire tinteds.

"But Miss Kaigh, I can't see without them," Ginger protests.

"I can't either," Timmy says.

"You can see well enough," she says, bolstered by the uncannily prescient warning she remembers from Biblical Costumes: Glasses should not be worn onstage even by those who claim they cannot see without them.

"But I really can't."

Likewise now she looks for wristwatches. "Off," she says to Rory. "Girls, that goes for jewelry, too—rings, bracelets, everything." After snatching all the articles from them—not, it occurs to her, unlike a thief at a holdup—she stows them in a shopping bag and checks to make sure everyone's wearing sandals. With them stripped of all obvious traces of twentieth-century-ness, she says, "All right, then," but is unprepared for what happens next: suddenly they break from the arc and huddle about her, bare eyes blinking up—each of them, even Kevin's, void, for the first time she can remember, of any trace of a squint or smart-aleck gleam; indeed, they're in dead earnest, the eyes of frightened children, looking to their teacher. Surely, she should say something to them, something rallying, some last important bit of advice. But what?

Down in the audience, in a seat Mr. Loughlin was kind enough to add to a row near the side door, Carol silently belches from an attack of indigestion and rummages feverishly and inefficiently through her pocketbook for Tums, chiding herself the whole while for eating all three candy bars on her walk to the school. How could she have done something so stupid? Doesn't she have any self-control? She wishes she could throw up, wishes, even, that she'd miss a good portion of the performance while heaving somewhere outside. She'd prefer that to the torment of sitting here and waiting for her son to humiliate them both before this army of Catholic youth—CYA, as she's begun to call it. She wonders if they even had this many for Oklahoma!, her little bit of hell she'd so comfortably forgotten about, and that now, thanks to her budding playwright, she seems to be reliving all over again. Well, she doesn't want to relive it, goddammit. She's sick of having things pushed on her, sick of kids and their sneaky ways. Why do people insist on having babies anyway? Isn't it enough to go through all of this crap once? But now, Stop it, she tells herself, you're hysterical. Imagine the state she'd be in if she hadn't taken the Valium. And no sooner does she think this than she comes upon the plastic case again and, removing the second-to-last pill, rolls it between her fingers. Looking out the corners of her eyes at the boys to her right, she lifts her hand to her mouth in what she hopes resembles a thoughtful gesture and slips the pill between her lips.

This just as Liz, with a last gust of inspiration, paces and gesticulates before her blinking company in the girls' dressing room. "'Suit the action to the word, the word to the action!'" she cries, not with any genuine hope that they'll understand the line and make use of it, but more like a magical incantation, an invisible fairy dust that she sprinkles over the stage. What matter that they glance at each other with wrinkled brows? It's Shakespeare! Poetry! Better than any go-get-'em commonplace she might've come up with. What's more, she says it beautifully, with desperate force; it astonishes her own ears, raises goose bumps on her own arms. She is, this moment, for all the world a fretting Hamlet: "'Hold as 'twere the mirror up to nature!'"

This last line, nearly shouted, carries to Danny in the next room, rising above the steady, muted swells of chatter and murmurs that roll up from the audience and across the stage and in through the open doorway. Now he starts and once again urges himself, within his haze of terror and exhaustion and inwardness, to stop praying, and to dress, for the time is upon him, right now upon him. Yet he can't will himself to move or to unfreeze his body, heavy again as if weighted with the stone, as if he himself has become a kneeling stone statue. *God, anything is possible with You. You could take it all away—with one word, one wave of Your hand.* The very next moment, just as he's imagining the extent of his mother's fury and the beating he'll certainly get now from his father—one like he's never gotten before, perhaps even worse than Robby's—and his panic is reaching its blackest, most mangled pitch, the line whispers through him: *Not as you would have it, but as God would.* He doesn't think the line, but rather it's said: Arram, appearing close by, placing his darker hand on Danny's shoulder; and this message—solemn, miraculous—frees him. *Yes,* he says obediently. *'As God would.'*

With Arram's help, Danny rises to his feet and sheds his uniform article by article, every old vestige of himself, onto the floor. Then he fastens the towel about his waist, pricking his thumb as he pushes the safety pin through the thick, bunched material, and again when it springs open and he has to bend the point out so it will stay fastened, each time wiping the bead of blood across the snowy face of the cloth. Then he laces up his sandals and dons the tan robe and ties it and transfers the consecrated hosts—many in pieces now—to its right, godly pocket, the McDonald's ketchup packets to its left. *Hurry,* Arram says; at the same time Danny hears his teacher again in the next room, "'Go make you ready!'" followed by the hesitant clacks of her heels and the duller thumps and swishes of other shoes following her out of the room. *See, your betrayer is near.* The footfalls continue for an instant and then abruptly halt, and Danny gasps and braces for the call.

One, however, that's still moments away, for his teacher has yet to hurry down to the stereo and start up the music—or at least that was her intention until an instant ago, when she, together with her wad-dling sound-effects boy and foot-dragging narrator, emerged onto the open stage and were hit with the full, terrifying vista: row upon row upon row of seated, standing, murmuring students; a high sea of eight hundred or more, rippling wall to wall, and all the way to the back of the building; and here and there—like bits of debris floating among the plaid and the blue and all the young, pink, upstaring faces—teachers, taller, in beiges and browns; Sisters, in rich black veils and cardigans and overcoats, and one long, extended swath of black where all the rarely seens have flocked together. Good Lord, were there even this many at the Roman trial? Would their judgments be as harsh? With this last thought, she comes to and shudders and lowers her eyes. "Walk," she says, and, stiffly proceeding to the stairs, hisses in to Danny, "Listen for Patricia," but hears nothing in return; and now with Sister Regina, in the third row, staring eagerly up at her, she nods bleakly and continues on to the stereo.

"Okay, boys and girls!" *Boys and girls!* The nun raises her hands and turns to face the audience, the murmuring and chattering dying off about her in widening, concentric bands. "Let us turn our minds now to the real meaning of Holy Week," *Holy Week,* "and to this play that the 5A class—"

"5B," Mrs. Sullivan politely interjects.

"—5B class will now present. As they are ready to begin, let us say a silent prayer for the actors and for ourselves," *for ourselves,* "that we may all learn from the story of the suffering and receive God's blessing."

Then a deeper, weightier silence falls as she clasps her hands and closes her eyes and, in but the time it would take to say *Hail Mary, full of grace,* opens them again and sits down. Suddenly Liz, finding herself the target of every eye in range, experiences something akin to a switch thrown on her nervous system: her fuzzy-fingertipped hands be-gin to shake uncontrollably, her teeth to actually chatter. *Oh please,* she prays, glancing to Mrs. Burke in her chair beside the door, who just as quickly turns her head, then at Sister Regina, who furrows her brow and nods again for her to proceed. Is her trembling visible? Is she the picture of terror? Either way, it's clear she can't possibly operate the stereo. "Stephen," she whispers to the boy at her right, "do the music."

"Me?"

"Hurry."

His cookie sheet clatters to the floor as he kneels before the system.

"'Summer,'" she hisses. He nods, thick fingers and successive chins intent on powering the turntable and positioning the needle; astonishingly, he succeeds in placing it at the beginning of the track, and the soft opening notes of the violins rise, however faintly, over the first rows of the hall. "Good job," she mutters—regrettably, for then he bursts into a smile and jumps up excitedly, right knee bumping the turntable and sending the needle well into the galloping hysterics of Strauss's "Radetzsky March."

"Oh no. Stop it, quick!" and, over the giggles of shoe-swinging first-graders, "Not the right song." Mrs. Sales, in the second row, winces compassionately until, with a little scratch, the Vivaldi floats up again. Patty, from her station near the stairs, regards her teacher with as urgent an expression as her impassive face can muster: "Now?" Liz gives her a last pleading look before slowly nodding, then as the girl begins to climb, lurches backward to her chair, fairly collapsing on it. *God help them*, she thinks, stomach wrenching as it all trots away from her, into the lions' den.

The Passion of Danny Burke

Amid the moody pulsing of the violins, the girl shuffles to center stage and turns to face the audience. At once her habitually staid eyebrows tilt up slightly and she seems to sway backward, as if pushed by a wind. Then quite suddenly her eyes, momentarily stripped of their apathetic sheen, spark with pitiable intensity—*Shaking in her boots,* Carol thinks—before she glances down at her index cards, reads the top one, and looks up again. And when at last she breathes in, silver-glinting mouth yawning wide—*Don't do it, run!*—half the assembly slides down in its seat, bracing for the first offenses of her monotone lisp or just sensing, from the look of things, some impending blunder. But by the swells of laughter that soon break, particularly from the students along the walls and in the back, it seems no one was prepared for the startling volume the girl musters to announce the title of the play or the hissing ferociousness with which it echoes through the hall, as though it had gotten into her head that she'd have to scream at the top of her lungs to be heard by such a mob: "THE PATHON AND THE RETHURRETHON OF CHRITHT!" *RETHURRETHON OF CHRITHT!* "BY DANIEL BURKE!" *DANIEL BURKE!*

Yeah, she can sure project it, Carol thinks, her own cheeks just slightly less colorful than those of Miss Whatsherface's in front, *probably heard her across the street in the beauty parlor.* And now she glares at the clutch of pimple-nosed hardy-hars carrying on to her right despite the shushing of the teachers, her revulsion just as strong and intact, it seems, as when their hair was shorter and they wore the old Immaculate Conception jackets. To her they're one and the same, these boys, a kind of generational constant; might even be sons of some of the brats she went to school with. Might even be her own sons, come to think of it, not too many years ago . . . and here she drops this vexed train of thought altogether and winces at the poor girl onstage, the principal-Sister advising her in front of everyone and calling her *young miss.* "Young miss, we'll be able to hear you if you lower your voice a little." *Voice a little.*

Practice what you preach, Sister Mary Bugle-Mouth, Carol thinks, a sentiment not altogether different from Liz's, her eyes presently narrowing at the principal's barking profile. Unbelievable! First she wants her to "speed things up," now she's telling her players how to say their lines? *Shut up already, stay out of it.* And then almost to Liz's gratification, Patty resumes at an only slightly less ear-splitting volume: "LEAVING JERUTHALEM, JETHUTH AND HITH DITHIPLES THOON REACHED THE GARDEN OF—" here looking down at Liz, who quickly shakes her head "—THE GARDEN," then over to the doorway of the boys' dressing room, where Paolo and Timmy huddle, casting goggle-eyed glances at her and Liz before turning back to the room. Patty continues hesitantly, "THITH GROVE OF OLIVE TREETH . . . HAD BEEN A FAVORITE RETREAT OF JETHUTH IN HAPPIER . . . DAYTH . . . BUT TONIGHT IT HAD NO CHARM FOR HIM . . . FOR HITH THOUL WATH TROUBLED WITH . . . WATH TROUBLED WITH . . ." Suddenly the boys disappear inside and Patty stands awkwardly, looking to Liz again, who in turn looks with increasing alarm to the dressing room, from which indistinct whispers are emanating. Oh no no no, please say it's not happening. Is it happening? Of course it is, just as she always predicted: two frustrated apostles, reemerging with raised hands. And still their words, already written in her mind—"Miss Kaigh, he's not coming!"—take her breath away.

"What?" She glances sideways at Sister Regina, then over her shoulder at Mrs. Burke.

Oh brother, looks like they've got another one, Carol thinks, *shaking in his boots.* And who's this now? Christ? The star of the whole thing, won't even come out on the stage? Too much. She looks down at the floor, touching her fingers to her temple. Well, maybe he's just a sensible boy, knows a disaster when he sees it. In fact, this could be the best outcome of all, the star getting terror-struck and the whole thing having to be canceled before Danny's king figures in. Oh God, she wonders if anyone fixed that robe of Gerry's, and at the same time takes solace in the thought that he'll be wearing some kind of crown—the crown will hide his hair and maybe disguise him completely. And then suddenly another belch sneaks up on her, the crisp double pop heard by the future ex-cons to her right, their eyes widening and hands flying to their mouths. "Oh, pardon me," she almost says, but instead casts an accusing look about her, enough to discourage the daring few who glance in her direction.

At front, the apostles abandon their whispers and call urgently into the dressing room—"Come on, everyone's waiting!"—and Liz, who's been miming her dismay and trying to find the courage, if not to rush up to the room herself, at least to call to the boy from her seat, is at last shaken from paralysis by Sister Regina's ardent glances, and by the way the nun huffs and leans forward, on the verge of standing up. "Okay! Okay, everyone!" Liz says quickly and has the presence of mind not to use his name: "Okay, players, let's take it from the top again, and everyone BE READY!" Then she motions to Stephen to restart the track. "Don't jump."

And once again Patty: ". . . FOR HITH THOUL WATH TROUBLED WITH . . . WATH TROUBLED WITH . . ."

And this time, as all look to the dressing room, the wigged and bearded Danny pokes his head out the doorway, hand pressed to his tan-robed heart. Liz catches a glimpse of the jet hair, his left, fearfully peering eye, before he ducks inside again—too soon to perceive her mouthed *Get out there!* and sharp finger pointing at the stage. Then she tucks the finger beneath her crossed arms and glances about her, blushing on top of blushes to imagine what her expression must've looked like. Yet no matter how vicious or ugly, it wasn't half the rage she feels, half an indication of the vitriol stomping through her mind: *Little bastard, you wanted to play Christ so much, got your little spoiled way, and now you won't even come out on the stage when the entire school's waiting? You make an ass out of me like this? Out of the whole company? I hope the ceiling falls down on your head!*

In the dressing room, Danny, swatting at the hands that try to grasp his robe and tug him forward, cries, "No, no, leave me! I'm-I'm-I'm-I'm coming."

"But you have to come now, we're supposed to be in the Garden," Paolo says.

"You go first, th-then I'll come."

"But we're supposed to follow *you*."

"It-It-It doesn't matter."

"All right, we'll go first," Paolo says, "but you have to come right after. You swear you're gonna come?"

And so they move toward the doorway again, and Danny follows at a distance until they clear it and pass into the open, then quickly retreats out of sight, stuffing pieces of host into his mouth. *Body of Christ, Amen. Body of Christ, Amen.* Just as the boys race furiously back in, he leaps toward the door again, nearly colliding with Timmy. "G-G-Go," he says, and again the boys about-face, while Danny, baby-stepping after them, looks at last to Arram, standing just inside the doorway, and even reaches a trembling hand toward his skinny, tan fingers. *Hail Master,* his friend says, touching his lips to Danny's cheek; then the next instant, he hears Patty cry, "—*HITH COMING PATHON!*" and emerges into the brilliant daylight.

Instantly he's doused with laughter, a great, spraying break from a sea he doesn't dare look up at. Instead he blinks at his bare, bluish toes, a long and violent shiver jolting his frame.

Liz groans and blushes below, for it's the same laughter she heard from her players in the morning, magnified a hundredfold, and rifled through with the vicious cackles of upper-class boys. She wants to turn and scowl at the entire assembly in full view of Mrs. Burke, so the woman can see how utterly she sides with her son, but then abruptly imagines the mother scowling back at her—*Look what you did to him!*—and so bows her head and stares fixedly at the red toes of her shoes.

And just as well, for behind her, Carol, the two Valium humming through her bloodstream, is covering her mouth and struggling to compose herself, despite her former glares at the boys. It's just such a travesty, this poor kid, finally stumbling out of the room for his big appearance in this pathetic wig and beard, looking more like Captain Hook with a hangover than Christ on His way to the Garden! And now she can't help it—a bubble of laughter escapes her fingers and spreads down the row like a contagion, attracting the attention of a gap-toothed nun who furrows her brow. Effectively chastened, Carol hangs her head with the others, staring at her blue flats and wincing at the echoed shushing and indignant calls of the principal for silence. At last, when the disturbance has died away, she looks up again. And quite suddenly, the cowering manner with which the boy teeters toward the neon trees strikes her as terribly, terribly familiar. She glances again at his robe, scrutinizing its material and color, and feels the blood recede from her face and hands.

At the same moment Liz, watching through half-opened eyes as Danny stops before the entrance to the Garden, tightly clasps her glue-sticky hands. *Pick up your head, dammit!* Didn't she tell them to make sure they looked at the audience? Not enough, maybe. And now everyone, including Paolo and Timmy, stares at him with expectation and dread, and she tries not to squirm as his mouth gapes dumbly open, then closes again. *Take a deep breath*, she mentally advises, and does so herself.

But the problem is that Danny, because his mouth has gone so suddenly dry, is unable to swallow the bits of hosts adhered to the back of his tongue. At present, he's trying to push them forward, so he can chew them more and force them down, yet they don't seem to want to move.

"My soul is sad. My soul is sad," the boys whisper.

What's he doing with his mouth? Liz thinks. Not chewing gum, is he? During the performance? Now it seems he may even be retching again!

"What's the matter with you?" Timmy asks. Danny points to his throat and mouths the words, "I can't speak."

"Is something stuck in his throat?" Paolo asks.

"Hit him on the back," Timmy says, swatting him.

And now behind them, the sea murmurs again, and Sister Regina leans forward, tossing her resonant whisper across several rows, "Miss Kaigh, is this part of the play?"

Liz clenches her teeth and tilts her head slightly, not quite answering before a loud, throat-clearing sound snaps their attention back to the front: Danny, quivering mouth open again, struggling to form the first word, "M-M-M- . . . M-M-M- . . ." She squints down at her shoes again, chanting beneath her breath, "My soul is sad, my soul is sad," and, a full, harrowing moment later, hears the line mumbled above, a long and sibilant string of stammers ending in *d-d-d-death*.

"Huh? What?" those in the audience who aren't giggling ask; "Daniel," Sister Regina says, "you'll have to speak louder." *Louder.*

Bewildered by the request and by the fact that his mouth, so recently touched by the consecrated hosts, should yet produce such graceless speech, Danny stumbles through the line again.

"Louder still."

Upon the third, mangled rendition—one punctuated by scattered surfacings of shushed and half-suppressed bursts of laughter—the nun relents, and he's free to stutter his request to the apostles to sit and watch, and to turn abruptly for the interior of the Garden, upsetting an olive tree and quickly righting it before collapsing to his knees and shaking his clasped hands heavenward, "F-F-F-F-Father . . ."

Carol, now rigid with rage and mortification, her mouth in an appalled, frozen O, tries to hum away the excruciating stutters, the mammoth silences. It's more than she can bear, an auditory torture, a soundtrack of hell: "L-L-L-Let this c-c-c-cup-p-p-p-pass Me by . . ." She's going to have to scream. *Stop! Stop this performance at once! March right up the aisle past that teacher's chair, I specifically forbid him to play Christ!* then storm onto the stage itself and yank him off by the collar of Gerry's robe. But now here, knowing she probably won't do any of this, she eyes the exit at her left. Only with her luck, the knob won't turn right, or the door will stick in its jamb—it looks like one of those old doors that would just stick like that. Then, too, she can't imagine moving with the kind of speed such an action would require; she feels suddenly old and infirm; it could take whole minutes to get up and over and through, and by then everyone would see her and know—*the mother, leaving!* Dammit, why did that ninny have to yell across the hall like that? Now she has to stay in this chair, hand pressed to her stomach, wincing at each whisper and giggle, incessant ripples throughout Danny's speech, the ripples rising into waves whenever he gets up awkwardly to shake his finger at the sleeping apostles, once tripping on his sandal and twice more upsetting a tree. Finally, with her pulse spiking so high she can feel it in her throat, Carol hears the call of the last pill in the case, the last lonely pill, fishes it out, and slips it on her tongue. There, she thinks, working up her scant saliva and swallowing it down, now all available help is on its way.

This just as her Son of Man above is betrayed into the hands of sinners: Frances, her long hair concealed beneath the hood of the striped Judas robe, approaching the Garden with the helmeted, swaggering guards. The claps and appreciative murmurs that greet the boys' entrance sting Danny, even in his sweating, breathless state, even as his heart gallops at such a breakneck pace he wonders how his chest can contain it—because they've only had to appear, wearing the armor he himself made, to receive applause; they've only had to be themselves. But now, glancing up bitterly from his ugly flipper feet, he finds himself recoiling from the boys' fierce expressions and zestfully brandished swords—"Hi-ya! Ya!"—actually taking a step backward.

"The man I shall embrace is the one!" Frances shouts over their battle cries, making no discernible attempt to disguise her nasal, girlish voice. "Arrest Him and lead Him away, taking every precaution!" And here she turns to Danny, as if happily greeting a friend, "Hi, Master!" but too sharply, for strands of her blond hair fly out of the hood. "Ah!" she screams, quickly tucking them away. Then as her lips approach, without quite touching, his cheek, Danny, grimacing and looking for Arram in the dressing-room doorway, sustains another raucous spray of giggles—though a lesser one, certainly, than if they'd gone with a boy.

"J-J-J-Judas," he murmurs, "do you betray the S-S-S-Son of Man with a k-k-kiss?"

Next Timmy, jumping ahead five lines, "Lord, shall we use the sword?" squints and swipes his tin foil weapon wide of Joey's ear. The boys, taken by surprise, scramble for a moment, at last producing the cardboard cutout and tossing it to the floor.

"Oh!" the players say too late, and Danny, retrieving the ear and pressing it to the side of Joey's wrongly grinning face, mumbles to Timmy to put his sword back where it belongs. But then, intending to secretly slip the ear into his robe pocket beside the ketchup packets, he drops it on the floor—evidence refuting the miracle—and looks at Brian. "Sh-Sh-Should I pick it up?"

"No," Brian says, stepping on it; and so Danny, neglecting all mention of angels and fulfilled Scriptures, says, "Th-Th-This is your hour—the triumph of darkness!" his voice at last spasming to a perceivable volume and carrying, to the passing surprise of Liz and the players, a whiff of genuine outrage and authority. But he cowers again as the boys rush upon him, tightly tying his wrists with a robe sash and pushing him toward the opposite side of the stage. As Patty relates how "JETHUTH WATH LED THROUGH THE DARK THTREETH OF JERUTHALEM TO THE HIGH PRIETH'TH HOUTH," the fleeing apostles, taking the trees with them, disappear into the boys' dressing room, from which Rory then emerges, crowned with a paisley bandanna and carrying a folding chair, followed by the also bandannaed Paolo. Rory opens the chair at center stage and sits down, Paolo standing beside him, and together they wait for the guards, who, crying their *Mush*'s and *Move it*'s, propel their tripping prisoner along the periphery of the stage. At each turn Danny, struggling to balance himself with tied hands, glances at his right pocket, horribly imagining the hosts spilling onto the floor; and then, once or twice, also, the boys themselves trip—no one, it seems, immune from the menace of oversized sandals—only to recover gracefully and push and jostle Danny harder.

And as much as Carol—prying her eyes from the door, cruelly close division between agony and peace—is conjuring mother-son torture scenes not entirely different from this one, she rankles at these little smart-asses doling out the insult and injury with such obvious relish. What, they don't like Danny? Or can they be such good actors?

"Here's the prisoner!" Brian cries, at last shoving Danny into the invisible house. "Here's the dastardly Jesus!" Joey adds, to the clear delight of many; then the two step aside, facing the audience with crossed arms, smug guards at attention.

Liz, leaning so far out of her chair now her knees are almost touching the floor, only glancingly perceives this brief respite from derision, determined as she is to have the third track on side two played. "The second big black groove," she whispers to Stephen, yet still he crash-lands the needle into the furious finale of *Swan Lake*.

"No, *Finlandia*," she says, and again, "*Finlandia!*" louder, looking back at the mother and her now vacant, numbed expression. Oh, what must she think of them? "The third song!"

"This one?" the boy asks, looking up from the whirling um-pa-pa's of "The Blue Danube Waltz."

"I said the third track, the third!" She's almost yelling now, about to rush up to the stereo herself, when at last the menacing horns rumble from the one good speaker before her. "Yes, yes! Leave it!" she says, just as Paolo, false-witnesser, claims he heard Jesus say He would destroy the temple and rebuild it in three days. Then Rory, not aghast enough, says to Danny, "Have You no answer. To what these men. Testify against You? I order You. To tell us under oath. If You're the Messiah. The Son of God."

"It-It-It is you who-who say it," Danny answers. "B-But I tell you this . . ." And just as he's describing the miracle they'll soon see, and his voice is again struggling clear of its stammers and approaching a genuine resonance—the beard, which has been gradually loosening from the sweat dripping down his hairline, detaches from the right side of his face, swings out, and, detaching from the left as well, plops to the floor like a shot bird. Amid gasps and snickers from the court, titters and groans from the sea—Liz's groan, and Carol's, louder, that her son should be this much more recognizable—Paolo snatches it up and helps press it back onto his face. But in a moment, when Danny lowers his bound hands, it drops again, and they all look to Miss Kaigh. "Forget it," she whispers. And Rory, who's supposed to leap up in a rage and feign to rip Danny's robe, uncertainly stands and says, "You heard the. Blasphemy," though clearly no one has. "WHAT. IS. YOUR. VER. DICT?" he adds, delivering the cue with special fracturing and volume. Then Paolo, joined by Stephen below and Kevin in the dressing room, shouts, "HE DESERVES DEATH!" the overlapping cry echoed throughout the assembly, first by a pocket of boys along the wall, next by a section of Liz's own class, like a continuation of yesterday's practice.

"All right, Miss Kaigh?" Sister Regina, seemingly pleased, calls across the rows.

"Oh, well, sure," Liz says, in no position to argue.

And the nun stands right up: "Let's all speak the part of the crowd. Ready? 'HE . . .'"

". . . DESERVES DEATH!" they scream, like a thunder.

"Very good!" Sister says, sitting down again. Yes, *wonderful*, Liz thinks. And, *Get me out of here*, Carol prays, as the smart-asses onstage push Danny from one to the other and pretend to spit at him—she hopes they're pretending—and now they blindfold him and swing at his face. "Play the prophet for us, Messiah!" the blond booms joyfully."Who struck you?" Then he and his sidekick explode with seemingly genuine laughter, continuing their jeers in pantomime as the squinting boy in the brown robe reappears at a stealthy remove to the left, hood raised. Right away he's approached by some kind of Spanish tray-toting girl, her hair tied up in a kerchief.

"Yoo-hoo!" she says, waving at the boy, her pink nail polish visible even from this distance. "Excuse me, mister! Aren't you a follower of Jesus?"

"I do not know the man," the boy says, slinking away.

And now some other boy pokes his head out a doorway, "Cock-a—!"

"No!" the girl snaps. "I'm not finished."

"Oh," the crower says, disappearing again.

"You were with Jesus of Nazareth!" she continues, tossing the tray and all its invisible contents to the ground.

"I do not know the man," the slinker says—Saint Peter, Carol realizes now, same schmo who gets the keys to heaven.

"You're one of them! Your accent gives you away!" the girl cries, stomping her foot. "I have a mind to smash you, like these plates!"

"I do not know the man."

"Now?" the boy in the room asks.

"Yeah," the girl says.

"Cock-a-doodle-doo!" he cries, joined by the fat hand at the foot of the stage and the death-rally boys along the wall, "COCK-A-DOODLE-DOO!" And so carried away do they get that Danny's teacher glares over her shoulder at them. "All right," she says, "enough crowing."

As the players all exit, leaving the chair at center, Danny, herded toward the boys' dressing room by the guards, turns to Timmy with a look *not of reproach, but of understanding and forgiveness,* as suggested in *The Life.* Stating his "Boo-hoo-hoo," the ashamed apostle rushes off before them, hands covering his eyes. Inside, as the pent-up Kevin greets the guards with back slaps—"You guys were cool!"—Timmy begins to search blindly around the room. "Does anyone know where Miss Kaigh put my glasses?" In the ensuing commotion and flesh-flashing changes of costume—guards to soldiers, high priest to governor—Danny struggles to keep his eyes to the floor and to stand aside inconspicuously. Then, remembering the whipping post and other scourging props that need to be placed outside the doorway, he quickly transports them, careful not to look up at the open sea when he crosses onto the stage.

Good Lord, Liz thinks, shielding her eyes from the spectacle of Christ arranging His own torture set—one that Carol can make little sense of. Isn't that a cat's scratching post? What the hell do they need that for? Can't they just crucify him quick and get it over with? Now Danny dashes back to the dressing room, finding the courage to sidle up to Timmy and whisper, "H-H-How did *I* do?" "Huh?" the boy says, moving his face closer and making slit-eyes, "Danny?" So he turns to Paolo, "D-D-D-Did I look stupid?" but the dark-skinned boy recoils with widened eyes, saying nothing. Finally he poses the question to Joey, and the boy, now tunicked, repeats loudly, "Did you look stupid?" then begins a chorus of yeahs: "Yeah." "Yeah," Kevin says. "*Yeah,*" Brian says, "you looked like a stupid dick." "You couldn't have looked more like a stupid dick if you were dead," Joey says. Sufficiently stung, Danny retreats to the corner, fingers picking through the hosts in his right pocket, heart scavenging for hope. Hadn't he just felt grace swoop briefly down on him? Hadn't his voice rung out clearly, even just for several words? Perhaps more next time, more clear words. *Please, God,* he prays, facing the wall and lifting the blessed shards to his tongue. *I am not worthy to receive You. Amen the Body of Christ.* And from outside, the elephantine lisp: "AT DAY-BREAK, THE ELDERTH AND THCRIBETH HANDED JETHUTH OVER TO PILATE . . ."

"Come on!" Rory says, rushing to the door, a hand steadying the glittered wreath pinching his blond hair.

"Wait!" Paolo says, pointing to the bowl and towel by the door. "Isn't this the scene you wash your hands?"

"Good call," Rory says, scooping them up and entering with unstately swiftness, followed by the spear-and-shield-toting soldiers, their costumes and weapon wielding once again garnering easy applause. When Rory reaches the chair and sits down, the admired pair standing at attention on either side, Paolo and Timmy, both now in the high-priest bandannas, come for Danny and lead him out again with copy-kitten heckling and boyhandling.

"What accusation. Do you bring. Against this man?" Rory asks, even before they've stopped walking, and there follows a confused and halting interrogation, in which Paolo, in his muttered list of claims, says he found Danny perverting the nation.

"*Sub*verting," Danny whispers.

"Sub-verting," the boy repeats, "the nation."

Rory bends to Danny, "Surely. You hear. How many charges. They bring against You?" As required, Danny says nothing, and the boy quickly leans back again and stage-whispers to the soldiers. "Psst. Psst."

"What?" Brian whispers back, a real question.

"Kevin," Rory says.

The soldier-boy glances toward the dressing room, within which the smirking, messy-haired stray waits in his tattered robe. "Oh yeah," he says, reaching for another sash looped around his belt, "come on." Together he and Joey hurry across the stage.

"You have a custom. That I should release. Someone to you. At the Passover," Rory says as Kevin's hands are tied behind his back. "Who do you. Wish me to release? Barabbas, the robber and murderer—?" At which point Kevin's dragged forward, writhing and roaring through his small, clenched teeth, "Rrr-rrr-rrr! Rrr-rrr-rrr!" and the audience ripples with the high-pitched squeals of the children in front; gawky, deeper delights in the back. Who would've guessed it? Liz thinks, her worst student, a tiny island of pride. "—or Jesus, the so-called Messiah?"

"Away with this man! Release Barabbas!" Paolo and Timmy cry. And Sister Regina, only half-standing this time, "Everyone?"

"AWAY WITH THIS MAN! RELEASE BARABBAS!" *RELEASE BARABBAS!*

Now Ginger, in her bordered tunic and gold headband, weaves and trips myopically toward the trial, stopping at last beside Paolo. "Husband," she says.

"No, not me. Over there," Paolo whispers, pointing to Rory.

So she weaves and trips on. "Husband," she says to Rory, "have nothing to do with this just man. I had a dream about Him today that upset me."

To no surprise of Carol's, the cross-eyed wife's prophecy is largely ignored, and the Pilate-boy turns back to the bandanna twins. "Then what am I. To do with. Jesus. The King of the Jews?"

"Crucify Him!" the two shout. And now the intrusive principal has but to raise her hand and the audience thunders, "CRUCIFY HIM! CRUCIFY HIM!"—Carol's line, which she immediately disowns with a frown, terrified to hear it echoing around her so, and to see them all wagging their fists like apes. Of course, she herself had wagged her fist in Danny's bedroom and had even made a furious kind of smile. But that was just horsing around; this—this sounds almost real, as if she's suddenly surrounded by those old, bloodthirsty Jews. She casts an alarmed glance at her son and finds his expression, as he stares into the heart of the crowd, not really like terror at all. She doesn't know what it's like, can't recall seeing it before. Dazed? Disoriented? Excited, even, in some crazy way? But she quickly dismisses this last thought and focuses instead on how annoying it is that he simply continues to stand there, silently, with them all carrying on—"CRUCIFY HIM! CRUCIFY HIM!"—even as she realizes that this is how it goes, the behavior of the original article. Well, she's sorry, but *she* could never have done it, then or now; she would've had to tell them to go somewhere, to shove something where the sun doesn't shine.

At last Pilate sits up. "Why? What has He done? I find no crime. Deserving of death in Him. I will therefore chastise Him. And release Him." With outstretched arm and finger, he orders the soldiers to scourge the pris-o-ner, but first they untie the unruly, teeth-baring Kevin, who struts in a circle and wags his clasped hands overhead, "I'm free! I'm free! Barabbas rules!"

Barabbas rules? Liz thinks, sliding down in her seat, her former impression of the boy restored. Then as the crowd cheers "YEA! YEAH!" and the soldiers yank and prod Danny toward the scourging station, she snaps, "Patricia!" and the girl, seemingly in a daze of her own near the steps, lifts her head and climbs up.

"TAKING JETHUTH TO A ROOM INTHIDE, THE THOLDIERTH FORTHED HIM INTO A THTOOPING PO-THITHON AND TIED HITH WRITH TO A LOW WHIPPING POTH."

And here Joey turns to Brian, "Are we supposed to pull the robe down first?"

"No," Danny says urgently, "not till the crucifixion."

"Why?"

It occurs to him to say: "If-If-If the whips leave marks, Miss Kaigh will stop you."

"What do you mean?" Joey asks.

"He means he wants us to really hit him," Brian says.

"Cool," Joey says.

As Danny stands with bent, robed back toward the audience, the mystery of the cat toy becomes clear to Carol. Oh Jeez, they're actually going to show this? she thinks, squinting and sliding down in her chair like a kid at a horror movie.

"THEN THEY BEGAN THEIR TATHK, LATHING HIM WITH LEATHER THONGTH TIPPED WITH METAL."

Metal? "One! Two! Three!" the boys holler, the whips cracking frightfully and sometimes looking very much like they're hitting her son's back. *Hey, watch!* she thinks, flinching as the strokes land and as the crowd begins to murmur and count along with the boys, "FIVE! SIX! SEVEN!" "Don't tell me they're going all the way to forty," she says aloud, her lone voice swamped by the force of the many around her, growing with the numbers. "We get the idea!" she says at eleven. At fourteen, "I hope they're not hitting him!" Then at sixteen she taps the shoulder of the pimple-nose to her right. "I hope they're not really hitting him," she repeats. The boy glances at his teacher before daring to whisper, "It's just a play."

"I know that," Carol says, pursing her lips at him—even as Liz's own stomach flutters with excitement: a guilty near-pleasure, for she, too, fears that whatever power the scene may have is coming at Danny's expense. These are the same boys he'd like so much to be friends with; not even in a play will they be kind to him. In fact, some of the lashes are clearly hitting his back—though the whips, of course, are just light rope. She glances warily over her shoulder, wondering if Mrs. Burke realizes this, but, oh dear, no, she doesn't look happy at all. What's she saying to that boy? *I could kill that teacher. Why is she letting them hit my son?* And the next instant, when the mother looks up in her direction and widens her eyes meaningfully, Liz snaps right around, waving her hand and even calling, "Boys?" But so engrossed are they in their charge—"Twenty-six! Twenty-seven!"—that they don't seem to hear or see her. Again she glances at Mrs. Burke, returning the meaningful glance, *I'm sorry. I'm trying to stop them.* And at the same time to her right, Sister Regina, making a move-it-along motion with her hand. "Yes, Sister," Liz says, waving at Brian's back.

Onstage, beneath the shouted numbers and snarled asides of the boys, *"Asshole!" "Queer!"* and even as the sweat drips down from under the wig, loosening the bobby pins and staining his face, Danny wishes the whips would hail down harder, that the mere stinging he feels were the deep, unendurable burning. But as it is, everything is a compromise, a weak approximation of the hugeness of the torture inflicted on Jesus; and he imagines his own slight shoulders and the pointed wings of his back covered with red hatch-marks, and the marks splitting open and oozing blood, and so grisly is this picture that he has to bite his lip to keep from groaning.

"Beat 'im! Harder!"

"Boys!"

"What's she saying?"

"I don't know."

"Thirty-seven, thirty-*pussy, faggot.* Forty!"

"FORTY!" the hall echoes. And as the whips are dropped, Carol and Liz and even Sister Regina sigh and sit back in unison.

"THEN THEY LOOTHED JETHUTH FROM THE POTH AND WRAPPED HITH MANGLED BODY IN A THCARLET CLOAK."

"A what?" Carol says under her breath, knowing, even before the boys produce it, that they're going to drape that screaming red robe Gerry bought her on him, a woman's screaming red robe. And as they do—"Son of a gun!"—Liz, too, exclaims, wishing for a cloak of her own to cover her blouse, for suddenly the connection of the reds is so clear, so absolutely exposed.

"THEY PLATHED ON HITH HEAD A HIDEOUTH CROWN THEY HAD WOVEN FROM THORNY PLANTH."

Joey plucks it up from the floor, too quickly. "Ow. This thing is nasty." Then as he warily raises it, the nearer audience ooohs—at its realness, it would seem. Carol, understanding now what the sticker bouquet was for, winces as the boy plants it ungingerly on her son's head.

Indeed, it pricks right through the mesh of the wig, sending shivers of pain across Danny's forehead and scalp, many times the intensity of the rope stings on his back. "AND IN HITH RIGHT HAND THEY PLATHED A REED, HITH THEPTER." But no sooner has he gripped it than Brian snatches it away again and smites him over the head, and there's another shivering and crisscrossing of a dozen points of pain. At last they kneel before him, arms raised in salute, and laugh uproariously, joined by the pointing and still-ambling-about Kevin, "Ah ha ha ha ha!"

Rory dips his hands into the washbowl on his lap, "I am innocent. Of the blood. Of this just man," then pretends to dry them with the glue-crusty towel. "See to it yourselves."

"His blood be on us and on our children!" Timmy and Paolo cry; and, "HIS BLOOD BE ON US AND ON OUR CHILDREN!" the audience bellows.

Good God, did they really say such a thing? Carol wonders.

"Look, I bring Him. Out to you. To make you realize. That I find no case against Him," Rory says. Then as the soldiers push Danny, with cloak and crown and reed, right up to the edge of the stage, the boy adds, "Look at the man!" and there's more, heartier laughter— perplexing to Liz, who can no longer tell if it's feigned, the crowd having gone fully into character, or real, aimed at Danny—not least of all now because his wig, beneath the crown, has shifted severely to the right. And here, on one of his rare glances up from his feet, she makes adjusting motions about her own head, but he only squints back with more bewilderment. "The wig!" she says, tilting her head now to one side; still he doesn't get it. Meanwhile the players behind him are all looking to one another: "What's next? Who goes?" she can hear them whispering. *'Crucify Him!'* she thinks. *Come on, somebody, say it.* And then just as her mouth is opening to form the line herself, she hears it rise up behind her, a female voice—"Cuh-*roo*-cify Him!"—and she spins around. Mrs. Burke?

And in fact, Carol, to her own astonishment, has just hollered the words, unable to tolerate the sight of Danny in her old red robe a second longer, and instantly the hall reverberates with the hysterical cry, "CRUCIFY HIM! CRUCIFY HIM!" Then someone starts, "AWAY WITH HIM! AWAY WITH HIM!" and the two collide and overlap, "AWAY, CRUCIFY! CRUCIFY, AWAY!"

Liz spins back to the front, "Stephen, ready with the Beethoven!" while Rory yells over the pandemonium, "SHALL I CRUCIFY. YOUR KING?"

"WE HAVE NO KING BUT CAESAR!"

And so he waves his hand and bows his head, "Take Him away!" Danny, beneath the cascade of cheers, is stripped of the cloak and pushed toward the dressing room. *Hallelujah*, Carol thinks; and "Hurry, Stephen!" Liz says. Yet not until the players have crossed the threshold does the delayed crash of the *Fifth!* rise weakly into the air: *Duh-duh-duh-DUH, duh-duh-duh-DUH.*

~ 20 ~

Danny in Ecstasy

"Quick," Liz says, rushing to the steps to detain Patty, "yell in to Danny to take off the wig."

"Take it *off?*"

"I'm sorry we put it on in the first place."

"You're thorry?"

"No, don't say that, just tell him to take it off. And Patricia," she adds, because now Sister Regina is signaling again, "tell them to move it."

"All right." And, "Mith Kaigh thezth for Danny to take off the wig," she relays at the dressing-room doorway.

"Take it *off?*" Kevin asks.

"And move it."

And so the request is repeated inside, replete with *Mith* and *thezth*. Rory, who's just untied Danny's hands, helps remove the prickly crown and the bobby pins at the base of the wig. When the last of the long, clingy hair pulls free of Danny's neck and ears, exposing his sweaty ringlets, it's as if a cold breeze blows over his scalp. As Rory suddenly sucks in his breath and cries "He's bleeding!" the breeze seems to flutter through Danny's stomach. "I am?"

"He is?" the others say, circling closer. "Where?" "Oh cool, real blood!" "Does he need stitches?" "Give him Pilate's towel." "Should we tell Miss Kaigh?"

"No!" Danny insists, backing off to the corner. "I-I-I'm all right. I-I-I swear," then waits with downcast eyes for them to resume their prop collecting and costume changing before turning to the wall and lowering the crown to his naked scalp. The thorn-pricks are sharper and more relentless, like clenching teeth, and he steels himself beneath them, holding his head stiffly to contain the throbbing. "THE WAY OF THE CROTH," Patty announces outside, and Brian and Joey rush to where it leans against the wall.

"I want to come, too," Kevin says. "That was cool out there."

"You can't come, you're Barabbas," Brian says.

"So? I'm free now. I can go wherever I want."

"Curly, does Barabbas go to the crucifixion?" Brian asks, and Danny, just then raising the blessed shards to his mouth, freezes and pretends not to hear. "Okay," Brian decides, "carry these," and passes the boy the Craftsman hammers and sponge-on-a-broomstick. "You can be our assistant."

And outside, louder now: "JETHUTH WATH MADE TO CARRY THE HEAVY WOODEN CROTH THROUGH THE THTREETH OF JERUTHALEM!"

"Let's go, Curly!" Brian calls, but as Danny turns, he feels a whirling in his head and runs upon an unexpected slant in the floor.

"What's the matter with him?" Joey asks.

"Now he's practicing his fall," Brian says.

"Yeah, Curly, wait till you get onstage," Kevin says. Then suddenly, "I'm going out first," Brian says, pressing the crucifix on Joey and striding right out before the waiting sea. "Bring out the prisoner's cross!" And so Joey hands it off, and Brian stands the towering prop beside him, an arm encircling its vertical beam, and at once—to Liz's wary relief, for clearly this isn't in the script—the assembly oohs and ahs. "Sister Ernestine, the cross!" several of the shoe swingers say. "Yes, children," Sister Ernestine says, "everyone bless: 'In the name of the Father . . .'" "'And of the Son . . .'"

"Bring out the prisoner!" Brian cries next, and Joey yanks him, wigless, onto the stage.

"Is that Jesus?" the children ask. "His hair turned red. What happened to his hair, Sister Ernestine?" But the nun doesn't answer, and likewise Liz refuses to look at them. Carol, moaning at the spectacle of her now clearly identifiable son, once again eyes the door: so close, two yards, two yards from peace. And after Danny and Joey, Kevin appears, arms laden with props—What's *he* doing in the scene? Liz thinks, stomach coiling tighter. As the cross is lowered to Danny's shoulder, he buckles so realistically that the first-graders scream again. "Is it heavy, Sister?" "Yes, children, it was very heavy," Sister Ernestine says. "Onward march!" Brian, the show stealer, cries. Then he and Joey fire their whips at Danny until he begins to trudge forward, his body locked in such an awkward, bent posture that both Liz and Carol look away. And now Paolo as John and Timmy as Simon join the rear of the procession, followed by the girls, streaming and tripping out of their dressing room, heads draped with shawls and Communion veils. "Hoo-hoo-hoo!" Juanita cries at the fore, one yellow-brown fist to her heart, one pink palm extended imploringly, "Hoo-hoo-hoo!" "Come on, girls," she whispers behind her, "wail and lament." "Hoo-hoo-hoo!" the girls say behind her, "Oh Jesus!" "Oh, my Son! My Son!" Juanita cries.

Son? Carol thinks. They've got this dark-skinned ham playing the Blessed Mother? What kind of nightmare is this? As she realizes further that the girl's wearing her old blue robe, her mind, whatever portion isn't humming or elsewhere, reels.

Via Dolorosa, road of sorrows, Danny repeats to himself, the hosts in another sticky, half-dissolved clump on the back of his tongue. He can't find the saliva to swallow them; his mouth, his throat, are very nearly *burning with thirst.* And just now, the tip of a rope catches the edge of his crown, driving the thorns on one side deeper into his scalp; with a shocking flare of pain, his vision blurs and stars and he finds himself on his knees, the cool, gritty floor under his left hand.

"THE FIRTHT FALL," he hears Patty announce over the screeches of the women-girls, their calls of "Jesus!" and "Son!" and then the audience shouts it again: "THE FIRST FALL!"

"Off the ground! Let's go!" the boys say, and Danny, staggering to his feet and trudging on, passes the forgotten ear, the fallen beard; and when at last they close in on the far wall, the procession horseshoes confusingly, bound back the way it came. "Faster! Put a move on!" Brian cries, his foot striking Danny's hip and sending him to his knees again. This time, as Danny's hand slides out from under him and his chin smacks the floor, the crown shifts on his head and there are many new flares of pain, dozens of brighter stars. "THE THECOND FALL." "THE SECOND FALL!" And now Frances, warily dodging the whips, rushes up to Danny, about to press the veil to his face, when she stops and cries, "You're bleeding!" But he shushes her and asks her to wipe the blood away, however much of it there is. She pats his forehead and the slicks of sweat along his jaw. By the time Joey pulls her back, "Get out of here, woman! Move away from the prisoner!" he's able to see better and finds energy enough to stand again and pick up his cross, the audience here murmuring with appreciation—not of this feat but of the miraculous impression on the veil, which Frances displays. Then right away the stage begins to whirl again—because he's stood up too quickly or because his hunger and thirst have weakened him to the point of collapse—and with the next whip that falls, he stumbles first to his knees, then to his face. "THE THIRD FALL!" And now despite the lashes and the kicking, he continues to lie there, chin to the floor, inhaling dust.

Finally, "Seize that man!" Brian cries, pointing to Timmy in the clutch of sympathizers, and Joey grabs the boy by the shoulder. "Carry the cross!" Then they yank Danny roughly to his feet and prod him on with their spears and insults, some loud and practiced: "Weakling! Think we got all day?" some whispered and new: "Phony Messiah! Daughter of God!" Soon, as they near the dressing rooms, the procession horseshoes again, bound at last for the draped milk crates at center stage. Here the weeping women, urged on by Juanita, hoo-hoo louder and beat their breasts, until suddenly the girl, breaking from the others, takes several unrehearsed steps to the front—"What's she doing?" Liz says beneath her breath—and addresses the audience with clasped hands: "No one knows the terrible pain I suffer as I watch my Son led off to be crucified!"

"Oh no," Liz groans.

"The beautiful fruit of my womb! My Sweet Jesus, treated like a dog!"

Stop! Liz is about to hiss, when Sister Regina, pesky hand temporarily retired to her lap, nods at her—not in so much of a rush now, it seems, to cut short this Mary soliloquy. And so Liz merely narrows her eyes at Juanita, the girl's round cheeks aflame with renegade inspiration:

"Tortured and spit at! How it makes the holy women weep! Poor Mary Magdalene, friend of Jesus!" she says, indicating the squinting, cross-eyed Ginger.

"My friend!" Ginger squeaks. "I love Him!"

"Poor Veronica!" indicating Frances, who once again displays the veil.

Would somebody please shut her ass up? Carol's struggling not to say, just as the brown-haired soldier lumbers up from behind and tugs her back to the procession. "Get up there!"

"All right, all right, I'm coming!" the recalcitrant Mother says. Then Danny, in his confusion, abbreviates the involved daughters-of-Jerusalem speech to "Do not weep," and Patty, realizing in the unyielding silence that he's not going to finish it, jumps to explain how they "CAME AT LATH TO CALVARY, WHERE OTHERTH HAD BEEN THTONED AND CRUTHIFIED BEFORE HIM. THE THUN THONE BRIGHTLY, BUT ATH THEY THTARTED TO ATHEND THE HILL, A DARK CLOUD THPREAD ACROTH THE THKY."

In the imaginary change of light, Timmy lays the cross before the stand and rushes to join the weeping huddle at left. At the same time Danny, dropping the ketchup packets nearby, is reaching into his godly pocket when Brian and Joey bear down on him, their eyes wide with eagerness and intention. At last their hands reach out, twenty tugging fingers, and he trembles uncontrollably. "No, wait," he begs as the robe is pulled from his shoulders, his titties, his belly button, his skinny legs. A collective gasp rises from the onlooking players, one which—as the boys carelessly toss the robe behind him and step back, exposing him to the audience—multiplies exponentially: a hissing, gathering wind whooshing to the back of the hall and then forward again, redoubled with murmurs and giggles.

Liz is astonished. The boy has no shirt on! In nothing but a bath towel! What on earth was he thinking? And now, "You can see his boobies!" a girl behind her whispers—loud enough to start a pool of outright laughter, which spreads and widens; and finally, along the wall, an emboldened boy cat-whistles, and a great burst surfaces.

"Maturity!" Sister Regina cries, leaping to her feet and pointing at the perpetrator, an upper-class Graybosch. As the boy is told to report to her office after the play and Mrs. Dillon swarms at him, all wagging finger and hot words, Liz coils up like a poked crab. It's her fault; she should've gone over this carefully, specified a tank top at least! But who would've expected him to be so literal?

By now Carol, her face submerged in the hottest blush of her memory, has slid down in her seat, level with the boys beside her. She should get up now, walk out; who cares if anyone sees? She can't endure a second more of this. Yet she remains, covering her face, and peers between a gap of her fingers, fearing that if she doesn't watch, something worse may happen. But what could be worse? Look at him up there, crossing his arms over his little chicken chest, staring down at his bare feet! He even seems to be shivering in this stuffy sauna. *Jackass*, she thinks, glaring at the back of Whatsherface's flip-infested head. Isn't looking back at her now; got some sense at least—because in the state Carol's in, she might very well flip her the finger, and wouldn't that be a sight? Make the whistler look like nothing, a little kidder; and now here, as he seems to have been adequately chastised, the principal aims another pink-faced frown at the assembly and turns to the front.

"Continue," she says without looking up. Then Danny, shocked into action by her words, turns to the cross and, in a series of tottering stages—kneeling to sitting to reclining—aligns himself over the painted beams, careful to cross his ankles and hold his head up slightly, so as not to bear down on the thorns. Quickly, when Kevin deals out the hammers, Brian and Joey squat on either side of him like operating doctors, their faces laughing and wild as they pound the floor by his hands and feet, making the boards beneath him vibrate, his ears ring with the monstrous clamor. All the while he can feel their close glances rake his twiggy arms and shrinking titties; he can feel the farther-off glances of the cluster of blushing disciples. Now he reminds Brian of the ketchup packets and, as Joey continues hammering, the boy blatantly tears one open with his teeth and spatters Danny's ghostly palms and foot tops with deep-red blobs, the sweet, vinegary smell spreading over the stage. "Mm, this is making me hungry," he whispers and, before Danny can stop him, makes a thick swath down his ribs with the whole second packet.

"No! Jesus isn't lanced till after He dies. Wipe it off."

"I'm not touching it."

Here Joey drops his hammer, and Timmy and Paolo rush over, holding up the white sheet. "WHEN THEY COMPLETED THE RUDETH PART OF THEIR CHORE . . ." Patty begins. "Get off!"

Brian says, rolling Danny to one side and yanking the cross out from under him. As he and Joey run to fit it into the stand, Danny sits up, the ketchup slowly running from his hands and side, and reaches for the discarded robe, picking out the hosts left in his pocket—not as many, it seems, as there were before The Way. Indeed, he spots a stray shard on the floor to his right, Jesus' Holy Body, and crawls toward it, snatching it up and stuffing it in his mouth with the others. On his knees still, he wipes the ketchup from his side with an arm of the robe, trying not to disturb the blobs on his hands, then hoists himself to his feet and feels another rush of dizziness, accompanied, suddenly, by an extraordinary shiver beetling down the length of his body, and he has to hold his arms out and breathe deeply before everything stills and rights. And then, stepping toward the tall cross, the boys already stationed on either side, he sees he's sprung the safety pin on the towel—just the tip of it now, glinting at the base of the knot, resisting his trembling attempt to bend it back in its catch. ". . . NOW BEGAN THE DARKETH HOURTH OF JETHUTH'TH THUFFERING."

Liz, uncoiling enough to slide to the edge of her seat, braces for what seems to her their last chance: if they could just get this part right, if they could just do it the way they did in practice, it might redeem them—not entirely, but somewhat; raise them a foot or two from this pit of shame. *Oh please.*

On every side, the boys are urging Danny with whispers—"Hurry! Get up there!"—but it's as if all his bones are falling out of joint, and he sways and totters and only half-raises his foot to the stand. Suddenly the soldiers, swarming and snapping their teeth, hoist him up by the armpits and turn him about. Then just as Patty repeats, *"THE DARK-ETH HOURTH OF JETHUTH'TH THUFFERING,"* and Miss Kaigh, spurred on by Sister Regina, cries, "Okay, boys!" he manages to raise his arms in line with the crossbeam, and the sheet's dropped. Instantly stricken by the extent of the gawking throng that pans out before him, Danny casts his eyes to the floor and wants to cross his arms over his titties again, but can't for the nails, and so his chest and soft heart remain bared to the surging hisses, the roiling laughter.

"Maturity!" Sister Regina yells louder. "Such a disgrace!" *Such a disgrace!* the phrase puncturing the remains of Liz's last irrational hope. She knows that even while it's aimed at the audience, it stands for the play as well, and for each of the actors, and for Danny, and for herself—herself especially: she, the teacher responsible for this catastrophe, has been disgraced, maybe permanently, like Hester Prynne. "No. No, Stephen," she calls to the boy, restarting the Beethoven for the third time. "Just turn it off now—nothing can save it."

When Sister Regina squelches the commotion and all wait in the musicless silence for Danny to speak, he at last pries his tongue from the roof of his mouth and, with a desperate effort, swallows down the last, sharp lump of hosts at the back of his throat. "F-F-F-Father—"

"Louder, please!" Sister Regina says.

"F-F-F-Father—"

"Help out, everyone. 'Father . . .'" And during the thundering completion, "FORGIVE THEM, FOR THEY KNOW NOT WHAT THEY DO!" a drop of ketchup rolls free of Danny's palm and plops to the floor.

"Ew!" Frances says, despite herself; and quickly Patty, to drown out the weeping women's giggles, "THEN THE MULTITUDE BEGAN TO UPBRAID CHRITHT IN HITH HUMILIATHON AND AGONY. 'VAH!' THEY CHORUTHED IN THARCATHM."

"Vah!" Sister Regina says.

"VAH!" the audience cries.

"What am I supposed to say now?" Brian whispers up to Danny.

"Jesus of Nazareth, King of the Jews," he answers, with minimal movement of lips.

"Jesus, King Jew!" Brian cries.

"Laugh," Danny tells him.

"Ah ha ha!" the boy says, pointing with derision. And here Joey and Kevin join in, "Ah ha ha!" and even Paolo, seemingly forgetting he's John, "AHH HAA HAA!"

Danny widens his eyes at the laughing apostle, who claps his hand to his mouth.

"Idiot," Juanita says. "Shut up, jerk," Paolo fires back.

"So You were going to destroy the temple," Danny whispers to Brian, "and rebuild it in three days."

". . . and rebuild it in three days!"

"Save Yourself now by coming down from that cross."

"Save Yourself now by coming down from that cross!"

"He saved others but He cannot save Himself."

"He saved others but He cannot save Himself!"

"AND NOW NEAR THE CROTH OF JETHUTH THERE THTOOD HITH MOTHER WITH THE DITHIPLE WHOM HE LOVED."

"I'm right here, Son!" Juanita waves to him. "Mama's been watching all the time! So's John!" But when she attempts to hold Paolo's arm, the boy pulls roughly away.

As the two darkies skirmish, Carol, who's now sunk below kid level, freezes with utter fear—because this, if she's not mistaken, is the behold-thy-Mother moment, and she's just had the nightmarish thought that Danny might look at her while delivering the line, he and the entire assembly in turn. *It's not my play, I'm not Mary.* And so for the dreadful duration of "W-W-W-Woman, there is your s-s-s-son," she stares down at the scuffed rubber tip of a chair leg before her, thinking, *Don't you dare, don't you even think about it,* and then has to suffer, too, through the parroting principal's rendition, and the audience's "THERE IS YOUR SON!" Oh, someone make it stop! Is he looking at her? No. But now here we go again with, "S-S-S-Son, there is your M-M-M-Mother," and if *anyone* looks at her she'll shatter— "THERE IS YOUR MOTHER!"—she'll fall in pieces to the floor. However, then quite suddenly it seems to be over, and no one has, and she hears Danny say, "I thirst."

"I THIRST!" the audience echoes, while onstage Brian raises the sponge, its coarse dryness roughing over Danny's cheek and lips. At last Danny glances up at the audience, directly at his mother by the door, whose face, with its glassy, unreadable expression, turns immediately away. And then he glances at his teacher, leaning forward with crossed legs, crossed arms, as if struck with terrible cramps. And then he glances at the teeming rest, the hundreds and hundreds to the back of the room, all still looking—at him and at his near nakedness: boys and teachers and astounded, wide-eyed girls; and here several cover their faces and whisper nervously to each other, there a row of Sisters with stunned, red cheeks stare down at their black shoes. And then as he looks up from them all to the ceiling, his brow furrows, stoking the ring of pain about his head; and at the same time, the pain in all the other portions of his body seems to rejuvenate and cry out in a chorus:

his whipped back, his booted hips, his splintered calves; and even in those places where the ketchup smears his hands and feet, he believes he can feel the searing fullness of the stakes that split his flesh, and pushed apart his bones, and snapped his veins. *Please, God*, he prays, *come near. I have no one to help me. Look how they surround me, roaring like hungry lions. I am like water poured out; all my bones are racked. My heart has become like wax melting away in my chest. My throat is dried up like baked clay, my tongue sticks to my jaws; to the dust of death you have brought me down. Save me from the mouths of the lions, my wretched life!*

He stops and waits—one second, two—but still there's no blessing, still there's no voice. "My God, My God," he murmurs, meekly at first, then takes a long, hissing draft of air, closes his eyes, and cries it: "MY GOD! MY GOD! WHY HAVE YOU FORSAKEN ME?" A clear, ferocious, crackling howl that fills the immense room, leaping and ricocheting from far wall to far wall. So startling is the sudden leap of his voice that the entire audience seems to jump in its seat at once before it dashes apart again, a circus of gasps and guffaws and grunts, reprimands from the teachers; he hears Sister Regina's words as if from another room: how disgraceful that they should laugh at the Lord's cry, His terrible pain! And when at last the noise fades, he opens his eyes again and fixes on a water stain in the high, pocked ceiling, his heart pounding wildly, his blood thrumming so loudly through his ears as to block out all sound below. And then just here, just when he's abandoning all hope for guidance and courage, it comes again, whispering through his mind: *Soon you will see the Son of Man seated at the right hand of God*; and, glancing to the dressing room, he sees Arram—his friend!—long, tan body framed in the doorway. He wants Danny to understand what he means: *Seated at the right hand!* he says urgently.

The right hand, Danny repeats.

And coming on the clouds of heaven.

Clouds of heaven.

Hurry! Arram says.

What? Danny says.

Do it! Now!

I can't.

You can!

I can't.

Yes!

All right! Danny says. *All right! Yes!* And takes a last, long breath and holds it. Then with eyes fixed on the water stain, he twists his hips in such a way that the knot slides free of the gaping pin.

And for an instant, the towel hesitates, as if held by an angel's finger, then it falls, right past his stiffening, magic-markered dickie, to the floor.

The roars hit his ears like sledges. All at once, he sees Sister Regina at the center of the standing mob, pointing and slapping her habit-veiled thighs, "Cover him! Cover that devil! Blessed Mary!" Miss Kaigh, lurching toward the stage, "Daniel! Daniel, what's happened? Brian, Joey, get something!" His mother, stooped, hand to her face, slipping out the side door. As the boys, crowing and flush-cheeked, come at him with the bright, uncovered hammock, he smiles savagely, the ecstatic blush bursting over his body and slowly seeping inward, as if to his very bones. "Oh God, God," he murmurs, the rough canvas chafing his skin, the boys' hands and arms pressing in about his waist, and at last he gazes into their dull, unfathoming eyes, "It is finished."

CURTAIN

Acknowledgments

With special thanks to my ever-faithful agent, Mitchell Waters.

Thanks also to my editor, Alexandra Shelley; and to all who helped carry this book along the way, especially Joe Pequigney, Adele Glimm and Vincent Brandi; Jean Ayer, Myriam Chapman, Miriam Finkelstein, Eleanor Hyde, Elisabeth Jakab, Maureen Sladen and Marcia Slatkin; Bob Acker, David Ebershoff, Victoria Kingsley, Vince Lardo, Michael Lowenthal, Sarah Ruhl and Rob Stuart.

And thanks finally to The MacDowell Colony and Ragdale Foundation for their generous and important residencies, and to the editors of *New England Review* and *Other Voices*, who first published portions of this book in slightly different form.